LOVE *and* MONEY

RUTH HARRIS

"Harris will keep her fans engrossed as she accentuates the riskiness and unpredictability of lives spent obsessed with money, setting them against a backdrop of dizzying social change and a volatile stock market."

Publishers Weekly

"She can tell you [about men and women] with more style and verve than many others who have won fame and fortune writing in the same vein."

Liz Smith

Also by Ruth Harris:

HUSBANDS AND LOVERS*
A SELF-MADE WOMAN*
THE LAST ROMANTICS
THE RICH AND THE BEAUTIFUL
DECADES

*Published by Fawcett Books

LOVE *and* MONEY

RUTH HARRIS

FAWCETT CREST · NEW YORK

To MICHAEL,
with love

CONTENTS

PART ONE

*The
Past /
1944*

"Time present and time past
Are both perhaps present in time future,
And time future contained in time past."

—T. S. ELIOT
Four Quartets

"Those who cannot remember the past are condemned
to repeat it."

—GEORGE SANTAYANA
The Life of Reason

I

RICH GIRL

*H*er *name was Deedee Dahlen and she had been famous*
from the day she was born. The tabloids, anxious for a respite
from war news and ration stamp scandals, called her "The
Million-Dollar Baby" because of the million-dollar trust fund
her grandfather established for her on the day after her birth.
At a time when the minimum wage was thirty cents an hour
and the Dow stood at 144, at a time when stagflation, Arab
oil embargoes and double digit inflation had never been heard
of, a million dollars was a huge amount of money. A million
dollars seemed, even to rich people, like all the money in the
world.

The gossip raged from Park Avenue to Wall Street, from
Locust Valley to Newport. The table-hoppers at the Stork
Club and El Morocco, the shoppers in the fitting rooms at
Mainbocher, the Scotch sippers at "21" and the lunchers at
the Colony all speculated about what Luther Dahlen's million dollars was buying. Was the trust fund simply a loving
gesture from a rich and indulgent man to his first granddaughter?

Not if you knew how tight Luther Dahlen was, according
to the people who knew him best. They said Deedee
Dahlen's trust fund was more than simple generosity. But
what was the something more? Was it blackmail, bribe or
hush money? Was the million dollars buying silence, security or secrecy? Only the family knew, and the family
wasn't talking.

* * *

Although Dolores was her real name, everyone always called her Deedee. Her father was handsome, the sole heir to the Dahlen fortune. Her mother was charming and beautiful. Her family was Park Avenue WASP. It all looked perfect—from the outside.

Deedee was born in Manhattan's fashionable Carnegie Hospital almost three weeks late. As if, she would always say, she knew ahead of time exactly how complicated her life was going to be and needed all the time she could get to prepare for coping with its difficulties. The first questions her pale and anxious mother asked when her brand-new daughter was brought to her were: "Is she all right? Is she going to live? She won't die, will she?"

Joyce Torngren Dahlen was a poor girl who had married rich. Her first child, little Luther, born two years before, had lived for only eighteen hours. His death had been due to a defect in his tiny lungs, and throughout her second pregnancy Joyce had feared delivering, once again, an imperfect child, a child born only to die.

"You have an absolutely perfect baby this time," said the doctor, coming into Joyce's room a moment later as the nurse helped Joyce settle her brand-new baby in her arms. Julian Baldwin, head of obstetrics at Carnegie, had delivered little Luther, and he knew how devastated Joyce had been by her son's death. A cigar-shaped man with perfect pitch in bedside manners, he was delighted to be able to reassure her about Deedee. "This time you'll leave the hospital like all the other new mothers—with a perfectly healthy baby."

"Are you sure?" asked Joyce anxiously, remembering how crushed she had been when she had left the hospital two years before with empty arms and an aching heart. She was a woman who had been doubly wounded—by a disappointing marriage and by the death of a child. Those wounds, psychological and emotional, showed in her hurt and apprehensive expression.

"I'm absolutely sure," said Julian Baldwin with another smile. Joyce was very pretty and had a very pleasing personality, and Julian Baldwin, although a happily married man, was not immune to her considerable charm. Joyce Dahlen elicited his protective instincts. So did the thought of a handsome gift to Carnegie from the grateful Dahlen family. "All you have to do is enjoy her!"

"Oh, I will!" said Joyce, visibly relaxing at last and hugging her baby close to her. She literally glowed with happiness and pride. "I will!"

Her fears finally allayed, Joyce abandoned herself to the baby in her arms. She kissed Deedee's forehead and fists. She checked the in-and-out regularity of her breathing and examined her tiny fingers and toes. She caressed her silky, sweet-smelling skin and dark wisps of hair and, assured that her baby was perfect, absolutely perfect, began to weep with a simultaneous outpouring of love, exhaustion and immense relief. *This* baby was healthy. *This* baby would live! Joyce could not believe how happy she was nor how much she already adored her infant daughter. She would gladly be her slave for life.

Then, getting her emotions under control and wiping away her tears, Joyce had two more questions: "Where is he? Is the son of a bitch here yet?"

She was referring to Russell. Her husband.

The answer, which Joyce had dreaded but half expected, was no. Russell Dahlen still hadn't arrived at the hospital and no one knew where he was.

"The baby's grandparents are outside, though," said the nurse much too brightly, trying to skip over the moment of awkwardness. "They're very anxious to see their new grandchild. Can I let them come in?"

"Why not?" replied Joyce, not bothering to hide her bitterness. It was just like Russell to disappear. It was just like him to leave her alone to deal with his aloof and intimidating parents. Joyce had given up trying to love them. She had settled for respecting them.

"Tell them their new granddaughter is looking forward to meeting them. Be sure to say exactly that," Joyce cautioned defiantly, smiling down at her baby and then up at the nurse. Then she repeated herself, emphasizing the noun. She wanted to make sure that there would be no misunderstanding. She wanted to make sure that Luther Dahlen knew exactly what to expect.

"Their *granddaughter.*"

Why not let them come in? Why not let them see their new grandchild? They were entitled, thought Joyce. Besides, she had something to tell them.

Luther Dahlen was a very rich man and, like most very rich men, he was used to getting his way. He was a hard-headed, no-nonsense male chauvinist of the old school. He had been terribly disappointed when he learned that his long-awaited grandchild was only a girl, but, ever a realist, he told himself that Russell and Joyce were still only in their twenties. They had already produced a boy once. There was still plenty of time for them to produce another. Meanwhile, he stood at his daughter-in-law's bedside, his wife Edwina beside him, and smiled with surprising warmth for such an ordinarily restrained and formal man. Even his pale blue eyes, usually so warily watchful, seemed to soften and glow with genuine emotion.

"Can I hold her?" he asked Joyce, clearly ill at ease at having to ask permission. "I promise I won't drop her."

"Of course you can hold her," said Joyce, handing over her precious baby, aware that for the first time since she had first laid eyes on Russell, she had something the Dahlens wanted.

Luther took the baby into his arms as carefully as if she were made of moonbeams and gossamer. He cuddled her close to him and smiled down at her. He touched her tiny hands and traced his finger across her cheeks and forehead. Then, bending down to her, he kissed her face and her warm neck. Joyce watched, more than a bit surprised. She had never seen Luther Dahlen express physical affection to any-one, not to Russell, not to Edwina and certainly never to herself.

"She's gorgeous, isn't she?" asked Joyce, ecstatically, al-most unutterably proud of herself and the healthy baby she had managed—finally—to give birth to. Because of her belated arrival, Deedee had none of the red, wrinkled appearance of so many newly born infants. Her silky dark hair, ivory skin and intriguingly slanted cat-shaped eyes gave her a slightly foreign and even rather exotic appearance. She looked faintly Oriental or, perhaps more accurately, even a bit like an Eskimo. Joyce's mother had always sworn that the Torngrens were not pure Scandinavian but had a sprinkling of Lapp blood somewhere not too many generations back in the past.

"She's a Dahlen," replied Luther, putting such nonsense as gorgeous or not gorgeous firmly aside. He himself, tall, white-haired, bristly-mustached and militarily erect, was an impressively distinguished-looking man and, as such, could easily afford to dismiss such trivialities as mere good looks. Beside, he loathed words like gorgeous. They belonged in movie magazines—and in the mouths of the empty-headed idiots, like Joyce, no doubt, who read them. "It doesn't matter what she looks like."

"She *is* lovely," said Edwina, taking her grandchild from her husband and mildly contradicting him. Edwina, tall and straightforwardly handsome, shared her husband's disdain for anything as superficial as looks, preferring instead to place her values on more important considerations such as character and intelligence. She was nevertheless impressed and indeed almost dazzled by the child's unusual comeliness and, like all the Dahlens, the moment Edwina felt a strong emotion, she felt compelled to deny it. "Not, of course, that anyone cares what she looks like."

Joyce, who was very, very pretty in a conventional candy-box, snub-nosed, blond, blue-eyed way, hardly flinched anymore at her in-laws' dismissal of the one quality other than her youth that they seemed to think she had to offer. Instead, asserting her prerogative as the child's mother for the first time, Joyce held out her arms and Edwina obediently but reluctantly handed the baby back.

There was a moment of strained silence. Everyone was thinking the same thing. Where was the child's father? Where had he gone? What had happened to him? Where was Russell?

* * *

That night passed and so did the next morning with no word. Neither Russell's parents, the police nor the private detective Luther had hired had been able to track down Russell. There was no report of an accident, no emergency room admissions of unknown persons, no unidentified bodies, no entries on police blotters. Russell's secretary said that he had left the office just after speaking to Dr. Baldwin and that was the last anyone had heard or seen of him. Russell Dahlen, sole heir to his family's Wall Street fortune and brand-new father, had apparently vanished off the face of the earth.

"Not being here when Deedee was born was the last straw," Joyce said tearfully the next afternoon. Her eyes were red with weeping and she was torn between hurt and fury. Russell Dahlen, she thought, could be unbelievably weak and cowardly. As a young bride blinded by the Dahlen name and the Dahlen money, Joyce had thought that she had married the confident and sophisticated heir to a Wall Street fortune. Instead, as the early years of her marriage went on and romance turned to reality, she realized that she was wed to a man uncomfortable in the role his birth and his family had conspired to impose on him and unable or unwilling to rebel against the restrictions and rewards that inescapably accompanied both love and money.

Russell Dahlen, Joyce knew, could not face conflict. Confrontation was a word that simply did not exist in his emotional vocabulary. She knew perfectly well how much Russell feared his father and she wasn't exactly surprised that Russell had, once again at a crucial moment, taken off and disappeared. What she couldn't, in her heart of hearts, forgive or forget was how he had apparently abandoned her and their brand-new baby.

Didn't Russell care about her? Wasn't he interested in his new baby? Didn't he want to see Deedee? Considering little Luther's tragic death, didn't Russell even want to know if Deedee would live or die? Didn't he want to hold her and to kiss her? Even cold and aloof Luther had held her and kissed her!

"Russell doesn't even care about his own child," said Joyce bitterly. "Not to mention whether I'm dead or alive."

"Of course he cares. He'll turn up. He always does," said Luther, trying to soothe Joyce.

"Sure," said Joyce, refusing to be placated. "When it's too late to be of any help."

"He'll probably show up any minute now," Luther said as if Joyce hadn't spoken. "No doubt he's been out celebrating."

"No doubt," said Joyce. "I suppose he'll do me the honor of showing up when he gets out of whatever gin mill he's in."

"He'll be here!" said Luther, abruptly turning his anger at Joyce. Like Russell, he hated confrontation. He hated even more being reminded of Russell's weaknesses.

"But I won't," said Joyce, finally getting it out. "I want a divorce."

"No divorce!" said Luther instantly.

"Oh, yes!" replied Joyce, knowing she had hit a sore spot. "I don't want to live like this. I don't want to bring my baby up with a father who doesn't give a damn about her!"

"I said, no divorce," Luther snapped, the steeliness that had helped make his fortune obvious in his voice. "There's never been a divorce in the Dahlen family and there isn't going to be one now!"

"Yes, there is," said Joyce adamantly. She had nothing to lose except a marriage that had turned out to be a bitter disappointment. The Dahlens may have had money, but money wasn't everything. Joyce had found *that* out the hard way. "And I'm taking Deedee with me."

Luther, who had said all he planned to say on the subject, did not even reply. There was going to be no divorce, and that was final.

Luther Dahlen had always considered women—except for Edwina—flighty and incapable of logic. He had never taken Joyce or Joyce's wishes seriously. He knew perfectly well why she had married Russell—for his money. For the Dahlen money. Money was what she obviously wanted and money was what he would give her. Luther, who had made his fortune being able to calculate very finely the price of a stock, began to calculate the price of his granddaughter. The price he came up with was one million dollars.

"The money will be placed in a trust fund. It will become Deedee's free and clear when she turns twenty-five," Luther said. "There is only one condition: no divorce. Not now. Not ever. Deedee is going to be brought up a Dahlen. With all the advantages that implies. Including a mother and a father."

"No," said Joyce, thinking that she wasn't going to let Luther dominate her the way he dominated everyone else. "You can't buy me. And you can't buy my baby."

"Deedee's not just your baby," said Luther. "She's a Dahlen baby."

"The Dahlens aren't the Rockefellers!" said Joyce, irritated at the way Luther always carried on about the Dahlens, as if they were royalty or something.

"They're a damn sight better than the Torngrens!" said Luther coldly. "Now what do you want? A custody fight you're going to lose or a million dollars for Deedee and a life of comfort for yourself?"

Joyce had no response and Luther did not go on to spell out the financial and legal weapons at his disposal. He did not have to. Joyce was well aware that people like the Dahlens used their money and their power to get whatever they wanted. In any legal battle, she knew that she would eventually lose, the way Gloria Vanderbilt had lost custody of little Gloria just ten years before. Joyce simply did not have the resources, financial or emotional, to fight the Dahlens on their terms and win.

Unable in the end to turn down a million 1944 preinflation dollars and the lifetime of security it represented for Deedee, Joyce finally accepted Luther's offer and, by the time Russell showed up late that afternoon, shaky and pale and obviously hung over, the deal had been made, the papers signed, sealed and delivered. Luther did not want to take any chances on Joyce's changing her mind, and Joyce, who had married her husband for love, was now wed to him for money.

* * *

Joyce pretended to believe Russell's excuses about having suddenly been called away from New York on urgent business the very day Deedee was born, and she continued to live with him in the comfortable Park Avenue apartment just beneath her in-laws' penthouse. Everything seemed to proceed exactly as usual except that, although Joyce continued to be Russell's wife and even to share his bed, she made sure that she never again became pregnant. Joyce did not want Deedee to have to share her inheritance with anyone—not even another Dahlen child. Deedee was the one source of Joyce's power against a rich and dominating family, and Joyce, shrewder than Luther had ever dreamed, did not want to dilute her one advantage.

Instead, Joyce focused all her attention on Deedee, lavishing love and affection on her and seeing to it that Deedee, who would get everything, *had* everything. Joyce made sure that Deedee had only the best. The best schools, the best clothes, the best toys and the best companions.

Pampered and spoiled, Deedee would be the center of everyone's attention in an often divided family. She would grow up with an exaggerated sense of self-importance paradoxically undercut by an almost total lack of self-confidence. Utterly indulged on the one hand, told that it was too bad she was only a girl on the other, Deedee was an heiress in bondage, invisibly yet almost fatally crippled by the contradictory double message.

She would wonder what she could possibly ever do to make up to her family for not having been born a boy. She would also wonder why her father had not been present at her birth.

What, Deedee wondered, could possibly have been more important? Or, it would sometimes occur to her as she grew older, who? It was a question, rarely asked, that was never answered.

I I
POOR GIRL

*H*er mother named her after the movie star and she grew up in a mean house in a mean town in central Massachusetts. For as long as she could remember, all she ever wanted to do was get out. She was even born six weeks prematurely as if, she would always say, she couldn't wait to get out into the world and take charge.

Unlike Deedee, Lana was her mother's first-born. However, like Deedee, Lana's birth brought with it a price—a price not of a million dollars but a price of guilt and secrecy.

From the moment she skipped her first period at the end of January of 1944, Mildred Neill knew she was going to have a baby. When she met her rich and handsome lover in the Eagle Luncheonette and told him she was pregnant, he told her something she hadn't known—that he was married.

"Married?" Mildred had repeated, her creamy Irish rose complexion blanching pale, her deep blue eyes blinking involuntarily. She was stunned. Absolutely shocked. Married? At nineteen and madly in love, the possibility had simply never dawned on her. "Why didn't you tell me?"

"I didn't think it mattered," said Russell Dahlen as his eyes shifted uncomfortably away from hers, telling her that of course he knew it mattered.

What Russell Dahlen also didn't say was that his wife was pregnant, too, and that he felt trapped. Trapped by the idea of becoming a family man, trapped by his father's obsession with a third-generation male heir to carry on the Dahlen name and inherit the Dahlen fortune. Trapped by his wife's hopes that children would help him settle down and trapped by the idea of another generation in hostage to the Wall Street company his father had helped found and seemed to care about more than anything on earth.

As a married man and as his family's sole surviving son, Russell Dahlen was doubly exempt from military service. He was in Wilcom, Massachusetts, because his father wanted him to work in a small brokerage firm where he would be able to learn about everything from administration and management to sales and back-room operations. He was also there because he wanted to get away from his wife and his family, all of whom expected him to be responsible for a new baby and an old company.

Now, as Russell Dahlen looked across the marble table at another woman who was telling him that he was responsible for something else, he wanted to scream. He wanted to cry. He wanted to break down and sob. He wanted someone to tell him why his life was such a mess and, why, no matter what he did, he seemed helpless to change it.

"There's a very good clinic in St. Thomas. It's in the Virgin Islands," Russell said finally, still unable to meet Mildred's eyes. He had heard about it while he was at Princeton and knew a number of classmates and their debutante girlfriends who had used its services. "You'll have the operation and a nice week at the beach, besides. I'll pay for everything."

"Kill my baby?" Mildred said, appalled at Russell's apparent indifference to the life he had helped create. Mildred had assumed that when she told Russell about the coming baby that he would do what any of the boys she had grown up with would have done: offer to marry her. She had not taken into account the enormous social and cultural differences between her and her handsome, green-eyed lover. She had never even dreamed that he might already have a wife. She had never even dreamed that instead of marriage, he would offer to pay for an abortion. "It's the same as murder! It's a sin!"

"Then what are you going to do?" said Russell, bewildered. He was astounded by her reaction. Mildred had always been on his side, had always seen things his way, had always been so willing to go along with whatever he had wanted. It was one of the reasons he had fallen in love with her. Now he was seeing a side of her he had never dreamed existed. Mildred had been brought up a strict Catholic; Russell an indifferent Presbyterian. The Roman Catholic concept of the sanctity of life was an abstraction to Russell, an idea without much meaning since he had been brought up, however inadvertently, to conclude that money was the answer to every problem.

"Don't you mean what are *we* going to do?" Mildred replied. In 1944, being pregnant and unmarried was to be marked for life. In 1944, no one, including Russell Dahlen, had even heard the phrases unwed mother or single parent—the stigma was simply too enormous, the very thought quite simply unthinkable. Unwed pregnancy was a stain and a humiliation from which no woman could ever recover.

"I thought you knew how to take care of yourself," Russell said, evading Mildred's question and answering it at the same time. He blinked rapidly and looked everywhere except at her: at the beveled mirrors, at the white-painted tin ceiling, at the hand-lettered sign over the soda fountain that listed the eight flavors of homemade ice cream. His marriage, begun with such high hopes, had turned into a disaster. Now the affair that had once seemed to promise such happiness had turned into another trap.

"Think over what I said. The offer is still good," Russell added, wanting, as he always did, to do the right thing and wondering, as he so often had, why the right thing was so frequently not enough. He then got up and quickly left the booth at the Eagle Luncheonette as a stunned Mildred sat in silence, wondering whether to believe him and trying to decide what to do next.

When Mildred called Russell's office later that afternoon, thinking that she would ask him point-blank if he would get a divorce and marry her, she was told that he had left Wilcom. One of the secretaries thought he might be in New

York. One of the brokers thought he had heard Russell say something about Canada. No one had a forwarding address or phone number for him, and when Mildred called the Lancome & Dahlen office in New York, she left message after message. None of her calls was ever returned, and finally she was told that Russell was out of town. There was nowhere he could be reached, and he had given no date for his return.

Mildred Neill found herself in the same frustrating situation as almost everyone who had ever had anything to do with Russell Dahlen. He was the nicest, kindest man in the world, and yet, when she needed him, he was nowhere to be found. He was, she thought bitterly, hiding behind his money, allowing her to face the consequences of their love alone.

Two weeks later, Mildred received a check signed by Russell Dahlen for one thousand dollars along with a note with the address of the clinic in St. Thomas. Mildred cashed the check and tore up the note. She would never have an abortion. Never!

She spent part of the money for diapers, baby clothes and a crib and put the rest in the bank, a savings account for her unborn child's future. She did not hear from Russell Dahlen during the rest of her entire pregnancy, nor did she ever expect to again.

When Mildred began to show, Will Bantry, who had been sweet on her since she had been old enough to go to high school, was the only person in Wilcom who was nice to her. Mildred, guilty and scared and still not quite believing the shocking abruptness of Russell's abandonment, was more than grateful.

"I don't know what I would have done without you," she told Will as she entered her seventh month. Mildred's pregnancy had made her a pariah. People she had known her entire life actually crossed the street so as not to have to speak to her. She looked upon Will as a rock and a savior, the only person in Wilcom, including her own father, who treated her decently.

"You know I've always liked you, Mildred," Will said earnestly. He had always been drawn to Mildred, but he had been afraid that he might be too old for her. Now, with the younger men gone off to fight the war and Mildred in trouble, Will dared express the feelings that once had seemed embarrassing and unacceptable. He was a mechanic at the Wilcom Carpet Works, a good worker, a man of strong feelings and few words. "I'd be proud to marry you. We'd have babies of our own."

"And my baby would have a name?" Mildred asked anxiously. She had decided to name the baby Cary, if the child were a boy; Lana, if it were a girl. The movies were the world that Mildred dreamed of: a world where people were beautiful, where every problem had a solution and every ending was a happy ending. The first names were no problem. It was the question of a last name that had haunted Mildred. She didn't want to call her baby Dahlen because she didn't want to be reminded of her charming but cowardly lover. Her father would kill her if she gave her illegitimate child his name, Neill, the fine Irish name of which he was so proud. The fine Irish name he would not permit to be sullied by his daughter's shameful carryings-on. "Would you give my baby your name?" she begged Will. "Would you let me call my baby Bantry?"

Will thought for a moment. A lifelong bachelor, he wanted to marry Mildred. She wasn't the prettiest girl in Wilcom, but he saw in her all the things that Russell had seen. She had a sparkle to her blue eyes and a lilt in her walk that made her seem so much more alive than other, prettier girls. She was as bright as a button, a sparkling companion and yet at the same time a down-to-earth, entirely level-headed young woman. The fact was that Will liked everything about her—except for the fact that he wouldn't be first. He couldn't get over the idea that she was soiled. If only he could forget that Mildred wasn't a virgin.

"Could I call the baby Bantry?" Mildred asked again, touching Will's callused hand gently. Her anxiety about her baby's last name was making her ill. She had been losing, rather than gaining, weight. Her constant nausea was not morning sickness but the result of guilt and fear.

"I don't know," Will said, the conflicting emotions showing on his blunt, meaty face. "I just don't know . . ."

"But will you think about it?" Mildred urged, desperate for her baby to have a name, desperate for her baby to escape her shame.

Will shrugged uncomfortably and, despite Mildred's entreaties, refused to be pinned down to a definite answer. Mildred went into labor in an agony of anxiety, not knowing what her baby's surname would be and fearing that an innocent child would have to pay the price for her own indiscretions.

When Julian Baldwin called Russell Dahlen at his office and told him that Joyce had finally had her baby and that it was a girl, Russell left his office in the Lancome & Dahlen building at Broad and Wall and got into a taxi. He gave the driver the address of the Carnegie Hospital and, as the taxi headed uptown, Russell sat back and wept, crushed by a familiar and devastating sense of failure.

Russell had given up his own dreams for the sake of his father's and, like his father, he desperately wanted a boy, a son to replace little Luther and to reap the benefits of the lifelong sacrifice he had made. Russell wanted his son to be the hard-driving, hard-nosed businessman he knew he could never be. He wanted a son he could be proud of and—even more important—that his father would be proud of. He wanted, for once in his life, to have done something his father would admire him for unequivocally, something for which his father would have nothing but words of pride and praise.

Another boy to replace little Luther, a son and heir to the Dahlen fortune, would have been that perfect something. Now, though, knowing that his new child was a daughter, Russell could just imagine the cutting remarks his father would make about his latest failure. He would tell him that he couldn't do anything right. He would fault him because the baby didn't have a stem. He would say that he wasn't man enough to produce a boy.

Just the thought of his father's wicked tongue made Russell cringe. When the taxi, heading uptown on Madison, passed the Roosevelt Hotel, Russell, on a sudden impulse, told the driver to stop. He had never been in the Roosevelt Hotel in his life, nor had he ever known anyone who had ever stayed there. Its anonymity made him feel safe. He decided to have a drink to prepare himself for facing his father. One drink, however, led to another and at some point Russell checked into a small suite, drew the blackout curtains, ordered six old-fashioneds from room service, drank them one right after another and passed out.

The next morning, Russell woke from a hotly erotic dream about Mildred Neill with semen dribbling stickily down his side and opened his eyes to a vicious headache and a sour stomach. Almost sixteen hours had passed since Joyce had given birth, and Russell had now added the sin of lateness to the sin of producing a girl instead of a boy. He had no idea of how he would be able to face his father, not to mention himself.

He called room service and ordered a vanilla milk shake, a Coke, black coffee and a bottle of aspirin, his usual hangover remedy, and, still in the grip of his dream, decided on the spur of the moment to call Mildred. He felt guilty about the way he had dumped her and he wanted to talk to her and ask her if everything had gone smoothly in St. Thomas. He also wanted to make sure that she wasn't mad at him and didn't bear him any grudges.

"Mildred's in the hospital," Louise Neill said sourly, recognizing the voice of her daughter's onetime, here-today-gone-tomorrow suitor. "Having *your* baby!"

Russell was shocked by the news so bluntly and cruelly delivered. He had sent Mildred a check for the abortion. She had cashed it right away. Russell had received the canceled check to prove it. He had taken it for granted that Mildred had taken care of herself. Now he had been told that she hadn't. He had been told that there was a baby. A second baby. The impact of the revelation staggered Russell and questions rushed through his mind.

How could Mildred have gone ahead and done anything so irresponsible as having a child who would grow up without a father? Mildred knew that he was married. She knew that, no matter how passionately Russell felt about her, he was a Dahlen and therefore he would not be able to divorce his wife for her. Didn't she care about her reputation? Didn't she care about the child's future? How did she intend to support her baby? How would she bring it up without a father? What would she name it?

Russell knew that Mildred was stubborn, yet he had never for one instant believed her when she had threatened to have their child. He had never heard of a woman who deliberately went ahead and had an illegitimate child. No one had. Even the possibility was inconceivable to Russell. Mildred's decision seemed to him selfish and reckless. He wondered who she had wanted to punish? Him? Herself? Their child?

Now, Russell realized, he had two children, one who would be a Dahlen, one he could raise, one to whom he could give everything, a daughter he would love even though she was only a girl. That sudden thought of Russell's triggered a sudden, crazy hope. Outlandish . . . impossible . . . but perhaps, just perhaps, the answer to his prayers.

Russell showered and dressed rapidly, checked out of the Roosevelt, took a cab uptown to the garage and got into his Buick. Using the last of his ration stamps, he filled the tank of his car and headed for the Triboro Bridge and New England. By the time he got to the tiny Mercy Hospital, he had talked himself into believing that even though he had failed to produce a son with Joyce, things might have turned out better with Mildred.

Russell wasn't exactly sure what he had in mind, but he thought he would offer Mildred a few thousand if the baby was a girl; if it was a boy, he decided that he would divorce Joyce and marry Mildred. Then he would bring up the boy on Park Avenue as his rightful son and heir. How he would work out the details hadn't really occurred to him, but he was sure it could be done. One of the advantages of being a Dahlen was that almost anything could be arranged.

"Maternity?" Russell asked the receptionist.

"Second floor. Turn left."

Russell nodded and smiled. Maybe, he thought, things would turn out well after all.

The delivery, although several weeks premature, had been an uneventful one and Mildred was in bed looking tired but happy. The baby, wrapped in a blanket, was in her arms and Mildred was amazed to see Russell Dahlen on the threshold of her room. Painfully she had forced herself to forget him and now that she had just about succeeded, here he was! He waved and was about to say hello when Mildred suddenly covered her mouth and screamed.

"Oh, my God!"

"What?" replied Russell, startled.

Wordlessly, Mildred pointed.

Russell turned and saw a man coming up behind him, a strong, muscular man in a red-and-black-checked wool hunting shirt and heavy field boots. It was the beginning of hunting season, and Will Bantry planned to go up to the Canadian border after he made sure Mildred was all right.

"Get out of here! You already caused enough trouble!" Will said loudly, almost shouting. He knew Russell by sight, just as he knew everyone who had ever set foot in Wilcom by sight. On the way to the hospital, Will had had a few to give him the courage to face the woman he wanted to marry and the kid who wasn't his. He grabbed Russell by the arm and began to push him toward the door.

"I just wanted to see Mildred and the baby," Russell explained, twisting away and moving further into the room, away from Will. "I wanted to give you some money . . . for the baby," he added, valiantly standing his ground. He addressed Mildred but included Will in his offer, hoping to mollify him with money.

"We don't want your money," sneered Will. Will Bantry was a union man. He had a good job, a good paycheck and good benefits. He could well afford to support a wife and a family. The last thing his pride would allow would be for him to accept money.

"Suppose we ask Mildred?" said Russell in the big-city accent that sounded so offensively affected to Will.

"Suppose you just get out of here?" mocked Will, imitating the snotty-sounding upper-class accent. He stepped toward Russell and grabbed him by the arm. He twisted it up behind Russell's back, propelling him toward the door. Once again, Russell twisted away.

"It's my baby, too," insisted Russell stubbornly, although the blanket was pink and the baby was a girl and Russell wished he had never set foot in the state of Massachusetts. "I want to help."

It was exactly the wrong thing to say. It reminded Will once again that Mildred wasn't perfect and that the baby wasn't his.

"Help? You ran out on Mildred!" Will snarled, sounding almost like an animal. The smell of whisky on his breath collided sickeningly with Russell's hangover as Will stepped in front of Russell and shoved him toward the door. "Now you can get out of here and stay out."

"I want to see my baby!" Russell said, shoving back.

"Never!" said Will and he stepped back half a pace and took a swing at Russell, hitting him in the jaw and causing him to stagger toward the wall. Russell ricocheted off the nightstand, upsetting a carafe of water and sending it crashing to the floor. Mildred began to scream and Russell, who had never been physically threatened and did not know how to defend himself, sagged helplessly toward the floor as Will, fists raised, head down, came toward him again.

Mildred, terrified that the two men might crash into the bed and hurt the baby, rolled out of bed to the floor, her baby in her arms, as the floor nurse and an orderly, attracted by the ruckus, ran into the room. The orderly seized Will from behind and wrestled him off balance, while the nurse grabbed at Russell, pulling him away from Will and propelling him out of the room.

"If I ever see you again, I'll kill you!" shouted Will, escaping from the orderly and chasing Russell as he fled down the corridor and into the parking lot. "I mean it! I'll kill you!"

As Russell scrambled into his car, Will went to his truck and grabbed the hunting rifle from the cab. When Russell gunned the ignition Will took quick aim and fired. The shot nicked the rear fender, chipping the glossy paint. As Russell made a hard right into traffic, three beefy security guards, alerted by the floor staff, ran into the parking lot and pinned Will to the ground.

Saving her baby's life almost cost Mildred hers. Her leap to the floor from the high hospital bed so soon after the delivery caused her to hemorrhage. It took half a dozen transfusions to bring her back and, when she left the hospital with her baby two weeks later, the first thing she did was go to the county jail where, using part of the money Russell had sent which she had deposited in the bank for Lana's future, she bailed Will out. With the rest, Mildred hired a lawyer to defend Will and, persuaded by her testimony, the judge let Will off with a warning not to drink during the hunting season.

At their marriage before the justice of the peace a month later, Will vowed to love, honor and cherish while Mildred vowed to love, honor and obey. The promises they made to each other before the marriage, though, were even more solemn.

Will promised to give the baby his name and bring her up as if she were his own. Mildred promised never to tell anyone that another man was the child's father. She also promised never to see Russell Dahlen again and never to accept so much as a dime from him.

"I'm the man in this family and I'll pay the bills," Will said, refusing to admit even to himself the depth of his hatred and resentment toward Mildred's handsome, upper-class lover, a man who had had everything handed to him on a silver platter. A man who had had everything Will had never had. Including Mildred.

In the next two years, Mildred had two more children, John and Kevin. Will showered all his love on the two children he knew were his, while Lana grew up in an atmosphere of poisoned resentment and crushing rejection.

"What did I do wrong? Why does he hate me so much?" Lana asked her mother over and over as she grew up. She could not understand why her father ignored her and, when he wasn't ignoring her, criticized and humiliated her with a vicious tongue.

"Nothing," Mildred said, keeping her promise to Will. "*You* didn't do a thing wrong." She was also never able to explain what Will meant every time he got drunk and repeated his murderous threat.

"I wasn't *that* drunk. I meant what I said," Will would say as if daring someone, anyone, to challenge him. "If I ever lay eyes on him again, I'm going to kill him."

"Who?" Lana would ask, terrified of her father's violent temper. "Who is he going to kill?"

Will would threaten anyone and everyone: the boss, the foreman, the shop steward, Mildred's boyfriend from before they had gotten married, the widow next door whose dog barked all night long, the bitch at the power company who threatened to turn off the electricity if the bill wasn't paid on time. Sometimes, even though it didn't make sense, his anger would be so fearsome that Lana was afraid that he really meant her. That he wanted to kill *her*.

"Don't pay him any mind," Mildred would say. "He'll forget it as soon as he sobers up."

Except that he always got drunk again and Lana swore that, just as soon as she could, she would get out of that house. She would leave and never return. She would get even with Will for ignoring her and abusing her. She would make him notice her and admire her. She would make the whole world notice her and admire her.

*   *   *

Deedee and Lana. Rich girl, poor girl, socialite and rebel. They should never have known each other. They should never have met. Yet their lives were joined by love and money and by not one man but two: the charming but sadly flawed father they would both love but could never count on and the brilliant outlaw with the Midas touch they would both love but never possess. A man who would forever transform their ideas about love and money and themselves . . . a man from nowhere named Slash Steiner.

III

THE MAN FROM NOWHERE

He couldn't remember his mother and he never knew his father and he never knew for certain when his birthday was. Although he would never know it, his mother, Edith, had been a dancer and actress with a U.S.O. theatrical company that toured army bases during World War II. Edith was the quintessential nice girl who couldn't say no. She was sleeping with the company's director because he was older and very sophisticated and also because he could help her career. She was sleeping with the leading man because he was so handsome she just couldn't resist, and she was sleeping with the leading man's understudy, who was also the script man, publicity man and troupe photographer just because she liked him.

It was long before the Pill had been invented. Young, unmarried women did not blithely go to their doctors and ask for a diaphragm and, as Edith learned to her dismay, the Coca-Cola douches the girls recommended backstage weren't foolproof. Any one of the three could have been the father; none of the three cared to take the slightest responsibility.

"Who, me?" said each with varying degrees of surprise, denial and/or blank ignorance.

Edith gave birth to the seven-pound, three-ounce boy on a Monday, not a matinee day, thank heavens, in a hospital near the rundown theatrical boarding house in Seattle where the troupe had been staying on its tour of the Pacific Northwest. The baby was so healthy and so well formed that even the nurses, used to newborns, exclaimed over him. From the earliest hours of his life, he had a magnetism that made him absolutely irresistible.

"I know a nice couple who'd love to have him," one of the ward nurses told Edith. "They'd give you a thousand dollars." A thousand dollars was a fortune. The only people Edith had ever heard of who had that kind of money were movie stars or gangsters.

"Sell my baby? Never!" said Edith, horrified. "I'm going to keep him. I'll bring him up by myself!"

"It won't be easy," warned the nurse, a dour and very practical woman. "A thousand dollars is a lot of money," she pointed out unnecessarily, not adding that a nice 10 percent commission would be hers if she could deliver the newborn boy to the waiting couple.

"It's *not* a lot of money!" said Edith vehemently. "It's nothing compared to my baby."

From Seattle to Boise, from Cheyenne to Omaha to Des Moines to Chicago to Philadelphia, true to her brave words, Edith took her baby along with her on the tour. However, in New York, unable to dance, go to rehearsals, pack and unpack, take care of diapers and formula and 4 A.M. feedings and be on time for showtime, Edith tearfully caved in to reality. Because she was ashamed of what she was doing and didn't want anyone to know, she bundled up her precious baby and took the train to Long Island City, where she had heard there was an excellent orphanage, the Saint Ignatius Residence for Boys. Although run by the Catholic church, Saint Ignatius accepted boys of all races, colors and religions. Black and white and yellow, Catholic and Protestant and Jewish, God loved them all and so did the priests and nuns who staffed Saint Ignatius. The nun who took him asked for his name.

"Boy Doe," replied Edith. She had fallen in love with the unusual name on the blue beaded bracelet the Seattle hospital had placed around his wrist at his birth. Wanting to conceal her unwed state, Edith had given her name at the hospital as

Edith Doe, thinking of it almost as a stage name. She had never anticipated the bracelet, and she had never anticipated that her child would be a boy. She was so sure the child would be a girl that she had already decided to name her Sarah, after the divine Bernhardt. When they told her she had delivered a son, she had to ask for time to think of a name.

The minute Edith saw "Boy Doe" on the tiny beaded bracelet, she realized it was perfect. It was short and therefore ideal for a marquee. It was memorable, always a plus for those in the public eye, and it was easy for anyone to pronounce. Edith decided to keep the name for good and bring her son up as Boy. In fact, when she got enough money, she would legally change her own name to Doe. She had already decided to tell the publicity man to change her billing to Edith Doe. She would use it as her stage name. Perhaps it might change her luck.

"What?" repeated the nun, not believing her ears. "That's not a name!"

"Yes, it is. His name is Boy," insisted Edith in a voice that made the nun back down. "I never wanted my child to be ordinary."

Ordinary or not ordinary, the nun had never heard of such a thing. Although she most certainly did not approve, she was too timid to give the child the name she, herself, would have picked—Malachy, after the saint—and in the space provided for the Christian name, she inserted a bold diagonal slash, leaving it to the other sisters or perhaps even one of the priests to name him. None of them ever did, though, because when Edith left she promised with tears in her eyes that one day she would come back and get her boy.

"How could I abandon my beautiful Boy Doe?" Edith asked the last time she held him and kissed him before returning to the city for the eight-thirty performance. "I'll be back for him. I promise."

"The mother should name him. It's only right," everyone at the Saint Ignatius Residence agreed, moved by Edith's tears and taking her at her word. The war had torn families apart, and often parents were forced to leave their children at Saint Ignatius for a while. When they could, they always came back for them and everyone believed that, one day, as soon as she could, Edith would come back, too.

Edith, despite the sincerity of her promise, was not to be heard from again, and Boy grew up with no family or relatives at all. No uncles or aunts, no cousins or grandparents, no brothers or sisters ever came to visit him or to take him home for the holidays. No kin, however distant, however dubious their claims to relationship, ever inquired after him. No letters or packages ever arrived for him. No telephone ever rang for him and no car ever drove up to take him away, not even for an afternoon's outing.

Alone of all the boys who stayed at Saint Ignatius, Boy seemed to have no one, seemed to be connected to no one. He had no parents who, temporarily, could not afford to support him, no family who, one day, would come back for him, no relative, however distant or far removed, who seemed to care if he lived or died. Boy lived a lonely and isolated life with only a lonely and isolated future seeming to await him. He seemed to be someone who had all the odds against him.

Boy Doe grew up with the director's savvy, the leading man's good looks, the understudy's way with words and publicity—and his mother's sense of drama. When Boy was five, Father Hugh, the director of Saint Ignatius, agreed with the nuns that it was time for Boy to choose a name for himself, something to replace Boy. Boy, who had nothing, no family or relatives or friends, did not even have a name.

"At least," said Father Hugh, asking the other priests and nuns for suggestions, "Boy should have *one* thing everyone else has: a proper name."

The nuns suggested John or Malachy and the priests suggested Peter or Paul, but Boy didn't like any of the suggestions. He said that he already knew what name he wanted. He pointed to the bold penciled slash on his admission documents.

"I want to be called Slash," he said, his gray eyes intense with the seriousness of the decision he was making. The name was his own invention and he had fallen in love with it. Slash sounded invincible, invulnerable, unconquerable. Slash sounded like everything Boy had always dreamed of being.

"Slash?" said Sister Beatrice, the one with the mustache, not believing her ears. "I've never heard of it! No one has!"

"That's no Christian name," said Father Timothy, his round, red face turning beet red in his irritation. Father Timothy had no tolerance whatsoever for the slightest deviation from the conventional. "That's not even a heathen name!"

"You can't call yourself Slash," said Father Paul, more calmly, trying to talk Boy out of his outrageous idea. "No one's ever heard of such a name!"

"That's all right," said Boy with the enigmatic smile that even then seduced as it concealed. "They will."

Such was the force of his will and persuasiveness that sooner or later everyone, including Sister Beatrice and Father Timothy, called Boy Slash. In no time at all people couldn't remember any other name. It seemed so perfect for him.

Edith would have been proud of him. It was the kind of name people would remember.

And it would have been wonderful on a marquee.

Topic A at Saint Ignatius was adoption. The parentless boys at the orphanage talked incessantly about being adopted, and their fantasies were all directed toward being part of a real family. They lived for the day, once a month, when prospective foster parents came to meet the boys. Bathed and brushed and on their best behavior, they were anxious to please, waiting to be chosen.

"Not me," declared Slash to the others, "I'm going to do the choosing."

It was not the only outrageous statement Slash had ever made.

"I'm going to make my first million before I'm thirty," Slash had declared for the first time just after his eighth birthday. The birthday had passed, like all the others in

Slash's brief, bleak life, with no cards, no phone calls, no festively wrapped gifts, no special outing with family, friends or relatives.

Sister Anne, the cook, made him a cake frosted with chocolate and decorated with eight small blue candles. The priests gave him a picture book of the lives of the saints. Their kindly gestures, however, did not fill the deep sense of abandonment which nothing seemed to heal. Nothing, that is, except the collections for which Slash had become celebrated. Marbles, baseball cards, stamps—whatever it was that the boys of Saint Ignatius most craved, Slash always had the most.

"One day," he told Father Hugh, "I'm going to have the most money, too."

Father Hugh cautioned Slash against the worship of mammon, but his words went unheard. The thought of having the most, of having more than anyone else, much, much more, was the only dream that helped fill the deep inner emptiness that pursued Slash everywhere, even in his dreams.

Slash knew exactly what he wanted: not only a way out but a way up. Even then, even in his very earliest years, Slash hated being poor. He hated eating inferior cuts of meat, hated wearing shabby, hand-me-down clothes, hated washing with cheap, lye-smelling soap and sleeping on rough, hard sheets. The way out—and up—came in the form of Richard and Belle Steiner. Unable to have children of their own, the Steiners decided to adopt. They visited Saint Ignatius because of its excellent reputation and because it was the closest orphanage to their Long Island City home.

The first time they came to Saint Ignatius, Slash noticed Belle's mink coat and he learned that Richard Steiner, an accountant, had wanted to be a lawyer but hadn't been able to afford law school. His dream, Slash had also learned, was to have a son who would do what he had never been able to do.

"My real father was a lawyer," Slash told Richard proudly, although Richard Steiner knew perfectly well that the identity of the boy's father was unknown. The brave but sad little lie touched Richard's heart. "That's my dream, too."

"And when I'm successful," Slash promised Belle, "I'm going to buy you a Cadillac to go with your mink coat."

Slash also told the Steiners that his real parents were Jewish. The other boys were shocked but Slash didn't understand why.

"After all, maybe they were," Slash shrugged. "Nobody knows for sure."

Belle and Richard Steiner adopted Slash, and he grew up solidly middle class in a quiet, pleasant neighborhood of Long Island City. Slash never made a secret of being adopted and never had any interest in finding out about his real parents.

"They weren't interested in me. Why should I be interested in them?" he said, quite logically and without hostility. Even as a child, the past—over which he had no control—did not interest Slash. Only the present—and that to an extreme degree—attracted his attention. He would always be the first to be aware of current events and current trends. News fascinated him. History bored him. Now was all. Then was irrelevant.

Slash was well coordinated and graceful but uninterested in athletics. He was a good student and well liked although too aloof and self-contained to be really popular. Slash was noted for always being different. He was the only kid on the block with his own subscriptions to the *Wall Street Journal* and the *Racing Form*, and he caused a sensation in school by writing a senior English composition based on the *Variety* headlines.

He preferred the cool complexities of progressive jazz to the simplicities of pópular music and amassed a valuable collection of John Coltrane, Miles Davis and George Shearing records. He was equally disdainful of the conventional values of the squares and the avant-garde philosophies of the Beats. He aspired neither to a neat, suburban house with a white picket fence nor to a picturesque beatnik pad with orange-crate bookshelves and a mattress on the floor.

"I don't want to be an organization man in a gray flannel

suit," Slash told his best friend, Pete Oney. "And I don't want to be a so-called poet writing crap no one wants to read and starving in a cold-water flat."

"Who *do* you want to be?" asked Pete, who wanted to have fast cars and fast girls just like he imagined James Dean had.

"J. P. Morgan," said Slash soberly, picking a name out of the air. "I want to be the richest man in the country."

As Slash became accustomed to his adoptive home, he seemed to have shed the memories of Saint Ignatius completely. Only at night, when dreams of being back at Saint Ignatius turned into nightmares, did the stark, emotional bleakness of Slash's past intrude into the enviable life he had chosen and created for himself.

"It's all right," Belle would soothe, awakened by Slash's screams and running to his room in the middle of the night to comfort him. "It's all right. You're still here. You're still with us."

"We haven't taken you back," Richard would tell him. "We'll never take you back to Saint Ignatius. Never. You're ours now. Forever and always."

They would hold Slash and reassure him, and eventually Slash would be comforted and fall back to sleep. Yet, deep down, Slash didn't dare believe them. After all, his own mother had abandoned him, apparently without a second thought, and if his own flesh and blood could abandon him, why couldn't and wouldn't the whole rest of the world? Deep down, Slash feared that one day the Steiners would change their minds about him and take him back to Saint Ignatius, rejecting him as they might reject an unwanted visitor. To deal with his fears, Slash cultivated an almost intimidating self-sufficiency, and he permitted himself to depend on no one.

"Sometimes I think that boy is a hundred years old," Belle told Richard when Slash, all of eleven years old, suddenly and without warning returned his allowance, telling Belle that he no longer needed it. He told Belle that he had been lending out the money he made on his paper route and charging a small but profitable amount of interest. He now had enough money for all his needs and no longer required the allowance the Steiners gave him every Friday. Belle and Richard were impressed by Slash's independence and vaguely hurt by his unwillingness to depend on them.

"I sometimes wonder if he needs us at all," Richard said wistfully when Slash turned fourteen and gave them a television set for Chanukah. "I thought we adopted a child. Sometimes I think he adopted us instead."

Richard and Belle were thrilled with the television set, a Philco no less, that they had hesitated to buy fearing it was beyond their budget. They were slightly in awe of the poised and self-possessed teenager whose only symptom of vulnerability was the nightmares that still plagued him, nightmares of being sent back to Saint Ignatius.

"Will I ever stop having them?" Slash asked Belle in one of the few moments he revealed any uncertainty.

"I hope so," said Belle, knowing from the way Slash woke up sweating and screaming just how much the nightmares disturbed him. "You'll never have to go back to Saint Ignatius," she told him, wanting to comfort him. "Not as long as we're alive."

"Never?" asked Slash.

"Never," she said, holding him tight.

Slash, who rarely believed anyone or anything, believed Belle, and his fear of being sent back to Saint Ignatius eventually faded. In its place emerged an obsessive fear of death.

I V
MINK AND
MOUTON

*W*ith the charm that had been his since birth, with seal-straight dark hair, clear gray eyes and a classic profile, Slash resembled a matinee idol and most certainly could have been a model or a movie star. His inclinations, though, in no way followed the theatrical bent of his mother. He meant what he said when he told Pete that he wanted to be the J. P. Morgan of his time. And just as his nightmares went with Slash when he went to live with Richard and Belle Steiner, so did his dreams.

"I'm going to be rich," he declared to his adoptive parents. "One day I'm going to have all the money in the world."

Richard and Belle, used to Slash's extravagant imagination and wild flights of fantasy, tried to bring him back to earth. Comfortable with their own modest aspirations and frightened by Slash's too-extravagant ambitions, they cautioned him to be realistic and to think about the future.

"Go to law school," Richard said, remembering Slash's own words about his real father.

"Or become an accountant like Richard," advised Belle, trying to persuade Slash to be practical. "Accountants can always find work. Perhaps if you study hard, you might even become a CPA."

Slash was much too kind and far too considerate or, perhaps, to put a less kind interpretation on his behavior, much too manipulative to say that his ambitions went far beyond becoming a mere lawyer or a CPA. Instead, he said that he would think about it.

* * *

Several weeks after he went to live with the Steiners, Slash had learned that Belle's coat was not mink but mouton.

"Good heavens! It's not mink!" said Belle, laughing at Slash's naive error. "We could never afford mink."

"One day you'll be able to afford mink," said Slash seriously, determination on his face. "The best mink in the whole city! And," he added, just as seriously, "I'm going to get you a Cadillac to go along with it just the way I said."

Slash's naive error became a family joke, a joke that Slash took seriously, a joke that he remembered for the rest of his life. In later years, after he had become enormously rich, Slash still liked to say that wanting to buy Belle Steiner a mink coat was the real motive behind his huge success.

Slash loved the Steiners but, clear-eyed and determined to be realistic, he never thought of them as his real parents. His favorite Steiner was Sammy, the black sheep of the family. A bespectacled, cigar-chomping fireplug of a man, Sammy Steiner was Long Island City's biggest bookie. Slash often spent weekends in Uncle Sammy's smoky, beery bachelor flat manning the phones, toting up the wagers and personally delivering the bigger payoffs. While working for Uncle Sammy, Slash discovered that he loved the risk and thrill of gambling. He also learned something that school had only barely hinted at: that he had an extraordinary facility with numbers.

Numbers and the way they worked, their mix of symmetry, certainty and plasticity had, for Slash, a fascination nothing else could match, and his ability to work with them was as instinctive as a poet's ability to work with words and wrest from them their magic. Even as an eleven-year-old, Slash Steiner could calculate odds, payoffs and pools in his head faster and more accurately than any adding machine ever made.

As a fifteen-year-old, Slash lied about his age and got a summer job as a page at the New York Stock Exchange, running orders from the brokers to the floor traders. He fell in love with the beat of the street, with the view of the Statue of Liberty from Battery Park and with the stone and granite buildings of Wall Street, whose solid, unyielding faces seemed to guarantee riches, power and invulnerability. At night he took accounting courses at Long Island University, and by the time he graduated from high school the money, the action, the adrenaline highs of risky gambles and fast profits were in his blood. Wall Street had everything Uncle Sammy's betting parlor had except that it was legal and the profits were higher.

By the time Slash was sixteen, he knew he wanted to get his stockbroker's license. College was something to be gotten through as quickly as possible, and right after Slash's graduation from Adelphi in 1960, disaster struck. Disaster that Slash would turn into opportunity.

Richard Steiner believed in old-fashioned loyalty and hard work, in respect for authority and obedience to the rules. He had had the same job at the same company for almost a quarter of a century. To him the company he worked for was a benevolent and all-powerful institution and the people who ran it were wise, authoritative figures to be neither questioned nor disobeyed. The name of the company was Lancome & Dahlen. The name of his boss—who was only a few years older than Slash—was Trip Lancome. One of *the* Lancomes. The name of his boss's boss was Russell Dahlen.

"One of *the* Dahlens," Richard always said, proud at the association. According to Richard, it was the Lancomes who had the class. The Dahlens who had the brains.

Slash had grown up hearing his father's stories so often that Lancome & Dahlen and the men who ran it had become legends. There was old Luther Dahlen, a stock market wizard, the financial brains of the company. Luther's partner, Hamilton Lancome, Sr., now dead, had provided the crucial social contacts that meant entree into the world of the rich and powerful. Russell Dahlen, Luther's son, oversaw the internal operations of the company, and Junior Lancome, Ham Senior's heir, continued to cultivate the social contacts that brought the right clients and the right money to Lancome & Dahlen. Trip Lancome, Junior's son, was the only member of the third generation of the original founders to work at the firm. Trip Lancome was the sole heir to the presidency of Lancome & Dahlen because, said Richard, he was the only third-generation male descendant. The Dahlens, unfortunately, had no living male heir.

"I feel sorry for the Dahlens," Richard said, identifying as he always did with his superiors. "Their little boy died. They only have a girl. It's a shame. Girls can't inherit."

The girl's name was Dolores, Richard had told Slash, although everyone always referred to her as Deedee. She wasn't important, though, Richard said. A girl couldn't be. Not on Wall Street.

Richard Steiner spoke of Lancome & Dahlen and of his employers as if they were perfect, their words to be reverently heeded, their ideas to be unhesitatingly carried out. Lancome & Dahlen seemed, to the young Slash, a place of virtual magic, its power immense, its influence unlimited, the people who worked there specially blessed and anointed. The heavenly saints of Slash's early youth had been replaced in his adolescence by more temporal deities.

However, because Richard Steiner was the wrong religion, because he had gone to the wrong schools, because he wore the wrong clothes and had the wrong parents, he would never get out of the back-room bullpen into a private office. He would never have a title to impress people or the salary, perks and benefits that went along with the title. Yet Richard never complained.

Son of a delicatessen owner who had gone bankrupt in the Depression and ended up washing dishes to support his family, Richard was extremely proud of his hard-won white-collar status. He was always aware of how short the step was from wearing a clean shirt and neatly pressed suit every day to working in a sweat-stained undershirt in a steaming restaurant kitchen for the minimum wage. To Richard, Lancome & Dahlen was the protective and mostly benevolent but sometimes frightening father to whom he owed everything. He was grateful for the opportunity to work long and diligently at such a prestigious place, and he had impressed on Slash the virtues of hard work, thrift and loyalty.

"Just remember," Richard had told Slash a thousand times, speaking from the heart, "what you give, you get."

Much as Slash had secretly suspected, Richard turned out to be wrong. Eight months before his retirement Richard Steiner was fired. Trip Lancome called him in on a Friday morning.

"Overhead has been getting out of control," Trip said, making it sound as if he were confiding in Richard. "Profits are being adversely affected. I'm sorry," Trip continued, telling Richard that his job was being cut. "Very sorry."

Trip Lancome handed Richard two weeks' salary and told him that he was not to return on Monday. In a seven-minute interview, Richard Steiner lost his benefits, his pension, his security—everything he had worked almost twenty years to earn.

Paradoxically—and to Slash, infuriatingly—Richard refused to get angry. Instead, he seemed to be on the company's side.

"I'm not angry," Richard Steiner kept insisting in his quiet voice, his brown eyes hurt but resolutely dry behind his thick glasses. "They had to trim the payroll. It was a necessity. The overhead was getting way out of control."

To Slash's amazement, even when they double-crossed him, Richard Steiner still thought that Lancome & Dahlen was perfect.

Slash absolutely could not believe Richard's meek acceptance of his undeserved fate, and in a beer-fueled rage, Slash and his best friend, Peter Oney, went to a classically columned white granite building on the corner of Wall and Broad late that same night. Chiseled in chaste Roman letters above the entrance was the name of the company that owned it and whose offices were inside: Lancome & Dahlen.

Using a key swiped from Richard, Slash and Pete let

themselves in through the unguarded employees' entrance. Not knowing exactly what they had in mind, they walked through the ground floor, looking into the impressive reception areas, trying out the cushy leather chairs in the elegant conference rooms and finally wandering up to the partners' offices and stenographic, trading and filing areas on the second floor.

"Jesus Christ!" said Pete, impressed at the marble staircase, the crystal chandeliers, the Oriental rugs, the polished antique furniture. "They must be made of money!"

"I hate them," said Slash grimly, refusing to be impressed. Instead, he felt all the rage Richard couldn't. He wanted to kill his father's boss for what he had done. He wanted to find Trip Lancome and personally strangle him.

"Richard gave his life to them and they treated him like a piece of shit," Slash said and, with that, picked up a typewriter and crashed it to the floor. Taking a cue from Slash, Pete hurled a white china cup filled with pencils against the wall.

"I hate rich bastards just on principle," said Pete, pleased with the destruction they had caused. Pete's father, also an accountant, worked for a Long Island City bakery, and Pete shared Slash's dreams of money and freedom and his hatred of the people that he thought possessed them.

Together, Slash and Pete trashed the entire second floor back-office bullpen, smashing typewriters and desks, pulling out phones by their wires and throwing the contents of filing cabinets all over. Using his Zippo, Pete began to set fires in wastecans while Slash, using his penknife, ripped chair cushions and curtains.

Like guerrilla fighters, Slash and Pete moved methodically through the rear offices, steno and trading areas, destroying everything they could. When they got to the door of the big corner office in the front, they were shocked to come face to face with another intruder: a handsome and distinguished-looking man with wavy, chestnut hair and expensive, slightly disarranged clothing. He was embracing a voluptuous, flashy-looking redheaded girl, a girl young enough to be his daughter.

"Who are you?" the man demanded, turning from the girl and looking straight at Slash. "What are you doing here?"

"Oh, shit!" blurted Pete as the girl, startled, froze and seemed momentarily unsure about what to do.

Her eyes met Slash's for an instant—intruder acknowledging intruder, outsider acknowledging outsider. Then she turned and fled, disappearing into the private bathroom that adjoined the office.

"What are you doing here?" Russell Dahlen repeated, squaring his shoulders and straightening his jacket.

"I could ask you the same thing," Slash replied coolly, recognizing the green-eyed, chestnut-haired Russell Dahlen as one of the "big bosses" his father spoke of with such awe.

"I belong here," Russell said, his hands checking the knot of his tie.

"*She* doesn't," said Slash, standing his ground and indicating the girl who had disappeared into the bathroom.

"At least I'm not destroying private property," Russell replied, ignoring Slash's inference and maintaining his dignity. "I suggest you leave. Now."

"You gonna tell?" Pete asked, with unsteady bravado.

Russell, thinking over the risks of calling the police and the certain tabloid publicity that would undoubtedly follow, was silent for a moment. The Lancomes would ask a lot of questions about what Russell had been doing in the office that late at night. Joyce would be angry and suspicious. Luther would hit the ceiling, demanding to know why he hadn't thrown the intruders out before they had done any damage. Meanwhile, the smell of smoke was getting stronger.

"Hell, no!" Slash said, aware of Russell's hesitation and sensing his guilt. He turned toward Pete. "He's just as scared as we are. Now let's get out of here!"

Slash and Pete ran along the corridors and down the front steps to the ground floor as the fire spread through the back offices while Russell Dahlen and the girl, holding wet towels to their faces, ran through the burning corridors behind them. A heavy filing cabinet, buckling with the heat as the papers inside burst into flame, sagged drunkenly and crashed on Pete, pinning his legs and trapping Russell Dahlen and the girl in the burning corridor. Flames licked up behind them. The heavy, burning cabinet blocked their exit.

"Slash!" screamed Pete, beating ineffectually at the flames with his bare hands.

Russell and the girl, choking and coughing, tried to help Slash as he pulled the cabinet away just enough to free one of Pete's legs and to allow Russell and the girl to escape.

"Run!" Slash shouted at them. "Run!"

He shoved Russell through the flaming passageway and pushed the girl after him. Russell hesitated indecisively for a moment and then grabbed the girl by the hand and ran along to the ground floor exits. The girl glanced back. Fire licked up around the two young men.

"They're going to die!" she screamed. Her red hair was mussed and wild and there was a dark smudge along her cheek. She started to run back toward the trapped young man and his friend, thinking that she could help move the cabinet.

"Get back!" shouted Slash at her. "Get out!"

"Get out!" urged Russell, repeating Slash's instruction. He grabbed the girl by the hand again and dragged her along with him. "Come on, Lana. There's nothing you can do!"

Slash never hesitated. Taking off his jacket, he beat out the flames engulfing Pete and, with one last, enormous effort, shoved the cabinet away with all his might and half carried, half dragged Pete from the burning offices to the sidewalk. Russell and the girl had just disappeared into a taxi. Slash watched the yellow cab make the left turn as the light on the corner changed.

Lana, thought Slash. It was a perfect name for a hooker.

"I hate those rich cocksuckers!" Pete said a moment later when he and Slash were safe in the street. In a delayed reaction to his close call, Pete began to shake and with trembling fingers lit a cigarette even though he knew how much

Slash hated smoking, despising it as a weakness. "I'd like to kill them all."

Slash was silent.

"Not me," he finally said, his blind anger dissolving as his mind worked. The sumptuous luxury of the place and its aura of invincibility had made an indelible impression on Slash. His ambitions, fueled by enormous energy and intelligence, hitherto somewhat scattered, had, that night, found a focus.

Slash had always wanted to be rich. But what did rich mean? J. P. Morgan was just a name out of a history book. It had no reality for Slash. Richer than who? Richer than what? Suddenly, Slash knew. He wanted to be richer than Russell Dahlen and he wanted *his* name to be chiseled on the front of the building that was a combination of fortress and temple.

Slash watched as the taillights of the taxi disappeared and he turned to Pete. "Why get mad when you can get even?"

While Slash was lost in thoughts of money and power and revenge, Pete thought about the girl they'd seen in Russell Dahlen's office. He wondered who she was and what she was doing with Russell Dahlen who, even though he was loaded, was old enough to be her father.

"You know perfectly well what she was doing with him," said Slash contemptuously. "I just hope she soaked him plenty."

What he didn't say was that he, too, had noticed a girl, a girl with exotic, slanted eyes and glossy blue-black hair whose photograph in a silver frame stood on the cabinet behind Russell Dahlen's desk. She looked rich and remote, regal and unavailable. She was clearly a girl who came from a different world than the girl he had just seen in Russell Dahlen's office.

As the fire engines, sirens screaming, roared up to the burning building, Slash wondered who she was. And he wondered what he'd have to do to get her.

On Monday Slash telephoned Russell Dahlen.

"You don't know me and you don't know my name," he said, introducing himself. "But I saved your life on Friday night. Your life and Lana's life. We have something to talk about."

"She wasn't what you thought," Russell said, ignoring the young man's innuendo. He guessed what was coming and wanting to forestall open-ended blackmail. "I'd like to remind you that I didn't start the fire. Nevertheless, I'd like to give you a reward. You've earned it."

"I'm not interested in a reward," said Slash. "I want my father's job back."

"And who is your father?" Russell asked, taken by surprise.

"Richard Steiner," said Slash. The name was familiar, but Russell could not quite place Richard Steiner. "He worked in Accounting. Until Trip Lancome fired him. On your orders."

"I'll look into it," promised Russell, cautious and wary, grateful for being saved but afraid of being cornered. Although Russell had ordered the cutback, he had known none of the specifics about the low-level firings. He had allowed Trip to make all the personnel decisions. Russell called for Richard Steiner's employment file, found his records impeccable and told Trip that he was making an exception to his order for a cutback in overhead.

"Richard Steiner was valuable. He was with the company for almost twenty years. Shouldn't he be rehired?" Russell said to Trip. As usual at Lancome & Dahlen, an order was never directly given. The style at Lancome & Dahlen was indirect. Russell's order was couched as a suggestion, but Trip did not for one moment misinterpret it.

"Whatever you say," replied Trip, annoyed at being overruled by his father's partner. "As long as I don't have to do it. I don't like to look weak or indecisive in front of the help."

Russell Dahlen returned Slash's call personally, but only after he had checked Richard Steiner's files *and* taken the precaution of finding out as much as he could about Richard Steiner's brash and nervy son. He had telephoned Adelphi for Slash's transcript and checked Slash's former boss at Merrill

Lynch. The college transcript showed straight A's. His former boss said that Slash Steiner was the sharpest kid who had ever come through the office. Bar none.

"Your father will have his job back. And you can have a job, too," Russell said. "Of course, we expect you to be discreet."

"That's a payoff, not a job offer," said Slash.

"Then suppose I just offer you a job?" said Russell admiringly. Slash Steiner had the kind of *cojones* Russell wished *he* had.

"How much are you paying?"

"Seven thousand." It was five hundred dollars more than the standard beginner's salary.

"Make it seventy-five hundred," said Slash, "and I'll think about it."

At first the young man that Russell Dahlen hired for a starting salary of seven thousand five hundred dollars a year didn't seem particularly different from any of the other young men of that very last year of the Eisenhower era. He wore a studiously shapeless gray suit, a button-down oxford cloth shirt, a soberly striped rep tie. His shoes were shined, his hair was neatly trimmed and his degree in economics was brand new.

His ideas of love, like those of other Americans in that last of the pre-Pill years, had been formed by Doris Day and Elizabeth Taylor movies, by songs that rhymed June with moon and asserted that love and marriage went together like a horse and carriage. His ideas about money, no less conventional, were that money, real money, was inherited and not earned, that money was for the old, not the young, and that money, hard to earn, was to be handled prudently and carefully invested, something to put aside for the rainy day that would inevitably come.

In 1960, when fitting in was everything, Slash Steiner was good at fitting in. The only thing noticeably different about him was his white MG sports car, and the only thing particularly noticeable about *that* was that he always parked it illegally and never got a ticket.

Slash had by no means given up his dreams of becoming rich, but how he was going to get that way, given the circumstances of his background and the tenor of the times, was a question to which he did not yet have the answer.

V

OLD MONEY/ NEW RULES

*L*ancome & Dahlen wasn't one of Wall Street's biggest firms, nor one of its oldest. It considered itself, however, one of Wall Street's best. Lancome & Dahlen prided itself on being safe, conservative and prestigious. Lancome & Dahlen did not seek out clients. Clients sought out Lancome & Dahlen. Lancome & Dahlen, its senior partners liked to say, didn't handle just any money; it handled the right money. Old money, respectable money, conservative money, money beyond reproach. Money that came with the right names and the right addresses and the right schools. Money that meant tradition and safety. Money that never had to say I'm sorry.

Portraits of the two founders and the eight original partners of Lancome & Dahlen hung in its paneled hallways. Not one, of course, was female. They were the kind of men who enjoyed Cuban cigars with Chivas Regal and patronized the same Savile Row tailors their fathers had. Each was a model of probity, caution and sobriety. Not one looked a minute under a hundred and ten.

"Not a rebel in the group," Junior Lancome liked to say, always with pride.

The offices matched the partners: well bred, well tailored, well proportioned. Rebuilt and redecorated after the fire, the offices looked the way they had the day the building was originally finished: as if they'd been there forever, muted and paneled and reeking with upper-class understatement.

Oriental rugs covered the gleaming parquet floors, green-shaded lamps stood on the desks and by decree unanimously passed at a board meeting the only telephones permitted were black. The partners' dining room was furnished with mahogany tables and Hepplewhite chairs. Madeira linen, fresh flowers, English silver and bone china were used daily. No alcohol was served, much to the dismay of the chef, a ruddy-cheeked Burgundian hired away from the Chambord.

The atmosphere, as Luther Dahlen and Hamilton Lancome, Sr., had intended it to be, was one of permanence and security much appreciated by the Republican businessmen, wealthy widows and family trust lawyers who kept their brokerage accounts at Lancome & Dahlen. Even though Lancome & Dahlen's business was making money, that crass activity was so covered over in encrusted layers of prestige and social polish as to be almost invisible.

For the first year, Slash played by the rules and did what he was told to do. He pored over quarterly reports, research department recommendations and Dun & Bradstreet ratings. He tallied buy and sell orders, tracked the profits and losses on individual portfolios and listened to the complaints, problems and suggestions of clients whose money was being invested by Lancome & Dahlen's senior account managers. He worked at a plain wooden desk in the open-area bullpen on the third floor, one floor above where Richard Steiner had spent his life and where Slash did not plan to spend his. It was a lot of hard work for not very much money.

"To tell you the truth," he told Pete Oney, disappointed in the lack of action and longing for the good old days at Uncle Sammy's, "it's a pain in the ass. A *boring* pain in the ass."

It was, however—and Slash knew it—a free education, and he made the most of it. He learned the mechanics of trading and the ins and outs of stocks and bonds. He absorbed the differences between preferred and common and the significance of price/earning ratios and the tell-tale asterisked items tucked away on the bottoms of balance sheets.

Because he had no social contacts and no old school ties to cash in on, Slash was given the clients no one else wanted—the widows who had plenty of time to call and second-guess every move, the third-generation heirs who treated their trustees as a combination babysitter, travel agent and headshrinker and the small potatoes accounts who, for one reason or another, were owed a favor.

"I run the Sanitation Department," Slash told Pete in disgust after a day of dealing with petty problems and complaints. "I get all the garbage accounts no one else wants."

"There's money in garbage," Pete reminded Slash when he was down in the dumps. "Just ask the Mafia."

In the long run Pete would turn out to be right, but at the time, Slash didn't see the gold in garbage. Mafia or no Mafia, on Wall Street, he told Pete, crap was crap.

Meanwhile, Slash began to follow the career of his first hero, Gerry Tsai, the brilliant Chinese-American mutual fund manager who was making his Fidelity Capital Fund the talk of the Street. Gerry Tsai was turning conventional investment wisdom on its ear with his razzle-dazzle market timing, frankly speculative stock picks and penchant for buying huge blocks of only a few stocks. Gerry Tsai broke all the rules and did it successfully. He was everything Slash wanted to be: rebel, outlaw, millionaire.

The partners at Lancome & Dahlen, like Queen Victoria, were not amused. They considered Gerry Tsai at best a flash in the pan, at worst a disruptive element in an orderly market. They said that he and his techniques were a passing fad like the hula hoop or elephant jokes.

"Of course they can't stand him," Slash told Richard. "For one thing, he's not a thousand and ten percent WASP. For another, he's making money hand over fist. Anything over four percent a year gives them the bends."

However, no matter how critical of Lancome & Dahlen's investment policies Slash was, there was nothing he could do for his clients except follow the Lancome & Dahlen party line. He could, however, do anything he wanted for himself and so, starting with seventeen hundred dollars saved from his salary and track winnings, Slash began trading his own account as 1960 turned into 1961. He did not buy the safe and sure blue chips like General Electric and U.S. Steel and AT&T that Lancome & Dahlen recommended for its clients. Instead, he bought shares like Polaroid and Xerox—stocks so outrageously speculative that they were considered nothing more than crapshooting. He ran his own account the way Gerry Tsai ran Fidelity Mutual.

"You're not investing," said Arthur Bozeman, a junior stock analyst who had been hired at the same time as Slash. With his three-piece suits and already receding hairline, Arthur, who had an accounting degree at a distinctly non-U Brooklyn college, seemed to have been born old. Arthur's ambitions went no further than Richard Steiner's and he could not imagine that the flashy and irreverent Slash would eventually change his entire life. "You're gambling."

"As long as I'm right," replied Slash unperturbed, "it's not gambling."

By the middle of 1962, Polaroid was up and so was Xerox. Despite the Cuban missile crisis of October, Slash, trusting his instincts, turned aggressively bullish. Buying on margin, Slash put every nickel he could lay his hands on into the stock market.

"The ride is just beginning," said Slash that fall as he watched his own account steadily increase in value. "Missile crisis or no missile crisis."

The youngest president in history was in the White House, hemlines were going up and old barriers coming down as the first black entered the University of Mississippi. Beatlemania was about to sweep the country, and when the Americans and the Russians stared at each other over the Cuban missile buildup, it was the Russians who blinked first. There seemed to be no barriers, no limits. The old had given way to the young, prejudice had given way to opportunity, and, as Slash was fond of pointing out, even the sky was no longer the limit as John Glenn, launched by rocket, orbited the earth.

By the end of the year, Slash's own net worth had risen a staggering 68 percent and the money he had invested for Richard and Belle gave the Steiners the first nest egg they had ever had. Even Uncle Sammy had to admit that going legit could have its points.

Slash, emboldened by how right he had been, began to ignore the Lancome & Dahlen buy recommendations and invest the portfolios that had been turned over to him exactly as he pleased.

"Aren't you afraid of getting fired?" Arthur asked. At Lancome & Dahlen no one ever rocked the boat. There was too much prestige, status and money involved in saying that you worked for Lancome & Dahlen.

"Of course," said Slash. "But I'll cross that bridge when I get to it. *If* I get to it."

November 22, 1963. For an entire generation, it was the day history began.

The early reports came at about one o'clock and were first heard on the small portable radio in the mail room. One of the secretaries immediately turned on the television set in the conference room, and everyone who had not gone out to lunch was glued to the first stunning reports about the shooting of a president in Dallas. While the presidential limousine was still on its way to Parkland Hospital, even before it was known for certain whether the president had been hit, even before it was known whether he had been injured and, if so, how badly, Slash left the conference room. He ran to his desk and got on the telephone to Wilson, Sykes, Lancome & Dahlen's trading firm.

"Sell, goddammit!" Slash could be heard shouting into the phone in his urgency. "Everything! Now!"

Heads turned in the conference room. More than one censorious glance was exchanged. More than one pair of eyebrows was raised.

The value of the market declined by thirteen billion dollars that one afternoon—the greatest slippage in value in the stock exchange's 170-year history—and Slash's fast action saved his clients' money. Slash earned even more criticism on November 26, the first day the market opened after the assassination, by buying in at the sound of the opening bell and catching the market back on the upswing.

Hamilton Lancome, Jr., considered Slash's attention to profit at a moment of national crisis unseemly.

"You're disgusting. All you can think about is money," Junior told Slash. An aristocratically tall and handsome man, Junior looked at Slash as if he were looking at a ragpicker in Tiffany's.

"I'm just doing the job I'm paid to do," Slash replied, infuriating Junior with his insolence. Slash always said, right out loud, that he had trouble respecting a forty-five-year-old man whose name was Junior.

Slash refused to apologize, continued to do as he pleased and followed the market up until the end of the year when the Dow, breaking the seven hundred mark, hit an all-time high. Slash was finding out that even on Wall Street breaking the rules could pay. Slash was beginning to discover the answer to the question of how a young man from nowhere could make his dreams come true. He was beginning to discover just how he could get rich.

Most of all, he was beginning to see that there was new money to be made and that the old rules just didn't apply any more.

In the middle of December, the time of the year when bonuses, raises and promotions were traditionally decided upon, Junior Lancome told his partner Russell, not for the first time, that he had made a big mistake in hiring Slash.

"He doesn't fit in here," said Junior. Junior didn't like anything about Slash: not his wrong-side-of-the-tracks accent, not his table manners, not the sunglasses he sometimes wore in the office, not his insolence, unpredictability or irreverence. He didn't like the length of his sideburns or the width of his ties. Junior called Slash a gambler in search of flashy but overly risky profits. Furthermore, he was still offended by Slash's preoccupation with money as a young president lay dying. "He's not our kind."

"What kind?" asked Russell, sarcastically.

* * *

Just as their two fathers had been partners, the two sons, now in their mid-forties, were partners. The difference was that while Luther and Ham Lancome, Sr., had chosen each other, Russell and Junior had inherited each other. Each felt he had been stuck with a dubious bargain, and theirs had been a guarded and suspicious relationship from the very beginning.

Junior Lancome was sick and tired of being considered a lightweight, with only a Social Register listing and a background of the right schools and the right clubs to his credit, especially since, over the years, Lancome & Dahlen's richest and most powerful clients had come to the firm through the Lancomes' connections. Russell Dahlen, on the other hand, had had a lifetime of having the Lancomes' precious social superiority thrown into his face, and he was more than fed up with it, especially since, over the years, it had been money earned by Dahlen brains and Dahlen savvy that had paid for Lancome social status.

"We're supposedly in business to make money for our clients," Russell told Junior, defending Slash. "No one has been better at doing that than Slash."

To that, Junior had no answer. He also had no real answer for Alicia Fulton, who was on the board of the Chelsea Child Care Association when she wanted to know why the association's portfolio, handled by the Lancome & Dahlen senior investment committee, was up 5 percent while her own modest trust, handled by Slash personally, was up over 16 percent.

"That's almost four times better," Alicia pointed out.

"There a big difference in handling a personal account and a public one," Junior said reassuringly. It was an explanation that was not an explanation, and Alicia, who had been brought up not to question what men did, did not press him. Junior, however, although he concealed it from Alicia, was boiling mad and confronted Slash.

"You have not been following the Lancome and Dahlen recommendations in investing for your clients," he told Slash, confronting him with his sin. To Junior, the Lancome

& Dahlen buy list was like all ten commandments rolled into one. It was never to be broken, never to be deviated from, never to be questioned.

"The Lancome and Dahlen recommendations are a joke," said Slash, not even bothering to lie and deny Junior's accusation.

"No one gave you permission to set aside research department recommendations," Junior said coldly. He was tall and his sandy hair was turning a distinguished silver. Only a faint whitening around his mouth revealed the extreme degree of his annoyance. Slash, unaccustomed to the Lancomes' icy, patrician way of showing fury, did not realize to what degree he had infuriated Junior. If he had, he said later, he wouldn't have cared anyway.

"That's right," said Slash. "No one gave me permission. I took it."

Slash knew he was being flippant. He did not know how dearly he would one day pay for his insolence.

"He's nothing but an outlaw," Junior warned his son. "Slash Steiner is not one of us. He doesn't play by our rules. He's an enemy. One day he's going to get the firm into a lot of trouble."

Trip Lancome would eventually inherit, along with his sister, Nina, the Lancome half of the company. He had already inherited his father's ambition and grandfather's ruthlessness, both hidden beneath impeccable tailoring and impeccable manners. He was a shark in a Savile Row suit.

"So let's get rid of him," said Trip, who didn't like Slash any more than his father did. He didn't like Slash's attitude or Slash's ties or Slash's crass ambition. He considered Slash an unappetizing cross between Sammy Glick and a Broadway tout and thought of his presence at Lancome & Dahlen as an embarrassment to the company.

"Russell won't hear of it," Junior said. He had already spoken to his partner about Slash and gotten nowhere. "Slash is his fair-haired boy these days."

"Why did Russell hire him anyway?" Trip wondered. The juxtaposition of the mysterious fire, the abrupt reinstatement of Richard Steiner's job and the overnight hiring of his son, who had no Wall Street connections and only a bachelor's degree from an unregarded college, had made Trip suspicious of Slash from the start.

"Who knows why Russell does anything?" Junior shrugged, annoyed at how much of their valuable time was being wasted on Slash Steiner. "Let me talk to Russell again. One way or another, Slash Steiner's days here at Lancome and Dahlen are numbered."

In the end, though, Junior did not act. For one thing, Junior was always a superb politician and Slash Steiner, a low-level portfolio manager handling insignificant accounts, was not worth what would certainly be a major confrontation with his partner. For another, Lancome & Dahlen had an unwritten policy of never firing any employee who had anything to do with the clients. Lancome & Dahlen did not like to admit that it could make a mistake.

Besides, Junior reluctantly admitted, Slash's clients never mentioned his lack of family connections, his occasional insolence or his wrong-side-of-the-tracks accent. Oh, no. They looked at the bottom line and seemed to think he walked on water.

"Rules? What rules?" Slash said when Junior Lancome's words got back to him, "Wall Street has no rules. That's what I like about it. You just make them up as you go along."

"And break them, too?" asked Arthur Bozeman.

"Sure," said Slash. "What good are they otherwise?"

Arthur shrugged and shook his head and told himself that he should have known all along what the answer was going to be.

To a young man coming of age in the sixties, interested not in what was but what could be, everything seemed possible, and what Slash wanted at twenty-three was what he had wanted for as long as he could remember—to become a millionaire by the time he was thirty. What he also wanted was Russell Dahlen's daughter.

PART TWO

Rich Girl /
1962-1964

"Whenever I looked at her I saw money. She looked
rich, she sounded rich, she smelled rich. Her money
was such an integral part of her that I sometimes
thought that without it she might cease to exist. The
sad thing is that she seemed to think so, too."

—ANNETTE GWILYM

"She was one of the first of the society celebrities. The
press loved her. From the day she was born, money
and scandal surrounded her. She attracted attention
like a magnet and although she said she wanted
privacy and always refused requests for interviews, she
always smiled for the photographers. Haven't you
noticed that you've never seen a bad picture of her?"

—NINA LANCOME

"People said she was dumb. I think they were dead
wrong. After all, she ended up with a husband who
worshipped her and more money than even she knew
how to spend. That's not my definition of dumb."

—PAUL GWILYM

I

THE

DEBUTANTE

"*Slash Steiner?*" *Deedee repeated in disbelief the first time* her father mentioned the name. It was right after the Kennedy assassination, and the offices at Lancome & Dahlen were still buzzing about Slash's insistence on business first— even at a time of national crisis. "Is that a real name?"

"Apparently," said her father. "It's the only one he ever uses. It's an advantage, too. No one who hears it ever forgets it."

Deedee didn't forget it, either. The name stuck in her mind. Anyone who had a name like Slash Steiner had to be . . . well . . . *interesting*. Deedee wondered what he was like. Particularly after Trip, quoting his father, told her that Slash Steiner was nothing more than an outlaw.

"An outlaw!" Deedee told Annette Gwilym, one of her best friends. "Don't you just love it?"

Annette saw the excitement in Deedee's eyes and thought, not for the first time, that Trip, who had graduated Yale cum laude, could certainly be dumb when it came to handling people.

Deedee Dahlen was the gilt-edged product of upper Park Avenue, Westport, Connecticut, a private island with an Indian name off the coast of Maine and other points elegant. She went to boarding school in Virginia, to junior college in Connecticut and made her debut in 1962, a transitional year between the end of the age of Society with a capital "S" ruled by old names and old money and the advent of the era of the

Beautiful People, which celebrated the mutually beneficial fusions among society, fashion, art and publicity.

Deedee had not one but two coming-out parties, one just after Christmas at the River Club and another, less formal, in June at her grandparents' Locust Valley house. At the River Club, Deedee's dress was white peau de soie, which she wore with a strand of real pearls. In Locust Valley, she wore white tulle and a Beatles button.

Although Deedee would often be referred to as a society girl, the expression was not entirely accurate since her family, although rich, was not, as the Lancomes liked to remind the Dahlens on every possible occasion, really top drawer, grade-A, blue-chip, crème-de-la-crème, Social Register social.

The Dahlens were simply another one of New York City's millionaire families. They did not belong, like the Lancomes did, to the Knickerbocker Club or Piping Rock. They did not, like the Lancomes did, give to the right charities nor were they, like the Lancomes were, on the boards of the Met and the Philharmonic. Their lack of social status was due partly to Luther and Edwina's genuine lack of interest and partly to Russell's inappropriate marriage. Joyce, although pretty and personable, had never learned to remake herself over to Manhattan requirements. Her thin vocabulary and inconsistent grammar revealed her indifferent attention to a public school education, her hair color was too obviously from a bottle and her clothes were always just a bit too tight and just a bit too bright.

It was, in fact, through Bunny Lancome, Junior's wife and Trip and Nina's mother, that Deedee had even been included on the Cotillion lists. It was, however, through Deedee's own efforts that her photograph, in which she wore a Van Cleef & Arpels tiara of blue-white diamonds, was on the cover of December *Town & Country.*

"Cover girl!" her father teased her.

"At least Bunny won't be able to go around anymore thinking of me as one of her charities!" Deedee replied. She was as fed up as the rest of her family with the Lancome's precious social superiority. All she knew was that she wanted to fly, she wanted to soar. How, exactly, she would find her wings, she did not yet know.

Although Deedee knew that by old-line standards the Dahlens weren't *really* social, she was aware from an early age that, thanks to Luther, they did have money and plenty of it. She also knew that she was the beneficiary of a one-million-dollar trust fund established by her grandfather at the time of her birth. The trust fund would be all hers when she turned twenty-five, and Deedee adored it when columnists and society writers called her the "million-dollar baby." It made her feel that she was someone special.

Money, the power of money, the flattering, golden aura of money hovered invisibly over Deedee's entire childhood, and from her earliest years the importance of money had been made very, very clear to her. Money, Deedee had been taught in lessons both spoken and wordless, was what made the Dahlens different from other people. Money, Deedee had learned, bought power, attention, respect. Money guaranteed safety, status and identity, and Deedee's greatest hopes and greatest fears, like those of her family, all centered around money, lots and lots of money. Deep in her secret heart, Deedee thought that money was magic.

She thought, without quite exactly realizing that she even thought it, that if she had enough money, she would no longer be a disappointment to her family. She had the idea, only barely recognized, that if she had enough money, she would no longer be an inferior substitute for a brother who had died before she had been born. If she had enough money, a huge, huge amount of money, even Luther would be proud of her and, almost more than anything, Deedee wanted to earn the respect and admiration of the man to whom her family owed everything. She wanted to feel that, even though she was only a girl, she was somebody, too.

For as long as she could remember, Deedee had been told that, one day, far, far in the future, she would inherit the Dahlen wealth. She would inherit the houses and antiques, art and silver, crystal and china outright. The Dahlen money, of course, would also be hers, but only in trust.

Girls, Deedee was told, could not receive their inheritances outright. Girls needed someone, someone wiser, someone more responsible, someone male, to take care of their money for them, to invest it for them and to make it constantly grow for them. The alternative of handling her own money herself was a possibility so heretical that it was simply never raised. It was made clear to Deedee that it was up to her to marry someone who was worthy of the Dahlen fortune. Meanwhile, she was warned about adventurers and fortune hunters.

"You can't be too careful," everyone told her, pointing out examples of heiresses like Barbara Hutton, who had been fleeced by a series of playboys, and Gamble Benedict, who had run off with a chauffeur. "You have to marry someone from your own background, someone who has your best interests at heart and who knows how to take care of your money for you."

That someone, they all agreed, was Trip.

Trip was, as the Dahlens had pointed out a thousand times, just as rich as she was. Deedee need never fear that he loved her for her money. He was also, her mother said, really top drawer, Social Register through and through. Deedee would be able, through him, to enjoy the social life Joyce yearned for but never achieved, having naively assumed as a young and inexperienced bride that the Dahlen money guaranteed social status as well. Trip was perfect, her mother said. So did her father and her grandparents, who pointed out that Trip's and Deedee's children would one day inherit all the Lancome & Dahlen stock, thus keeping everything right where it belonged: in the family.

For one of the few times Deedee could recall, everyone agreed. Trip was perfect.

His full name was Hamilton Lancome the Third, but everyone called him Trip, which stood for Triple, which came from the Third. His name—and his nickname—were exactly right for him. Trip Lancome was rich and handsome, blond and blue-eyed, tall and well built. His clothes never seemed too new and his cars never seemed too old. The thick comma of blond hair which fell over his forehead and concealed a star-shaped, raspberry-colored birthmark of which he was terribly ashamed was his only unruly, imperfect physical feature.

Like many other young men of his class, Trip had had the rebellion and the individuality bred out of him from an early age. On the day of his birth his father had him registered at St. Paul's, and at his christening he wore the same hand-embroidered linen sacque his father and grandfather had worn before him. From the elegant Eton suits and neat knee socks he wore as a boy to the dancing classes and debutante balls he attended as a young man, Trip had been brought up to know his place.

His place, Trip had been told over and over, was at the top. Specifically, at the top of Lancome & Dahlen. Mindful of the privileges that had become his at birth, Trip conformed brilliantly to the role that life had prepared for him. He had the right accent, the right manners, the right friends. He belonged to the right clubs, enjoyed the right sports and read the right newspapers. He voted Republican, worshipped Episcopalian, drove within the speed limit and respected his elders. However, beneath his patrician manners and distinguished pedigree, Trip was far more like Slash than he consciously imagined.

Slash and Trip each felt, for different reasons, that the rules didn't apply to him. Slash, because he had nothing to lose. Trip, because he felt above the rules. Under his perfect manners and purebred attitudes, Trip saw himself as a man who had been born to get anything he wanted. He would be rich and powerful not because of an accident of birth but because he was shrewd and smart and tough. His drive and his ambition, concealed by his seemingly bland perfection, revealed itself in a vicious, although rarely expressed, temper and in a lifelong passion for rough games and blood sports.

"The moment of the kill, the moment when the bullet hits home and the bird falls to the ground," Trip told Deedee when he returned from the annual quail shoot at his family's estate in North Carolina, his eyes glittering in remembered excitement, "it's the greatest thrill of a lifetime!"

"As long as it's birds and not people," said Deedee, shuddering. She could not, for the life of her, understand how anyone could get a thrill out of killing. Even if the killing was of the terribly chic variety, committed with hand-tooled Purdeys and taking place in luxurious privacy on a three-thousand-acre private estate.

Trip, his father made clear, had been born not only rich but damn lucky, too. Just as the Dahlens had made clear to Deedee the benefits of a Lancome-Dahlen wedding, Junior Lancome spelled out the benefits of such a marriage to Trip.

"It's a hell of a thing to say, but you're damn lucky little Luther died," Junior Lancome had told his son a thousand times. "One day Deedee will inherit the entire Dahlen half of Lancome and Dahlen. If you marry Deedee, Lancome and Dahlen will be all yours," Junior pointed out in case Trip hadn't noticed.

"Nina will go along with anything you want," Junior added, taking his daughter's acquiescence in financial matters for granted. "You'll never be stuck with a partner the way I've been stuck with Luther and Russell."

Having to deal with Luther, who was literally old enough to be his father and who thought he knew all there was to know about Wall Street, had always been a strain for Junior. Being saddled with Russell, who had his head in the clouds half the time, had been another ongoing problem. If Trip married Deedee, Trip wouldn't be stuck with anyone. He could run Lancome & Dahlen exactly as he pleased without any interference or second-guessing. Junior would never have admitted it but he envied his son's future.

"One day," Junior kept telling his son, "Lancome and Dahlen will be yours. All yours."

Trip never doubted his father's words. Nothing in his entire life had ever given him any reason to.

* * *

Just as the Dahlens thought Trip was perfect, the Lancomes agreed that Deedee was ideal even though she did tend to draw too much attention to herself. Junior and Bunny thought of Deedee as almost their own and Nina, Trip's sister, had been one of Deedee's best friends since boarding school. Trip and Deedee had known each other since they were children and everyone, including them, had taken it for granted that they would marry.

Trip taught Deedee to ride her bike when she was eight, kissed her when she was ten and gave her a gold-and-pearl friendship ring when she was fifteen. They dated throughout college and, although she didn't consider herself fast, Deedee slept with Trip, romantically viewing sex as a sign of their love and commitment.

When Deedee turned eighteen two weeks after her coming-out party in June, Trip gave her her engagement ring. It weighed three carats and had once belonged to Trip's grand-mother. People like the Lancomes didn't buy diamonds. They had them.

"Now it's official," Trip said, slipping the ring on Deedee's finger with a feeling of relief and triumph. Deedee was not only rich and well connected, she had also been very popular and, in becoming engaged to her, Trip had a gratifying sense of having made a very desirable conquest. Trip told himself that he loved Deedee, but he also viewed her as an acquisition. She would be a perfect wife for the kind of powerful and influential man Trip knew he would one day be. "We're going to get married and you're going to be my wife."

"Mrs. Hamilton Lancome the Third," Deedee sighed, thrilled at the thought. Mrs. Hamilton Lancome the Third! Even Luther, she knew, would be impressed.

"I love you and I always will. We were born for each other," Trip said, kissing her deeply and solemnly, showing her that he not only loved her but respected her.

Trip was never happier than when doing what was expected of him—both by others and by himself. His values were traditional and conventional and he was exceedingly proud of them.

* * *

Like all engaged girls, Deedee's dreams were dreams of ideal and unshadowed happiness. She dreamed of being a beautiful bride, a perfect wife, a celebrated hostess and, above all, a loving mother to a big brood of children.

Deedee adored children and she wanted a lot of them. There would definitely be more than two, maybe even as many as four. There would be boys and girls. Brothers would have sisters. Sisters would have brothers. No child of hers would have to bear the burdens of being an only child.

No child of hers would grow up in a silent house, surrounded by strict governesses and remote, obviously unhappy adults. No boy would have to shoulder the immense, weighty responsibility her father had had to bear of being the sole male heir to a company that had been in the family for generations. No girl would have to be responsible, as she had been responsible, for making the one, absolutely, sensationally perfect marriage. Things would be different for her children.

Her children would be free to follow their talents and their instincts. *Her* children would not have to subordinate themselves to the interests of the company that had dominated the family for three generations. *Her* children would not grow up in a tense and unhappy marriage. *Her* children would be happy although, without even stopping to think about it, Deedee took it absolutely for granted that at least one of her sons would follow in the family tradition and rise to the head of Lancome & Dahlen.

"No only children for me!" Deedee swore to Nina and Annette, her two best friends, her eyes shining with dreams of the future.

The Dahlen-Lancome wedding was planned for May of 1964. As 1963 drew to a close, everything, from the official announcement in the *New York Times* to the selection of silver and china patterns at Tiffany's, was proceeding according to schedule, and if Deedee felt no *frissons* of excitement when Trip touched her, she told herself that passion would come. And, if she had to persuade herself that she was in love, she also persuaded herself that *grands amours* were for other people.

She, Deedee told herself sternly, was too sensible to be swept off her feet, too down to earth to indulge in the theatrics of high romance. Love, she told herself, was a fantasy. Love, she told herself, was a myth. And why shouldn't she? After all, as Annette had pointed out, Deedee had grown up in a family where love was never mentioned and money was all that seemed to matter.

"I guess I'm just not the passionate type," Deedee told Nina, trying to account for her sane and sensible love life. "I could never give up everything for love the way Ingrid Bergman did."

"*Everyone*'s the passionate type," said Nina who, exempt from the expectations that fell to Trip, was free to be the family rebel. Nina was in the throes of a passionate romance with a thrice-divorced Argentinian polo player twenty years her senior. Deedee breathlessly followed the ups and downs of Nina's volcanic love life, wishing they would happen to her, glad that they didn't.

She envied Nina and she pitied her and she couldn't wait to get married so that she wouldn't have to torture herself wondering about love anymore.

I I
THE GIRL WITH EVERYTHING

*The Lancome & Dahlen Christmas party was, like every-*thing else about Lancome & Dahlen, traditional. In 1963 it was held, as it had been held every year since the company's founding in 1926, in the big oval partners' conference room on the afternoon of Christmas Eve.

A large pine, decorated with red satin ribbons, silvery tinsel and traditional white lights, stood next to the fireplace as it had for as long as anyone could remember. Carols were playing on a portable stereo system the way they did every year. The chef served Belon oysters, beluga caviar, smoked salmon, fresh goose liver and a luscious homemade *bûche de Noël* with meringue mushrooms the way he always had. Because it was Christmas, the no-alcohol rule was temporarily suspended the way it always was and dignified waiters in starched white jackets passed silver trays of Perrier-Jouet in crystal flutes.

The mood was particularly festive that year because on December nineteenth the Dow had closed at 767, a record high for the year. Everyone was looking forward to the generous year-end bonuses that were traditional on Wall Street in a good year. Executives, junior executives, secretaries, research assistants, stock analysts and back-room employees sipped champagne and toasted the profitable year.

People stood in small groups, joking and gossiping, and everyone looked forward to the coming holidays. Everyone except Slash.

* * *

Slash loathed the holidays. Holidays inevitably brought back memories of the worst moments of loneliness at Saint Ignatius and always depressed him. He remembered how everyone had someone—except him. He remembered the way the nuns had taken pity on him and made him Christmas cookies and knitted him mittens. He remembered the books carefully selected by the priests and wrapped in red ribbons. Their touching gestures, lovingly intended, only made Slash feel even more excluded and even more unwanted.

The holidays reminded Slash that even today—except for Richard Steiner—he still had no one. Belle had died unexpectedly of a heart attack three months after Slash had begun working at Lancome & Dahlen. Two weeks later, Uncle Sammy had been killed by a speeding taxi as he crossed the street to get a newspaper. Even today, fifteen years after he had left Saint Ignatius, Slash still carried its memories and its scars. He still felt uncomfortable and out of place, an interloper amidst all the year-end festivities.

He had come to the party for only one reason—and she was the reason.

Slash's first impression was that she was a girl who had everything and knew exactly what to do with it. He couldn't decide if she were pretty or beautiful and he soon realized that, in her case, pretty or beautiful was irrelevant. It was what she had done with herself that counted. Her gleaming blue-black hair, fresh from Kenneth's, was teased into the stylish bouffant of the moment. An A-line gabardine dress, fashionably knee length, showed off her slim, finely boned legs, and skillful makeup emphasized her exotically slanted green cat's eyes. She wore a Kenny Lane copy of a David Webb bracelet and so much Joy that she seemed to have bathed in it. She reeked of class and style and money and Slash, who had first seen her silver-framed photograph on the cabinet in her father's office, knew exactly who she was.

"You look like you're on your way to the Peppermint Lounge after this is over," Slash said, going over to Deedee the moment Trip left her side. The Peppermint Lounge was a wildly, if inexplicably, fashionable dive in the West Forties where socialites did the twist to the loud rock music of Chubby Checker.

"I don't want to disillusion you, but I've never been there," Deedee replied, aware of how his sleek, racy looks made him stand out in the room of long-boned, horse-faced blue bloods and dressed-in-their-Sunday-best back-room drones. His clear gray eyes, she noticed, seemed to see everything—and to find everything slightly humorous. He was, she thought, the most attractive man in the room. Except, of course, she added loyally to herself, for Trip.

"Never?" he asked, raising his eyebrows. Her high-pitched, slightly breathless voice with its elegant vowels and precise consonants even *sounded* rich. Slash made a conscious effort not to be impressed.

"Never," she confirmed. "Trip absolutely refuses to take me and my family warns me about the riffraff I might meet there. I, on the other hand, play 'Twist and Shout' constantly. Have you ever been there?"

"Of course. I make it my business to go everywhere," he replied. He was tempted to invite her to the Peppermint Lounge on the spot, but instinct made him hesitate. He had a feeling that she was used to men throwing themselves at her. He didn't want to be too obvious. In addition, of course, there was the minor detail that she was engaged to Trip.

There was a moment of awkward, electric tension between them. It dissolved as Trip came up.

"Slash is our office trend-spotter," Trip said, feeling compelled to make the official introduction. He was irritated at the way Slash was monopolizing Deedee. It was so pushy. So aggressive. Just like him! Trip had overheard the tail end of their conversation. "Slash is one of our junior portfolio managers and an expert on doing the twist."

"I've never heard of any of the senior managers doing the twist. They're usually much too arthritic," Deedee said, apparently oblivious to Trip's condescending put-down of Slash's expertise. She was thinking that with his lean, dark good looks and streetwise accent, Slash Steiner *did* seem like an outlaw—a gentleman gangster. Despite herself, she wondered what it would be like to go to bed with him.

"Actually, the twist is just about passé. The frug is going to be next," Slash said, addressing Deedee as if Trip weren't there. "They're definitely too arthritic for *that.*"

"See? I told you Slash was the office trend-spotter," said Trip, inserting himself between them, annoyed with them both but trying to hide it. Although Trip prided himself on having an excellent sense of humor, the way that Slash and Deedee made fun of the senior managers irritated him. He didn't expect much more from Slash, but Deedee should have known better.

"Now, come along," Trip said, taking Deedee possessively by the arm. "There are a lot of people who want to say hello."

Together, Trip and Deedee greeted Trip's secretary, several of the auditors, the switchboard operators, young stock analysts, senior portfolio managers, research associates and vice presidents. Deedee remembered everyone's name and the names of their husbands and wives and children and made a personal comment to each person. Hers was a polished and very impressive performance, and Trip was proud of her. Deedee, poised and gracious, would be the perfect wife.

"She reminds me of Jackie Kennedy," Andrew Macon, one of Lancome & Dahlen's senior partners, told Trip. Andrew Macon had a Santa Claus nose and excellent Washington connections through his college roommate, who was at the Federal Reserve. "Deedee has the same patrician manners and the same delightful charm that Jackie does."

Trip glowed with pride at the compliment. Yes, he thought, Deedee would be an ideal president's wife. Not the presidency of the United States, which didn't interest Trip at all—not with its connotations of political horse trading, back-room deals and the constant pandering to popular tastes—but the presidency of Lancome & Dahlen, which did interest Trip. He had been born to it, and although he knew he didn't even have to want it to get it, he wanted it more than anything. His whole life, he had once told Deedee, revolved around one goal: becoming the president of Lancome & Dahlen.

As Deedee made small talk, she kept glancing around the room, looking for Slash Steiner. She noticed that he was watching her, too, and, as the party began to break up, Deedee and Slash found themselves standing next to each other opposite the double doors.

This time, it was she who spoke first.

"I'm dying to know," Deedee said, speaking so softly that Slash had to lean forward a little in order to hear her, "where did you get your name?"

"I made it up," Slash said with his patented fighter-pilot's grin. It came straight from the gene pool that had produced Errol Flynn's—wicked, rakish and irresistible—and Slash knew just how to use it.

"Made it up? What did your parents say?" Deedee asked, her green eyes widening in amazement. She had never heard of such a thing. Trip was motioning to her from across the room, and although she saw him, she pretended not to.

"I already had the name when I met them," Slash said.

It took Slash five minutes to explain how he got his name first and his parents second and he made being an orphan seem the most enviable state in the whole world. Imagine, Deedee thought, being able to pick not only a name, but parents! She thought for a moment of her own parents and their unhappy marriage. She shocked herself by wondering for the first time since she and Trip had gotten engaged whether she, too, was doomed to be unhappily married.

"Deedee!"

She could hear Trip now calling to her from across the room. Irritated. Impatient. The crown prince unaccustomed to being kept waiting.

"Would you take me to the Peppermint Lounge some night?" Deedee blurted to Slash. Until the words were actually out, even she hadn't known she would say them. For an instant, Slash seemed surprised, then he picked up her left hand and touched the diamond engagement ring.

"You're engaged," he pointed out.

"Oh. That."

Deedee felt her face turn hot and she knew that she had turned crimson. Almost violently, she jerked her hand away.

"Yes. *That*," Slash said with another insolent grin.

Deedee couldn't quite tell if he were chiding her or teasing her. Either way, he made her feel flustered and uncomfortable.

"Deedee!" Trip said, coming up to her, exasperated. "Didn't you hear me? Let's go!"

Trip took her by the arm again and led her away. She left a trace of perfume behind her, and as Slash inhaled her scent, he thought with amazement that she even *smelled* rich. For a moment Slash wondered uneasily just exactly what he was letting himself in for.

Joyce, about to leave the party, saw the exchange between Slash and Deedee. As she stood in the double doors waiting for Russell, she noticed the way Slash touched Deedee's engagement ring and the intense way he spoke to her.

What, Joyce wondered, had Slash Steiner said to cause Deedee to turn crimson?

"What were you and Deedee Dahlen talking about for so long?" Arthur Bozeman asked Slash when they'd left the Christmas party and gone to a nearby bar for a real drink. Arthur himself was too shy to go up to Russell Dahlen's daughter. He wouldn't have known what to say to her. Yet he was dying of curiosity to find out what she was like.

"Frugging," said Slash.

Arthur had never heard the word and he blushed, not exactly sure whether frugging and fucking were the same. Arthur wasn't the least bit ashamed of being a square but sometimes he had to admit that it could be a disadvantage.

"I mean, seriously?" he asked. "What did you talk about?"

"I just told you," said Slash.

What he didn't tell Arthur was that he had already decided to marry her. He had heard about the million-dollar trust fund but he also made it a rule never to believe everything he heard. Before he saw Deedee Dahlen again, there was one thing Slash wanted to know. He wanted to know exactly how rich she really was.

The fact that it was Christmas Eve meant nothing to Slash. That evening, after he and Arthur had finished their drinks, Slash returned alone to the empty office as he so often did. However, instead of going to the block trading desk to check on the unexecuted orders, he went into the central file room. Using the key the librarian had lent him when they had had a brief affair and which he had had copied before returning it to her when they broke up, he removed the records of Deedee's trust fund, photocopied them, returned the originals to the files, put the copies into a plain manila envelope and took them home with him.

Sitting at the desk in the small living room of his bachelor apartment, Slash went over the figures again and again. He checked and rechecked the calculations. He couldn't believe what the figures told him. At first, he thought that there had been a mistake. But his own calculations proved that the calculations on the statements were indeed correct.

Slash was amazed to see that, after almost twenty years of Lancome & Dahlen's investing, Deedee's million-dollar trust fund was worth just over a million four hundred thousand dollars.

Even though the interest had been withdrawn and not allowed to accumulate, the figures were absolutely shocking. A pathetic 40 percent increase in over two decades of the richest economy the world had ever seen? A mere 40 percent growth in the same time that had seen the Dow jump from 150 to over 765?

Slash himself, by comparison, had just made almost 70 percent on his own investments in the three months between October and December 1963. Deedee's trust fund, handled by the Lancome & Dahlen investment committee, had been, in Slash's view, almost criminally mishandled. Already impatient with Lancome & Dahlen's ultraconservative ways, Slash realized that he had just been handed the opportunity of a lifetime. Deedee Dahlen, he realized, was the girl with everything—except enough money.

Three days later, Slash picked up the telephone and called Deedee. He didn't even have to look up her number. He had memorized it on the first day he had ever heard her name.

I I I
N E R V O U S
Q U A D R I L L E

His voice on the phone was calm but intense, the accent unmistakably streets-of-the-city. Even before he identified himself and said that he wanted to invite her to lunch, Deedee knew who it was. Ever since the Christmas party, she had had the feeling she would hear from Slash Steiner again. Half of her had waited impatiently; the other half, sensing danger, had told herself that she was mistaken and that she would never hear from him again. Now that he was on the other end of the telephone, Deedee's hands began to shake with involuntary excitement. Slash Steiner had made much more of an impression on her than even she had realized.

"The Plaza?" Slash suggested. He had thought it over and chosen carefully. The Plaza, he had concluded, was ideal, both expensive and impersonal. It would show her that he cared enough to impress her but that his intentions, although obviously not strictly honorable, were at least superficially innocent. After all, had anyone ever gotten into serious trouble at the Plaza? "Friday at one o'clock?"

Slash got there five minutes early. Deedee arrived at the stroke of one and, once again, Slash, who had prepared himself to be impervious, was dazzled by her.

More than just pretty but not exactly beautiful, she had a quality that made it impossible not to look at her. Slash had somehow forgotten the sheer physical impact Deedee had on him. She was both taller and slimmer than he had remembered, almost as tall, in fact, as he was.

In a black wool suit with an ivory satin blouse and a waterfall of gold chains with red and green and blue stones set off by a jeweled Maltese cross, Deedee was the woman Chanel must have had in mind. Her hair gleamed with blue-black highlights, her seemingly poreless ivory skin glowed as if it had been polished and her perfume, not Joy this time, but something else, reeked of wealth and privilege and for a moment Slash wondered if he had, finally, set his sights on something that he simply would not be able to get. Had his grasp, finally, exceeded his reach? Trip's ring still glittered possessively from her finger.

"You're not even late," Slash said, his killer smile hiding his anxiety, his dreadful fear that he might not be good enough for her. "Didn't your mother tell you to keep men waiting?"

"Actually, it wasn't my mother. It was my father," Deedee replied, matching his teasing tone perfectly. "I just could never follow his advice."

Slash laughed and Deedee did, too. As the captain seated her and handed them menus, she studied him for an instant: knifeblade-narrow face, high cheekbones, die-straight shiny dark hair, almost transparent gray eyes and pale, almost translucent complexion. He projected a sexy, slightly sinister aura and she could sense barely banked fire and more than a hint of danger. *Outlaw* was the word her father had used about him. *Outlaw* was the word that Trip had used about him. *Outlaw* was the word that came into her mind, and just the thought excited her.

Always conscious of her weight, Deedee ordered the chef's salad while Slash ordered a steak, well done. If she got to know him better, Deedee thought, she'd have to do something about that. No one ever ordered steak well done.

As they waited for the food, Slash talked about the Thalidomide controversy, the new popularity of folk singing and the relationship between hemlines and the Dow Jones averages. Both were going up rapidly. Both were cause and reflection of the rapidly changing attitudes toward love and sex, materialism and money. Changing attitudes, in fact, that made their lunch with each other even possible.

Just a year earlier, before the Beatles had made the wrong class and the wrong accent suddenly chic, Deedee would never have dreamed of meeting someone like Slash for lunch, would never have seen him as potentially attractive and even, perhaps, desirable.

"Do you know *everything*?" Deedee asked, when the food came and Slash finally stopped talking. She was impressed and slightly intimidated by Slash's conversation. The people Deedee knew talked about parties, clothes and servants. She had never known anyone who could talk about so many things so knowledgeably.

"Not *everything*," he said, mimicking her inflection and making her smile. But as the waiter served Deedee's salad, Slash continued to impress her with the breadth of his knowledge and the liveliness of his intellect.

He picked up where he had left off and described the effects of the Thalidomide controversy on drug stocks. He told her how the millions of dollars worth of Bob Dylan and Joan Baez albums being sold caused the record companies' stock to go up. He told her about the theory that connected periods of rising hemlines with periods of rising markets. The last example, Slash said, had been during the 1920s. A more recent example was happening this very moment. Skirts were going up and so—in a big way—was the market.

"And that's why I invited you to lunch," Slash said, getting down to business. "I want to talk to you about money."

"Money?" repeated Deedee stunned. No one she knew *ever* talked about money.

"I looked up your trust records after the Christmas party," Slash said calmly, as if snooping into other people's finances—and admitting it—was something people did every day of the week. "Your trust fund isn't worth nearly what it should be. If you let me handle it for you, you'd be the richest girl in the city."

"Let *you* handle it?" Deedee asked, shocked. Her tone of voice suggested that he had just proposed that they take off their clothes right then and there and jitterbug naked on the table. She could just imagine herself going to Luther and Junior and asking them to turn her trust fund over to Slash Steiner! She could also, she realized suddenly, imagine herself getting rich. She would *love* to be the richest girl in the city and, from what she had heard about Slash Steiner, he could probably do exactly what he promised.

"I'm good," Slash said, unperturbed. "Damn good. I could make you really rich."

"I'm already 'really rich'!" Deedee said, withdrawing defensively into a frosty altitude. Talk of money upset her. So did her own fantasies of being really rich. Somehow, they always made Deedee feel guilty. Her dreams of being terribly, terribly rich made Deedee feel disloyal to Luther and the Lancomes—the people she loved and to whom she owed everything.

"No, you're not," Slash said, ignoring the sudden change in climate. "You're minor-league rich. It's peanuts compared to what it could be."

"Peanuts?" Deedee repeated, suddenly sarcastic. Slash had unknowingly gone too far and given Deedee a reason to reject him. "Really, Slash, I expect fortune hunters to be a little more subtle."

"Don't flatter yourself," he said. "Your so-called fortune isn't worth hunting. At least not by me."

Deedee stared at Slash in disbelief, not sure whether to be outraged or insulted or just to laugh in his face.

Or to take him up on his offer.

Then the moment passed.

She decided not to give him the satisfaction of any reaction at all.

"I think I'd better go," she said, finally. She looked at her watch, amazed to see that, somehow, it had gotten to be almost four. She picked up her handbag and began to pull on her gloves. "Thank you for lunch."

"Don't go!" he said, suddenly reaching out for her hand. His smile, not wicked now, but embarrassed and chastened, melted her heart.

"I was a schmuck," he said. "Forgive me?"

"You're outrageous," she said.

"But am I forgiven?"

She thought for a moment and then, deciding that anyone that obvious couldn't be dangerous, shrugged.

"I guess so," she said and smiled in spite of herself.

"Then we'll stay for tea and later I'll take you to the Peppermint Lounge," he said in a transparent and successful attempt at bribery. "I promise I'll never mention money to you again."

Deedee got home at four the next morning.

Joyce, in a nightgown and robe, was still up. She wanted to know where Deedee had been and who she had been with and she was, as Deedee had feared, furious.

"I didn't put up with your father and his parents for all these years for you to run off with some no one," Joyce said, furious. Deedee was her only child and Joyce literally lived for her. She completely identified with Deedee and wanted only the very, very best for her. She simply was not going to permit Deedee to throw away her carefully planned future on an impulse. "You're not to see Slash Steiner again. Ever! Do you understand?"

"Mummy," replied Deedee in her best boarding school drawl, knowing that her mother hated to be called mummy. Joyce said it made her feel like a dead Egyptian. Elated by her thrilling evening and apparent conquest of Slash, Deedee felt courageous and confident and full of herself. "I'm twenty years old. I can see whoever I want."

"Not as long as you're wearing that ring!" Joyce snapped. She had given up her youth, her energy, her vitality to get out of that shack in the weeds behind the gas station. She had endured a joyless marriage, an unhappy and withdrawn husband and years of interfering in-laws who controlled the purse strings with a tight fist. She had not gone through all of that just to turn around and let Deedee throw away her lifelong sacrifice.

"Then I'll get rid of the ring!" Deedee said rebelliously, suddenly not giving a damn about the ring and the very proper marriage it symbolized. She touched Trip's ring as if to twist it off. For a second Joyce feared she would do just that.

"Deedee! Your ring! Don't! Think about the future!"

At her mother's words, Deedee seemed suddenly shocked by what she had been about to do.

"I'm sorry," said Deedee, dropping her right hand and leaving the ring on her finger, instantly repentant. She and her mother had always been best friends and the look of shock on her mother's face had sobered Deedee up. She might have had the most exciting evening of her life but she was not about to defy her mother. After all, for her entire life, Deedee and her mother had shared the same dreams for Deedee's future. "I didn't mean it. I'd *never* take Trip's ring off. Never!"

Deedee suddenly leaned forward, hugged her mother hard and kissed her goodnight. She disappeared into her bedroom where, rather than waste time trying to sleep, she tried to remember everything Slash had said to her and everything she had said to him. She had never had such a wonderful time with anyone in her entire life and she wondered what it would be like to kiss him.

Not, of course, that she ever would.

Joyce, too, did not sleep that night. She had spoken to Slash Steiner at the Christmas party and sensed that his Brooks Brothers disguise was just that. An outsider herself, Joyce knew perfectly well that Slash did not really fit in at Lancome & Dahlen. She also knew, from the way he looked at Deedee, that whatever he had in mind, it wasn't just being nice to the boss's daughter. When she had mentioned it to Russell, though, he had defended Slash.

"Why shouldn't Deedee talk to him?" Russell had said, pooh-poohing Joyce's concerns about Slash Steiner's motives. Slash had brought a fresh breath of life and vitality into the office and his clients raved about him. The more Russell observed Slash, the more convinced he was that he had been absolutely right to offer him a job. "Slash Steiner was the most interesting person there."

Now, as Joyce sat up in the darkened living room, smoking cigarette after cigarette, she wondered whether Deedee had gone to bed with him. Not that the possibility of sex bothered her that much. What bothered her was what sexual intoxication might lead to, for she had no doubt that Slash Steiner, who was apparently very good at work, was also very good in bed. She wished that May 10, the date of the wedding, were five hours away, not five months away.

The next morning at breakfast, Deedee apologized to her mother for upsetting her and told her that the evening had been perfectly harmless. Her mother accepted her apology but didn't seem completely convinced by Deedee's contention of the evening's harmlessness.

"Even if the evening was harmless," Joyce said, dubiously, "your going out with someone other than Trip just doesn't look right."

Russell listened to the exchange between mother and daughter and said nothing, but Deedee noticed that her father didn't seem the least bit upset that she had gone out with Slash. *Au contraire.*

Nineteen sixty-four was the beginning of the four-year period that would later be called the sixties. It was referred to as Youthquake and focused on the interests of the young: music, clothes, sex, dancing and shocking the elder generation. Its effects would totally transform previous ideas about love and money.

The Pill had first been introduced in 1960, and by 1964 love was no longer synonymous with marriage but, increasingly, with sex. The Four Tops' recording of "Baby, I Need Your Loving" made it obvious that the loving being referred to was not the platonic kind. Julie Christie in *Darling* was clearly living with a man to whom she was not married and, although he would later get into trouble for it, Lenny Bruce was using four-letter words in public and finding large, responsive audiences among the young and the hip.

Money, now that the Dow was close to nine hundred and Congress had voted a tax cut, was plentiful. There was enough to finance two wars: one abroad in Vietnam; the other at home against poverty. Furthermore, for the first time in history, everyone could see that even the young could earn a fortune. The Beatles and the Rolling Stones and dozens of other groups made millions by selling records. A very young Joe Namath was about to make history by signing a contract that would pay him an astronomical $389,000 over three years, and models like Jean Shrimpton and Twiggy, not even out of their teens, could make hundreds of thousands of dollars a year. Money was no longer exclusively for the very old.

Carnaby Street mod was taking over the world as go-go dancers bumped away in discotheques, and Slash had been right when he said that the twist was on the way out and the frug was on the way in. The frug, however, was followed in swift succession, according to the speeded-up tempo of the times, by the swim, the watusi, the surf and the monkey. Society was changing and Slash, always fascinated by the present, had become virtually addicted to change and knew how to take advantage of it. He began to dance a nervous quadrille with a tentative but clearly intrigued and increasingly receptive Deedee.

In the month following their lunch date at the Plaza, Slash took Deedee to the Dom, a dingy Lower East Side Polish bar with a certain slummy beatnik chic, to the back room at Max's Kansas City where artists and rock musicians in tie-dyes and fringes talked shop and traded drugs and to a screening of *Dr. Strangelove*, a mordantly satiric movie directed by Stanley Kubrick and starring Peter Sellers and George C. Scott that would later be seen as one of the first salvos in the era's bitter war of the young versus the Establishment.

Thanks to Slash, Deedee learned to recognize the still somewhat unfamiliar smell of marijuana, threw away her bras in favor of a body stocking and bought a little nothing dress from Tiger Morse at 2 A.M. in the ladies' room of Daly's Dandelion. Deedee had lived in a New York defined by the boundaries, both physical and social, of the River Club and

Park Avenue her entire life, and yet she felt she had never known the city until she saw it through Slash's eyes.

"Aren't you afraid Trip is going to find out about us?" Slash asked Deedee the third time they'd been out together. He was beginning to feel slightly more sure of himself and he wanted to find out just how far Deedee was willing to go.

"Trip never gets out of the Racquet Club," replied Deedee confidently.

Besides, she wondered, what was there to find out? Nothing ever happened. The Beatles were singing "I Wanna Hold Your Hand" but Slash didn't seem to get the message. He, literally and almost unbelievably to Deedee, had never even taken her elbow as they crossed a street, much less tried to hold her hand. He acted as if she were as untouchable as if she were in quarantine, and Deedee wondered from time to time if Slash was even interested in girls. After all, she told herself, bewildered and finally offended by his utter lack of physical interest in her, Slash Steiner certainly knew a lot of people who made a point of their highly unconventional lifestyles.

Control. Slash sensed that if he wanted Deedee—and now that he was becoming more confident of her response to him, he did, more than ever—that control was the key. She was a spoiled rich girl, used to having everything she wanted when she wanted it. The only way to capture her interest was to tantalize her with something she might—or might not—be able to get. Deedee, as a rich girl and an only child besides, was also used to a great deal of attention, Slash realized. The only possible way to get her off balance and to capture her interest was to act as if he didn't particularly care.

Control, Slash soon decided, meant apparent indifference, a take-it-or-leave-it attitude. He never called on Monday for Saturday. He never asked for another date at the end of an evening. He never talked about the future. Control meant unpredictability. He never said when he'd call or even if he'd call and when he did call he never called at the same time twice. Control meant never doing the expected. Slash never did what other suitors might have done. He didn't send flowers or candy, perfume or love notes. Control meant hiding his feelings. Control meant keeping his distance. Control meant waiting until she came to him.

Slash never said another word to Deedee about money or her trust fund or not being rich enough. When he took her home, he dropped her off in his MG and waved a casual goodnight as the doorman looked on. He never held her hand and he never put his arm around her. He never even tried to kiss her and, although he had convinced himself that he was taking the right approach, he wondered how much longer he could hold out. What had started out as a game had become an obsession.

Slash was falling madly in love with Deedee, and she was driving him crazy. With her shiny, gleaming hair. Her perfect ivory skin. Her exotic cat's eyes. Her ravishing perfume. The expensive clothes whose secrets he longed to uncover and the elegant voice that he dreamed would whisper words she had never learned on Park Avenue.

Control, Slash reminded himself. Control was the key, and as January turned into February Slash continued, with increasing difficulty, to control himself.

Slash Steiner was elusive and mysterious, apparently out of reach but definitely not out of mind, and Deedee couldn't stop thinking about him. She had never met anyone who looked like him, who spoke like him, who thought like him. He was a native of another world and Deedee spent hours trying to interpret the cool irony in his eyes and the thousand nuances in his voice. She tried to remember whether his eyes were steel gray or velvet gray and finally decided that, depending on his mood, they could be either. She wondered whether he was gay or straight; whether he had a dozen girls or none. She stayed at home like a lovesick fourteen-year-old waiting for the phone to ring at the same time that she vowed never to see him again.

Nevertheless, whenever Slash called, Deedee dropped everything for him and on the nights she didn't see Trip, she saw Slash. She was mortally afraid that Trip would find out about her dates with Slash even though those dates, as she kept telling her increasingly fretful mother, were completely—and frustratingly—innocent.

As Valentine's Day approached, Deedee decided to take romance into her own hands. Slash had taken her to a screening of a quasipornographic, solemnly artistic Scandinavian film during which he had not even taken her hand. After, they had gone to dinner in the back room of a Ninth Avenue spaghetti factory, a spot so in that neither Eugenia nor Suzy had yet mentioned it. When they were finished with dinner, they got into Slash's MG and he headed uptown through the park. He was, Deedee thought, simply the best driver she had ever ridden with—swift, sure, utterly in command.

"Are you ever going to kiss me?" she asked, trying to sound casual. She had been rehearsing the line for days.

"Of course," he said. "But not yet."

"Then when?" she said, abandoning all pride.

There was a long silence. His scheme was working, Slash thought, forcing himself to control his excitement. He had forced himself to hold back and wait and his strategy had paid off. Now she was coming to him just the way he had hoped. He wanted to stop the car and take her into his arms and tell her exactly how much she meant to him and how much he wanted her but, once again, he fought his impulse. His feelings for Deedee were no brief affair, no momentary lurch of the heart, no fleeting uprising of the hormones, no quick twitch in the groin. This time he was playing for keeps, and he wasn't going to back down now.

"When you give Trip his ring back," he said finally.

"I could never do that!"

"Then I guess I'll never kiss you," he said and lapsed back into silence.

Deedee sat stiffly, expectantly, sure that, this time, despite his words, he would slow down and park in a dark, romantic spot, reach out for her and smother her in his arms and scald her lips with hot, demanding kisses. He *had* to feel the same way she did, didn't he? He *had* to sense the electricity that sizzled on a live wire between them, didn't he? He *had* to crave her touch and yearn for her mouth. *Had* to be almost wild with longing and crazed with wanting. *Had* to know, as she knew, that what was happening between them was a once-in-a-lifetime fusion of sexual attraction, personal chemistry and profound emotional connection. He *had* to sense what she sensed. *Had* to feel the way she felt. Didn't he?

Well, didn't he?

Obviously not, because Slash drove the whole rest of the way to 999 Park in dead silence. He let Deedee out of the car, waving a comradely goodnight in full view of the doorman and a few late-night dog walkers. Once again kissless, Deedee went upstairs to her parents' apartment and her own room, where she tossed and turned, able to find no comfort in the virginal white, canopied bed that had been hers since she'd been a girl.

The next day both the spaghetti joint and Slash's date with Deedee made Eugenia.

"Oh, my God!" Deedee told Annette, showing her the *Tribune*. Deedee was obviously frightened almost out of her wits at having been caught quite so publicly. She felt guilty and afraid. Guilty at having sneaked around. Guilty at having lied to her mother and guilty at having gone out with another man and lying to Trip about it. She did not want to let the dreams she and her mother had shared go up in flames. She was also afraid. Afraid of what her mother might do or say. Afraid of Trip's violent temper.

The worst part of all was that Slash had still not so much as touched her! Deedee realized the bitter irony was that she risked losing Trip—for nothing! She was white and shaking like a leaf.

"My mother is going to be furious and Trip is going to kill me. Or maybe Slash!" Deedee fretted.

"You knew you were playing with fire," said Annette, realizing that although Deedee sounded melodramatic, she was also being serious. Unlike Nina, the rebellious one, or Deedee, the glamorous one, Annette, the third of the three best friends, was the realistic one. She knew about Joyce's dreams and Trip's temper. She knew that Deedee wanted to soar but was also afraid to. "You knew all along that you might get caught."

"I knew it but I didn't really believe it," said Deedee, looking absolutely miserable. "Now I feel like a criminal."

"That's what you get for associating with an outlaw," Annette said, remembering the first time Deedee had ever mentioned Slash and trying, but failing, to make Deedee smile.

"Slash is good at being an outlaw. He's got the confidence," said Deedee sadly. "I'm a terrible outlaw. I'm afraid I'll get caught and so I always do."

Deedee could not decide which she feared most: her mother's anger or Trip's temper. Like a convicted criminal awaiting sentencing and punishment, she paced and wondered, dreading the next turn of events.

I V

THE BEAUTIFUL
PEOPLE

Nina Lancome, like almost everyone else she knew, was an avid reader of the gossip columns. She read Winchell and Earl Wilson, Eugenia Sheppard and Cholly Knickerbocker. She knew who had been seen with whom at what disco of the moment, who was divorcing, who was expecting, who was engaged or engaged-to-be-engaged and who was doing what with whom and why.

She often wondered why Deedee's name appeared so much more often than her own. Her pangs of envy crested the moment she saw the Eugenia Sheppard item about Deedee's dinner with Slash Steiner. She called her brother instantly. Excited and agitated, Nina spoke quickly and breathlessly.

"Deedee is going out with Slash Steiner!" Nina began, agog with the news. Nina was a younger child, a girl who had grown up with the extreme disadvantage of being someone of whom little was expected. Her rebellions, although frowned upon, were not taken seriously—even by herself. It was one thing to rebel with glamorous Argentinian polo players. It was another to sneak around with someone like Slash Steiner.

"He took her to someplace I've never heard of on Ninth Avenue," Nina continued, remembering Slash Steiner from the Christmas party. She had noticed his brooding air, his almost sinister sensuality. She had also noticed that he had barely looked at her. "They were having dinner together and then seen leaving together."

"Don't believe everything you read in the newspapers,"

said Trip, unwilling to think that Deedee would do anything so disloyal. "I don't."

"Well, I do!" said Nina, impatiently. "She's making a fool of herself—and of you!"

The last thing Deedee needed, Nina said, was a fortune hunter. The last thing Trip needed, Nina said, was to be made a laughingstock. She hung up only after she had finally forced Trip to promise that he would get the *Tribune* and see for himself.

As he read the item, Trip began to understand what Deedee's recent headaches and broken dates were about. Furious at being cheated on and doubly furious that it was Slash who Deedee had two-timed him with, Trip stalked down the hall to Slash's desk.

"I suppose you're proud of this!" Trip said, standing in front of Slash's desk and holding up the newspaper. The whitening around Trip's mouth was a sign of the intensity of his anger. Underneath the comma of thick blond hair, the star-shaped birthmark had turned bright red.

"Not specially," Slash said, shrugging indifferently.

"You mean you don't deny it?" demanded Trip. He was almost incredulous. The least he had expected was a denial, a lie, some attempt to protect Deedee.

"We had dinner," Slash said. "Sue me."

Trip leaned threateningly over Slash's desk, almost as if he were going to hit him.

"Keep your hands off Deedee!" Trip warned.

"Relax," said Slash, holding his hands palm out in a gesture of innocence. He leaned back in his chair, put his feet up on his desk, folded his hands behind his head and smiled up at Trip, a perfect, one-in-a-million screw-you smile. "Deedee's perfectly safe. My hands have never been anywhere near her."

Trip glared at him.

"If I find out you've touched her, I'm going to finish you," Trip warned. Then, not wanting to make a scene in the office,

Trip threw the newspaper on Slash's desk and walked away, swallowing his fury but not forgetting it.

When Trip had disappeared down the corridor, Slash called Deedee and told her about Trip's jealous fit, the way he had flung down the newspaper and his melodramatic warning.

"He warned me to keep my hands off you. He said he'd finish me if I didn't," Slash said, laughing and quoting Trip's exact words. "I feel like a half-made sandwich."

"Be careful," Deedee warned. Slash's words underlined her own fears. "Trip has a terrible temper."

"So what?" asked Slash. "What's he got to be jealous of?"

Deedee thought for a moment.

"Nothing, I guess," she replied.

Then, together they made fun of Trip and how silly he was to be jealous.

Jealous! Jealous of what?

Jealous of everything. Jealous of Deedee's popularity. Jealous of her charm and her easy way with people. Jealous of the way men looked at her and jealous of the way women admired her. Trip was jealous of Deedee the way he would be jealous of any prize he had won with difficulty. Although everyone had always assumed that Trip and Deedee would marry, Deedee had been hard to get and now, Trip was finding out, hard to keep.

All through school and college and her debutante year, men had flirted with Deedee, wooed her and courted her. They had been attracted by her glamor and her charm, by her smile, by the mystery and the promise in her green eyes and, perhaps, some of them, because of who she was and who her family was. They had sent flowers and slim volumes of poetry. Their convertibles were lined up in front of her apartment building. They waited to take her to dances, to the movies, to dinner and to parties. And Deedee had not spurned their attentions.

She was always smiling and laughing, dressed beautifully

and smelling of perfume, encouraging their gifts and their compliments, raising their hopes and stirring their dreams. Trip had finally won her because he had been more patient than the others, more dogged, more persistent and, in the end, more passionate. Trip not only loved Deedee, but he was possessed by her. She had the sparkle that brought life to Trip's seriousness, the energy that lifted his weightiness, the laughter that made him smile. He had fought hard to win her. He would fight harder to keep her.

"It's not because I'm jealous," Trip told Deedee later that evening, telling her that he had seen the item. He tried, as he always did, to be logical and reasonable despite his intense anger. He spoke earnestly, lovingly and, he thought, with her own best interest foremost in mind. "You shouldn't be going out with anyone except me. After all, I don't think I have to remind you that we're engaged."

"They weren't really dates," Deedee said, a bit defensively, convincing herself that because Slash had never been the least bit romantic, she wasn't lying. "Just a few dumb dinners."

"I still don't think you should go out with anyone else," Trip insisted. "You're making a fool of me and, worst of all, you're making a fool of yourself."

"It wasn't any big deal. Just dinner," Deedee repeated, shading the truth a bit. She loved Trip and she respected him. She did not want to do anything that would make him think less of her.

" 'Just dinner' is plenty! It looks terrible!" said Trip. He loathed Slash and he loathed the idea of Deedee's spending any time with him. He wished he could get rid of Slash Steiner once and for all. He was a constant irritation and annoyance at the office. Now he was intruding into Trip's personal life.

"I'm sorry," said Deedee, ashamed of herself. "I didn't know it disturbed you so much. I won't see him again."

"You promise?"

"Yes," said Deedee, avoiding his eyes.

"Yes, what?"

"Yes, I promise."

* * *

Deedee not only promised Trip she wouldn't see Slash again, she promised herself. Why look for trouble? Why embarrass herself over a man who apparently had no interest in her? Above all, why hurt Trip, who loved her?

Deedee remembered the way she and Slash had laughed about Trip, and she felt profoundly ashamed of herself. Trip did not have Slash's glamor. He did not have Slash's advantage of being a forbidden outsider. Trip was solid and responsible and adult. The way, Deedee cautioned herself, she should be.

"I'm ashamed of myself," Deedee admitted to her mother the next day. Afraid that her mother would yell at her, Deedee had been first to admit that she was wrong, first to admit that she had snuck out with Slash Steiner, first to admit that she was embarrassed by her own behavior. "I treated Trip terribly. I won't do it again."

"Trip is very patient with you," said Joyce. "He's a fine man. He doesn't deserve being made a fool of."

"I know," said Deedee. "I won't see Slash again."

"I hoped you'd come to that conclusion," said Joyce relieved. She had feared Slash from the first time she'd met him. She did not dismiss him as Trip did. She saw, as perhaps only another woman could see, Slash's allure.

"Do you hate me?" Deedee asked forlornly, feeling that she had let everyone down.

"No," said Joyce, understanding the temptation and how Deedee had been unable to resist. "You're just young."

Deedee smiled in relief, and she and her mother gratefully reconciled the small but dangerous split between them.

Deedee resolved to be a perfect fiancée, just as she had resolved to be a perfect wife. She turned down Slash's next invitation to dinner and felt that she had grown up. Deedee thought that her sin was forgiven, that her indiscretion was firmly in the past. She told herself that she would never have broken her promise if only Trip had taken her word.

Instead, a man possessed, Trip began to act like a policeman. He grilled Deedee on her doings and whereabouts. He questioned her friends about where she had gone and what she had done. He telephoned her three times every evening they didn't spend together and, two weeks later, on a Friday, Trip was right there, standing on the sidewalk on Fifty-fourth Street, when Deedee left Kenneth's at five-thirty.

"What are you doing uptown so early?" Deedee asked, surprised and at first pleased to see him.

"Meeting you," Trip said, taking her by the arm.

"Meeting me?" she asked, suddenly breaking away and turning to face him. "Or checking up on me?"

There was a moment's silence.

"I just wanted to make sure you were where you said you'd be."

A week later Slash invited Deedee to see Margot Fonteyn and Rudolph Nureyev in *Swan Lake*. It was a test: Slash knew about Deedee's promise to Trip not to see him again. She had told him about it herself when she had turned down his dinner invitation. Slash let ten days pass before he called again. He wanted to see if Deedee would break her promise for him. If she broke a promise, Slash thought, his nervous quadrille on the verge of turning into an unconventional but definite courtship, she might also break an engagement.

"I thought it was impossible to get tickets," Deedee said. Nureyev and Fonteyn, the tempestuous Russian defector and the brilliant titled English ballerina, were the hot ticket, the Liz and Dick, the Frankie and Ava, names in the sizzling headlines of the moment.

"Impossible," confirmed Slash. "But not *that* impossible."

Even though they were speaking over the telephone, Deedee could *hear* his patented, one-in-a-million, drop-dead killer smile. She wrestled with herself, torn between her promise to Trip and her attraction—increasingly irresistible—to Slash.

Deedee knew that she was playing a dangerous game, but between her resentment at Trip's suffocating possessiveness and her inability to forget the effect Slash had on her, she was unable to resist the prospect of seeing him again. The danger made it even more exciting.

Made heady and courageous by the rebellions, minor and major, ranging from civil rights protests to family fights over the length of hair, Deedee got out of a dinner with Trip and his squash partner by pleading her period and a bad headache. She spent the afternoon at Kenneth having her hair teased high and wide, put on a brand-new skin-tight gold lurex minidress, black fishnet tights and soft suede thigh-high boots. Knowing that she looked more than just sensational, she met Slash at the Met.

"I bet your mother didn't approve of that outfit," said Slash, who, along with a score of papparazzi, obviously did.

"Well, actually she didn't see it," admitted Deedee, proud and embarrassed at her clever sneakiness at leaving her room with her coat already on. "I knew better. She would never have let me leave the house!"

They laughed in a rebellious collusion that Deedee found a brand-new and amazingly pleasurable experience. It was fascinating, she told herself, how *safe* she felt with Slash.

After the performance and a dozen clamorous curtain calls, Slash took Deedee to a party at the Russian Tea Room. Deedee, along with the rest of the Beautiful People, watched Nureyev devour caviar with sour cream on a baked potato and wash it all down with champagne. Balanchine was there and so was Margot Fonteyn. Baby Jane Holzer, her lion's mane of hair adding inches to her height, was with Andy Warhol, but Verushka, at six feet, towered over everyone. Leo Castelli, vulpine and elegant, was there along with the Sculls, Bob and Ethel. There were the usual social faces: Amanda Burden and Carter, Christina Paolizzi, whom Avedon had photographed nude from the waist up for *Harper's Bazaar*, Diana Vreeland, whose hair was the color of black patent leather, along with the Reeds, the Eberstadts and the Peabodys.

Society, money, talent and power, Manhattan-style, were all prominently represented. The people were more glittering than the conservative old-line WASPs Trip associated with and more glamorous than the dull-as-dishwater businessmen and lawyers and bankers her father and grandfather dined with at "21." They were interesting people, exciting people, people Deedee wanted to know. Slash, once again, was opening Deedee's eyes to the city she had always thought of as hers.

"His cheekbones are even higher than yours!" she told Slash, referring to the dashing defector. She had not been able to take her eyes off Nureyev. He exuded sex, temperament, genius and ruthlessness. He reminded her of Slash.

"I'm only an American stockbroker," Slash replied. "Not a wild Tartar from the steppes of mother Russia."

"How did you get invited to the party, anyway?" Deedee wanted to know.

"Who says I was invited?" he replied with his witty, dangerous smile and Deedee thought once again that Slash Steiner was the most exciting person she'd ever known. By comparison, he made Trip seem rigid, boring and old-fashioned. Deedee had taken a big chance in breaking her date with Trip to go out with Slash again but she felt the risk had been well worth it.

"When I'm with you I feel I'm living life in the present tense," Deedee told Slash later. She sparkled with a rare sense of freedom and a whole world of newly glimpsed possibilities. She had spotted Edie Sedgwick and was wondering if she'd ever be daring enough to cut off her own hair and have it silvered.

"Is there any other way?" Slash replied. A man with little history of his own, Slash did not understand how heavily the past could weigh.

Deedee, not wanting to be disloyal to Trip, did not want to say that more and more she was beginning to feel that Trip was living in the past tense. He was shocked by the antiestablishment attitudes expressed even by people his own age. He despised protests and protestors. He loathed the music of the time, calling it barbaric noise. He detested long hair on men, beards, hippies, Afros, flower power, drugs, dashikis, disco and Dylan.

"Trip says that people are losing their standards," Deedee said finally, wanting Trip's point of view to be represented.

Slash shrugged wordlessly as if what Trip said or thought made no difference and Deedee, backing down, let the moment, ripe with the potential of conflict, pass.

Later, when the evening was over, Slash waved another casual goodnight from his car, leaving Deedee once again kissless and agitated. Now that Slash was gone and she was alone, Deedee felt both guilty and frightened about having lied to Trip and, although she hated to admit it to herself, Slash's total lack of physical interest in her was an unaccustomed rejection.

"It's one thing to cheat on your fiancé for a wild, mad fling," she confided to Annette Gwylim. "It's another to make an ass of yourself over someone who doesn't even seem to notice that boys and girls are different."

There was a sexual revolution going on, and Slash Steiner, who supposedly knew all there was to know about everything, apparently hadn't heard. With a combination of relief and almost unbearable disappointment, Deedee finally decided that he was definitely gay and she swore that this time she really meant it when she said she'd never see him again. She had taken a risk and won but, she told herself firmly, once was enough.

She wanted to fly. But not at the risk of crashing.

Deedee would have gotten away with it except that her photograph, taken at the Nureyev party, made the Suzy column. Trip, alerted once again by Nina, did not waste his time on what he knew would be Slash's insolence. Instead, he barged into the Dahlen apartment and, brushing the butler aside, called for Deedee.

"What the fuck is this?" Trip demanded, waving the folded newspaper at Deedee as she came into the living room.

"Shhh!" cautioned Deedee, closing the door. "The servants!"

"Just what the fuck is this?" Trip repeated. He slapped the newspaper against the end table, and the noise made Deedee jump. "You're sneaking around with some Sammy Glick from the office and you say 'Shhh! The servants!' Are you my fiancée or some goddamn slut?"

"Shh, Trip. Really . . ." said Deedee, stepping back as Trip advanced toward her. She was frightened by Trip's anger and she was afraid that her mother or the servants would hear. "It was just a party."

"And you're just a liar! Your word doesn't mean shit!" he shouted and continued to come toward her, waving the folded newspaper in his hand. Deedee wasn't sure if he meant to hit her or not, and she moved back, afraid of him. The star-shaped birthmark flamed crimson as Trip's usually neatly combed hair became disheveled in his agitation. "You promised you'd never see him again! You swore!"

Trip yelled at her, losing his temper, and he loomed over her, threatening her with word and voice.

"I'm sorry, Trip," Deedee said, almost in tears now, cringing and afraid of him. She held up her hands to protect herself. "It was stupid. I was stupid. I'm sorry!"

"Sorry? You break a promise and the most you have to say is that you're sorry?" Trip imitated her, mocking her inflection. He stood in front of her, his face directly in hers, the newspaper ominous in his right hand. The birthmark throbbed a dangerous red and, physically afraid of him, Deedee moved back another step as Trip decided what to say next.

"If you ever see him again, I want my ring back. If you ever see him again, the engagement is off!" Trip said. He was literally shaking with anger, his breath hot on her face. "Do you hear me? Do you understand me?"

Deedee nodded silently as, step by step, she backed away from him. Trip had made the most serious threat he—or she—could imagine. He meant every word of it and Deedee knew it.

"Well, do you?" he demanded. Using the rolled newspaper like a club, Trip began to swing it in the air near Deedee's face, almost hitting her with it as she moved away from him, stepping backwards, bumping into a chair and almost falling. "Do you hear me? Do you understand me?"

"Yes, Trip. I understand," Deedee said in a choked voice, trying to regain her balance at the same moment that she instinctively held her hands up to protect her face.

"You'd better understand!" Trip snarled. Then, visibly controlling himself, Trip flung the newspaper viciously against the wall, where it made a loud *pop* and then slid to the carpet. Still not relieved of his rage, Trip grabbed the poker that stood next to the fireplace and, like a madman splitting invisible logs, began to bring it down on the newspaper time after time, reducing it to shreds. Deedee, terrified by Trip's display of temper and literally shaking with fear, cowered in a far corner of the room, afraid to scream, afraid to move, afraid to remind him that it was she who was the cause of his rage.

As Trip continued to vent his rage against the newspaper, Deedee remembered the time, several years before, when Trip, angered by a horse who had refused a jump for the third time, had suddenly dismounted, taken a split rail from the jump and beaten the animal. Deedee, infuriated by his cruelty, had finally ripped the log out of his hands. Then—and again now—there was a moment of naked, silent recognition between them that was rare in their carefully choreographed relationship: Trip, when threatened, could be dangerous and they both knew it.

When, almost exhausted by rage, Trip had finished his attack on the newspaper, he raised the poker high over his head and, in one final spasm of fury, brought it down viciously, smashing a valuable glass vitrine. Stalking from the room as the shards of glass tinkled to the carpet, Trip paused for a moment at the doorway and turned back to face a pale and shaking Deedee.

"I mean it, Deedee," he said in a low, lethal tone, his eyes filled with murder. "If you ever see him again, our engagement is off. I want the ring back and the announcement made."

* * *

Deedee made up with Trip that night, but she realized that there was a side to Trip she had sensed but rarely seen before, a dark side that scared her. Still though, she had meant it when she said she wouldn't see Slash again. She hated sneaking around, she hated feeling guilty, she hated hurting Trip. Above all, she knew that Trip meant exactly what he had said about wanting his ring back if she ever saw Slash again. Unlike her own vows, Deedee thought in chagrin, Trip's meant something. Chastened, she told herself that she would not throw away her dreams and her family's dreams for a nobody like Slash Steiner.

"I learned my lesson," she told her mother. "This time I mean it. I'm never going to see Slash Steiner again."

Her resolution turned out to be easy to keep, since it was never tested. Slash simply never called again. It was as if he had dropped off the edge of the earth and Deedee, guilty, bewildered and confused, did not understand what was happening to her. She approached the date of her wedding in slow motion, like a prisoner approaching the gallows.

V

PARADISE

The early sixties marked the first time in social history when the man who came to dinner—and stayed for dancing after—was a hairdresser. Much of the time he wasn't gay and spent plenty of evenings proving it. This confluence of society and style turned out to be one of the sixties' more enduring legacies, lasting into the eighties, and a chain of friendship, mutual benefit and reciprocal usefulness linking a star hairdresser, a millionaire salon owner, a powerful public relations agent and a socialite named Paul Gwilym brought Deedee and Slash together once again.

Deedee had known Paul Gwilym and his sister, Annette, from the days they had all attended Miss Browning's Park Avenue dancing school. Paul and Annette were not only independently wealthy but independent-minded. Of all the girls Deedee had grown up with, Annette was the only one who worked. She had her broker's license and, using her social contacts, personal charm and quite considerable brains, sold cooperative apartments.

Of all the boys Deedee had grown up with, Paul was one of the few who was neither a lawyer nor worked on Wall Street. Using *his* social contacts, personal charm and quite considerable brains, Paul had become an up-and-coming public relations executive. He worked for Nellie Sanderson, whose public relations firm specialized in fashion and beauty accounts, although Nellie was definitely not fashionable and by no means a beauty.

* * *

Nellie Sanderson was four foot nine and had the disposition of a viper. Her voice reminded people of fingernails on a blackboard, and the only curves in her tubby figure resembled those of a beer barrel. She carried great wads of cash in a cheap black pocketbook bought from S. Klein and worked out of a dusty, low-rent office over a kosher delicatessen in the middle of the diamond district on West Forty-seventh Street. She had been known to hit recalcitrant taxi drivers with her umbrella and reprimand insufficiently diligent employees with flying staplers and other assorted office equipment.

Nellie was a widow, her husband having died, no doubt, of exposure to Nellie. Her best friend was a retired buyer of scarves and accessories for Saks Fifth Avenue of such vile and vicious temperament that only she was unruffled by Nellie's frequent tantrums. Paul's job was to escort Nellie to every party that mattered and to see to it, one way or another, that Nellie's clients and their parties got into the newspapers.

One of Nellie's most important clients was Marx & Marx, a huge and highly profitable company that ran hairdressing salons in department stores all over the country. Although the company was called Marx & Marx, there was, in fact, only one Marx, and most people said one was more than enough. Leon Marx, at five foot five, was more than a match for Nellie. *He* had been known to attack people who displeased him with heated curling irons.

Nineteen sixty-four, which saw the introduction of the Touch-Tone telephone and movies on airplanes, also marked the beginning of precision haircutting in America. It had been invented in London a few years before by Vidal Sassoon and Roger Thompson and Leon, knowing a trend when he saw one, was one of the first to jump on the bandwagon. When Vidal Sassoon opened his salon on Madison Avenue, Leon retaliated with his own Limey (as Leon referred to Roger right to his face) and hired him, for a staggering sum, to be Marx & Marx's artistic director. To introduce Roger to the press and to store executives, Leon gave a party at

Arthur. Pete Oney, Leon's assistant vice president for marketing, was, naturally, invited. Pete asked Slash to come along.

"There'll be lots of girls," was how Pete put it. "They'll all be on the Pill." The sexual revolution was being waged with peak intensity, and Pete was one of its greediest beneficiaries.

"How can I resist an invitation like that?" laughed Slash, although casual sex, like casual anything, never interested him in the slightest and Pete, who seemed interested only in casual sex, knew it.

What Slash hoped, as he hoped every time he went anywhere, was that Deedee would be there. He had something to tell her. Something to give her.

"Maybe tonight will be the night," Nina confided to Deedee, referring to her designs on Paul Gwilym. The Argentinian, Nina said, had come (giggle, giggle)—and gone. Nina now turned her attention to Paul. He was rich, attractive, socially acceptable and married, a state which did not seem to faze Nina. The fact that he was widely known to be stubbornly monogamous only added to the sense of challenge.

However, although Nina liked to shock with blunt talk about her sex life and although she dressed in hippie fringes, had a personal mantra and otherwise proudly acted the part of the sixties rebel, she was afraid to walk into a party alone. She asked Deedee to go to the Marx & Marx party with her.

Deedee accepted Nina's invitation and said, "Me, too."

Deedee also hoped that tonight would be the night. The night she'd run into Slash. She hadn't heard from him and she didn't know why. She hadn't called him herself and she did know why—she was afraid. Afraid of being accepted. Afraid of being rejected. Afraid, most of all, of Trip. Wedding plans were going forward at a breakneck pace, and the closer Deedee got to May, the more reluctant she felt and the more she worked at convincing herself that in marrying Trip she was doing the right thing.

Everyone—all the Dahlens and all the Lancomes—seemed, for once, to be so happy. Yet everywhere Deedee

went and everything she did, she did with one purpose: somehow, to see Slash again. If she ran into him accidentally, she
told herself, Trip's threat couldn't possibly apply.

Nina and Deedee giggled in boarding school cahoots, put
on Gernreich minis, Dynel falls and false eyelashes, and went
to Arthur, which was a psychedelic cave of noise and smoke
and music. In the darkness and the confusion of energetic
dancers crushed together on the dance floor, the first person
Nina saw was Paul, who was introducing Roger Thompson
to *Time* magazine's style editor. The second was Slash. He
was dancing with a beanpole-thin model in a geometric haircut, Courrèges boots, corpse-white lipstick, Vampira black
eyeliner and the shortest mini Nina had ever seen. His eyes
seemed riveted to her and he seemed almost hypnotized.

"There's your flame," said Nina, pointing out Slash and
thinking that the evening was turning out even better than
she had hoped. Maybe now, Deedee would see once and for
all how utterly unacceptable Slash Steiner really was.

"Ex-flame," said Deedee. "If you can call him that."

"God, he looks like he wants to screw her right there on
the floor," Nina said.

Nina, although blunt, was, from the look of things, apparently correct and Deedee, although she would have died
before admitting it to Nina, was devastated. Afraid of Trip's
temper and knowing he meant his threat, unwilling to see
Slash and risk breaking her engagement and bear the certain
anger and disapproval of both her family and the Lancomes,
Deedee was nevertheless crushed and bewildered by Slash's
sudden and inexplicable disappearance from her life.

Feeling like a robot going through the motions, Deedee
had helped make out guest lists for her wedding, select a
florist and go over menus with the caterers, choose brides-
maids' dresses and attend fittings for her own lavish gown.
The whole time she kept telling herself that while she loved
Trip with the mature part of herself, the part of herself that
was still young and irresponsible was somehow absolutely
crazy out of her mind about Slash. Deedee knew that her
feelings about Slash were irrational and impossible and could

lead to nothing but problems. Those feelings, however, were stronger and more intense than any she had ever experienced. She didn't understand how or why that should be, and she was at the mercy of her own raw and confused emotions.

At the sight of Slash looking absolutely mesmerized by another woman, Deedee suddenly could contain herself no longer. She wanted to go home. She wanted to be alone with her shame and humiliation. She wanted to understand why she even felt shame and humiliation since, in fact, as she had been truthfully telling everyone all along, absolutely nothing had happened between her and Slash.

Turning abruptly away from Nina, Deedee burst into tears, and, without another word, fled into the coatroom.

"You sound lousy," Slash said.

Deedee hadn't heard him come in after her and she stood there in the stuffy cubicle crammed with minks from Maximilian and funky fun furs, feeling exposed and ugly, miserably aware of the mascara running down her cheeks. Slash handed her his handkerchief and automatically Deedee reached out for it. At the last minute, she snatched her hand back as if she were about to be burned.

"I have some Kleenex, thank you," Deedee said, stiffly, reaching into her evening bag. She was suddenly unbelievably angry at Slash for not calling her, at the same time she told herself that, if he had called, she would have refused to see him again. "I don't want anything from you!"

"You look lousy, too," he said, smiling jauntily and ignoring her haughty rejection. Helpfully, he added: "There's mascara all over your face."

Deedee tightened her mouth and, ignoring Slash, she took her coat and put it on, silently shaking off his offer of help. Without another word, she left the cloakroom and fled into Fifty-fourth Street looking for a taxi. One materialized as if by magic and pulled up to the curb. The door opened.

"Get in," he said.

"I'll get my own taxi!" Deedee snapped, wondering how on earth Slash had gotten a cab so quickly.

This time, it was he who ignored her. He simply reached out and, touching her for the first time, took her by the hand and pulled her into the cab. Reaching across her, he shut the door.

"Where's your car?" Deedee asked, yanking her hand away from his and sitting as far away from Slash as she could. She had never known him ever to use anything except his beloved MG, and she was acutely aware of being alone with him in the dark. She felt edgy and uncomfortable and wildly excited. She wanted to bolt from the taxi, but she felt suddenly paralyzed. At the touch of his hand, her heart began to pound in her chest, deafening her and almost taking her breath away.

"In front of Arthur," Slash said.

"Parked illegally, I suppose?" Deedee's voice sounded choked and suffocated as the sledgehammer in her chest pounded heedlessly away. In the crush of cars, taxis and limousines, Deedee had not noticed the MG.

"Of course," he said. "Even I have my standards."

"I thought you never took taxis," she said, gulping for air. Her attempt at sarcasm wrestled with her breathlessness. "I thought you hated taxis."

"I do," he said. "But this is different."

"Different?"

"I wanted to be alone with you. And I didn't want to have my hands on a steering wheel," Slash said, reaching for her hand again.

She snatched it away again.

"I'm going to get out at the next light," Deedee said, edging even closer to the door. Her excitement had become unbearable, unendurable. All she wanted to do was escape. His presence was threatening. Threatening to her precarious sense of control, threatening to all the *shoulds* of her life. "I don't want to see you. I don't want to talk to you. I don't want to be with you."

"Not even for a ride on a cold night?" he asked.

"Not for anything," she said. "I told you. I don't want anything from you. Not one thing!"

"Not even this?" he asked.

* * *

Slash handed her a small box and, unable to contain her raging curiosity, Deedee opened it. Even in the dim light of the taxi, she could see that the diamond, emerald cut and surrounded by two huge triangular baguettes, was enormous. It was what was vulgarly called a rock. Deedee had never seen a ring so big outside a jeweler's window. No one she knew or could conceive of knowing, no matter how rich, wore a stone that size. She supposed it weighed eight or nine carats.

"Ten," Slash said, reading her mind.

"What am I supposed to do with it?" she asked numbly. Trip's warning floated distantly through her mind. *If you ever see him again, I want my ring back.*

"Wear it, I hope," Slash said, bringing Deedee back to the present tense.

Slash's voice was tender. His eyes asked for her mercy and her love. All along he had wanted her more than he had ever wanted anything or anyone, and all along he had been afraid that his chances were too remote and that his dreams, for once, were too big. Knowing that the plans for the big wedding were gathering momentum, Slash had decided not to make a fool of himself. Reluctantly, but deciding caution was the better part of valor, he had stopped calling her. It was, ironically, Trip himself who gave Slash the courage to continue to seek her out.

Trip had repeated his threat to Slash, telling him that he was never to see Deedee again unless he wanted to be responsible for breaking the Dahlen-Lancome engagement. Trip intended the threat with deadly seriousness. Trip himself would never interfere with another man's engagement. Nor would any other man Trip knew. He assumed that Slash, however insolent, shared the same gentleman's code. He never imagined that Slash would take his threat as the challenge and the opportunity he had been waiting for.

On the same afternoon that Trip delivered his ultimatum, Slash cashed in his stocks and went to Harry Winston. He then spent his evenings going from party to party, looking for Deedee. He hung around the restaurants he knew she frequented and he posted himself outside her apartment building, hoping to surprise her. He hoped that chance would be in his favor but, if it wasn't, he would find another way to see her, to touch her, to let her know that he would risk anything, dare anything, just to have her.

Deedee looked at Slash for a moment, Trip's threat suddenly forgotten. His gray eyes were tender and intense, he looked at her as if she were no mere mortal but a goddess. She realized that she had been right. She hadn't been the only one who had felt the electricity. She hadn't been the only one to think that something special was happening between them. Taking her eyes away from his and without a single word, Deedee slowly and deliberately removed Trip's ring from her finger and replaced it with Slash's.

She held her hand out, showing him her decision.

"I thought you'd never ask," she said, suddenly, the sledgehammer gone, replaced by a feeling of giddy and ecstatic joy. She flew. She soared. And she knew that she would never crash.

"I never did," he reminded her and, letting out a shout of joy, took her into his arms. His mouth on her mouth was the answer to a thousand prayers, said and unsaid. His tongue, insistent and probing, was an exquisite invasion. She yielded to him and responded to him, heat finding heat, desiring meeting desire. She did not even know, as he continued to kiss her, where the boundaries of her ego and her identity ended and his began. Her self merged with his and her surrender to him, although complete, seemed insufficient.

"It's the biggest diamond I've ever seen in my life," she told Slash later when she could speak again. She was unable to take her eyes off it. She turned her hand this way and that so that the facets of the stone reflected and refracted light in the dim back seat of the taxi, sending out sparkling arcs of red, green, blue, yellow and violet light. "The biggest and the most beautiful!"

"It's not big enough. It's not beautiful enough. We're not close enough," Slash said, pulling her next to him and turning her face to his with gentle hands. "I'm going to change all that."

His words were exciting and filled with an infinity of promise. The touch of his hands was electric. No one had ever spoken to her like he did. No one had ever thrilled her like he did. No one had ever kissed her like he did in the back of that taxi.

He took her back to his apartment and opened a bottle of champagne.

"I don't drink," Deedee said.

"You're not going to," he replied.

He dabbled the wine on her throat as if it were perfume and began to lick it off. No one had ever done anything remotely like it to her and Deedee closed her eyes, reveling in paradise. He allowed the wine to trickle down her shoulders and arms, between her breasts and down to her belly.

"Vintage Deedee," he whispered and kissed the trail of wine as its drops coursed in sparkling rivulets down her body.

Naked except for the ring she wore, Deedee gave herself completely to him and, in doing so, found paradise.

VI

BY MUTUAL
CONSENT

ove, everyone said, had nothing to do with it. It was the money—Deedee's money—that mattered. The small notice on the *New York Times'* society page informing the world that the Dahlen-Lancome engagement had been broken said merely that it had been broken by mutual consent. The words sounded undramatic, but Deedee's announcement that she was breaking her engagement to Trip in order to marry Slash Steiner came as nothing less than a bombshell.

No one seemed able to believe for one minute that there was one thing about Deedee other than her trust fund that could conceivably have attracted Slash. Slash was thought to be nothing but an ambitious and predatory fortune hunter. Deedee was accused of everything from being a traitor to her class to an infantile, immature spoiled brat who was risking not only her own future but the future of Lancome & Dahlen for the sake of a momentary impulse. No one seemed to think that Deedee was heading into anything but utter and total disaster.

Luther, whose money had made him accustomed to acquiescence if not always obedience, felt double-crossed. He had always spoiled Deedee and had always seen her, inevitably on the receiving end of his affection and largesse, as loving and grateful. It had never occurred to him that she had thoughts and feelings of her own, and the realization that she did—and that they were not always the same as his—shocked him.

He was beside himself that the dynastic union by marriage of the Lancomes and the Dahlens was suddenly not to be.

Instead of a future dynasty and an assured line of succession, Luther foresaw division rather than unity. Stunned by what he saw as Deedee's betrayal of not only his personal wishes but his hopes for the future of Lancome & Dahlen, he lashed out at her.

"You've inherited your father's unreliability and your mother's flightiness," Luther told Deedee, his blue eyes blazing with anger. He insisted that Deedee return Slash's ring. Deedee refused.

"And *your* stubbornness," Deedee retorted, shocking the old man with her defiance. She told her grandfather that she wanted to marry Slash and that she was going to marry Slash and that no matter what he said or did nothing would change her mind. "Marrying Slash is the best thing I could possibly do. For myself. For the whole Dahlen family. One day you'll thank me."

"Never!"

Grandfather and granddaughter found themselves locked in an unprecedented battle of wills, and Luther tried to persuade Deedee to change her mind. He offered her a first-class trip around the world "to think it over" and Deedee replied that bribery would get him nowhere. He told her how much Lancome & Dahlen meant to the family and how much it would, one day, mean to her and she told him that although Lancome & Dahlen meant a great deal to her, Slash Steiner meant more. He told her how much Trip loved her and she replied that Slash loved her more. Finally, unable to persuade Deedee to change her mind, Luther looked for a way to force her.

"Marry him and you'll never inherit a cent from me!" Luther said, finally turning to the ultimate weapon of every rich parent. More than anything, Luther dreaded that his worst fears might come true: that one day someone who was neither a Dahlen nor even a Lancome might head the firm. "I won't have some fortune hunter end up with the Dahlen money. I mean it, Deedee. If you go ahead and marry this Slash Steiner, I'll disinherit you."

*   *   *

Edwina, who had never seen Luther so angry, not even at the moments Russell had disappointed him most, was concerned about more than Deedee's sudden announcement that she was breaking her engagement. Edwina feared that Deedee's act of rebellion might be fatal to Luther.

"You're going to kill him!" said Edwina, after a conversation with Luther's doctor. Luther's blood pressure had skyrocketed. He was complaining of stomach pain and chest pain. The doctor had prescribed rest, a bland diet and no emotional upset.

"He's doing this to himself," retorted Deedee, with more confidence than she felt.

"You're breaking your grandfather's heart," Edwina said, sadly. "And mine, too."

"And *my* heart will break if I don't marry Slash," Deedee said. She had tears in her eyes but she refused to be swayed.

Silently, Edwina shook her head.

Didn't Deedee realize that when it came to marriage that love—if that's what it was—wasn't all that mattered? Hadn't she learned anything from the example of her own parents' mismatched and unhappy marriage? Didn't she understand that because she was a Dahlen, money counted, too? Not only money but family and background and all the things that the young these days thought so trivial and insignificant.

Apparently not, because, no matter that Luther's blood pressure rose along with his anger and his threats, Deedee still refused to return Slash's ring.

"Luther's making himself sick," Deedee repeated, bitterly. "I'm not. Slash is the heir Luther has always wanted."

"You're throwing away every single thing I struggled to get for you, starting with a million-dollar trust fund and ending with the right marriage to the perfect man!" Joyce said, frustrated as Deedee refused to cave in to her family's threats and fury. Joyce had come from a poor family herself and she remembered what it was like to be poor: how it smelled and how it tasted and how it felt. She was sure she understood Slash and how he felt. Nevertheless, she did not want Deedee to marry him. Joyce, more than anyone, had perceived Slash's magnetism right from the beginning, and she alternated between blaming herself for not absolutely forbidding Deedee to have anything to do with him and blaming Deedee for not being able to resist him.

"*This* is the right marriage and Slash is the perfect man!" Deedee replied, refusing emotional blackmail as defiantly as she had resisted financial blackmail.

"He's a nobody," Joyce told Deedee bluntly. "A nobody from nowhere."

"And the Dahlens aren't the Rockefellers," replied Deedee. "Not to mention the Torngrens!"

Deedee's stinging reply outraged Joyce and she had to restrain herself from slapping Deedee.

"He's obviously marrying you for your money," Joyce said coldly, after a moment, deciding to get down to the real issue at hand.

"The way you married Daddy?"

"I did *not* marry your father for his money," Joyce said, stunned by Deedee's defiance. "I married him because I loved him."

"That's why Slash is marrying me," Deedee replied adamantly, refusing to give in. "And that's why I'm marrying him. Because we love each other. Besides," she added, "he says I'm not nearly rich enough. So how could he be marrying me for my money?"

"Not rich enough!" exclaimed Joyce, thinking that Slash Steiner had really gone too far. "You're one of the richest girls in the city!"

"Slash doesn't think so," said Deedee, imitating Slash's insouciant tone. "He says if I marry him, I'll really be rich!"

"He's just saying that to get his hands on your money!"

"He swears he'll never touch my money! He says he's going to support me," Deedee said. "He says we're going to be richer than Luther. *Much* richer!"

"I'll believe that," said Joyce bitterly, "the day I see it!"

If freedom, as the lyric goes, is just another word for nothing left to lose, then rich people have the opposite problem.

Rich people always feel, on some level, that they have everything to lose.

The Lancomes, like the Dahlens, felt they had everything to lose. The Lancomes, like the Dahlens, reacted to the broken engagement out of fear and anger. Anger at Deedee for the way she had blatantly cheated on Trip and then summarily rejected him. Fear that one day Slash might even, through Deedee, try to oust Trip from his position at the head of Lancome & Dahlen.

"He's ambitious," Junior said, fearing that marriage to Deedee might be the first step in Slash's master plan to take control of Lancome & Dahlen. "Too ambitious."

"He's a nobody," Trip said, echoing Joyce and dismissing his father's concerns. "How could he possibly take over Lancome & Dahlen?"

Trip hated Slash. He didn't fear him. Not yet.

Nina told Deedee that she was making the mistake of a lifetime. She said that Slash was immoral and unethical and that shame and a lifetime of humiliation were the most Deedee could possibly expect from someone like Slash.

"He'll probably go through your money and then, when it's all gone, he'll dump you for someone richer," Nina predicted.

"The ring is vulgar and nouveau riche," Bunny Lancome told Deedee the first time she saw the diamond Slash had given her. *This* time, Bunny thought, Deedee had gone too far. It was one thing for Deedee to go mod and have her pictures all over the newspapers; it was another to wear her money on her hand. "I'd be embarrassed to wear it if I were you."

"He's a fortune hunter," sneered Junior Lancome, telling Deedee that she was a fool to fall for Slash and his sleazy charm.

Deedee paid no attention to Nina.

"She's just jealous," she told Slash.

She thought that Bunny, with her inevitable cashmere twin sets and single strand of pearls, was living in the nineteenth century and she thought that Junior Lancome could have benefited from a bit of charm himself, sleazy or otherwise. She was, however, genuinely afraid of Trip, and she even feared, although she told herself that she was being ridiculous, that he might turn physically violent. Instead, he turned verbally vicious and told Deedee that if she went ahead and married Slash, she would have nothing but regrets.

"You'll be sorry," Trip said, his jaw clenched tight with the icy, tight-lipped Lancome fury. "Slash Steiner is *not* one of us."

"Trip, you make it sound like we're royalty," said Deedee, aware, not for the first time, of the way money tended to elevate people's opinions of themselves. "But we're not. We're just ordinary people with ordinary feelings."

"You're being naive," said Trip, feeling suddenly almost sorry for Deedee and what she was getting herself into.

"Or maybe," he added witheringly, the moment of compassion gone, "Slash Steiner has blinded you with love."

Trip almost made it seem that he had been doing Deedee a favor by agreeing to marry her. He contended that his motives were pure and even altruistic while Slash's could only be completely cynical.

"He doesn't care about anything or anyone except money," said Trip after he wordlessly took the ring Deedee returned and put it into his pocket. "He used your father and now he's going to use you."

"That's ridiculous!" replied Deedee, unable to see the slightest flaw in Slash. "He loves me."

"Love?" repeated Trip sarcastically. "Most people would call it ambition and greed. He's a fortune hunter," Trip said, echoing Joyce and Luther. "He wouldn't look at you if you weren't a Dahlen."

"Neither would you!" snapped Deedee.

Trip looked at her for a moment with almost murderous venom. Deedee had been right and Trip hated her for it.

"You'll be sorry," Trip said finally as he brushed past her

and walked out of the room. He turned back and, with a cold smile, added, "I'm going to destroy Slash and you along with him. Then you'll come crawling back to me, Deedee, and I won't take you. Marrying Slash Steiner is the worst mistake you'll ever make. You'll regret it in a thousand ways and I won't do one thing to help you. Not one thing! Mark my words."

Trip's words were melodramatic, but the intensity with which he had uttered them sent a chill through Deedee.

"He threatened to destroy you," Deedee told Slash. "And me, too."

"Don't be silly," said Slash. "The worst Trip could do to me would be fire me and I can get another job with one phone call. As for you, what could he possibly do to you?"

Deedee thought about Slash's question and realized that Slash was right. There was nothing Trip could do to her. Nevertheless, Trip's words and the passionate anger that had produced them stayed with Deedee, an ominous portent hanging over her future as everyone continued to tell her that she was making the mistake of a lifetime.

"You're not, are you?" Deedee asked Slash as the attacks against him continued. She felt like a punching bag instead of a bride-to-be. She was bitter that no one seemed to share her happiness, wounded that no one seemed to wish her well. She spoke timidly and tentatively, but the relentless attacks by her family and the Lancomes on Slash's motives continued to upset her and finally began to undermine her confidence in her own feelings.

"Not what?"

"Marrying me for my money?" Deedee said, finally, putting her worst fears into words. She could barely look at him.

"Your family is getting to you," said Slash.

"Yes," admitted Deedee. "But it's me you love, isn't it? Not my money?"

"It's you I love," Slash told her, knowing that she wanted to be reassured and not really blaming her. The viciousness of the reactions toward their engagement angered Slash and made him feel that he was rescuing Deedee from a den of tigers. He was happy to be able to give her the reassurance she wanted, and he held her close. "But if you want me to prove it's not your money, I will."

"Could you?" Deedee asked, almost pleading. Part of her was vulnerable to her family's suspicions. Part of her believed that her money *was* the most interesting and attractive thing about her. Part of her wondered, just wondered, if what everyone was saying was true. Did Slash love her? Or her money?

"I will do anything if it will make you feel better," Slash promised and made an appointment with Van Tyson, an idea already forming in his mind.

Russell was Deedee and Slash's only ally.

"Why on earth shouldn't she marry him?" Russell asked, standing up not only to Joyce but to his parents and his partners as well. "Slash is smart, energetic and hardworking. He may not have a past but he has a tremendous future. Deedee's right about him."

When Deedee repeated Trip's threat to destroy Slash, Russell told her not to worry.

"Slash can take care of himself," Russell said, remembering the way Slash had taken charge in the burning building. Slash had saved not only himself but also his friend. And Russell never forgot that he owed his own life to Slash. His own—and Lana's, too. "I wouldn't worry about Slash."

"But what about me?" asked Deedee. "Trip threatened to destroy me, too."

"There's nothing he can do to you," said Russell, repeating Slash's reassurance. "Besides, I'm here to protect you and so is Slash."

During the same week in early May that Deedee would have married Trip Lancome, Slash went into Luther's big corner office at Lancome & Dahlen and shut the door behind him. He wanted to get everything out into the open, and he wanted, once and for all, to put to rest Luther's suspicions about him and his motives.

"I know exactly what you think of me," said Slash, looking the old man straight in the eye. "You think I'm an opportunist. You think I want to marry Deedee for her money. Well, I'm not and I don't and I am going to prove to you that you're wrong."

"And how do you propose to do that?" Luther asked, not even inviting Slash to sit down. Being proven wrong was not something that had happened to Luther very often in his life and his attitude made *that* perfectly clear.

"By not touching a penny of Deedee's money. Not ever," said Slash. He stood across from Luther, resting his hands on the back of one of the leather visitor's chairs. "And that's not just a promise. It's a fact."

"It is?" replied Luther. A cynic both by inclination and experience, he was far more dubious than convinced.

Slash nodded politely, refusing to be insulted.

"I'm going to be Deedee's husband whether you like it or not," he told Luther calmly. "I am not, however, despite what you and everyone else may think about me, either a gigolo or a fortune hunter. I plan to support Deedee on *my* money. I've spoken to Van Tyson and I've asked him to draw up a codicil to be added to Deedee's trust fund saying that I am never to touch a cent of Deedee's money."

"You don't have to go that far," said Luther sarcastically, impressed despite himself as Slash handed the document containing the legal provision across the desk to him.

"But I do have to," said Slash, his gray eyes steady as he watched Luther read the language of the codicil. "I know what you think of me. I want to change your mind."

Luther, of course, agreed to have the codicil added to the terms of the trust agreement although, as Slash had known he would, Luther called Van Tyson the moment Slash left his office.

"Is the codicil foolproof?" Luther asked his lawyer. One of the things Luther had learned in his very long career was that it always paid to double-check.

"I drew it up, Luther," said Van Tyson. "It's absolutely unbreakable. Slash won't ever be able to touch a dime of

Deedee's. Not even if she wants him to. Not even if *you* want him to."

Luther snorted and unwittingly echoed Joyce. "That will be a cold day in hell!"

"Even if it freezes over down there, you won't need your overcoat," the lawyer reassured him. "The codicil is absolutely ironclad."

Nevertheless, Slash's promises and Slash's deeds all seemed almost too good to be true and Luther, unimpressed by promises and good intentions, still had lingering doubts. Slash had come too far too fast, and Luther was infinitely suspicious of this knifeblade-thin, gray-eyed young man with the right ideas and the wrong attitude. He knew almost everything—Russell had never told him about Lana—about the circumstances under which Russell had hired him, and he still wondered whether Russell had done the right thing. Giving in to blackmail, however subtly applied, was dangerous.

"Words are cheap," said Luther when he told Edwina about the codicil. "Follow-through is what counts. Let's see what he *does.*"

In the end, though, afraid that Deedee would be alienated from them permanently and persuaded by the signed codicil, the Dahlens relented and gave Deedee their reluctant blessing. Deedee, who had never wanted anything as much as she wanted Slash, literally glowed with victory and satisfaction.

"It's *me* he loves. *Not* my money," she told Annette joyfully, referring to the codicil. "I knew it all along, and this just proves it."

VII
PETALS

The Dahlen-Steiner wedding at the St. Regis in June of 1964 was the major social event of the early summer. The guest list of five hundred ran the gamut from old society to new money and symbolized the vast social changes taking place. Rhinelanders and Paleys mixed with pop artists and fashionable hairdressers. French champagne and Iranian caviar were served in public, while in private the young passed joints of marijuana and hashish and traded tabs of LSD and mescaline. Pete Oney made a date with one of the Cushing girls. Nina Lancome, who had given up on Paul Gwilym and was flitting in and out of a subsequent romance with a famous but often impotent movie producer, went home with a brooding actor named Mario di Pinto whose family came from the Bronx.

And Deedee and Slash had gotten their way.

Richard Steiner, like the Dahlens, did not really approve. He warned Slash about the perils of marrying too far above him—warnings that sounded positively Victorian to Slash. He also warned Slash about the potential hazards of marrying a spoiled only child—one who had always gotten everything she wanted. Including Slash.

"Make one mistake, just one, and she'll get rid of you the way she got rid of Trip," Richard said. Richard Steiner had worked for and around rich people for over twenty years. He had been a victim of their whims and capriciousness and he wanted to warn Slash.

"Deedee's not like that," Slash said, surprised by a cynical side he had never seen in Richard Steiner. "Besides, I can handle her."

Richard wasn't entirely convinced, but he knew better than to argue with a young man madly in love.

Despite all the doubts, spoken and unspoken, everyone put the best face on everything. Deedee's French lace gown was from Bendel's, the wedding gifts came in Tiffany boxes and the romantic honeymoon destination was halfway around the world in Bali.

"Bali?" replied Deedee in surprise when Slash told her where he was planning to take her on their honeymoon. "But I don't know a soul there."

"That's the whole point," he said. In Paris or London or Rome, in Bermuda or Acapulco or Barbados, there would have been friends or friends of friends and Slash and Deedee would have been part of Deedee's world. "I'm going to be your husband, not your gigolo. We're going to be leaders, not followers. What we do, your friends will do, not the other way around."

Slash thought they could be stars and trend-setters. He would make the money and Deedee would set the styles. They were young and beautiful, bright and energetic. She had the contacts and he had the savvy. Slash's vision of who they could be excited Deedee and ignited an ambition she barely knew she had, and his dreams became her dreams.

Bali was warm and sensuous and ravishingly beautiful. Hand in hand, Slash and Deedee toured small villages where woodworkers and jewelers practiced their trades. Arm in arm, they visited exotic, walled living compounds where religion and ritual were part of everyday life and every household had its own shrine. They marveled at the lovely terraced rice fields and the way the Balinese—both men and women dressed in sarongs—seemed to be the most graceful people in the world. They purchased lengths of batik in rich colors and patterns, swam in the warm seas and feasted on each other.

Deedee, who had daringly slept with Trip at a time when nice girls didn't, thought that because she wasn't a virgin, she knew everything there was to know about sex. What she found out was that she knew only Trip's conventional and rather inhibited lovemaking. Slash, who was brisk and efficient about everything else, took his time when it came to sex, drawing out the act and the pleasure with imagination and inventiveness until Deedee thought she would die with ecstasy.

"Where did you learn all this?" she asked when she could speak.

"I read a book," he replied and muffled her reply with his mouth.

"In the beginning, I wasn't even sure you liked me," Deedee confessed. It was sunrise. She and Slash were walking along the edge of a terraced rice paddy. The humid air was warm and sensuous, the soft quacking of the ducks an idiosyncratic refrain. The rising sun was just beginning to refresh the shadows.

"I more than liked you. I just didn't want you to know," Slash admitted. "I thought that if I made my feelings obvious, you'd lose interest."

"You were probably right," Deedee said, knowing perfectly well that he was. She had been very popular all through school, and the only boys who had ever interested her were the ones who didn't throw themselves at her. "How did you know me so well?"

"Instinct, I guess," Slash said. "I knew you were used to men like Trip. I thought I'd be the opposite."

"You almost drove me crazy."

He traced a finger down her throat and onto her shoulder and grinned lasciviously.

"Good," he said. "Now let me do it again."

"Do what?"

"Drive you crazy . . ."

"Here?" she asked, startled, glancing around at the lush green paddies and the narrow, grassy walkways between. At a distance, she could see the duck master with his triangular pennant flying high from his bamboo pole.

"Here," he replied, following her eyes and seeing what she saw. "Now."

He wet his forefinger with his tongue and began slowly to run it around the inside of her ear.

The honeymoon was more than love and kisses, whispered words and passionate moments; it was a blueprint for their future. Slash and Deedee talked about the places they would live, the friends they would have, the successes they would achieve, the way they would win her family over and the children they would have.

"Three or four," said Deedee, who told Slash that the attention she had received as an only child had been more than offset by the devastating sense of insignificance she had felt in being only a girl in a family that valued boys. "Maybe even five."

"Three or four," Slash confirmed and added with a laugh: "Maybe even five if I have the strength."

Slash, too, longed for children of his own. He would give his children the love and attention only a real parent could. He would lavish them with toys and ballet lessons, ponies and sailboats, birthday parties and trips and excursions of every kind. He would protect them from anyone and everyone. He would give them everything he had never had, and he and Deedee agreed at how amazing it was that he who had been an orphan and she who had grown up with her real parents, both felt so deprived of the normal experiences of an ordinary childhood. Their children, they solemnly promised each other, would know what it was like to be young and carefree and happy. Their children, they promised each other, would have the one thing neither of them had had: a normal childhood.

During the second week of their honeymoon, Deedee got her first taste of Slash's flair for theatrical generosity. It happened at the open market in Batur.

"Gardenias! My favorite flower," Deedee exclaimed at the sight of an entire stall massed with hundreds of the fragile, fragrant blooms. She had never seen so many of the exquisite white flowers in her life and she turned to Slash. "Can I have one?" she asked.

"No," Salsh said. Before Deedee could protest, he continued: "One's not enough."

Slash turned to the flower vendor. "We'll take them all," he said, handing over a bill in such a large denomination that the vendor bowed and then smiled.

Slash turned to Deedee, motioning toward the opulent display.

"Take them. They're yours," he said.

"All of them?" Deedee asked, still stunned and not quite sure whether or not Slash meant what he said.

"All of them!" Slash ordered.

Deedee, who was accustomed to being spoiled and indulged, lit up with delight. She was overwhelmed not only by the scale but by the apparent impulsiveness of Slash's largesse.

"You shouldn't have!" she reprimanded, clearly thrilled despite herself as they walked toward their hotel, followed by three young boys Slash had hired in the market to carry the flowers. "You shouldn't have . . ."

When they got back to their room, Slash spread the gardenias on the carved and painted Balinese wedding bed that furnished their room. Naked, Deedee lay back, luxuriously crushing their heavy, velvety petals with her body and releasing their sultry, seductive perfume into the room.

"You shouldn't have." Deedee said again, intoxicated by the scent and reeling from Slash's entravagance.

"You're going to have to learn," Slash told her, chiding her for being an uptight WASP, "that only the Shakers and the Japanese have found happiness in too little. For the rest of us, too much is just the right amount . . ."

"Are we really going to be richer than Luther?" Deedee asked later, stroking Slash's long, narrow back. She was referring to a promise Slash had made before the wedding, a promise Deedee had repeated to her mother.

"Much," he said, aware not for the first time of the way this rich girl was turned on by the prospect of money. "Much!"

Deedee shivered deliciously in greedy anticipation, imagining how wonderful it would be to have her own money to do with exactly as she wished and to feel free, finally, from her grandparent's caution and her mother's hovering protectiveness. Although she wasn't consciously aware of it, Deedee, as anyone else would have, had adopted her family's attitudes as her own. To her, money was more than just dollars and cents, money was her very identity, and the more she had, unconsciously, the more she imagined herself to be. Of all the things that money could buy, it was a sense of identity and the self-confidence that came along with it that was the most essential. Enough money, Deedee thought, could even make up for being only a girl.

It was during their honeymoon that Slash first began to realize the exquisite irony of it all and became aware of the source of his eventual, almost mystical, power over Deedee: it wasn't he who had married for money. It was she.

It would be several years, however, before Slash would completely understand his insight and be able to put it into practice. Meanwhile, he adored Deedee and was constantly amazed that he, a poor boy from St. Ignatius with no family and no resources other than his brains and energy, had actually married her.

People who knew them said that he treated her like a goddess, and they were right.

"I'm going to make you fall in love with me. Heart and mind. Body and soul," Slash said on the last day of their honeymoon. Their plane had stopped over in Singapore and they were in the garden of the Raffles Hotel drinking freshly squeezed juice from Malaysian pineapples—far better even, it was said, than Hawaiian.

"But I *am* in love with you," she said, leaning forward in

her intensity, wanting him to know that she was his and only his.

"No, you're not," he replied, his gray eyes deadly serious. "Right now, you're just infatuated with me . . ."

Later, Deedee would look back and realize that Slash had been right. But at the time, intoxicated by the heat and humidity, by the heady scent of gardenias, by memories of romantic, exotic Somerset Maugham tales of love in the simmering climate, she thought Slash was just being his usual, extravagant self. What she did think, then and for years after, was that everyone except her father had been wrong and that she was the luckiest woman in the world.

PART THREE

*The Man
with the
Midas Touch /
1964-1976*

"He never made a mistake. For years, everything he touched turned to gold. People began to think he was infallible. I was one of them. So, unfortunately, was he . . ."

—ARTHUR BOZEMAN

"With an evening coat and a white tie, even a stockbroker can gain a reputation for being civilized."

—OSCAR WILDE

"Wilde was wrong."

—SLASH STEINER

I

THE SEDUCER

"*The most important rule in getting someone to fall in love with you is to fall in love with them first,*" Slash told Deedee on their honeymoon, confiding to her how he had felt about her from the very beginning. "Now I want your family to fall in love with me, too."

"By falling in love with them?" asked Deedee, thinking of Luther's suspicions, Edwina's disapproval and her mother's broken-hearted opposition. *Lovable* was not exactly the first word that leapt to mind.

"When it comes to your family, the first rule doesn't apply," said Slash with his killer grin. "The second rule does."

"And what's that?"

"The second rule of getting someone to fall in love with you," he said, "is to make them rich."

Deedee smiled and nodded. Slash, it seemed, understood her family very well.

"How are you going to do that?" she asked.

"I have a good track record," Slash said, refusing to tell her the details, "and a great idea."

One of the secrets of Slash's success was an unblinking, clear-eyed realism that allowed him to face facts, however unpleasant and/or unflattering. He knew that Deedee's family, now stuck with him despite themselves, wanted their suspicions of him eased and, just as Slash had once seduced Deedee, he now set out to seduce her family. The codicil, he knew, had been a good start. But it was only a start.

Slash knew that the Dahlens still considered him an opportunist and a fortune hunter, and he searched for ways to ease their worries about his motives. Love and good intentions, he knew, were not enough. Not with rich people like the Dahlens.

With rich people like the Dahlens it was money that counted, and just as Slash had gone to Van Tyson with an idea before the wedding, he went to Russell with another idea after the wedding. He reminded his father-in-law that for the past fifteen months, the monthly performance of his portfolios had been number one on the Lancome & Dahlen internal rankings.

"I'd like to do for the partners what I've been doing for my clients," Slash told Russell. "I'd like to make them rich."

"They're already rich," Russell pointed out.

"But not rich enough," Slash replied, using a line he'd used once before. Deedee hadn't fallen for it, but he felt sure that men whose business was money would have a far different reaction. "You know my track record. Suppose Lancome and Dahlen establishes a partners' portfolio and suppose I invest that portfolio? *My* way."

"The partners think you're reckless," Russell pointed out.

"The clients don't," Slash reminded him. "Not when they look at the bottom line."

Russell nodded.

"I'll speak to Junior," he said.

By the end of the week the first Partners' Portfolio in the history of Lancome & Dahlen had been established. The portfolio was open only to partners in the firm, and the minimum investment was one hundred thousand dollars. Not one partner chose not to participate, and even the Lancomes, both Junior and Trip, who, although they despised Slash, knew as well as anyone how much money Slash was making, wrote checks made out to the brand-new Partners' Portfolio. Russell, knowing the depth of their resentment toward Slash, was amazed. Slash, on the other hand, wasn't the least bit surprised.

"Now all I have to do is make them rich," he told Deedee.

"And will you?" she asked anxiously.

"I better," he said, and, if he was the slightest bit apprehensive, Deedee never saw the remotest sign of it.

It was called the Partners' Portfolio and it was, in the fashion of the time, a hedge fund. Privately held, the Partners' Portfolio was free from federal laws forbidding publicly held funds from operating on margin or making short sales. Slash could—and did—pyramid debt and sell short, playing both sides of the Street, minimizing risk and maximizing profit. Slash began to invest its assets with his usual sure-handed aggressiveness in July. When that month's internal performance sheet was circulated, the Partners' Portfolio led the list. It continued to lead that list throughout that summer and fall.

"For an opportunist, he's remarkably generous with his talents," Russell pointed out to Luther in late October. "Lancome and Dahlen is making far more money from Slash than the other way around."

"Let's see how long it lasts," said Luther sourly, adding that anyone could have a four-month hot streak. The old man was still dubious about Slash and his intentions and, no matter what Russell said, he still found it impossible to keep an open mind.

Slash also attempted a seduction of the Lancomes. He knew that Junior and Trip despised him. He also knew that he would have to work closely with them. While money certainly counted with the Lancomes, Slash also knew that Junior and Trip valued loyalty, discretion and responsibility and he gave it to them—at least superficially—in abundance. Junior, like Luther, was highly dubious about the depth of Slash's conversion, but he was well aware of how much money Slash was making for the partners and how much the clients liked him.

"He's a little shit," Junior told Trip as Thanksgiving

neared, trying to see the good side of the outlaw they both felt had been shoved down their throats. "But at least he's *our* little shit and he's right where we can keep an eye on him."

Trip was not so forgiving.

"Codicil or no codicil, mutual fund or no mutual fund, I still don't trust him," he told his father, still stung by the sudden and very public embarrassment of having lost Deedee to a nobody. "The sooner we see the last of Slash Steiner, the better off we'll all be."

However, in public, Trip was just as unfailingly polite to Slash as Slash was to him. Trip even sent Deedee and Slash a wedding gift of crystal candlesticks. He hadn't done it out of the kindness of his heart. He'd gone to Tiffany's because it made him look good.

For her part, although she had attended the wedding for appearance's sake, Nina's feelings toward Deedee had changed. She felt that Deedee, who had dumped Trip, was no longer to be trusted. Even though it seemed ludicrous in the rebellious atmosphere of the sixties, Nina couldn't help but feel that Deedee was a traitor to her class.

"I don't understand how you can be so forgiving," Nina told Trip, unable to understand how Trip had been able to send a wedding gift.

Trip smiled tightly.

"What makes you think I've forgiven anyone?" he replied, his Southampton blue eyes as cold and unforgiving as the tundra.

"You sent a wedding gift," Nina pointed out.

"I have to work in the same office with him every day," Trip said and let the matter drop.

Even to those who knew him best, Trip appeared to be a man who had forgiven and forgotten. Only to himself did Trip admit the truth: if, for the time being, he couldn't destroy Slash, he would use him.

* * *

There was yet another seduction that Slash pursued: the continuing seduction of the million-dollar baby who was now his wife. With more passion and intensity than ever before, Slash wooed and courted the heiress he had married. He wanted her, as he had told her on the last day of their honeymoon, to fall deeply and irretrievably in love with him. He wanted her, as he told her a thousand times, to be all his. Heart and mind. Body and soul.

"I want you to love me the way I love you," he said.

"But I do," Deedee protested.

"Not enough," Slash said. "Not enough."

Deedee found that the elusive, maddening suitor who had reduced her to sleepless nights and tears of frustration before marriage became, after marriage, the most loving, accessible and passionate of men. The mysterious lover had become an adoring husband. Slash telephoned her three times a day, and Deedee who was accustomed, as an only child, to being the focus of attention, was overwhelmed by the intensity of Slash's attentiveness.

"I love you," he would say.

"Buy yourself something pretty," he would order. "I put some money in your wallet before I left for work."

"Meet me at the office," he would suggest. "We'll go to Chinatown for dinner. Just the two of us. Alone together."

"I wish I could kiss your ear," he would whisper.

"Do you miss me?" he would ask and before she could answer, he would tell her how much he missed her.

"Wear your lace panties," he would say and then tell her what they'd do when he got home.

He showered her with gifts and surprises. A bouquet of daisies bought from a street peddler or a telegram in celebration of nothing that said "I love you." A taxi-yellow vinyl raincoat from Paraphernalia or an appointment for her first Sassoon haircut. A dozen lipsticks in colors ranging from the palest pink to the deepest fuchsia. Supposedly impossible-to-get tickets for a Beatles concert, one of Rudy Gernreich's topless bathing suits which she wore in the privacy of their bedroom, a dozen bestsellers from *The Spy Who Came in from the Cold* to *How to Be a Jewish Mother.* He gave her credit cards of her own and never questioned the bills. When she would chide him for being too extravagant, Slash always had the same answer.

"You'd better get used to having everything you want," he would say, encouraging her to indulge herself in every whim and every wish and forbidding her ever to touch a penny of her own money. "This is only the beginning."

Christmas approached and, for the first time in his life, Slash looked forward to the holiday. His marriage was still in the honeymoon stage and, although he was far too realistic to think that there might be a honeymoon with Lancome & Dahlen, he was well aware that attitudes toward him were gradually shifting. Even though he still had the wrong attitude and the wrong accent, he was beginning to become respected, however reluctantly, for his dazzling performance with the Partners' Portfolio.

He definitely wouldn't go so far as to call it love, Slash told Deedee in November the day that Andrew Macon, one of the most senior of the senior partners, invited him to lunch for the first time, but it sure was beginning to feel like the ice might be thawing.

"You mean the second rule of seduction is working?" Deedee asked.

"I might have to make it the first rule," Slash replied with the killer smile that told Deedee that, even though Slash wanted to be accepted, another part of him despised the people he wanted to be accepted by.

As the Stones' lyric put it, time, time, time was on his side. Slash followed the Dow straight up in the great bull market of 1964 and by the end of the year he could point to an almost incredible 63 percent return on the assets in the Partners' Portfolio. His own portfolio, traded even more aggressively, had done even better, and he could promise Deedee anything and know that any promise he made, he could keep.

"All I want is you," Deedee would reply truthfully. "And a houseful of children."

But the fact was that the money didn't hurt, and little by little, without even knowing it, Deedee was becoming addicted to money—and to the man who provided it.

Just as Slash was working at getting rich, Deedee spent her time trying to think of ways to please her new husband. She switched from Cole Porter to rock and roll, from nightclubs to discos, from rich girl's A-lines to sexy girl's see-throughs. She wore miniskirts with maxicoats, Dynel falls and pants suits, ruffled gypsy rags à la YSL and acid colors that went with acid rock. She became assertive in bed and comfortable with her own sexuality. She tried all the positions in the *Kama Sutra*, became accomplished at oral sex and occasionally went to dinner parties without wearing panties because Slash said that he liked to look at her, all dressed up, and know that, underneath, she was available to him.

As the early months of their marriage sped by, Slash counted his profits and Deedee counted the days of the month. She looked forward to the moment when she could tell Slash that she was pregnant and that he would no longer have to be an orphan. She looked forward to the moment she could tell him that he would have what he had never had and so deeply wanted: a family of his own.

I I
THE SEDUCTION

For the first year of their marriage, Slash and Deedee lived in a comfortable but unpretentious apartment on East Fifty-fifth Street just off Sutton Place. Billy's became their favorite restaurant, and on Sunday afternoons they would walk along the promenade down to the United Nations and then, heading further south, would explore the pretty brownstone-lined streets of Murray Hill. They would continue walking down to Little India in the East Twenties, where they would have a spicy curry dinner before heading home again.

On the Sunday of their first wedding anniversary, Slash mysteriously changed direction and headed uptown. They walked along First Avenue and Slash turned west on Seventy-fifth Street.

"Do you still like it?" Slash asked, stopping in front of an elegant gray stone townhouse located between Lexington and Park avenues. Its shutters were lacquered a glossy black, and its stone façade was painted a soft dove gray. Its windows gleamed, seeming almost to float with their transparency. Immaculately whitewashed boxes of brilliant red geraniums and glossy green trailing ivy flanked the black lacquered front door.

"Absolutely," Deedee said, lighting up with the memories of the way the house had always seemed magic to her, the way its harmonious façade and trim boxwood hedges seemed to promise happy lives and laughter inside. The house had always seemed to Deedee that ideal combination of perfect elegance on a life-sized and welcoming scale. "Don't you remember? It was my dream house. I used to pass it every day on the way to school and stop and daydream about the glamorous people I was sure lived there."

"Do you still feel that way?"

"Of course."

Without another word, Slash took Deedee by the hand and led her to the lacquered door. As she turned questioningly to him, the door opened, as if magically, from the inside. A butler bowed silently and disappeared, leaving them alone. Banked in the foyer were enormous glazed terra-cotta jars filled with white gardenias. Slash picked Deedee up and carried her over the threshhold.

"Did you buy it?" Deedee asked, when she could catch her breath, finally beginning to understand that here was yet another of Slash's lavish surprises. "Is it yours?"

"Yes, I bought it, but no, it's not mine," he said, putting her down gently and kissing her. "It's ours. We'll bring our children up here."

The subject of children had become a painful one. In the sixth month of their marriage, Deedee had become joyously pregnant. She went to Doubleday and bought out their section of child-care books. She turned the spare bedroom into a nursery and painted it soft yellow. She had her own wicker bassinet repaired and repainted. She went to Saks and bought a layette. She began making lists of names and lists of schools. She bought a baby carriage, a baby scale and a bottle sterilizer.

"This kid is going to be better equipped than an invading army," Slash teased.

Deedee giggled and didn't deny it. Then she went to F.A.O. Schwartz and bought a teddy bear, a panda and a Raggedy Ann doll like the one she had once had.

In the tenth week of her pregnancy Deedee woke up early in the morning with slight cramps. She went to the bathroom and in her groggy, half-asleep state thought that she had gotten her period. Confused, she looked closer and realized that she hadn't gotten her period. She cried out as the cramps increased and Slash ran in to catch her as she swayed and almost fainted from an intense spasm of pain. He called Myron Kligman, who told him to bring Deedee to his East Ninety-third Street office immediately.

"It's a good thing," Dr. Kligman told Deedee after he had examined her and she was dressed again and back in his softly lit, comfortable office. On the wall behind his desk was a Miró, a Calder and a Robert Indiana that spelled LOVE. Expensive modern art for an expensive modern practice.

"Good?" she repeated numbly. How could a miscarriage be good? Deedee was pale and shaky and held a shredded and soggy Kleenex in her right hand.

"You wouldn't have wanted it," he said. Myron Kligman was tall and thin and stoop shouldered. He had a quiet voice and prided himself on being honest but never cruel with his patients. His East Side offices had the air of a club, and his patients, feeling that they were all in this adventure of child-bearing together, called themselves "Myron's girls." Deedee told Slash that the atmosphere in the always crowded waiting room reminded her of a boarding school for blimps.

"I would have!" exclaimed Deedee, contradicting him. "It was my baby! My baby!" she said and began to cry. Her sense of loss was devastating. She felt more than just empty, she felt vacant. Vacant except for the pain.

Myron Kligman shook his head gently.

"Nature has its ways," he said, coming around from behind his desk and putting his hand on Deedee's shoulder. He was a calm and comforting man and, when Deedee had quieted down, he continued. "You might think it's the end of the world," he said, "but it isn't. You're fine and you and Slash will go on to have other children."

Deedee tried to smile but managed only to nod. She couldn't think of a thing to say. She picked up her bag and got up to leave.

"I'll see you soon," said Myron Kligman confidently. "You'll be pregnant again in no time."

Deedee tried once again to smile and this time managed a wan upcurve of the lips. She went home and began to count the days again. When another six months went by, she began to wonder just how long no time would be.

It took Deedee almost a year to decorate her new house. She hired Dorsay Miller, a young interior decorator who worked on Sister Parish's staff. Deedee wanted to use the batiks she and Slash had bought in Bali. For one thing, she felt sentimental about them. For another, she knew that no one in the whole city had used batik. It was Deedee's idea to put the batik on the walls instead of wallpaper; it was Dorsay's idea to glaze and lacquer it. The final result was both elegantly informal and extremely sophisticated. Photographed by *Vogue*, the headline writer called it a beautiful house for beautiful people. Dorsay told Deedee that other clients were beginning to ask for batiked rooms.

"I told you we would lead and others would follow," Slash told Deedee.

"I never thought *anyone* would want to copy me," Deedee replied, thrilled by the supreme flattery of imitation.

Deedee had always felt she was a nobody, the disappointing replacement for a dead brother who could have done all the things she couldn't do: carry on the family name and the family line and cause the family fortune to grow. Now—thanks to Slash and thanks to Slash's money and the way he encouraged her to spend it—she felt she was a somebody, that she, even though she was only a girl, counted, too. People were beginning to notice her. People were beginning to copy her. The glamorous, exciting people Deedee had once wanted to know now wanted to know her. The feeling was intoxicating.

By the second year of their marriage, Deedee's life began to fall into a pattern as she devoted herself to the business of being a successful man's wife. She spent mornings on the telephone, tending to the details of running her household, chatting with friends, finding out who was going where and doing what, whose husband was on the way up or down, making lunch and dinner and weekend plans that would involve them with the people who most mattered—a combination of business and pleasure, of self-interest and interest in others.

At eleven-thirty she would begin to dress for lunch with friends from school, with wives of other men who mattered, with women she had recently met whom she wanted to know better. She devoted her afternoons to shopping for the clothes that would make the perfect impression and for the thoughtful gifts that people would remember years later. She could always tell the press who had designed her dress, and she always smiled radiantly at the *Women's Wear Daily* photographers when they snapped her picture coming out of Lafayette or La Grenouille. She began to give parties that got noticed, and Nina, who did not want to be left out, made up with Deedee.

"I feel like a fool," she told Deedee, apologizing for her behavior. Nina was a blond beauty in the classic Newport–Palm Beach mold and her cornflower blue eyes avoided Deedee's as she confessed what she now thought was the real reason for her coldness. "I guess I was just jealous."

"You're forgiven," said Deedee, putting her hand over Nina's. Deedee was in love and love made her generous. "I can understand how you feel. Slash is just wonderful. If I were someone else, I'd be jealous of me, too."

Her life was perfect and Deedee did not want to admit her one disappointment. Every month, as regularly as clockwork, her period arrived, announcing that no, she wasn't pregnant. Not yet.

Not yet, Deedee kept telling herself firmly, but soon.

Slash and Deedee would be known as sixties people and their parties were sixties parties. The parties they gave in their house on Seventy-fifth Street were an exciting combination of Slash's extravagance and willingness to break rules and Deedee's social talents and connections. Deedee, who had grown up instinctively learning to handle the often warring members of her family, was virtually a genius at charming people and bringing out their very best.

Deedee and Slash skillfully combined old money with new energy, youthquakers with diamonded dowagers, chic radicals with blue-haired members of the D.A.R., pop artists with con artists and tough-talking, cigar-smoking taxicab tycoons with bangled, spangled pot-smoking pill-popping rock stars. The food was wonderful, the drink was the best, the mood electric, the gossip wonderful and, of course, Slash's stock tips never seemed to miss. Everyone had a wonderful time and Deedee's parties became the talk of the town. Inevitably, many of the people Slash and Deedee entertained eventually became clients.

"*My* clients. Not Lancome & Dahlen clients," Slash told Deedee, proud of what he and she had accomplished together. She could introduce him to the right people; he could make their investments grow faster than they had dreamed. Together, Slash and Deedee seemed invincible.

Quickly, with sure instincts, Slash began to build his own client list. However, Slash's clients were not the wealthy widows or estate-appointed trustees of old family fortunes that Lancome & Dahlen had traditionally specialized in. Instead, the money that Slash began to handle was new money, earned money instead of inherited money, money without a past, money without a history and, some said, money without a conscience.

Seventh Avenue money, show-biz money and offshore money earned more money as Slash bought and sold, breaking every rule in the book. His clients came into the office wearing not three-piece suits and pure silk ties but denim and granny glasses, Nehru jackets and turtlenecks. They weren't all male, either. Some of them wore miniskirts and even knew the difference between the SDS and the SEC.

Slash's investment policies were as outrageous as his clients. He turned portfolios over an astounding 150 percent in a year. He daringly concentrated portfolios in a small handful of stocks and singlemindedly chased the Dow up, up and up.

Nineteen sixty-five was a bull trader's dream, and by early 1966 the Dow stood at an astounding 1,000. The value of the original shares in the Partners' Portfolio had quintupled, and

Slash's own portfolio, even more aggressively invested, had increased even more. When people began to speak of the go-go market and the gunslingers who made it go, Slash was one of the hot young money managers people were suddenly talking about.

"Are you *always* right?" Deedee asked. People were beginning to tell her that her husband was a genius, that he could do no wrong, that his market timing was infallible. They talked about Slash's golden gut and Midas touch. People told her that they thought he was a magician. "Don't you ever lose money?"

"Not so far," Slash said. "I get paid for being right."

He was becoming increasingly sure of himself at work. He was still unsure of himself with Deedee, still not quite convinced that he had really won her, that he really deserved her, that she really loved him. It was a secret that he kept from her. It was a secret that he tried to keep from himself.

Deedee had a second miscarriage in late 1965 but in the spring of 1966, just as Myron Kligman had promised, she had become pregnant again. Deedee sensed from the beginning that something was wrong but both Slash and Dr. Kligman told her that she was simply hypersensitive because of the previous miscarriages.

"There's no reason you can't have a normal pregnancy," said the doctor. His examinations had revealed nothing unusual and when Deedee, apprehensive, had asked about an X-ray, Kligman had advised against it. Since his examinations indicated no signs of any abnormalities, he said, he did not want to take the risk of exposing the very young fetus to radiation.

"You'll be fine," Slash said, noticing that, as always when she was pregnant, Deedee was extraordinarily lovely. Her skin became lush and velvety, her nipples slightly enlarged and extraordinarily sensitive. Their sex life, always satisfying, became even more profoundly and exquisitely exciting than before.

Still, from the moment her periods had stopped, Deedee had a deep sense of foreboding. She felt that something wasn't right, although she couldn't exactly describe it. One Saturday morning at the end of her eleventh week as she and Slash were in the foyer about to leave for Locust Valley for lunch, Deedee felt an explosion inside her. She dropped her canvas carryall and cried out.

"Call Kligman" was all she could say. Then she doubled over in agony, sweat pouring out of her hair as Slash ran for the phone.

Slash picked her up and carried her downstairs, where he shouted the neighbors out of the way and commandeered their waiting taxi. He rushed Deedee to meet Kligman at Mount Sinai. Deedee spent three hours in the operating room, and when Kligman emerged, he was white and shaking.

"She's fine," he told Slash. "She'll be all right."

The pregnancy had been ectopic, a result most likely, Kligman said, of the series of ovarian inflammations Deedee had had in college. It had ruptured, fortunately, in a very early phase of the pregnancy. Otherwise, Kligman said, things might have been serious.

"You mean she might have died?" asked Slash. Always pale, he turned ashen.

Kligman nodded.

That same afternoon, Slash bought Deedee a huge diamond pin in the shape of a gardenia.

"I love you," he said, giving it to her later that day.

Before Deedee could say a word, Slash broke into tears.

"Don't die," he said, grasping her hand. "Don't leave me!"

He thought that if she were to die and leave him, he would die, too. He could not bear to be orphaned a second time, and the pin was a hostage against that fate. If she owned it, she would have to wear it and if she had to wear it, she couldn't die, could she, and he wouldn't be abandoned again, would he?

Death was the one thing Slash couldn't control. Death was the one thing Slash dreaded above all others.

I I I
THE FIRST
MILLION

*W*hile stories of hawks and doves, black power and white backlash, pot and protest filled the front pages, the news on the financial pages was also about revolution, rebellion and razzle-dazzle. Conglomerateurs like James Ling, Harold Geneen, Meshulam Riklis and Charles Bludhorn were revitalizing corporate America. Price/earnings ratios were going through the ceiling and go-go money managers on the track of red-hot profits pirouetted through the market like go-go dancers in a disco.

Even though the Dow reversed itself by the end of 1966 and backed off to 790, Slash's holdings—Ling-Temco-Vought, Litton and Textron—bucked the trend. Slash's clients fared well and the Partners' Portfolio continued to perform brilliantly. That year, at the age of twenty-six, four years ahead of schedule, Slash personally made one and a half million pre-Vietnam-inflated dollars.

"A million and a half!" exclaimed Pete Oney. Pete had known that Slash was doing well; he hadn't imagined how well. "What does it feel like to be rich?"

"I don't know. I'm not rich," Slash told the astounded Pete.

Through his marriage and his increasing visibility at Lancome & Dahlen, Slash now moved in circles where a million dollars, although hardly to be sneered at, was nothing to brag about, either. When Slash remembered how he had once bragged to Deedee about wanting to make a million dollars before he was thirty, he cringed in embarrassment.

Lancome & Dahlen and its clients were the happy beneficiaries of Slash's shrewd trading. Slash's extraordinary trading performance with the Partners' Portfolio had begun to shift the opinion of the senior partners in Slash's favor. Even though Deedee hadn't married Trip, things had turned out far better than Luther had dreamed. Russell seemed happier than he ever had as Luther publicly credited him with bringing Slash into the firm. Starved for recognition his entire life, Russell blossomed with his father's praise. He became more confident and more outgoing, and even Joyce noticed the difference. She attributed it, correctly, to Slash.

"I was wrong about you," Joyce admitted to Slash. "I thought you would pull the family apart. Instead, you seem to have pulled us together."

Slash, the seducer, was succeeding. He did not, however, have any illusions about the reasons for his new acceptability.

"If you buy a stock at forty and sell it at fifty, it doesn't matter if your sideburns are too long, your ties too wide or your prep school was Saint Ignatius," Slash told Pete. "Everyone can read the bottom line."

"Even the Lancomes?"

"Especially the Lancomes."

Slash had developed the irritating but profitable habit of being right, and he was right once again. Both Trip and his father were forced, at least in public, to change their minds about him.

"He's a maverick," said Junior, rephrasing his earlier words. "But he's our maverick."

"He's making us look good," Trip admitted to associates, knowing that they admired him for his generosity to his former rival. "And he's making us rich."

Loyalty mattered to the Lancomes and Slash gave them loyalty. Looking good mattered and Slash made them look good. Making money also mattered and Slash was helping them make money. Lancome & Dahlen had always been small and exclusive. It was now, thanks to Slash, small, exclusive and very profitable.

Trip temporarily put aside his vow to destroy Slash. Why destroy someone who was making you rich, Trip asked himself. Slash was not a Dahlen, therefore Trip did not consider him a threat. Confident that Lancome & Dahlen would be his one day, Trip worked with Slash every day, praised him in public and, in private, continued to do what he had been doing since Slash's wedding: he used him. When Slash stopped being of use, Trip told himself, there would be plenty of time and plenty of opportunity to get rid of him. Unless, of course, he self-destructed first. Trip wondered how long Slash's hot streak could last. He wondered how long Slash could go on being right all the time.

Luther Dahlen, not a religious man, believed in nothing. Nothing except the balance sheets. Between Slash's performance for his clients, the profits in the Partners' Portfolio, the apparent change in the Lancomes' attitude toward Slash and Luther's own growing realization that the codicil was indeed ironclad, Luther gradually began to change his mind about Deedee's husband. The fact that Slash had supported Deedee on his own money and had forbidden her even to touch a dime of her own also weighed heavily in Luther's change of mind. Edwina wasn't surprised when, in the spring of 1967, Luther said that Slash Steiner didn't seem so bad after all.

"Maybe Deedee knew something the rest of us didn't," Luther said.

At seventy-six, Luther Dahlen seemed twenty years younger than his age. Luther's erect bearing, his alert blue eyes, his brigadier-style mustache, his full head of wavy white hair, his energetic walk and quick movements made him seem like a man who had learned the secret of stopping time. As he had since 1926, Luther Dahlen went to his paneled corner office at Lancome & Dahlen every morning. He asked Slash if he'd like to drive downtown with him.

"I leave at six-thirty," Luther warned when Slash accepted his invitation.

"That late?"

Luther Dahlen had made his first big money in the bull market of the twenties and lost almost all of it in the Crash of '29. It was a lesson he never forgot. In the thirties, Luther had been a scavenger, buying stock and real estate at artificially depressed prices. By the time the economy rebounded during World War II, Luther was in a position to make a second fortune. During the fifties, he always said, any damn fool could make money, and Luther was no fool.

As a result of his losses in the Crash, however, Luther had become overly cautious. He stuck to the conservative blue chips although, by the mid-sixties, the blue chips were no longer the place to be. Luther knew that he could be making much more than he actually was and he knew that his caution was costing him money. He knew he was out of touch with the inflated earnings, quick profits and pepped-up multiples of the go-go market. Among Luther's greatest strengths, however, had always been his great intelligence and timely opportunism. He saw that Slash was making a fortune and he didn't want the Dahlens to be left out.

"I want you to do something for me," Luther said to Slash in the early winter of 1967. Slash and Luther were in the back seat of Luther's chauffeur-driven Lincoln as it headed downtown to Wall Street. It was the first time Luther had ever asked for anything, and Slash looked at him with well-concealed curiosity and waited quietly for him to go on.

"Deedee's twenty-fifth birthday is this year," Luther continued. "Her trust fund will revert to her. Its terms will no longer be valid and, of course, the codicil will no longer be in effect. I'd like you to invest it for her."

Despite the raging bull market, Deedee's trust fund under Lancome & Dahlen's management had grown to barely $1.8 million, and that increase was mainly accumulated interest because Deedee, ever since her marriage, had not touched a cent of her own money. She had been living on Slash's money.

The blue chips in which her trust had been invested had not fared well in a market propelled by the new kids on the block, the Littons, the Textrons, the ITTs and the Gulf & Westerns.

"You mean you've finally decided I didn't marry Deedee for her money?" Slash replied, in a tone perfectly poised between humor and insolence.

"I was a horse's ass," said the old man, not looking at Slash. It was as much of an apology—and an admission—as Luther could bring himself to make. "Will you?"

"No, Luther," said Slash as the car headed down the East River Drive. Slash was aware of the funky smell of the East River through the limousine's powerful ventilation system. "I told you that I'd never touch a cent of Deedee's money and I meant it."

"But you're one of us now," said Luther, not used to having his requests turned down. "You're a Dahlen."

"Thank you," said Slash, knowing that Luther's admission meant that, finally, all the suspicions about him and his motives had been put to rest. "But I meant what I said. I won't touch Deedee's money. Not a penny. You were right about me. I'm too reckless. I'm too much of a gambler. Her money wouldn't be safe with me." ·

At first Luther told himself that Slash was being coy, but Slash's continuing refusals only made Luther more determined. Unwilling to be thwarted, Luther did everything he could to get Slash to change his mind. He cited Slash's track record with the Partners' Portfolio. He reminded Slash of how he had been right at the end of '66, when the Dow had gone down but Slash's stocks had gone up. He appealed to Slash's pride, to his ego and to his devotion as a husband but Slash would not change his mind. There was no way, he said, that he would ever touch a penny of Deedee's money.

"I'm too much of a gambler," Slash told Luther. "Besides," he added, indulging in the pleasure of having the last word, "I married Deedee for love. Not money."

When Deedee herself asked Slash to invest her money for her, he refused. Even when, in the early spring of 1967, she told Slash that she was pregnant again and asked him to handle her trust fund—for her and for their coming child's future—Slash gave her the same answer he had given Luther.

"No," he told her. "Suppose I screw up and lose it? I'd never be able to forgive myself."

"But you said you never lose," Deedee reminded him. "You told me you get paid for being right."

"I know," said Slash, continuing to refuse. "But there's always a first time. I don't want to be wrong with your money on the line."

Nevertheless, Deedee kept after him. She wanted Slash to invest her money for her. He did it for other people. Why wouldn't he do it for her? Deedee kept insisting. Slash kept refusing. He was afraid to touch his wife's money, afraid of what would happen if his Midas touch deserted him. Slash remembered what Richard Steiner had said about rich people. Even though he had sneered at the time, Slash sensed that Richard was right. He did not want to make even one single mistake. He did not want to risk Deedee's faith in him or gamble on the depth of her love.

"You'd never forgive me if I lost money for you," Slash said, explaining his refusal to invest Deedee's money for her.

"Yes, I would," replied Deedee.

"No, you wouldn't," said Slash, thinking that he knew her better than she knew herself and wanting to end the dialogue.

Slash, far more than Deedee, already realized how essential money had become to their marriage. Money had become the currency of their emotional exchange, the basis of Deedee's new self-confidence, the tangible and increasingly crucial cornerstone of their profound connection to each other. Slash had been right when, on their honeymoon, he had realized that it was she who had married for money, not he.

Money, Slash realized, meant even more to Deedee than it did to him. To him, money was merely a way of keeping score. To her, because of the family she'd grown up in, money was ego, identity and self.

"Please, Slash," Deedee would plead, pointing out that he

was even making Trip rich. "You're making a fortune for everyone. Why not me?"

After all, she said, what was the point of being married to one of the smartest men on Wall Street if she wasn't getting the benefit of his expertise, too?

I V
THE BIG
MONEY

Their first child was a boy. The baby Slash and Deedee had been waiting for since the earliest days of their marriage was the male heir the Dahlens had been waiting for for two generations. A quarter of a century had passed, and everyone agreed that the wait had been worth it.

He was born in late 1967 and his name, chosen by Slash and Deedee, was Russell Richard Steiner. Russell after Deedee's father; Richard, after Richard Steiner, whom Slash always honored in both word and deed. The birth was a time of unshadowed joy and unmarred celebration for Slash and Deedee, made poignant by the fact that Richard Steiner, dying of cancer, would live just long enough to hold his grandson.

"I was afraid I wouldn't be able to give you a child," said Deedee, holding the newly born Russ in her arms and showing him to Slash for the first time.

"I wasn't," said Slash, his voice hoarse with emotion. His own parents had abandoned him. Belle and Uncle Sammy were gone. The doctors gave Richard six months. Russ was his, thought Slash, and always would be. He would never have to wonder if anyone loved him ever again. He was no longer a man from nowhere. He was a man with a son, a man with a family, a man with a future. A man, finally, with everything. He smiled at Deedee and swallowed hard. "I always knew you could do anything."

* * *

Luther and Edwina, needless to say, were absolutely over-joyed with their great-grandson, the fourth living generation of Dahlens, and Russell and Joyce, for once united, were thrilled with their first grandchild. The rifts and tensions between generations were healed in excited talk about Russ, about his future, about where he would go to school, about his talents and triumphs and accomplishments. Russ was the son and heir the Dahlens had been afraid they might never have and their pride and admiration knew no bounds. They agreed that he had the Dahlen coloring, the Torngren cat's eyes and Slash's sleek greyhound bones.

"Cat's eyes and a dog's body? Poor kid!" commented Slash, with an ecstatic, giddy grin. Nevertheless, everyone agreed that Russ was a beautiful child who faced a beautiful future. The Dahlen family, for the first time that Deedee could remember, seemed united not divided, generous not suspicious, trusting not wary. No threats of divorce, no calcula-tion of trust funds, no shadow of infidelity marred the joy of Russ's birth, and if Russell remembered another birth, another baby, he revealed nothing outwardly.

Inwardly, he felt guilty and disappointed. He had spent the past seven years searching for Lana. He began with the only clue he had: Mildred's mother's telephone number. The ac-count, he learned, had been canceled in 1951, and the tele-phone company records had no further reference to Timothy and Louise Neill, Mildred's parents. The elder Neills, Russell had learned from a search of local newspapers, had died within four months of each other in 1951.

As for Mildred herself, Russell could not find out what had happened to her. He had the marriage certificates in the state of Massachusetts searched for the years between 1944 and 1966. Unfortunately, the Bureau of Registrations informed him, the records for the Ms through the Os for the years 1943, 1944 and 1945 had been destroyed when a pipe had burst in that wing of the State Hall of Records. Unable to provide the groom's name, Russell was forced to abandon his search of marriage licenses.

He had then hired an investigator to contact the licensing

bureau of cosmetologists and hairdressers. That list, the investigator learned, was kept for only ten years. Records from the early 1940s had long since been destroyed, and Russell Dahlen's search for his other daughter had come to an end.

What had happened to Lana? Was she sad or happy? Married or single? Did she have children of her own? Did she ever think of him? Why had she never tried to contact him again? Russell didn't know and he didn't know how to find out. He had questions but no answers and, having no other choice, he tried his best to shut his memories of his other daughter away and concentrated on a future that seemed, at last, to gleam with infinite promise.

"You're so lucky. Slash is madly in love with you," Nina told Deedee wistfully at Russ's christening. Nina had noticed the way Slash looked at Deedee and the way he couldn't keep his hands off her. He acted more like a lover than a husband, more like a suitor than a man who had celebrated several wedding anniversaries. "He's the ideal husband."

Nina was talking indirectly about her own not-so-ideal husband. She had married Mario di Pinto, the actor she had gone home with after Deedee's wedding, at a romantic dawn ceremony on a hilltop near Watch Hill, Rhode Island. Bride and bridegroom were barefoot and Nina wore a milkmaid's dress of eyelet and a wreath of flowers in her hair. A sitar played and the ceremony included readings from Khalil Gibran's *The Prophet*. After less than a year of marriage, Nina had learned that Mario had the bad habit of turning his onstage romances into offstage affairs. Whenever she confronted him, he never denied it. It's my way of getting into the role, he would explain, a double-entendre defense whose humor totally escaped Nina.

"The only competition you have to worry about is the Dow Jones," Nina told Deedee, pointing out that Slash was that apparently rare creature: an extremely sexy, very charming man who was not a womanizer. A wildly desirable, highly magnetic man who was blindly in love with his wife.

Deedee smiled. What could she say? Nina was right.

* * *

Five months after Russ's birth Deedee became pregnant again, and fourteen months after her son's birth, in September of 1968, Deedee had her second child, a girl. Deedee's labor was difficult and the child was finally delivered by cesarean section.

"No more babies," Myron Kligman told Deedee when she visited him in his office after her long recovery. "Between your history of ovarian infections, the ectopic pregnancy and the difficulties you had in delivering Claire, another pregnancy would not be safe."

"But we want a big family," said Deedee, certain that Dr. Kligman was being overly cautious.

"No," said Myron Kligman firmly. "It's too dangerous."

"We planned for three at least," Deedee said, trying to persuade him. She leaned toward him, pleading with her eyes. "Couldn't I risk just one more pregnancy?"

"No," repeated Dr. Kligman. "Not if you want me or any other reputable doctor to take care of you. The danger is not only to your health, Deedee, but possibly to your life."

Second and third opinions confirmed Myron Kligman's fears, and Slash was on the doctors' side.

"Two is enough," he said. "I don't want you to risk your health much less your life. You mean too much to me."

Reluctantly, and sure that she would one day regret it, Deedee agreed to the operation that would prevent her from ever conceiving again.

Deedee named her daughter Claire, after her mother's mother, a sweet-tempered, plump woman who had died when Deedee was ten. Claire Torngren, Deedee remembered, had been a wonderful baker, seemingly always in the kitchen producing a parade of savory Scandinavian delicacies scented with dill and caraway and rich pastries smelling of honey and cardamom. She seemed simple and loving, a healing contrast to the difficulties of her own parents' marriage and their thorny relationship with the Dahlens. Deedee had loved Claire Torngren passionately and had been inconsolable when she died. Having a daughter to name after her was a particular blessing.

"I hoped the baby would be a girl," said Slash, who was absolutely thrilled by the idea of having a daughter to spoil. He had often told Deedee that he thought her family's obsession with boys was ridiculous. Luther and Russell's hang-ups about a male heir had, after all, cast a shadow on Deedee's entire childhood, causing her to feel inadequate and incompetent, neither of which, Slash constantly reminded her, she remotely was. "I want her to be exactly like you."

By 1969, thanks to Slash's daring and sometimes almost reckless investments, he was a multimillionaire. He had tripled his money in Fairchild Camera, quadrupled it in Boise Cascade and almost doubled it in American Home Products. He was also getting nervous. Inflation was beginning to run away like young men on their way to Canada to avoid the draft. Nixon had replaced Johnson in the White House and, while wages and prices continued to go up, the government's annual figures on the gross national product indicated that business activity might be cooling down.

Like a gypsy reading tea leaves, Slash spent December and early January in his office watching the tape and searching for a clue to the future. The wave of mergers continued. It was the new guys versus the old guys, the kids versus the adults, David versus Goliath. Feisty Resorts International was rumored about to take over sedate Pan Am. New-kid-on-the-block Northwest Industries would take over Establishment Goodrich Tire and Rubber. Upstart Leasco, worth a mere four hundred million, would take over venerable Chemical Bank, worth an impressive nine billion. There seemed to be lots of money and lots of action.

Nevertheless, there were ominous signs: the Fed, worried about inflation, constricted the money supply, thus sending interest rates up. Trading volume on all exchanges from the Big Board to OTC was shrinking below 1968 levels. Between the reduction in trading levels and the increased costs in downtown personnel salaries and facilities, brokerage firm profits were definitely anemic. Mutual funds, now worth a hefty fifty billion, were moving vast amounts of money in and out of the market, turning accounts over at a 50-percent-a-year clip.

Like Scarlett, who had decided to think about it tomorrow, the Dow seemed to ignore the negative and accentuate the positive. The averages went up and up, the way they had ever since the early sixties when Slash had first gone to work at Lancome & Dahlen. Could the Dow continue to rise? Wasn't there an end in sight? Could profits always lead to more profits? The shooters and garbage stocks showed sensational returns. Nursing homes, leisure activities, environmentally sensitive business, weight loss plans—all cashed in on trends of the times.

Still, Slash sat in his office and waited and wondered and worried. It was one thing to hold your nose and make money on garbage stock. It was another when even the profits couldn't seem to make the stink go away. Finally, on the Monday after Joe Namath defied the oddsmakers and led the New York Jets to a 16–7 victory over the favored Baltimore Colts, Slash defied the Dow and made his move.

Slash sold everything: his clients' stock, the stock in the Partners' Portfolio, his own stock. Almost overnight, he had gone from 100 percent invested to 100 percent cash. He had gone against the market trends, against the prevailing wisdom, against the tides and tone of the decade. He was as alone as he had ever been. It was a feeling he had almost forgotten. It was a feeling as disturbing as any he had experienced at St. Ignatius or alone at night, deep in a nightmare, at the Steiners'.

"I got scared," he admitted to Deedee, wondering if for once his Midas touch had failed him and he had miscalculated. "Maybe I panicked."

That winter and that spring, Slash began to think he'd made his first big mistake. Everyone seemed to have—and spend—more money than ever. Private schools were swamped with applications, and Deedee began to worry about whether Russ would get into Collegiate. Tables at expensive restaurants were at a premium, and there was a long wait for delivery of a new Mercedes. That summer, so many people went to Europe that planes were stacked up at JFK for hours waiting for clearance to take off or land. The Dow continued to rise, reaching 970 in May, only a few points below the all-time high of January 1966.

"I'm out millions of dollars," Slash told Deedee, adding up the profits he had missed out on by selling. "Aren't you glad I didn't agree to invest your money for you?"

"No," said Deedee, loyally. "I'm sure you're right. Just be patient."

Deedee tried to buoy Slash when his confidence flagged. Nevertheless, the Dow continued to rise and Slash was left out, a wallflower at the dance, and Trip and Junior alternated between secret glee that Slash had finally miscalculated and concern about once-adoring clients who were becoming fretful and restless.

"Michael told me at lunch today that he's thinking of taking the Hemerding estate to Avery, Lansing. He's disappointed in the last quarter's results," Junior told Trip. Michael was Michael de Rosnay of MetroBank. Avery, Lansing was one of Lancome & Dahlen's closest competitors. For years the plum accounts in MetroBank's Estate and Trust Department had gone, almost automatically, to Lancome & Dahlen. "I asked Michael to give us another chance. I reminded him that Slash wasn't the only stock picker over here at Lancome and Dahlen."

Andrew Macon was more than just slightly disturbed when longtime client Freddie Dunbarton said that he was thinking of switching his grandchildren's trust accounts to another investment firm.

"Jesus Christ, Freddie Dunbarton's father was one of the original Lancome and Dahlen clients," said Andy, his Santa Claus nose even redder than usual, as he sat in Slash's office, moaning about the ominous phone conversation he had just had with his old pal, Freddie. "Other clients will lose confidence if Freddie moves the accounts and the word gets out."

"I don't blame you for being disturbed," Slash told the senior partner. "I'm pretty disturbed myself. I'm not used to being wrong."

Slash wondered if he should buy back in but, uncharacteristically, he still hesitated. The negatives, which everyone was blithely ignoring, were still there and they were still, Slash thought, as ominous as ever. He began to wonder if he was a Cassandra, doomed to be ignored. Then he remembered that Cassandra had been right. He, it seemed, was wrong.

Nevertheless, in May, his heart in his mouth, Slash took his biggest gamble ever. He held his breath and shorted the market. He sold stock he didn't own for his clients, himself and the Partners' Portfolio. Day by day, he hunched over his Quotron, sweating out the tape. He lost his nerve a thousand times but a thousand and one times, he stuck to his guns and his risk was rewarded. In June, the prime rate jumped to 8.5 percent, the highest ever, and the Dow began to slip.

"A technical correction," the pundits said.

"A technical correction my ass," said Slash, suddenly sure of himself again.

By July the Dow had fallen to 800. Transitron, which had sold for sixty dollars early in the decade, was now selling for less than ten. National General had slipped from 66 to 35, Litton from 100 to 50, Fairchild Camera from 88 to 52.

"No one's using the word 'crash,'" said Slash. "But that's what it is."

Slash, his clients and the partners were now richer than ever. They had made money on the way up and on the way down.

"Don't you ever make a mistake?" a hundred people asked.

"Sure," said Slash but he didn't really believe it anymore.

By the end of 1970 the word recession was being used in public and the old guard was in deep trouble. The Dow Jones sank below 650 and the Penn Central suffered a bankruptcy whose shock waves rippled through the economy. Hayden

Stone, one of the country's oldest, most prestigious securities firms, the one in which old Joe Kennedy had made so much of his money, also came close to going under. People were talking about doomsday. People were afraid. People also noticed that Slash was one of the few who had seen the handwriting on the wall. Slash's clients were safe and the enormous profits in the Partners' Portfolio were intact. Slash's own profits had been protected and whatever reservations people still had about Slash now seemed to have utterly disappeared.

"I missed the signs in '29," said Luther, congratulating Slash on his timing and decisiveness. "But you didn't. You saw what was coming."

"You had more balls than I would have," Andrew Macon admitted, telling Slash that even if he had had the sense to sell, he would have bought back in and gotten creamed.

"I knew you were right," Deedee said. She knew that all her friends had seen their portfolios shrink alarmingly. Her rich friends suddenly talked poor. But Slash was safe. If Slash had been handling her money, Deedee realized, she would have been safe, too—and she would have been richer than ever. More than ever before, Deedee wanted Slash to invest her money for her. More than ever before, still unnerved by the close call, Slash refused.

Deep down, part of him still couldn't really believe that the boy from Saint Ignatius had won the Park Avenue princess. He still did not want to take the slightest risk with Deedee's money—and with the way she seemed to feel about him. He remembered Richard Steiner's words and even though he tried not to believe them, part of him was constantly on guard, constantly on alert. One false move, Slash feared, and Deedee would send him back to the limbo from which he had come.

Even the Lancomes joined in the congratulations. Father and son complimented Slash on his reading of the market and on his timing. For the first time since he had come to Lancome & Dahlen, Slash was offered carte blanche.

"Whatever you want to do next, whichever way you want to turn," Trip told Slash, his widespread hands showing the virtually limitless extent of his backing, "Lancome and Dahlen is behind you. One hundred percent of the way."

The last—and the toughest—of Slash's seductions was, it seemed, complete.

As the new decade began, the bears drove out the bulls, the Dow dropped like a stone, finally settling at 631, and the price of gold fell below the official price of $35 an ounce. Stockbrokerages began to fail, mutual funds were wiped out, interest rates went up and inflation spiraled out of control.

Slash, who had foreseen it all, sensed that big money could be made in the midst of crisis. How, precisely, he didn't yet know, but he smelled money and now he was a man not only enslaved to a wife he adored but a father to two children, his living shields against death, the children who meant everything to him.

Like a hunter, Slash stalked his quarry through a dangerous jungle. He searched the pages of *Barron's,* listened to the gossip on the Street and tidbits overheard at dinner parties, paid attention to profit and loss statements, buy and sell orders, trends and fads, boomlets and bust-outs.

The seventies beckoned and Slash's greatest successes were still in front of him. Their roots went back to his childhood and his oldest friend, the man whose life he had once saved.

V

THE DIOR OF
THE DOW

*N*othing *about Pete Oney had ever promised excellence.*
He had been a fat child and a skinny adolescent. His marks
in school had ranged from fair to failing. He was too near-
sighted, even with Coke-bottle-thick glasses, to be any good
at sports. When it came to music, he had a tin ear. On the
plus side, he was extremely personable and, in the East
Meadow High School magazine subscription drive, had sold
more magazines than anyone else. He was also girl crazy. By
1965, when Slash had been married a year and was beginning
to set profit records at Lancome & Dahlen, Pete was being
fired from his third job, this one in a bank's trainee program.
As an adult, his childhood pattern of failure seemed to be
dogging him.

"They were right to fire me," Pete admitted to Slash. "I
hated banks, bankers and banking, and I was lousy at it."

"So what do you like?" asked Slash.

"Beautiful women," said Pete. At East Meadow High, he
had been renowned for his collection of pinups, the biggest
and best in the entire school. "And plenty of money," he
added, inspired by Slash's success.

"What about the cosmetics business?" asked Slash, who
was always practical about reaching goals. That week the
Lancome & Dahlen research department had recommended
the purchase of shares in the toiletries, cosmetics and personal care sectors to cash in on the booming youthquake

market. "There's plenty of money in it and you'd meet a lot of beautiful women."

"How bad could it be?" Pete replied, not yet having had the pleasure of Leon Marx's acquaintance.

Slash made a few phone calls and Pete Oney found himself with a job at Marx & Marx Cosmetics. Marx & Marx, which ran hairdressing salons in department stores, also had a cosmetics division which sold a popular-priced line of lipsticks, blushers, eye shadows and nail polish in drugstores, variety stores and supermarkets. Pete's job was in the marketing department. Marketing, he found out quickly, was the art and science of selling people things whether they wanted them or not. He also learned that Leon Marx, the founder of the company, conceived of marketing as the tail that wagged the dog.

Marketing, according to the commandments of Leon Marx, controlled advertising, promotion, selling, packaging and even production. As Leon, ever a master of the well-turned phrase, put it: how can you make a buck if the stuff costs too much to make or you don't get it in the stores in time for the holidays or the customers don't want it in the first place?

Pete, who had never seemed to be much good at anything, finally found the perfect outlet for his energies and abilities. He turned out to be a guy with a golden gut for psyching out what women wanted.

By 1969, when Slash had become Lancôme & Dahlen's top producer, Pete had become Leon's vice president in charge of marketing. It was Pete who was responsible for Bee Pollen Night Cream, gold frosted lipsticks and eye shadows, chip-proof nail polish in Ferrari colors and glitter eyeliners in fuchsia, sapphire, emerald, lemon, lime and raspberry. He was also responsible for the large profits they brought in.

As Pete became more successful, he emulated Slash as much as possible. He shared Slash's barber, tailor, accountant, lawyer, and Mercedes dealer. He had Deedee's dermatologist plane the acne scars off his face and Slash's

ophthalmologist fit him with contact lenses. Although Pete
had become a key executive and a man who fit in anywhere,
Leon Marx, a true animal, never let him forget that he had
turned up for work on his first day in an avocado green suit
with stitched lapels, his hair in a greased pompadour.

"Leon needs money," Pete told Slash in 1970, just after
Slash had sold all his stock and was sitting on cash, not sure
which way to jump next. "The beauty supply business is
going through the roof and Leon wants to build another
plant. If you can help get him the financing he needs, you'll
make a fortune."

Slash bought a hundred thousand shares of Marx & Marx
at the market price of four dollars for himself and his clients.
He arranged for Lancome & Dahlen ("We're behind you one
hundred percent of the way," Trip reminded him) to lend
Leon a million dollars.

Within eight months, bucking a swiftly sagging market, the
stock went to 6 and Slash's four-hundred-thousand-dollar
investment was worth six hundred thousand dollars, a 50
percent increase in less than a year. It was almost like the
good old times at the height of the go-go market of the sixties,
but the profit, in post-Vietnam-inflated dollars, was a cream-
puff profit. Impressive but insubstantial. Seductive but not
satisfying.

Slash complained to Deedee that he felt he was running
just to stay in the same place.

"The seventies are here," he told her, excited by the vision
gradually forming in his head. "And I'm still playing by
sixties' rules. I was too conservative, too conventional. Next
time I'm going to buy the whole damn company . . ."

He expressed the same feelings to Trip and once again Trip
repeated himself.

"Don't forget, Slash. You're our boy. Whatever you want,
we're behind you. One hundred percent of the way."

The second company was in the fast-food business. It was
called Hot Dog! and what it sold was the all-American, all-
beef frank. Customers could choose toppings ranging from

melted cheese to chili to bacon bits and a meal of a hot dog, a Coke and a side of French fries was good, fast, cheap and fun. The small chain had started in Phoenix, spread throughout the Southwest and was, in some cities, doing better than McDonald's.

Slash had first become aware of the company when Deedee had taken him to Santa Fe, where, inspired by one of her idols, Millicent Rogers, the Standard Oil heiress and leader of style of the thirties, she bought silver and turquoise Indian jewelry. Noticing the gay red-and-white-striped Hot Dog! stands and the full parking lots in front of them, Slash had sent for a financial statement.

The shares, regionally traded, seemed undervalued, and in late 1971, Slash began buying them at six dollars and then six and a half dollars. When Slash had acquired 17 percent of the company, the founder of Hot Dog!, an ex-circus owner, afraid that Slash would oust him from the presidency of the company he had founded, offered to buy him out for nine dollars a share. Slash's profits were two and a quarter million dollars and, inflation or no inflation, it was no cream-puff profit.

Slash had quickly discovered that he did not even have to buy the whole company to make a sensational profit. He just had to look as if he were going to. He had been right when he said that Wall Street had no rules and that all you had to do was make them up as you went along. His words had once been considered sacrilege. Now they seemed like prophecy.

"Everything is fashion," Slash told a *Barron's* reporter, explaining his current shift in investment philosophy. "I just follow fashion."

"Follow or lead?" asked the reporter.

Slash's answer was a drop-dead, you've-got-three-guesses smile, and the reporter's headline called Slash the Dior of the Dow.

Slash quickly turned away from the hot issues and market leaders that had made his fortune in the sixties to small, thinly traded companies brought to his attention by his handpicked, fanatically loyal staff of eight headed by Arthur

Bozeman. He began to buy big blocks of stock in them and, scared at being taken over, managements voted to buy back Slash's shares at more than he paid for them.

By 1973, three more companies—Electrix, a manufacturer of household appliances, Wheels, a rent-a-car company, and Small World, a tour group packager—had paid Slash to stay away. It was perfectly legal, stockholders loved him for increasing the value of the shares and the profits were virtually guaranteed. Slash seemed to have found the golden key to an endless spring of enormous riches and Trip now seemed to count himself as Slash's discoverer and main backer.

"We're behind you," he told Slash, putting his arm around him and asking him if he would like to be nominated for membership in the Knickerbocker Club.

"I know," said Slash, laughing and joining in as Trip repeated himself for the dozenth time. "One hundred percent of the way."

"I'm not just making money any more," Slash told Deedee with a new note of confidence and pleasure in his voice. "I'm building a future. I'm doing it for Russ. And for Claire, too."

Slash, who had grown up in an orphanage, now began to think like the founder of a dynasty. He was making money— for Russ and Claire. He was cultivating the right people—for Russ and Claire. He was changing himself from the outside in—for Russ and Claire. The man who had once thought only of the present had fallen in love with the future.

"Yesterday is still a drag," he told Deedee. "Today is interesting but it's tomorrow I live for."

Tomorrow, she knew, meant Slash's dreams for his children and most particularly for Russ, who would be his heir, his partner, his successor, his hostage against fate.

Slash was not only being asked to belong but, thanks to Deedee, he now looked and acted like a man who had been born to belong. Thanks to Deedee, Slash no longer had the anxious, insecure air of a desperate and hungry outsider.

Thanks to Deedee, his pseudo–Ivy League suits once

bought off the rack on lower Fifth Avenue had been replaced by custom-made hand-stitched models from an elegant Fifty-seventh Street tailor. Thanks to Deedee, his
shirts came from London and his shoes from Milan. Thanks
to Deedee, even Emily Post would have approved of his
table manners and, thanks to Deedee, he could make his
way through a French menu or a charity gala with equal
aplomb. His accent, still harsh and New York-y, only
added to his astonishing charm.

"Don't you dare change it," Deedee told him when he
wondered about going to a speech therapist. "It's one thing
to look like everyone else. It's another to sound like everyone
else."

Deedee, as always, with her exquisitely tuned sense of style
and status, was exactly right. She instinctively knew the difference between mere perfection and the flaw that was fascinating.

In early 1974, to celebrate their tenth wedding anniversary,
Slash bought the top three floors of 735 Park Avenue. The
apartment, originally built for a 1940s cosmetics queen, had
thirty rooms, including a room for silver, a fully equipped
gymnasium, and a ballroom. But, best of all, it was two
stories higher and one story larger than the duplex Luther
and Edwina occupied.

"It's spectacular," Nina said, after Slash had given her the
grand tour. She and Mario were still living in a dump in
Chelsea because, although Nina would have been willing to
use her own money to help support them, Mario's Italian
macho temperament did not permit him to take money from
a woman while he waited for the part that would make him
a star. Nina, struggling with the crummy walk-up and the
proud but unfaithful actor, could not even begin to suppress
the envy she felt, wondering, as she so often had, why it was
Deedee who always had all the luck.

"Not bad for a kid from Saint Ignatius," said Slash. He
tried to be casual but he could not hide the almost gloating
pride he felt at his spectacular acquisition. That pride was
fueled by such hunger and such driven ambition that, stand-

ing there next to him twenty stories above Manhattan, Nina felt almost singed by its force.

"Is it symbolic that the apartment is higher up than Luther's?" she asked.

"Still the psych major?" Slash teased. His gray eyes were smiling, but they reminded Nina of stainless steel, hard, burnished and perhaps a bit dangerous. He was, she thought, one of the most magnetic men she had ever met and she could not help but wonder what all that drive and all that energy would be like in bed.

"Answer the question," Nina insisted.

"Let's just put it this way," Slash said, walking over to the window and looking down, literally, at the entire city. "It wasn't a negative."

The Dahlens, like the English, could not deal with emotion. Sentiment was disguised as ceremony and love was expressed with money.

In late 1974, at his eightieth birthday party, Luther, still militarily erect, his white hair and brigadier-style mustache still luxuriant, took Russell aside and announced that although he was not planning on dying any time soon, he had been talking to Van Tyson about his will and the necessity of doing some estate planning. Luther was afraid, as so many rich men were, of inheritance taxes. Giving valuable assets away during his lifetime, Luther knew, was the way to avoid the heavy IRS bite and to preserve the Dahlen fortune for another generation.

"I worked my whole life to create Lancome and Dahlen," he told Russell. "I don't want the g.d. IRS to end up with it after I croak."

With that statement, he handed Russell the stock certificates for 50 percent of Lancome & Dahlen. The Dahlen half of Lancome & Dahlen had been transferred to Russell's name. There were no strings, no trust provisions, no tricky legal clauses, no ifs, ands or buts. One half of Lancome & Dahlen was now Russell's free and clear.

"It's all yours now," said the old man in his strong, young

man's voice. Then he smiled. "I hope to Christ you're not going to fire me."

"Not as long as you show up for work on time," Russell replied with a straight face and a stern tone, "and stop stealing the paper clips."

Luther smiled briefly, and the moment was over. Luther was eighty, Russell fifty-seven. Their teasing exchange was the closest father and son had ever come to admitting that they loved each other.

The outright transfer of the Dahlen stock from one generation to the next was the ultimate symbol of Slash's acceptance by the family he had married into. Luther's long-ago threats of disinheriting Deedee were completely forgotten. Luther's plan to put Deedee's eventual inheritance into an untouchable trust had also been forgotten. When Russell died, Luther made clear, Deedee would inherit the Dahlen stock outright and Slash would be there to take care of it. After Slash, Russ would come along.

"There will always be a Dahlen in Lancome & Dahlen," Luther told Slash with one of his rare smiles.

"Even if he is named Steiner," Slash said, responding with a smile of his own, a patented, trademarked and copyrighted I-wondered-when-you'd-wise-up model.

Slash knew exactly what the transfer of stock meant. It meant that Luther considered Slash, at last and in every way, a member of the family. It meant that the suspicions had been put to rest, it meant that seduction was no longer necessary. The Dahlens now thought of Slash as one of their own. Even the Lancomes seemed to agree.

VI
THE MIDAS
TOUCH

*A*t the end of 1974, a who-needs-it year of Watergate, *Jaws* and sharklike oil company profits, Junior Lancome officially offered Slash a full partnership at Lancome & Dahlen. Slash, in his early thirties, was by far the youngest man ever honored with such an offer. To Junior's utter amazement, Slash turned the offer down.

"I'm an outsider," he told a dumbfounded Junior. "I want to keep it that way."

"Then what *do* you want?" asked Junior. He knew that Slash was getting fat offers up and down Wall Street. Business, except for oil, was lousy. The Dow was wallowing around in the 660s, inflation was pushing prices up and economic growth, worldwide, had slowed to near zero. Slash, with his daring strategies and breathtaking profits, looked better than ever and Junior wanted to make Slash happy. He wanted to keep him at Lancome & Dahlen and would give him almost anything he wanted to induce him to stay— including a partnership. When Slash turned the offer down, Trip couldn't figure out what Slash had in mind. What did the little bastard want? The keys to the kingdom?

"To be relieved of the day-to-day hassles," said Slash, outlining his plans for the future. He wanted to concentrate his time and his energy on the big-ticket deals. He wanted to resign the clients whose money he managed. He wanted to turn the Partners' Portfolio over to the Investment Committee. "I want to be able to follow my nose."

"If that's what you want, it's yours," said Junior, relieved that Slash's requirements seemed so modest. "Just remember: we're behind you," Junior added, in anticipation of the profits that would keep flowing in. "Don't forget it and don't be shy."

Just as Slash had finally been accepted by the Dahlens, he was now accepted by the Lancomes. His salary, bonuses and perks were now equal to Trip's, and the size of his office, next to Luther's, was exactly the size of Trip's, which was next to Junior's. Wall Street watchers were already beginning to wonder if Lancome & Dahlen was big enough for the two of them. The wags at Solomon Brothers were switching from Polish and Italian jokes to son-and-heir and son-in-law jokes.

To most people, a Wall Street partnership was the holy grail, a license to print money, a ticket to power and prestige, a proof of brains and ability, the final A-plus a career on Wall Street had to offer. Most people worked and slaved, maneuvered, finagled, smiled, lied and kissed ass in the quest to make partner. Most people would have sold their mother down the river and thrown their father in as well to make partner. Most people groveled, sweated, plotted, snarled and otherwise worked themselves into incipient nervous breakdowns in order to make partner. To most people making partner was the be-all and end-all of a Wall Street career. To most people making partner signified the difference between the men and the boys, the chiefs and the Indians, the haves and the have-nots, the winners and the losers. Slash wasn't most people.

In the years he had worked at Lancome & Dahlen, Slash had learned that partners were required to keep their assets in the partnership pool. Thus, although the partners were rich men on paper, they did not have automatic access to their money. Whenever a partner wanted to make a substantial purchase—a house or an apartment, for example—he had to request permission from the board to withdraw the funds he needed. It sickened Slash to see fifty-year-old men having to ask permission to get their own money as if they were boys asking for an advance against an allowance.

A partnership didn't interest Slash. It hadn't for years.

What did interest him—what had interested him from the night he first set foot in the Lancome & Dahlen building—was the whole company. He wanted it for himself—and he wanted it for Russ.

"Neither Luther nor Junior will live forever, and your father is the first to admit that he's happiest in his greenhouse," Slash told Deedee, confiding his ambition and his dreams for Russ's future. "One day there's going to be a power vacuum at Lancome and Dahlen, and I'm going to be ready for it. I'm going to get everything and I'm going to get it for Russ."

"What about Trip?" Deedee asked. "I'm sure he expects to take his father's place."

"Trip's smart but he's a lightweight. Besides, he's too conservative," Slash said, quickly dismissing the man he had once defeated in love, the man who now depended on him for money.

"But you don't own any of the stock," Deedee said. Outsiders never had.

"Russell does and he's on my side," Slash said, reminding her of Luther's birthday gift to his son. "One day you'll own it and you're not going to throw me out. Are you?"

They laughed at the sheer impossibility of it and Slash, as he had from the day he decided that the Steiners would adopt him, was not planning to settle for what was allowed him. He intended instead to take what he wanted. Meanwhile, Slash continued to pursue his Gatsbyesque lifestyle and Deedee felt herself being increasingly swept along by the ever-faster-flowing currents of Slash's success.

The address was on Dune Road, the best Southampton had to offer. Shaded by huge oaks and shielded from the curious by high privet hedges, the weathered shingled mansion stood right on the beach, just a mile east of the Meadow Club. It had morning rooms and afternoon rooms, a living room big enough for a tennis court and a dining room only a bit smaller. There was an octagonal library upstairs and a cosy den downstairs, there were two master suites, six additional bedrooms and a kitchen that would have been fine in a hotel. The house, a relic of an era when household staffs of two dozen were easy to come by and keep, had stood empty for a decade. The locals nicknamed it the White Elephant and their children swore it was haunted.

In 1975 Slash bought it for Deedee. Gossip at First Neck Lane and Gin Lane cocktail and dinner parties, where real estate values were beginning to edge out adultery, face lifts and nervous breakdowns as conversational topics A through C was that he had paid the insane price of five hundred thousand dollars.

"*And* they say he's putting in another half million," said Adrian Adams, an advertising agency mogul whose main outside-the-office interests were young women and old money, cold martinis and hot gossip. Adrian liked and admired Slash and had, in fact, hired Slash to invest the agency's pension plan funds.

"At least," said red and rotund Billy Cosgrove. "Between the pool and the tennis courts and a special greenhouse just for gardenias."

"Don't say a word against him," cautioned Gil Lanahan, whose inevitable blue blazers matched his blue blood. "He more than doubled my wife's net worth."

"Not to mention the donations he's made to the Southampton Hospital," chimed in Dotty, Billy's thin and chic wife, who served on the board of the Southampton Hospital with Deedee.

People also said that Slash was giving nouveau riche a bad name. Slash was the first to admit that maybe they had a point. Still, he saw no reason to cut back.

"After all," he said, contending that he had an important function to fulfill, "someone has to set the standards for excess and conspicuous consumption."

Still, Slash's lifestyle was so spectacular, the house was so enormous and the price so astronomical that many people simply assumed that Slash was hocked to the gills. They could not have been more wrong.

"I'm not in debt. It's just that I spend it as fast as I make it," Slash said blithely. Then he thought for a moment and added: "Maybe even a little faster."

Deedee laughed along with everyone else, even though she had begged Slash not to buy it. It was too big, too extravagant, too pretentious. She knew that people would make catty remarks and she felt that their little family of four would get lost in it. Slash, however, had insisted and in the end, reluctantly but gracefully, Deedee had stopped trying to talk him out of it.

She had no idea of how much she would regret her capitulation. She had no idea that she was right. She had no idea that the children of Southampton were right, too, and that the house would be, for them, a haunted place.

"We're behind you," said Junior, every time Slash needed funds to pile up stock in another company. It was becoming Junior's theme song and Trip echoed the words and the sentiments.

"Don't worry about the money," Trip said, putting his arm around Slash and quoting his father almost word for word. "You have our support. One hundred percent of the way."

Trip and his father expressed their total confidence and unconditional support constantly and with utter sincerity. Over and over again they backed up their words with money, their compliments with cash.

Eventually, even Slash believed them. Who wouldn't have?

At the mid-decade mark, Slash seemed infallible. He was making money for himself, for his clients, for Lancome & Dahlen. His golden gut never failed, and financial writers now called him the man with the Midas touch. So far, Slash's biggest score had been the two-million-dollar profit he'd made on a five-month, six-million-dollar investment in a midwestern hardware chain in early 1974. His most spectacular was the 1975 hit and run on a greeting card corporation, when he made a million dollars in one month for an annualized return of over 800 percent on an initial investment of 2.1 million dollars.

People were beginning to say that Slash didn't simply make money, he invented it.

To celebrate his killing on the greeting card company, Slash bought himself a Rolls and Deedee a Russian sable coat. Of the softest, most supple golden skins, the coat was said to be the finest in the world. It had cost Slash a quarter of a million dollars.

"Pocket change, I suppose," said Nina in a bitchy mood.

"It's obnoxious," growled Leon Marx. "Even by my standards."

Deedee herself didn't know quite what to think of the coat. It was beautiful but at the same time she felt embarrassed by it. On the one hand, she felt that Slash was going too far, but on the other, she couldn't help but be touched by his pride and his pleasure in his extravagant gift.

Soon after Deedee received the coat, still buffeted by ambivalence, she modeled it for Annette. Like a runway model, Deedee twirled dramatically this way and that and when she was finished, she took the coat off with a matador's stylish flair and took a theatrical bow.

Her performance over, she opened her closet door to put the coat away. Through the open door, Annette glimpsed the contents of Deedee's closet: the dark mink reefer, the double-breasted fisher polo coat, the floor-length ermine evening wrap, the sweeping, horizontally worked chinchilla cape, the full-length shawl-collared lynx and the hooded Canadian wolf ski jacket. From a rich family herself, Annette had grown up with rich people. She was accustomed to comfort and luxury. She was used to fine furniture, priceless art, valuable jewelry, expensive automobiles and luxurious dwellings. She had never, however, known anyone, anywhere, who lived on the scale of Slash and Deedee. They lived, she told friends, like modern-day pashas.

"How do you feel?" asked Annette, impressed despite herself. She was thinking that Deedee's furs alone must be worth over a million dollars.

"Like a nobody," Deedee said suddenly, blurting out words that seemed to come from nowhere and then, slamming the closet door shut, she burst into tears and fled from the room.

Annette was so shocked that she literally didn't know what to say.

While Slash had been getting richer and richer, Deedee was all too aware of gradually feeling poorer and poorer, both literally and psychologically. Inflation was eating into the value of money and the recession that had begun in 1973 showed few signs of easing. The million-dollar trust fund that had once seemed such a fortune no longer did. Particularly when Deedee compared it to the huge numbers that Slash so casually talked about every day of his life.

Somewhere along the line, soon after their trip to Santa Fe and Slash's coup with Hot Dog!, Deedee had begun to feel that the tables had turned. As Slash had once predicted, he had indeed made her his: heart and mind; body and soul. What neither he nor she had foreseen, however, was that rather than feeling loved, Deedee felt the opposite. She felt as if she had, with her own consent, been taken prisoner. Her independence was gone. In its place was total dependence: on one man and the money he provided. Slash had replaced Luther and, at thirty-one, Deedee felt as powerless and as insignificant as she had at six.

Deedee had long been accustomed to being wanted and needed, to being pursued and courted, to being indispensable, to being the only child and the most popular girl in her class, to being a million-dollar baby and the richest girl on the block. She was accustomed, in a thousand ways, subtle and obvious, to having the upper hand. Now, suddenly, it was Slash who was the inevitable center of attention. Deedee, for the first time in her life, stood in the shadows while someone else hogged the spotlight.

In the beginning it was Slash who had needed her. Now, Deedee knew, it was she who needed him. It seemed that she owed everything to him: her clothes and her children, her social life and her private life, her houses and cars and furs and jewels, her identity and her ego, her present and her future.

Even at home, even within the confines of her own family, Deedee seemed to have become increasingly invisible and unimportant. Slash had replaced Luther there, too. Slash was now the one everyone turned to, the one everyone listened to, the one whose opinions everyone heeded, the one everyone wanted to please. His currency had increased in value. Hers had decreased.

Slash no longer seemed to remember that it was she who had tailored and groomed him, presented and packaged him. She rarely heard his passionate expressions of thanks for all she had done anymore. He hadn't told her lately that he owed almost everything to her. He hadn't let her know recently that she had given him a home, a family, an identity and, although he was making a fortune in one coup after another, he still refused to put Deedee's money into any of his ventures.

She was beginning to have the subversive feeling that Slash *wanted* to keep her down. He would give her toys, grown-up toys like jewels and houses and furs, but he wouldn't let her have money and money was what counted.

"It's too small," he had said of Hot Dog!, refusing to put Deedee's money into the deal. "It's only a regional business."

"I'm worried about the receivables," he had said of the Small World deal, explaining why he had been reluctant to invest Deedee's money. "I'm not sure we'll collect anywhere near a hundred cents on the dollar."

"The debt ratio is already too high," he had said of the greeting card company and the possibility that it might have to take out more loans. Once again, Slash didn't want to risk Deedee's money. "And interest rates are still going up."

No matter how Deedee begged and pleaded, argued and cajoled, Slash still refused to handle her money. He advised her to be conservative and he told her to put her money into good-quality, high-yielding bonds. He wanted her, he said, to be safe. He kept saying he was too much of a gambler. He kept saying that he was afraid of making a mistake. Deedee took his advice and bought the bonds but she no longer believed him. She was beginning to think that refusing to increase her wealth was Slash's way of using his money to control her, to rob her of her independence. When she reminded him of how, on their very first date, he had offered to invest her money for her, his response was brief.

"That was then," he said. "This is now."

If only she had more money, Deedee thought, she might not feel so invisible. If only she had more money, she thought, she'd feel like her old self again. If only she had more money, she thought, she wouldn't feel so ignored and so insignificant. She wanted to feel less dependent and she thought that money would make her independent. She knew, of course, that she could not invest her own money. She didn't know the first thing about the stock market or investing in it. But she did know someone who did. Someone who even Slash said was smart. *And* conservative.

Without telling Slash what she was planning, Deedee went to Trip Lancome late in the spring of 1976 and asked him to invest her money for her. She told him to cash in her boring bonds and put her money into the market. She was tired of quality, she told Trip. She was sick of safety, she said. She instructed him to be aggressive. She told him that Slash was making a fortune and that she didn't want to be left behind.

"Slash is so successful now that my puny little million doesn't interest him," she said, handing her portfolio over to the man who had once loved her and, who, she thought, probably still did. After all, Trip had unexpectedly married a girl he'd known since childhood four months after Deedee had married Slash. Three years later, there had been a quiet divorce. People kept saying that Deedee had been the reason for Trip's sudden marriage and consequent divorce. Deedee told herself—and other people who knew them all agreed— that Trip had married on the rebound. Trip, Deedee sensed, still carried a torch for her.

VII
CRASH

*The summer of 1976 was the summer of bicentennial cele-*brations all across the country, but it was Deedee's own declaration of independence that made her, for the first time in a while, feel good about herself. She had hated feeling like a child and, by taking control of her own money, felt that she had taken control of her own life.

Deedee, like many American women, was inspired by the promises and possibilities held forth by the women's movement. All across the country women were becoming powerful, visible, independent. Politicians like Barbara Jordan and Bella Abzug were making their voices heard and their opinions count. Betty Ford, outspoken and candid, was a new kind of First Lady. Two women, Barbara Tuchman and Frances Fitzgerald, won Pulitzer Prizes, and a third, Rosalyn Yalow, would win a Nobel Prize. Barbara Walters had just received a highly publicized million-dollar contract, proof that women could be just as overpaid as men. Jane Fonda, despised for her politics, praised for her screen portrayal of another talented, political woman, Lillian Hellman, in a film about a third woman, *Julia*, made the cover of *Newsweek*. Advertisers noted that "You've come a long way, baby" and Helen Reddy's *I Am Woman* put the feeling to music.

Women, it seemed, were taking control of their own lives and their own destinies and Deedee, inspired by their examples, felt that she was finally beginning to assert herself, that she was finally beginning to grow up.

* * *

"I told Trip that I want my money invested aggressively," Deedee told Annette, proud of her new feeling of independence. "I told him that I didn't want anything boring like bonds or money market funds. I told him that I was tired of feeling poor."

"And what did he say?" asked Annette, thinking that only in comparison to Slash could Deedee possibly imagine feeling poor.

"He said that the market was low," replied Deedee. "That it was probably the right time to buy. Bottom fishing, he called it."

Deedee kept her secret to herself and waited confidently for the first quarterly report. It felt good, she thought, to be assertive, good to feel in charge. Slash noticed the difference: at the dinner table, where Deedee announced her opinions more confidently. In bed, where she made her wishes known more clearly. And over breakfast, where she began talking about going back to school and starting a career. Now that Russ and Claire were both in school, Deedee had time for herself again. Inspired by Annette Gwilym and the exploding prices of the Manhattan apartment market, Deedee thought she might get her broker's license.

"You seem happy," Slash told her, saying that with her phenomenal social contacts and the design ability she had displayed in working with Dorsay Miller she might be very successful. She would be able to tell clients about an apartment's potential, to make them see how an empty space could become a dream. Slash was not immune to the new allure of liberated women, and he liked the idea of having a wife with a glamorous career.

"I am," she said, pleased with herself and encouraged by Slash's enthusiasm. "Why shouldn't I be? I have a husband I love, children I adore and a future that looks even better than the past."

After all, Deedee thought, her mood of discontent apparently behind her, she was finally the woman with everything. A successful husband, healthy and happy children, youth and confidence, love and money. She thought so and she knew that the world did, too. After all, didn't everyone envy them? Didn't everyone admire them? Didn't everyone want to be like them? Deedee felt that she, more than any woman she knew, was living a fairy tale, and she had no reason to think that she and Slash wouldn't live happily ever after.

The summer of 1976 was the happiest summer of Deedee's life. Her decision to take her money to Trip had turned out to be an excellent one. The Dow had reached 973 in August and climbed even further, to 990, in September. A Dow of a thousand, Trip told her, seemed certain. In a buoyant mood, Deedee looked forward to the fall and the beginning of a new school term and a new career. Slash would not be the only one to profit from trends.

Deedee told herself that she would indeed fulfill the promise of the times: she was on the way to becoming her own best friend. She understood that money was Power! She wanted to get it. She wanted to use it. She told herself that she was about to successfully negotiate a passage, one of the predictable crises of adult life. Feeling good about one's self was everything and Deedee felt good about herself. She frequently reviewed her inner landscape and decided that she was OK and that everyone around her was OK, too. She wasn't stupid and she wasn't frivolous. She was, like everyone else, influenced by the times in which she lived.

At first the Saturday morning of the Labor Day weekend of 1976 seemed like every other summer Saturday morning in Southampton. Deedee had gone into town to have her hair done while Claire was taking a riding lesson. Slash was in his study on the phone to Arthur Bozeman about a hot, hit-and-run corporate prospect, a surefire, can't-lose, ripe-for-the-plucking company in the beauty supply business. It was just waiting for Slash to move in, pick off a huge profit and ride off, richer than ever, into the sunset.

Annie, the au pair girl, was at the pool with Russ.

Tall and athletic at nine, Russ had inherited Slash's amazing facility with numbers, and he reminded Slash of himself at the same age: a passionate collector of everything boys wanted most—vintage comics, Beatles memorabilia and World Series buttons. Russ worshiped his father, and he followed the ins and outs of Slash's deals as if they were the latest James Bond movie. He had told Deedee a million times that he wished he could grow up faster so that he and his father could not only be best friends but business partners as well.

Annie was Danish, her short, plump figure and dark hair going against the tall, blond Nordic type. She was in her bathing suit, sitting in a lawn chair, writing a letter to her boyfriend back home in Copenhagen when the pantry telephone began to ring.

"Russ, go get the phone?" Annie asked, working on her letter and her tan simultaneously. "Your mother's expecting the caterer to call about tonight's party. Tell him she's out right now. She'll have to call him back later."

"Awwww . . . do I have to? I'm in a good part," Russ said. He was sitting on the edge of the pool, his bare feet dangling in the water, immersed in the new copy of *Fortune* that had arrived in the mail. He was looking, as he always did, for a mention of his father's name.

Annie was in a good part, too, writing to her boyfriend about the erotic dreams she'd been having of him all summer long. She was describing in juicy, purple detail exactly what she intended to let him to do to her just as soon as she got back to Denmark, which would be in just two weeks. The phone continued to ring and Russ, glued to the page, did not budge.

"Someday I'll be rich, too. Then *I'll* have someone to answer the phone," Annie sighed, putting down pen and writing paper and running for the house, sure that whoever it was would hang up the moment she got there.

It wasn't the caterer, it was Annie's boyfriend. He was calling all the way from Copenhagen just to hear her voice. He had been dreaming about her, too.

Annie shut the pantry door for privacy and began to tell him, transatlantically, all the things she had just been writing him. Almost twenty minutes later, when Deedee and Claire drove up in the station wagon, Annie was still on the pantry telephone, the door closed.

"Russ? Annie?" Deedee called, seeing that they weren't at the pool and that the tennis courts beyond were empty. She wondered where they had gone. "Russ? Annie?"

There was no answer. There was no sign of anyone. When Deedee got to the pool, she gasped. There was Russ, floating in the water facedown and fully dressed, in a dead man's float. His glasses were still on and the copy of *Fortune* was bobbing along, too, soaked and just out of reach.

"Russ! Get out of there!" Deedee ordered. This time one of his "sick" jokes had gone too far. Russ loved to imitate Chevy Chase imitating Gerald Ford. He liked to trip on stairs, stumble on carpets and fall all over his own feet, crashing dramatically to the floor. Claire and Slash thought he was a riot. Deedee, afraid that he might hurt himself, was often accused of not getting the joke.

Russ did not move.

"It's not funny, Russ!" Deedee shouted. "Stop fooling around and get out of that pool!"

Claire, walking toward the pool behind her mother, heard the sharp, worried tone in her mother's voice. She turned and ran toward the house to get her father.

"Daddy!" she yelled as she crossed the lawn, running toward the house. "Daddy! Something's the matter! Come quickly!"

"Russ? Russ!" Deedee shouted, aware of the first stabs of panic. The "joke" hadn't been funny in the first place; now it was becoming frightening. "Russ!"

Still Russ did not move. He floated gently, his dark, straight hair, exactly like Slash's, moving slightly with the currents generated by the filter.

"Russ! Russ!"

There was no movement, no response and without waiting a moment longer, Deedee kicked off her shoes and, fully dressed, dove into the pool and, swimming toward Russ, reached out for him. With a few strokes, she pulled him next to the ladder.

Annie, hearing the commotion, said a hurried goodbye to her boyfriend and ran out to the pool.

"Call 911!" Deedee screamed.

Annie grabbed the pool extension and dialed. In her panic, her English deserted her.

"Det er Russ!" she exclaimed. *"Han ligger i svømmebassinet!"*

She had to give the address three times before the operator understood her.

Meanwhile, running from the house and moving frantically, Slash lowered himself onto the pool ladder and, with Deedee's help, grabbed Russ under the arm. Holding on to the ladder with one hand, he used the other to pull a limp and unresponsive Russ out of the water.

"Is he all right?" asked Deedee. She was still in the pool as Slash, working frantically, put Russ down on the lawn. A stream of water poured from Russ's mouth, soaking the grass nearby.

"I don't know," said Slash, putting his mouth to his son's mouth, trying to breathe air into his lungs, life into his body as Deedee's blood-chilling scream of anguish seemed to echo and echo across the lawns and disappear into the horizon.

It was too late. Too late for everyone. Too late for Deedee to save her son. Too late for Slash to bring him back to life. Too late for the emergency medical squad. Too late for Russ. He was buried two days later in the Dahlen family plot at the Locust Valley Presbyterian church next to little Luther.

Deedee, heavily sedated, sobbed in Slash's arms and, as the small casket was lowered into the ground, she swayed and almost fainted. Claire, in tears, stood next to her parents while Luther, devastated, was supported by Edwina. Russell and Joyce stood by in stunned, stricken silence. With Russ's death, the dream that had united them had ended. The present was benumbed with grief, the future, a void.

Only Slash seemed in control, his expression stoic, his eyes dry. His usual paleness, however, had turned into an extreme pallor and he looked, said Annette Gwilym, like a ghost. He was a man who had lost his son. He was a man who had lost everything. He was a man who had been doubly orphaned—by the past and by the future. He was a man who would never recover.

To Slash's amazement, Luther insisted on an inquiry. It concluded officially what was already obvious: that Russ's death had been an accident. The report theorized that Russ had gotten up and, probably because of his wet feet, had slipped and fallen into the pool. There was a nasty bump on Russ's head where he had apparently hit either the side of the pool or the edge of the diving board. He had certainly been stunned, the medical examiner said, more probably even knocked unconscious. He had been taking antihistamine pills for his hay fever and the effects of the medication combined with the blow to his head had evidently caused his normal reflexes to stop long enough for him to inhale and fill his lungs with water. The cause of death was listed as accidental drowning.

The theory was logical, and the conclusion was obvious: Russ's death had been an accident. No one was at fault. No one was to blame. Not Annie. Not Deedee. Not Slash. Not anyone.

Tragedy can unite and tragedy can divide; tragedy can bring a family closer together or it can drive a family apart. Russ's birth had brought the Dahlens together. His death pulled them apart. Annie, scared and in tears, went back to Copenhagen and the family, floundering in grief, guilt, blame and anger, was left to deal with its loss.

Edwina became quieter than ever, her voice quieter, her words fewer, her gestures sparer. Always thin, she became emaciated. She sat silently for hours, not moving, seeming to hover in the background of her own life, more like a shadow than a woman. Joyce's smile disappeared and her eyes turned empty. Russ's death had left a terrible hole in Joyce's life. Never again would she hear his voice or kiss his cheek or glow with pride at his high marks or pretend to be shocked at the gross-out sick jokes he brought home from school and loved to tell. Russ was gone, and with him one of the few satisfactions of her unhappy and unfulfilling marriage.

Nearing the end of his own long life, Luther seemed almost unable to bear the ending of another young life, the final extinguishing of hope. Russ had been the fourth generation, the male heir who would ensure the continuation of Lancome & Dahlen, the great-grandson who would guarantee a kind of immortality for Luther. The future had been ripped away and its absence was unendurable. In his own anguish, Luther railed impotently against fate and looked in vain for someone to blame.

Unlike Luther, who was furious at fate, Russell seemed reduced by it. He was absolutely devastated by the second loss of a male heir and shattered that Slash, who had once seemed to be able to do everything he hadn't been able to do, hadn't been able to save his son.

"You should have been with Russ instead of at the hairdresser," Luther told Deedee more than once in a hard voice that brooked no defense. The old man's grief was transmuted into blame, his pain into accusation. "And Slash shouldn't have been on the phone. He should have been paying more attention."

Edwina stood mutely by and, with her paralyzed silence, seemed to agree with Luther. Russell and Joyce, like Luther, needed to find an explanation for the inexplicable, a way to comprehend the incomprehensible. They did not consciously mean to but their words, too, often seemed an indictment.

"If only you or Slash had been at the pool, Russ would be alive now," Joyce told Deedee, unwittingly echoing Luther's words. She was trying, like the rest of the family, to rewrite the events of that Saturday morning.

"Russ shouldn't have been left all alone with Annie. She's

just a teenager. She's not old enough to be really responsible,'' Russell said.

Deedee, almost constantly in tears, felt guilty and defenseless. They were right, she told herself. If she were a good mother, she would have been with Russ. She shouldn't have been at the hairdresser. Shouldn't have been thinking of herself and the party that night. Shouldn't have been so vain. The Valium the doctor gave her did nothing for the pain and when she did sleep, nightmares made sleep worse than tears.

Like Luther, Deedee raged against fate. She raged against Myron Kligman, who had forbidden her to have more children and convinced her to have an operation that made it impossible. She raged against her parents and her grandparents and their unintentional cruelties. She felt abandoned and guilty, responsible and helpless.

Slash dried her tears, but there were always more tears. He tried to offer solace and comfort and distraction. He held her in his arms but, for the first time, his arms weren't enough. He told her that he loved her but love, for the first time, wasn't enough. He told her that the world hadn't come to an end.

"But it has. At least for me," Deedee said, weeping and inconsolable. She could not forget the moment when she realized that Russ wasn't playing a game, that he wasn't trying to scare her. She went over and over that moment in her mind, reliving it, trying to make it all come out differently. It never did.

Deedee began to wait for fate's next blow and projected her fears on Claire. She became obsessed with loss.

"What if we lose her, too?" Deedee asked Slash.

"We're not going to lose her," Slash said, almost angrily. "We're not going to lose her!" he repeated, speaking as much to assure himself as to comfort Deedee. "Lightning does not strike twice. You have to believe that."

But it was clear that she didn't.

* * *

Deedee became wildly overprotective of Claire, insisting on accompanying her everywhere: to school, to riding classes, shopping on Saturdays and to friends' houses on Sundays. Claire, in response, alternated between extreme fearfulness that something would happen to her, too, and resentment toward her mother, whom she began to see as a jailer.

"Leave me alone, Mommy! I can walk two blocks to Tina's house myself!" she would lash out, wanting some independence.

At other times, she would cringe and cling to Deedee as they walked along a sidewalk.

"A car might run me over," Claire said, referring to a news story she had seen on television the night before about a taxi that had run out of control and killed three people in front of B. Altman's.

Slash told Deedee that she was making Claire neurotic, and she agreed. The problem, she said, was that she could not help herself.

Christmas passed and by the end of the year the Dow was almost at one thousand. Trip had been right, and the one and only good thing in Deedee's life was that the value of her portfolio had gone up. Thank God for that. Thank God for the money.

January passed and so did February. Spring finally came but Deedee seemed unable to get over Russ's death and to put her grief behind her. She wondered if her reaction were abnormal or excessive and she thought about seeing a psychiatrist but didn't. What, she asked herself, could a psychiatrist do? Bring Russ back to life? She thought about killing herself. But what would that accomplish? She couldn't abandon Claire. She visited a respected yogi, recommended by Nina, in search of help. She tried massages, meditation and a grief counselor. Nothing helped, and Deedee sank deeper and deeper into depression. The Dow, which had stood at a thousand at the beginning of 1977, began to fall.

Deedee was, she thought as the months dragged slowly by, a sister who had not been able to replace her brother, a mother who had not been able to help her son. She was also, by that spring, a million-dollar baby who was losing her money.

"I'm going to end up broke," Deedee told Slash in late February. The value of Deedee's stock began to shrink, week by week, month by month. The quarterly statements she had once looked forward to she now opened with dread.

"No, you're not," said Slash, trying to calm yet another expression of the panic and anxiety that had seemed infinite since Russ's death. "Your money is safe."

"No, it's not," said Deedee.

"Of course it is! It's in bonds," explained Slash patiently. "Bonds are solid."

"I sold the bonds," Deedee said.

"Sold?" Slash was shocked. "When? Why? What the hell did you do that for?"

"I wanted to make money. I sold the bonds and I gave the money to Trip."

"Trip?" Slash repeated in disbelief.

Deedee nodded.

"You wouldn't invest for me," she said. "So I asked him to."

Slash, always pale, turned white. He looked at Deedee in utter disbelief.

"You what?"

"You wouldn't handle my money," said Deedee. "You were making money for everyone except me."

"And so you went to Trip?" Slash asked, beside himself at the betrayal. She had gone to Trip? Of all people? What was the matter with her? What had she been thinking? And, why, above all, hadn't she spoken to him? Didn't she trust him anymore? Didn't she believe in him anymore?

"It was a mistake," said Deedee, unable to look at him, her voice barely audible.

"And you didn't even have the decency to tell me?"

"I was afraid."

"And now I suppose you want me to make back the money he's lost?" Deedee had never seen Slash so angry, so close to losing control.

"Would you?" she asked meekly. She seemed so chastened that she appeared physically diminished.

"I don't know. I'll have to think about it," he said, still so angry that he couldn't think straight.

He slammed the door and walked out.

That night, for the first time in his life, Slash went out and got drunk. Disgustingly drunk. Out-of-control, falling-down, piss-in-your-pants, puke-on-your-shoes drunk. He began with vodka martinis at the King Cole Bar, worked his way up Fifth Avenue to the Plaza and the Pierre, over to the Ritz Carlton on Madison, where he switched to Scotch, up to the Westbury and back to Fifth at the Stanhope, where he was refused admittance because of his obvious intoxication.

Slash headed east, stopping in a lesbian bar on Lexington, and a doormen's bar on Third, and finally turned north on Second Avenue, where he literally staggered into a dank Hungarian saloon called the Football Bar. He ordered slivovitz for the house and got into a fight with a covey of boisterous soccer players that ended out on the sidewalk. Slash, outweighed and outnumbered, ended up bleeding and almost unconscious in the gutter.

"Can I help you?" asked a black woman, a nurse who was on her way home from the late shift at Lenox Hill. She was not used to seeing expensively dressed men scratched and bleeding, lying in Second Avenue gutters.

"Can you get me into a cab?" Slash asked. As she flagged down a passing taxi, Slash thanked her and reached into his pocket and handed her all the money he had except for ten dollars for the taxi. She was amazed, when she counted it, to see that he had given her seventeen hundred dollars. Slash was amazed, when he got home, to see that he had gotten there in one piece.

"OK," he told a worried and almost hysterical Deedee as he brushed his way past her heading for the bathroom. "I'll do it. I'll pick up the pieces."

He meant the pieces of her life. He also meant the pieces of their marriage.

VIII
AFTERMATH

The news was inescapable. The news was bad. It flashed from a thousand headlines, a thousand television news shows. Gasoline prices were up and so were electric rates as the coldest winter of the century was followed by the hottest summer. Trade deficits were mounting, the English pound was at an all-time low and so was the Italian lira. New York City hovered on the brink of bankruptcy. The dollar was down and so was the size of automobiles. The economy was stalled and going nowhere, caught between inflation and recession. Businessmen did not know what to think of Jimmy Carter, the new president, and so did nothing. The Dow, in response, sagged listlessly.

The value of Deedee's portfolio had gone down by almost a third. Slash did not waste his time telling Trip how he had mistimed and miscalculated. Instead, he told him simply that Deedee wanted him to take over her investments.

"Deedee's upset by the losses," Slash told Trip. "She's asked me to see what I can do."

"It would have been nice if she had told me herself," said Trip sarcastically, handing Deedee's portfolio over to Slash.

"She hasn't been herself since Russ . . ." Slash said in explanation.

What Slash didn't say was that he hadn't been himself either. Slash had been profoundly changed by his son's death. The changes didn't show on the outside, as they did with Deedee. The changes were invisible and internal. Slash had always been a master of the self-created personality. He had made sure that he presented one side to the world, a side that was insouciant, cynical, outrageous and fatalistic. That image, a seductive fiction, had had little to do with the inner reality. Now, with Russ's death, the external image and the inner reality had become one.

Since Russ's death, nothing had really mattered for Slash. Not his money, not his reputation, not his ambition. Russ's death had been the death of the engine of hope that had always propelled Slash. Russ's death had changed Slash from a man who was always trying to a man who didn't really care.

What would be fatal was not the change itself or even the enormous anger that underlay it but the fact that neither Slash himself nor anyone around him was aware of those changes within him.

The company Arthur had called about on the Labor Day weekend was named Premiere. Slash had been about to move, about to begin buying up shares when Stan Fogel, the president and main stockholder, suddenly dropped dead. Slash put the project on the back burner and then in March, just after Slash had promised Deedee to handle her money for her, Arthur brought it up again.

The dust, it seemed, had never really settled since Stan Fogel's death, and Premiere seemed more troubled—and more desirable—than ever. The company carried little debt and maintained an attractive cash flow. In addition, the value of its assets—its manufacturing plants and offices, its subsidiaries and its regional warehouses—was worth more than the stock traded for. On top of everything else, its directors didn't own enough stock to control the board.

"The situation's a classic," Arthur told Slash, repeating the trade gossip about the troubled company. "When the founder died, all hell broke loose. Stan Fogel's kids and his old cronies are on the board. The kicker is that it's the girlfriend and not the wife and kids who inherited Stan's stock. No one knows why. However, needless to say, the girlfriend and the family are at each other's throats. The board is weak and in disarray. The company is ripe for plucking."

* * *

Stan Fogel, Arthur Bozeman's research revealed, was something of a celebrity in his business, a man known in the beauty trade as the king of the permanent wave. He had made his original fortune in the early fifties and had spent the years since multiplying it. The girlfriend, Arthur's research told Slash, was a former hairdresser who had owned a couple of small-town beauty parlors. A few people said that she had run the company since Stan's death although since she had no title at Premiere, no other business experience and not even a college degree, that seemed very unlikely.

Apparently, according to local gossip, the real story was that she had been Stan Fogel's girlfriend for years and that when Stan died, she had picked up some of the chips. As far as anyone knew, she was strictly a small-town beauty parlor operator who had fallen into the right bed and woken up lucky.

Slash's plan, enthusiastically endorsed by Trip, was to buy up Premiere stock and force Premiere to pay them to back off.

"Premiere's selling at seven," Slash told Trip. "It's a real bargain at that price. It's easily worth double," said Slash, reminding Trip of Hot Dog!, Electrix and Small World. "The least we'll take is fifteen dollars a share."

"If they don't come up with a price we like, we'll merge Premiere with Marx and Marx," Trip said, envisioning another scenario. "The merger would make Marx and Marx into the biggest company in the field. No matter what happens, we can't lose."

In a series of meetings, Slash and Trip engineered their strategy. Slash would personally buy a hundred thousand shares and he would buy another hundred thousand for Deedee. Meanwhile, Trip, acting for Lancome & Dahlen, would buy another two hundred thousand shares. Between them, they could dictate terms to Premiere.

Slash bought two hundred thousand shares on margin and placed half of it in Deedee's account. He would double her money—at least. He would double his own. And so would

Lancome & Dahlen. Everyone would win. No one would lose.

"It's going to be a slaughter," Slash told Pete Oney confidently, poised for the biggest kill of all in the deal of a lifetime. It would be another perfect deal by the man with the Midas touch.

When the price of the shares of Premiere went from seven to eight, from nine to ten, Slash wasn't surprised. His buying and Lancome & Dahlen's buying would have accounted for the upward pressure. However, when the price of the shares suddenly reversed themselves and began to fall, Slash, slightly surprised, wasn't the least bit worried. In fact, he saw the cheaper price as an advantage.

"We'll just buy more," Slash said confidently, planning on doubling up his holdings. Lowering the cost basis of the stock would only mean bigger profits in the end.

However, before Slash could act, the Premiere shares fell even further. Their price fell to five and a half. And then to five.

"What the fuck is going on?" Slash asked Arthur. The stock was behaving unpredictably, the bottom seemed to be dropping out, and Slash was disturbed at being taken off guard. When it came to the stock market, Slash was not accustomed to being caught off base. "Just our own purchases alone ought to keep the price up. I bought two hundred thousand shares and so did Lancome and Dahlen."

Arthur went back to his office and hit the phones. Ten minutes later he was back in Slash's office. Arthur, usually calm and contained, was clearly agitated. He looked like a man who had found a shocking and unappetizing solution to a mystery.

"*You* bought two hundred thousand shares," he told Slash. "Lancome and Dahlen bought zilch."

"The bastard!" said Slash, realizing what Trip had done. Trip had hated him for years. That secret hatred, hidden until now, was suddenly out in the open. "The double-crossing little bastard!"

* * *

Slash was utterly stunned to find out that Trip had gone back on his word. He was also stunned to find out that Premiere was getting no support in the market at all. No one except him was buying and someone was selling heavily. Someone was dumping Premiere stock on the market. Someone was causing the value of the stock to plummet. Someone was giving Slash a royal screwing.

The someone, in the early stages at least, although Slash didn't know it yet, wasn't Trip.

Only when the stock fell to five and one half did Trip realize that Slash's perfect deal was the perfect opportunity. The opportunity he'd been waiting for. The opportunity to get back at Slash, to repay him for taking Deedee and for ruining his plans to consolidate the ownership of the Lancome & Dahlen stock. Trip remembered a promise he had once made to Deedee and the memory triggered a plan. Whoever had been dumping stock provided the perfect vehicle for revenge.

"Why should Lancome and Dahlen buy Premiere?" Trip asked Slash calmly when Slash confronted him. "Premiere's in disarray. I wouldn't touch it with a ten-foot pole."

"But we had a deal!" said a furious Slash. "You and I had an agreement!"

Trip smiled.

"Well, Slash," he said calmly from behind the flawless wall of his blond WASP perfection, "so you're not the only one around here who likes to break the rules now and then."

The margin calls began to come in and Slash covered them himself using his own money and then when he ran out, using money he borrowed from Marx & Marx.

"I'll pay you back as soon as I can," he told Pete.

Soon was soon enough for Pete. After all, he owed Slash more than just a favor. He owed Slash his life. However, when Trip found out, he hit the ceiling. He didn't owe Slash Steiner anything. Not one goddamn thing. All he cared about was the money. He was furious at Slash for borrowing money from a company that Lancome & Dahlen controlled.

"You're treating Marx and Marx like a personal piggy bank!" Trip told Slash. Trip enjoyed having a solid reason, a reason no one could possibly disagree with, to be angry at Slash and he smiled bleakly as he spoke. "We have no guarantee of when you're going to repay!"

"I told Pete I'll pay the money back as soon as I can," said Slash. "It's good enough for him and he's the president of Marx and Marx."

"Well, it's not good enough for me," said Trip coldly. "And I own the goddamn thing."

Besides, Trip was now worried about another loan.

"We lent Marx and Marx a million dollars in 1970," Trip reminded Slash the next day. "I hope we're going to get repaid."

"For Christ's sake, don't worry about it," Slash said, irritated. He had made a fortune for Trip. He was furious at Trip's double-cross and infuriated by his demand that Slash repay the money he had borrowed from Marx & Marx to pay back the losses he had suffered thanks to Trip's failure to live up to his word. Now, he was beside himself that Trip was suddenly bringing up an old debt that hadn't been mentioned for years.

"I have to worry," said Trip pompously. "It's not just my money in Marx and Marx. I have Lancome and Dahlen's clients to worry about. They have money in it, too."

"Pious little son of a bitch," Slash told Pete. "He never says a word about the clients when we're making money. All he ever says is how much."

The price of Premiere continued to plummet. To four and three-quarters. To four and a half. The freefall ended at four dollars a share and the margin calls cost Slash four million dollars that he didn't have. But it wasn't only the margin calls that caused the debacle. It was Trip's demand for the instant repayment of the old loan on top of the margin calls that would push Slash to the wall.

It was Lancome & Dahlen he was thinking of, he told Slash. It wasn't personal. It was business. Slash reached into his own pocket for the one million dollars. Trip told him that it wasn't enough.

"Marx and Marx has tripled in value," Trip reminded Slash. "We expect to be repaid proportionately."

The figure that Trip had in mind was three million dollars. It was the coup de grâce.

Having no choice, Slash reached into the little that was left in Deedee's trust fund to come up with the additional money. It was not nearly enough, and Trip was not satisfied. Trip, on behalf of Lancome & Dahlen, filed suit against Slash for repayment of the old loan and for fiduciary crimes involved in borrowing money from Marx & Marx for his own personal use and the use of his wife. The financial pages had finally found a new angle: The man with the Midas touch had feet of clay.

The man with the Midas touch was bankrupt and the girl who once had had everything now felt that she had nothing and was nothing. The feeling was devastating and Deedee could not control the panic and the pain.

"How could you? How could you!" Deedee lashed out at Slash when she found out that everything was gone. The money. The stock. The trust fund. The pride. The reputation. The glitter. The dazzle. The shimmer. The myth. The loss Deedee had dreaded had finally happened. Her child was gone and so was her money. Her money, which equaled her identity. Her self.

"I was outsmarted," Slash replied, speaking quietly and almost inaudibly. His gray eyes were dark and almost opaque in his shame and humiliation and he was as close to being openly wounded as he ever permitted himself to be. "And Trip double-crossed me."

"Outsmarted? Double-crossed?" snarled Deedee, infuriated. Slash was not supposed to be vulnerable. He was supposed to be the strongest and the smartest. Invincible. On top and in command. He was supposed to protect her. He was supposed to take care of her. "*You?* How could anyone betray you? How could anyone outsmart you?"

"I made a mistake. I miscalculated," said Slash in the same quiet voice, the voice of a shattered man. Someone else who was interested in Premiere had outsmarted him. Then Trip, smelling blood, had moved in for the kill. Slash, who had always lived up to and even beyond every penny he earned, had helped set himself up. That knowledge, almost more than anything else, devastated him.

"But you're supposed to be perfect!" retorted Deedee. She was so lost in her own panic that she did not see what Slash was feeling, did not understand that for once it was he who needed her. "You're not supposed to make mistakes! Not with my money!"

"But I did," said Slash, refusing to shift the blame, refusing to hide behind rationalizations and excuses. "A huge mistake. A terrible mistake. I'll try to fix it. I'll try to make it right."

"Try? Try?" sneered Deedee, beside herself with fear and anxiety. "Try with what? There's no money left! No one will trust you anymore! No one will believe you anymore."

Slash was silent for a moment and he looked at her almost as if he had never seen her before. The pain her words inflicted was the worst pain of all.

"You mean *you* don't trust me, don't you?" Slash asked, stunned. Blindly, he reached out for Deedee's hand. "You meant that *you* don't believe me anymore, don't you?"

"That's exactly right! How can I? How can anyone? Get out! Get out!" Deedee cried hysterically, pulling away from him, her dreams smashed. She was unable to face the shame, unable to face the future, unable to let the man she loved and hated and blamed come close to her. She had wanted him to be perfect and now he had proven that he wasn't. He had proven he was human, and the disillusion shattered everything she needed to believe. "I never want to see you again!"

"You don't mean that!" Slash said, reaching out again to touch her, wanting to make contact with her.

"I do! I do!" she cried, flinching at his touch and pulling away from him. "They were right! I should have listened! I never should have married you!"

"But you loved me!" insisted Slash, begging her to remember the way she had felt, the way she had defied her family for him.

"I didn't!"

"You said you'd die if you couldn't marry me!" he reminded her.

"I didn't mean it! I didn't mean one word of it! I was young! I was crazy! I didn't know what I was doing!" Deedee sobbed, out of control. "I never should have done it. I never should have insisted. I should have done what they wanted. I should have married Trip!"

Slash stopped reaching for her, stopped wanting to touch her. Instead, he stepped back and stared at her. Her face was flushed and angry, her hair wild and disheveled. For the first time Slash could ever remember, Deedee looked ugly.

"You don't mean that, Deedee. You don't know what you're saying," Slash said quietly, trying to make her understand what she was saying. Trying to make her understand what she was doing to him, to *them*. He wanted to sober her up. He wanted to bring her to her senses.

"Oh, yes, I do!" screamed Deedee. "I mean every word of it!"

"Then go ahead!" Slash said, at that moment, for the first time ever, falling a little out of love with her.

"I will! I'll marry him!" replied Deedee defiantly. "Just you see!"

"And *you* see, too," said Slash, turning to walk out. "See what it's like to be married to a killer!"

Later, when they had both calmed down a bit, Slash told Deedee that he was sorry for everything that had happened and she replied bitterly that sorry wasn't enough. She told him that she never wanted to see him again.

"Never!" she said, shutting the door and her heart on him.

Slash disappeared then, and Deedee didn't hear from him again. One day passed. Then two. Then three. The debts, the scandal and the lawsuits piled up. The publicity, in the past invariably flattering, turned into notoriety. Deedee, always brushed with gilt and fairy dust, was now tarnished by innuendo and guilt by association.

A week went by and still there was no word from Slash, no sign of him, no letter, no card, no message, no telephone call. Deedee was frantic, beside herself with worry. She sank into a state of dread. She feared that Slash was somewhere in an anonymous hotel room. Alone. Dead or dying. By his own hand.

She flagellated herself because there was nothing she could do to save him. And because secretly, deep down, she felt that everything that had happened was her own fault.

Deedee, left alone, emotionally and financially bankrupt, shut herself into her apartment and brooded. Unable to bear the guilt she felt, she gradually began to project it on someone else. Someone she began to blame for all that had happened. Someone besides Slash. Someone *like* Slash. Someone who had come from nowhere. Someone who ran Premiere. Someone who had engineered the whole disaster.

Someone Deedee held responsible for the loss of her fortune, the collapse of her marriage and now perhaps the death of her husband. Someone she hated more than she had ever thought she could hate anyone. Someone named Lana Bantry.

P A R T   F O U R

Poor Girl / 1960-1979

"She wasn't the smartest person I ever knew, and, although she was extremely glamorous, she certainly wasn't beautiful. What made her special was her determination. She was the most determined person I ever met—determined to be successful, determined to be treated fairly, determined to be noticed. I always thought there was something sad about her."

—ED HILSINGER

"She was a money-hungry bitch and she deserved everything that happened to her."

—TONY MORELLO

"She thought like a man and fucked like an angel. She was the ideal woman. I loved her but I double-crossed her. Don't ask me why because I don't really know. Maybe she was just too much for me."

—STAN FOGEL

I

SILVER SPOONS AND SILVER FRAMES

Lana Bantry was a woman from the wrong side of the
tracks who made it to the right side of town. In 1980, the
town would be Manhattan. In 1960, when she was sixteen,
it had been Wilcom, Massachusetts. In the spring of 1977,
less than six months after Stan Fogel's death in September,
the town was Providence, Rhode Island, and the news, according to Kenny Conlon, was terrible.

Kenny was Premiere's controller, and he hated to be the
one to bring Lana the bad news about Premiere. Kenny knew
how much Lana cared about Premiere. She thought of it as
hers—her brains and her blood, her sweat and her tears—and
Kenny didn't blame her. Premiere was one of the leaders in
its field and Lana Bantry was the reason why.

"The absolute worst has happened," Kenny told Lana,
coming into her pink, white and silver office and waving an
ominous-looking 13-D, the obligatory disclosure form required by the SEC. "Premiere's the subject of a takeover
bid."

"Takeover?" Lana repeated, her heart sinking. She was
used to bad news but Kenny was right. This was the worst
yet. Ever since Stan had died, Lana had been struggling with
Premiere's board, which consisted of Stan's two sons, Stan's
banker and Stan's accountant. Struggling and, although Lana
hated to admit it, fighting what looked like a losing battle
over the future of Premiere. Now there was another threat.
Not from the inside but from the outside.

Lana Bantry leaned forward in the jazzy, eye-catching

black-and-white ponyskin chair she had designed herself and listened carefully as Kenny told her that a corporate raider had just bought 7 percent of Premiere's stock.

"Raiders have one object: money," Kenny went on, explaining the typical scenario. "They begin by buying stock in the target company. Once they accumulate a controlling percentage of shares, they have two alternatives: either they get rid of management and take the company over. Or they force management to pay them to stay away."

"They do?" asked Lana, immediately argumentative, refusing as always to be intimidated. "And who the hell is this raider?"

"Slash Steiner," said Kenny, wondering if Lana had ever heard of him.

"Slash Steiner?" repeated Lana, turning pale.

"The one, the only," Kenny replied grimly, thinking that of course Lana had heard of him. When it came to business, Lana Bantry never missed a trick and Kenny noticed that even Lana, who was afraid of nothing, looked scared.

What Kenny interpreted as an expression of fear was far more than merely fear. It was an expression of utter disbelief. Lana simply could not believe what Kenny had just told her.

Someone was going to try to put her out of business? Someone going to try to skim the cream off the company she had built? Someone was going to try to destroy her? Why? Why now? Why Slash Steiner?

Or, thought Lana with a sudden, sickening feeling in the pit of her stomach, was it *really* Slash Steiner who was out to destroy Premiere? Or was Slash Steiner just a front? Was Slash Steiner in fact acting on behalf of someone else?

Was it, Lana asked herself, really Russell Dahlen who was pulling the strings? Was it Russell Dahlen who had sired her and then abandoned her who was really behind the attack on Premiere? Was her real father planning to steal from her the way her stepfather had once stolen from her? Was the father who had ignored her for her entire life now out to take away everything she had struggled to build?

Lana had the doomed feeling that fate had finally closed in on her. She was filled with the grim foreboding that this time, just as in the past, no matter what she did or how she struggled, she was fated to lose. Nevertheless, concealing her feelings like the consummate tactician she was, Lana motioned for Kenny to continue.

"There's only one way to deal with a raider like Slash Steiner and that's to pay him off to stay away. It's called greenmail. I ran the numbers," Kenny said, running his hand nervously through his swiftly thinning reddish blond hair. "Premiere can afford to offer him fifteen dollars a share."

"If we pay him fifteen dollars a share, we'll cripple the company. There'll be no money for research and expansion. Cash flow will be cut to nothing. Premiere will be destroyed," said Lana, knowing what had happened to other companies that had given in to greenmail threats. The effects on Premiere would be no different. As she spoke, Lana's initial feelings of dread were already beginning to crystallize into her characteristic defiance and refusal to be defeated no matter what the odds. "I made Premiere what it is today and I'm not going to be greenmailed. Not by Slash Steiner. Not by anyone."

"But Lana, Slash Steiner doesn't play games. He already has almost enough stock to force a stockholders' meeting," Kenny warned, suspecting that Lana, as usual, might be being tight with money. "You know perfectly well that Premiere is worth even more than fifteen dollars a share. If you don't buy Slash Steiner off, he'll fire the board, get rid of you and either sell off the company's assets or merge Premiere into another company. Either way, the result will be the same: you'll be out on your ass and Premiere won't exist any longer."

"I don't plan to buy him off. *And* I don't plan to be out on my ass," said Lana, sitting up straight and squaring her shoulders.

Although she was a petite woman, barely five feet two, there was something about Lana Bantry, the combination of her assertive personality and the bold way she dressed, that made her seem big. Kenny had tremendous respect for her but, this time, he thought, even Lana Bantry had met her match.

"Lana, there's no way you can win," Kenny said soberly. "No way at all."

"Yes, there is," Lana said, putting her outspread hands down flat on the top of her blond wood desk in a gesture of iron determination. Her nails were long and perfectly manicured, their color a rich and vibrant fuchsia. Her determination, from long years of use, was equally well honed and cared for. "Slash Steiner, if that's really who is behind this, is going to be sorry he ever heard my name."

"I'm afraid the situation is the exact reverse," Kenny said, thinking that Lana was the one who should be sorry that she had ever heard Slash Steiner's name. "You're talking about playing Russian roulette with a bullet in every chamber, Lana. Slash Steiner never loses."

"Neither, if you will remember, do I," said Lana, her blue eyes narrow as she thought bitterly of silver spoons and silver frames and an entire lifetime of being treated as second best.

I I
THE WOMAN
WITH NOTHING

From the last years of the nineteenth century until the fourth decade of the twentieth, Wilcom, Massachusetts, had been a thriving and prosperous community. Its economy had been dependent on the carpet mills and shoe factories that dotted the area and provided jobs, pensions and loyalties that extended through generations. By the mid-1950s, however, the carpet mills were beginning to shut down. One by one, they left New England and moved south to the Carolinas and Georgia, where labor was plentiful and cheap. By the early 1960s the shoe factories, too, were closing down, unable to compete with inexpensive Italian and Brazilian imports.

In the years since Russell Dahlen's brief romance with Mildred Neill, the men and women of Wilcom had inexorably been thrown out of work. The local economy stagnated and Wilcom became a depressed area—depressed economically and depressed emotionally. Anyone who could, moved away. Those who couldn't, stayed, barely hanging on.

Lana could not remember one good thing that had ever happened to her there.

The man Lana called father, Will Bantry, had always worked with his hands. He was a mechanic, a damn good mechanic, and he had worked for the Wilcom Carpet Mills for over fifteen years, keeping its machinery in top-flight operating condition. Will was a proud, honest, and hard-working man whose life had been turned upside down by forces outside his control.

Six months after the Wilcom Carpet Mills had shut down, throwing Will out of work for the first time in his life, his union had gone bankrupt. Will's pension, his only source of income, had abruptly ended and, thus, Will found himself without work and without money. He wanted desperately to work, but there was no work to be had. Because of his age and because of Wilcom's depressed economy, Will was never able to get another steady job.

At the age of thirty-eight, Will Bantry found himself in the devastating position of being financially dependent on his wife. He felt like an impotent cipher and Will's humiliation stained, infected and finally destroyed his personality. Although his wounds were invisible, he was as crippled as if he'd lost an arm or a leg. Alcohol, which had once been an occasional Friday night drunk with the guys at work, became a morbid and eventually fatal disease infecting him and everyone who came in contact with him.

Except for odd jobs and occasional temporary seasonal construction work, Will's income was at zero. His dependence on Mildred's earnings was virtually total and so, consequently, was his rage. When he had money, when he could beg it from Mildred, when he could steal it from her purse, he went to the local tavern and drank until the money was gone and only his frustration remained.

He would stagger home, wake his family, scream abuse at them and sometimes beat them. When he didn't have the money to sit in the tavern, he would sit in the small, shabby, brown-varnished living room, drinking cheap whisky, spewing bitterness and blame. Sometimes he went upstairs and got his hunting gun out of its rack. He would come back downstairs and wave it around threatening to kill everyone from the union president who had bankrupted the pension fund to Mildred's former boyfriend, the man who had robbed him of a perfect wife.

There were nicks in the living room woodwork where, when Will's rage had become uncontrollable, he had actually fired his shotgun. The next morning, shaking and hung over, Will would further demean himself with guilty apologies and pathetic rationalizations. He would promise never to drink again, never to go near the tavern again, never to allow a bottle in his house again. His promises would be good—until the next time.

In consequence of Will's behavior, Lana hated him, pitied him and was terrified of him. She felt sorry for him because of the way life had conspired to beat him down, but he didn't want her pity or her understanding. He lashed out at her and her mother, often blamed them for his predicament, and Lana spent her childhood trying to protect her mother from him, becoming, in a way, her mother's parent.

Lana's one dream, the one thing that kept her going, was the idea of rescuing her mother from Will. One day, she and her mother would leave Wilcom together and never, ever return.

When Lana was eight, she ran away from home for the first time. When she was eleven, she sold magazine subscriptions and cosmetics door-to-door and hid the money she made in the bottom of a box of Kotex so that Will wouldn't find it and spend it on liquor. When she turned thirteen, she lied about her age and got her first paying job in the Wilcom Kresge's, working for less than the minimum wage. On the same day that she got her first paycheck she opened her first savings account, depositing the entire eighteen dollars and thirty-six cents. Money, Lana had decided, was the way out of Wilcom. She would work and save every penny until she had enough to get out.

"When I go, I'll take you too, Mom," Lana promised, her eyes gleaming with visions of freedom and beauty. "We'll go away together and we'll be happy."

Mildred Bantry was a beautician, a woman who, like her daughter, had worked for as long as she could remember. Mildred had never resented having to work but she had never expected anything from a job other than enough money to pay rent and put food on the table. From a decent, devoutly Catholic working-class family, Mildred had been brought up to be obedient and not to expect too much from life. That way, Mildred's mother had pointed out to her, she need never fear being disappointed. Lana, on the other hand, rebelling against church, school and family, expected everything.

As soon as Lana realized that she could make more money from tips than she could behind the notions counter at Kresge's, she began to spend her after-school hours and Saturdays at the Cut 'n Curl where her mother worked. Too young to qualify for the license that would have allowed her to work on clients, Lana did everything else she could think of to make herself useful. She swept up, kept the shampoo bottles refilled, handed roller papers to the operators, mixed permanent wave solutions, answered the phone, made the appointments, worked up the books and fetched coffee and doughnuts from the nearby luncheonette. Although Lana was not paid a salary, the tips and the occasional cash pressed into her palm by the Cut 'n Curl's appreciative owner added up little by little.

In her spare time, using herself as a guinea pig, Lana tried out all the new hairdos featured in the trade magazines that came into the salon. Using double mirrors, she cut and styled her own hair, experimenting with all the current fashionable looks the top stylists were showing. Methodically, she tried every brand of permanent wave on the market and dyed her own wavy chestnut hair every shade the Cut 'n Curl stocked from Doris Day blond to Rita Hayworth red to Elizabeth Taylor brunette.

Lana had skillful hands that could execute the most complicated and sophisticated styles. Whether it was a Grace Kelly French twist or an Audrey Hepburn poodle cut, an Annette Funicello flip or a June Allyson bob, whatever hairdo Lana was wearing was the hairdo the customers usually requested. Their admiration was flattering and encouraging, but it wasn't enough.

Lana was much too smart, much too ambitious and much too angry to settle for a drab life in Wilcom. Her aspirations went far beyond hairdo magazines, small-town beauty parlors and marriage to one of the local boys she had grown up with. She dreamed of respect and independence, wealth and happiness, power and glory. She saw herself as a winner mistakenly trapped in a loser's world and had for as long as she could remember.

Lana grew up in a bitter house of shouts and silence. She could not understand why her mother continued to live with Will. She could not understand why her mother put up with the cruel words, the drunken slaps, the alcohol-fueled threats, the constant, unending worries about money. She could not understand why her mother was, no matter what outrages Will perpetrated, so blindly loyal to him and so protective of him.

"Why do you put up with him?" Lana asked from the time she was seven and old enough to have an opinion. "Why do you let him treat you that way?"

"Will wasn't always like this. He was still working when you were a baby. He had a good job at the carpet mill. He gave us food and a roof over our heads. He was wonderful to me at a time when no one else was," Mildred said, defending her husband and remembering the extreme gratitude she had once, a long time ago, felt toward him and, even now, still felt toward him. "In a way, he saved my life. I owe him something."

"You don't owe him your whole life," said Lana, thinking that she would never, not for one single minute, put up with a man who treated her the way Will treated her mother. "Why don't you leave him?"

"Where would I go?" Mildred asked, thinking that only the young could be as unrealistic as Lana was being. "And what about you children? You need a father."

"Not him!" retorted Lana. "I don't need him! He's horrible!"

"Stop that!" Mildred warned. Lana's angry, defiant words shocked and frightened her and Mildred was sometimes afraid that Lana, forceful and outgoing, would one day turn as fierce and as violent as Will himself. "Show some respect!"

"Why? What did he ever do to earn it? He doesn't deserve my respect!" Lana would say, lashing out. "I hate him! I wish he weren't my father!"

"Don't say that!" Mildred would reply sharply, shutting her lips tightly together and avoiding Lana's blazing eyes. "Don't you even dare think it!"

There is more than one kind of poverty. There is poverty of the imagination and poverty of the intellect, poverty of vision and poverty of spirit. Although, as a young girl, Lana was not aware of any of those kinds of poverty, neither did she suffer from any of them. She suffered, instead, from still other forms of poverty, from material poverty and emotional poverty.

The first, material poverty, was easy to see and easy to define. The penalties of material poverty were clear even to a child. They included the threats of bosses, landlords and bill collectors and the indignities, large and small, that came with not being able to pay your own way. Lana could see clearly what material poverty had done to Will and to her mother. Material poverty meant dependence and powerlessness, and it had deprived her parents of dignity and choice.

Lana would perceive material poverty simply as an obstacle to be overcome. The tools with which to overcome it were hard work, thrift and self-denial. From the day Lana opened her first savings account, she went to the bank religiously every week and deposited every dime she could into her savings account. Her savings account was Lana's most precious possession and her most fiercely guarded secret. No one—except her mother—knew of its existence. No one—except her mother—knew that, all along, Lana was planning her escape. Lana's savings account was the key, the way she would, one day, get out of Wilcom, the passport to a happy life for herself and her mother.

It was the emotional poverty of her childhood that Lana would not know how to provide for. With nothing but the movies and the true love magazines that came into the salon as a basis of comparison, Lana could not by herself either define or effectively deal with the injuries intentionally and unintentionally inflicted by an abusive father and an exhausted, overworked mother.

There were no banks, no savings accounts, no compounding of interest to heal those invisible and crippling wounds. Wounds that would leave Lana hungry and hurt and that would cause her to build a defiant and brave shell with which to meet the world, a shell that was both constructive and destructive, a shell that was helpful and hurtful, a shell that helped her get what she wanted but a shell that inevitably held people at a distance.

"You don't seem to have any friends. Don't you like the other children?" Mrs. Fiori, the seventh-grade teacher, once asked Lana. Marie Fiori was concerned about the blue-eyed girl who was always alone, who always lunched alone and spent play periods alone reading under a tree.

"I'm too busy. I'm not interested in friends," Lana said, coldly, cutting off the teacher's concern.

Lana had no intention of telling Mrs. Fiori that she could not invite the other children home because she never knew how drunk Will would be. She had no intention of telling her that the other children teased her mercilessly about always having her nose in a book and called her stuck-up and accused her of thinking that she was better than everyone else. She had no intention of telling her that she was never invited to parties, to get-togethers, to join the team, to go on picnics, outings or shopping sprees. No one liked her and Lana, in retaliation, told herself that she didn't like anyone, either.

Instead, Lana did what she always did. She headed for the Cut 'n Curl the moment school was over. At the salon, Lana fit in. At the salon, Lana was wanted and appreciated. At the salon, Lana found companionship and a way to earn money. The salon was all she needed.

Meanwhile, every time Lana got her hands on a bit of money, she went to the bank and made another deposit into her savings account. Week by week, she watched as the dollars and cents added up and the interest accumulated slowly but surely. By her senior year in high school, penny by penny, dollar by dollar, Lana had painfully saved almost four hundred dollars. All her sacrifices, all her self-denial, all the impulses rigorously stifled seemed more than worthwhile when ninety dollars turned into a hundred, a hundred and eighty into two hundred and two hundred became three hundred.

Five hundred dollars was Lana's goal. If she could save five hundred dollars, she would have enough. Enough to make her escape. Enough to get out of Wilcom. Enough to save her own life and, one day, her mother's, too.

III

COMMENCEMENT

Graduation day. It started out as the happiest day of Lana's life.

Top marks in the graduating class meant a chance at the cash prizes donated by local merchants, and throughout senior year Lana's nose was stuck in a book more than ever before. Lana's determination and hard work paid off as her marks, always good, became excellent.

The 80s that gradually turned into 90s excited Lana almost as much as the mounting sum at the bottom of her bankbook and Lana was absolutely thrilled when the long, grinding hours of study won for her the English, Chemistry, Social Studies and Algebra prizes—twenty-five dollars each. Each time her name was called at the graduation ceremonies, Lana jumped up in excitement and almost ran to the stage to accept the applause and congratulations and the envelope containing the cash prize that came along with them.

"We were proud to have you here at Wilcom High, Lana. You were an ornament to the school," said Oliver Gershen, the principal, in front of the whole assembly as he handed Lana her fourth and final prize.

Flustered, Lana blushed and blurted her thanks. One hundred dollars added to the four hundred in the bank made five hundred, the five hundred Lana had been saving toward since she had been eleven. All she could think about was that she was finally going to escape. She would get out of Wilcom and never come back. She would never have to see Will again, never have to speak to him again. She would get out! She would be free!

Lana had turned work into magic, the magic that would change her life and make her dreams come true. *Her* life was going to be different from her mother's life and *she* was the one who was going to make it different. Lana put the hundred dollars into her purse and clutched it tightly to her. Never had an achievement meant so much to her. Never had a prize been so avidly pursued and so ecstatically won. Never before had Lana so truly understood that, if she wished it, her fate was in her own hands.

Parents and graduates mingled on the lawn and one person after another came up to Lana and congratulated her on the prizes she had won and wished her good luck for the future. Her mother stood next to her, tears of pride in her eyes, and Lana glowed with a sense of accomplishment and confidence about the future. Silently, she kept repeating Mr. Gershen's words over and over to herself. They seemed strange and flowery to Lana but she treasured them because she had heard so little praise and been singled out so rarely for positive attention. There had not been many perfect days in Lana's life. Graduation day was one.

"Now we're going to celebrate," Lana told her mother. "I'm going to take you out to lunch at the Paul Revere. *My* treat!"

Lana and her mother, a party of two, got into Mildred's car and headed for the Paul Revere.

"Could we stop at the bank first?" Lana asked as they passed the Wilcom Savings Bank. "I want to close out my account."

Mildred knew that later that day Lana planned to take the Greyhound to Worcester where she would register at the Acme Beauty School. One day, Lana had confided, she would rescue Mildred from her terrible life with Will. Together, they would buy a salon of their own and make it into the best salon in Worcester. Then they would be free, free of Will, free of worry, free of the past.

Dreams of success and independence sparkled like fireworks in Lana's eyes and, as Mildred sat in the car waiting for Lana to come out of the bank, she tried to remember what it had been like to be sixteen with the world beckoning like a brightly wrapped Christmas package before her.

The Paul Revere Restaurant was decorated in the style of an Early American tap room and the waitresses wore long, colonial-style dresses and old-fashioned bonnets on their heads. There was a candle in a brass holder and a tiny dimpled glass vase of miniature chrysanthemums on every table. The big, comfortable captain's chairs had soft red leather cushions. The stiff, parchmentlike menu was enormous and had a silky red rope with a tassel on the end running through its center fold. The various dishes and the explanations underneath were printed in an Olde English script and the dessert menu was so extensive that it came on a separate card. The Paul Revere was by far the fanciest restaurant Lana had ever been in and, although she was intimidated, she refused to show it. She told her mother to order anything she wanted.

"You're not even allowed to look at the prices!" Lana told her mother proudly, her eyes gleaming. Between the five hundred hard-earned dollars in her purse and the brand-new dress she was wearing, a graduation present from her mother, a dress bought for once in a store and not homemade, Lana felt richer than Onassis, the equal of Rockefeller. Even if it was only for lunch, she and her mother could have anything they wanted. Anything! Clams, shrimp cocktail, Maine lobster, porterhouse steak, chocolate mousse, crepes suzette. Lana was giddy with the possibilities and almost drunk with her feeling of power.

"It's awfully expensive," Mildred said anxiously, glancing at the prices. She did not want Lana to spend any of her hard-earned money on her.

"I don't care. I can afford it," said Lana, knowing exactly what her mother was thinking. "And if you dare order something cheap, I'm going to send it right back!"

* * *

The lunch cost fifteen dollars, more than Lana had ever spent in her life for a meal, and it was worth every single penny.

"One day we'll eat out all the time. *Every* day if we want!" Lana promised her mother when they were back in the car. Lana's eyes were shining with excitement and pleasure. She had seen what it was like to be rich. She had felt what it felt like to be rich. She just couldn't wait to get started at Acme. She knew she would do well. She knew she would get a good job. She knew that one day she would get her mother out of Wilcom. She knew that one day all her dreams would come true.

Mildred dropped Lana off at home and then headed back to the Cut 'n Curl for her afternoon appointments. Lana watched her mother drive off and then went into the small, shabby house that seemed even smaller, even shabbier after the luxury of the Paul Revere and the world of fifteen-dollar lunches. Lana's suitcase was in her bedroom, already packed. She would pick it up, come back downstairs, tell Will good-bye and take the four o'clock Greyhound to Worcester.

"You! Get in here!" Will yelled, as Lana headed up the staircase. Her heart sank as she obediently stepped into the brown-varnished living room. She could tell by Will's voice that he'd been drinking.

Will Bantry had been waiting for her, a half-empty pint of whisky on the tan formica coffee table. While he had been waiting, Will had been thinking of his bitter life. His thoughts, like a record stuck in a single groove, dwelled on his lack of luck, lack of the breaks, lack of money. He thought of the youth that was gone, the opportunities that had passed him by, the wife he needed but resented, the kid that wasn't his. He had been ready for Lana the minute she walked in the door.

"Four thousand dollars I spent on you!" Will shouted the instant Lana stepped into the living room. He leapt up from the sofa and waved a ledger at Lana, an old fashioned one with a rough gray cloth binding. Lana had never seen it before in her life.

"See? I've kept a record of every cent I ever spent on you!" Will shouted as he rifled the pages of the ledger under her nose. Snowsuits. Undershirts. Vaccinations. Shoes. School supplies. The history of Lana's life in material objects flashed before her eyes on the green-lined pages. Dumbstruck, she stared at Will. She did not know what to say.

"Four thousand precious dollars I wasted on you! Four thousand dollars I dumped down the drain! I expect repayment—with interest," Will yelled, hot with outrage. "Starting now!"

"*You* spent? *You?*" Lana demanded, suddenly finding her tongue. She was shocked by his crazy demand. She had never heard of a parent keeping track of how much he had spent on a child, much less demanding repayment. And, above all, she had never heard such a lie! The money that had bought her food and clothes had not been his but Mildred's and Will knew it! "You never earned a dime! That money was my mother's money!"

As soon as the words were out, Will's bloodshot eyes turned wild and his alcohol-blotched skin turned purple with rage. Lana realized she had made a fatal mistake. She had reminded Will that it was his wife—and not he—who had supported his family. She had reminded him of his dependence, his impotence, his failure.

For a moment, they glared at each other, motionless, not even daring to breathe.

Then, without a word, Will slammed the ledger to the floor. Like a rattlesnake striking, faster than Lana had ever imagined he could move, he raised his hand and slapped her so hard that involuntary tears sprang to her eyes. As Lana staggered back, stunned and off guard, Will grabbed her purse and ripped it from her hand.

"You won a hundred dollars today, Miss Einstein! Don't you think you ought to give it to the man who supported you your whole life?" Will snarled, clutching the bag. Will had heard about the prizes from John and Kevin, who, as members of the high school band, had played at the graduation ceremonies.

Outraged, Lana lunged toward him, reaching for her bag as Will pulled it away. It wasn't just the hundred dollars in prize money! It was the four hundred she had been saving since she'd been eleven! Lana jumped up in the air and grabbed at her bag again. A tall man, Will dangled it tantalizingly just out of her reach and opening it, he pulled out her wallet and threw the purse to the floor.

"Let's see. How much have I got here?" he said, opening her wallet and taking out the bills. Will grinned when he saw how many there were and he began to count them slowly, torturing her. "A hundred, two hundred, five hundred." he exclaimed and smiled evilly. "Well, Miss Einstein, I guess I hit the jackpot!"

Man and woman, adult and child, father and daughter, they stood two feet apart and stared at each other with years of naked hatred in their eyes. The only question was, who was going to attack next—and how?

"That's my money! I worked for that!" Lana shouted, a moment later. She reached desperately for the money as Will slapped her away, hitting the side of her face again. He was a big, powerful man, but Lana pressed forward, ignoring the pain and grabbing at him, refusing to give up.

Sadistically, Will danced away from her, waving the money at her, holding it high up, just beyond her reach.

"Just try to get it!" he challenged, toying with her, weaving slightly, his bloodshot blue eyes not quite focusing.

"Give my money back to me!" Lana demanded, jumping up and reaching for the money.

In rage and frustration, Lana grabbed over and over for the money Will Bantry held just beyond her reach. Her money! The money she had worked for since she'd been eleven! The money that was going to get her out of Wilcom! The money that was going to save her life—and her mother's life! Lana jumped up, almost able to touch the bills, but Will, amazingly agile, spun away on tiptoe, taking pleasure in tormenting her.

Slowly, he put the money into his back pocket and, grinning at her with sadistic pleasure, buttoned its flap down tight.

"What kind of father are you anyway?" Lana screamed, furious with humiliation and betrayal.

"John and Kevin's" Will said, patting his pocket and naming Lana's brothers, the sons he knew were his. He picked up his glass, staggered toward Lana and almost tripped. He caught himself and drops of foul-smelling whisky sprayed her arm and her cheek. "Not yours, Miss Illegitimate!" he snarled, paying her back for her crack about it being Mildred's money.

Lana was silent, stunned for a moment. She was used to Will's drunken threats and crazy ideas and she didn't even know whether or not to believe him. Her face showed her contempt and her disbelief.

"You heard me!" Will shouted, wanting to rub it in. "You're not mine! You don't belong to me! You don't have one drop of my blood in your veins!"

Lana stared at Will as the meaning of his words slowly began to register. He was telling her that what she had always secretly hoped her entire life was true: that Will Bantry was not her father. That she had nothing to do with him. That growing up in the same house with him had been a horrible mistake.

Someone else was her father? Someone else had brought her into the world? Someone else's blood flowed in her veins? Will was nothing to her? Nobody and nothing? Lana was almost giddy with the sudden fantasies that flashed through her mind. She was royalty. The lost daughter of a king. Of an aristocrat. Of a famous movie star, a respected professor, a famous artist, a wealthy tycoon. Her mind went on and on, whirling a million miles a minute.

"Good! I'm glad! That's the best news I ever heard!" she finally said, lashing back. Lana had always thought deep down that she was an orphan, that she'd been somehow switched at birth, that the ugly house and the ugly scenes with which she'd grown up had all been a terrible mistake. Now Will was telling her that she'd been right all along!

"Who wants a nasty drunk like you for a father anyway!"

Will glared back at her, his eyes going into and out of focus as he made up his mind what cruelty to punish her with next.

"I married your mother just to give you a name!" he confided with a drunkard's cruel cleverness. A nasty smile hovered slyly around Will's mouth.

"Some name!" Lana said, rage and contempt making her fearless. She was enraged that Will had taken her money, contemptuous of the weakness that drove him to the bottle. "You'd think you were a Rockefeller or something!"

"It's a better name than that playboy your mother spread her legs for!" Will yelled and suddenly he came after Lana again, his big, calloussed hand raised. Terrified, she turned and began to run and then she stopped and turned to face him.

"Name? What name?" Lana demanded. "Playboy? What playboy?"

"Dahlen," Will said maliciously. "Ask your mother."

IV

SECRETS

With no regrets, with no backward glance, Lana left that hated house for the last time. There was nothing to hold her, no reason to go back, no ties to bind her. Tying her suitcase to the rack on the back of her old red bike, Lana headed straight toward Main Street. She would tell her mother what Will had said and she would find out whether Will was lying or not.

As she pedaled furiously toward the Cut 'n Curl, Lana was torn between devastation and elation, vindication and annihilation, regret and relief.

"Is it true? What Will said? That he's not my father?" Lana asked her mother, barely able to get the words out. She was breathless. Breathless from her battle with Will. Breathless with the fury of being stolen from. Breathless from her breakneck bike ride to the Cut 'n Curl. Breathless from excitement, and from the shock of what Will had told her. Lana faced her mother, barely able to wait for her answer.

For a moment Mildred thought about lying. Why rake up the past? Why open wounds that might never heal? Why unearth memories better left buried? On the other hand, why not? Wasn't Lana entitled to the truth? Didn't she deserve to know about her past? Didn't she have the right to understand why Will had resented her so much?

Mildred had kept her end of the bargain. It was not she who had told Lana about the existence of her real father. It had been Will himself. *She* had kept her promise for all these years. A thousand times Mildred had thought of telling Lana the truth. A thousand times she had remembered her promise. To have her secret finally out in the open was a relief.

"It's true," Mildred said softly and turned away to hide the sudden tears that pricked at her eyes. Sixteen years after Russell Dahlen had disappeared from her life, Mildred was still hurt by the inexplicable way her lover had abandoned her.

"His name was Russell. Russell Dahlen," Mildred confirmed after she had gained control of herself. "He was working as a trainee in a stockbrokerage company here in Wilcom. I met him at the coffee shop. I used to go there several times a day to pick up sandwiches and coffee for the clients at the salon. Russell went to the Eagle for lunch. We began to nod and then to speak. One thing led to another . . ."

As Mildred continued, she recalled not only the facts but the feelings, not only the circumstances but the emotions. She remembered Russell as a young man; she remembered herself as a young woman. He had been bored and lonely; she had been naive and dreaming of romance. He had been unhappy in a job he wasn't cut out for; she had been understanding and compassionate. He had a father he feared and wanted to please; so did she.

Mildred Neill and Russell Dahlen had shared many similarities. However, their differences had been even more intriguing, even more of a magnet.

Russell Dahlen was unlike any of the local boys Mildred had ever gone out with. He was charming and sophisticated and rich. He had graduated from Princeton. He had traveled to Europe. He knew interesting, exciting people. He lived in a world that Mildred had only the sketchiest notion of—a world where people did not have the grinding, bone-wearying problems of too little money and dead-end jobs and sick children and limited horizons that were the only everyday life Mildred Neill had ever known.

Mildred Neill was unlike most of the girls Russell had dated. She was unspoiled and unsophisticated, straightforward and uncalculating. She admired him and she looked up to him. She never challenged him or questioned him. She seemed to love him for who he was and not how much money he had. She had never heard the Dahlen name and was therefore unimpressed by it. She made him feel that the Dahlen money didn't matter. She made him feel that *he* mattered. She made him feel that he was somebody.

"Russell Dahlen made me realize that my world wasn't the only world. He seemed to be the one chance I had to get out of Wilcom," Mildred told Lana, admitting part of the reason for her attraction to her lover, a reason that Lana, of all people, could understand.

"Did you love him?" Lana asked. Her mother's answer was important to her. She wanted to feel that once, even if had been long ago, her mother had loved someone. She wanted to feel that once, even if it had ended badly, her mother had been happy.

"Yes. I was madly in love with him," Mildred said with a smile Lana rarely saw, a smile that lit her entire face and allowed Lana to see how appealing her mother must once have been. Then Mildred's expression turned serious again as she went on.

"At least I thought I was madly in love with him. It was so long ago. It's hard to remember. Perhaps, though, I confused love with a way to get out of Wilcom," Mildred said, trying to sort out the feelings that were still jumbled, still confused. She had been so young then and it had been so long ago. She had been a different person then, innocent and inexperienced, and it was hard to remember what she had thought, what had gone through her mind. "But he didn't love me. At least, not enough. When I told him I was pregnant, he told me he was married. I didn't know until then that he had a wife. He offered to pay for an abortion."

"An abortion! He wanted to kill me?" Lana said suddenly, all fantasies of a long-ago romance disappearing as she realized that her real father, this Russell Dahlen, had wanted to kill her even before she had been born.

"I was shocked at the idea! I absolutely refused! 'Never!' I told him, 'Never!' " Mildred said, wishing she hadn't let it slip out about the abortion. Now the words were spoken. Now it was too late. "I wanted my baby. I wanted you."

Once again, Mildred's eyes filled with tears. Lana reached out to touch her but Mildred, unwilling to feel any more emotion, brushed her hand away.

"Did you ever regret it? Were you ever sorry you had me?" Lana asked, after a moment.

"Never!" said Mildred passionately. She loved Lana. She loved her even more because of the sacrifices she had had to make for her and the shameful secret she had promised to keep just to give her a name and a place in the world. "Never! Not for one single minute!"

Lana put out her hand to touch her mother and this time Mildred did not push her away. Mother and daughter stood closer together than ever, touching and touched, going to the point of tears and then beyond in a moment of utter silence.

"Have you ever heard from him?" Lana asked softly. She did not use the name but Mildred knew who she meant. The two women were talking in the small back room of the Cut 'n Curl where the supplies were kept and the coffee brewed. The smells of shampoo, permanent wave solution, half-burnt coffee and cheap whisky would always remind Lana of the betrayals and revelations of her high school graduation day.

"No," said Mildred. "Not since the day you were born. Will warned him not to come and he forbade me to have anything to do with Russell. Will even refused to let me accept money to help bring you up, although Russell offered."

"How could Will do that!" exclaimed Lana, in shock at the extent to which Will had caused her life to be even unhappier and more difficult than it had to be.

"His pride . . ." said Mildred sadly. "Will was once a proud man."

"You mean my father, my real father, offered money to help bring me up?" asked Lana, wanting to make sure that what she scarcely dared believe was actually true: that there was someone, somewhere, who cared about her.

Mildred nodded.

"Do you think he'd be interested in me? In how I turned out?" asked Lana tentatively.

"Of course. I'm sure he is. I'm sure the reason he never tried to get in touch with you is that he was afraid of Will," said Mildred. "Will threatened to kill Russell if he ever saw him again."

"Do you know where he is now?" asked Lana. Once again she didn't use the name. Once again, she didn't have to.

"In New York, I suppose," replied Mildred. "At least that's where his family is from. Are you going to look for him?"

"I'd like to," said Lana shyly.

"Are you sure you want to rake up the past?" asked Mildred, not sure if it was a good idea. "We haven't heard from Russell in so long. I don't even know if he's alive. I don't want you to get hurt any more than you've been hurt."

"I want to meet my father," said Lana, determinedly. "I'd like to know what he's like. But I can't go right now anyway. I can't afford it," said Lana bleakly, thinking that not only had Will stolen from her but he had fixed things so that her real father had never once come to see her.

"But what about your savings?" asked Mildred. "What about your prize money? Couldn't you use that?"

Lana shook her head and bit back tears.

When Lana finally got the words out and told her mother about the ledger and the five hundred dollars, Mildred nodded silently. What could she possibly say about the brutalities the bottle brought out in Will? Like Lana, Mildred knew that Will was probably already at the tavern, drinking up the money Lana had worked years to save.

A normally undemonstrative woman, Mildred Neill Bantry embraced her daughter for a moment, holding her tight. Then she released her and went to the owner of the Cut 'n Curl and asked for a fifty dollar advance on her paycheck. She handed the money to Lana and apologized that it was so little.

"I wish I could give you back the five hundred dollars," Mildred said, pressing the money into Lana's hand.

"It's OK, Mom," Lana said in a wavery, determined voice, accepting the money and putting it safely into the zippered compartment of her purse. "I've made up my mind. I'm going to go to New York and find my father. He'll help. He'll want to help."

Using part of the fifty dollars her mother had given her to pay for the ticket, Lana took the Greyhound to New York City. Her face was reflected back to her in the big window next to her as afternoon faded and turned into night. As the bus headed south toward a strange city and an unknown father, Lana's emotions careened wildly as if on a runaway roller coaster. The reality of what Will had told her in his drunkenness and what her mother had confirmed in the supply room at the Cut 'n Curl had finally sunk in.

Lana's initial feelings of righteous fury toward Will for stealing her money had turned to a profound sense of abandonment. She had hated Will for all the years she had thought he was her father. Ironically, now that she knew he wasn't her father, he suddenly didn't seem worth hating and Lana felt a strange, unfamiliar void. Where the hatred had comfortably and reassuringly dwelled, there was now a gaping vacancy.

Her emotions about her real father rushed in to fill that void. Lana's expectations soared as she imagined how happy Russell Dahlen would be to find her and how proud of her he'd be when she told him how well she had done in school, how she had won more academic prizes than anyone and how the principal had told her that she had been an ornament to the school. She dreamed of how impressed he'd be when she confided her dreams for the future and her plans for owning the nicest salon in Worcester.

Russell Dahlen would smile in approval. He would take her into his arms and into his life and she would finally have what everyone else had: a real father and a real family and a place in the world she could feel proud of.

*   *   *

As the Greyhound approached the Triboro Bridge, the air turned noticeably warmer and the fresh smell of grass and trees was replaced by the urban smells of fuel exhausts and polluted water. Maybe, Lana told herself in a last-minute failure of nerve, her mother was right. Maybe she shouldn't try to rake up the past. Maybe she was just asking to get hurt some more. After all, her father had wanted her dead. He had wanted her mother to have an abortion.

Maybe she shouldn't even get off the bus. Maybe she should stay right on and hand over her return ticket and go back home. Will would have sobered up. He would greet her with apologies and remorse, with solemn, sincere promises never to touch a bottle again. Maybe he'd even give her back the money he hadn't yet drunk up. Maybe, this time, things would be different.

But then again, why would they? Lana knew better. When it came to Will and the bottle, things were never different.

Even if Will gave her back the money he hadn't drunk up, Lana had been through the cycles of abuse and regret, threats and apologies, cruelty and remorse much too often to believe any more promises. Her mother was wrong, she thought. Food and a roof over your head were *not* enough. Food and a roof over your head were what they gave you in an orphanage.

Outraged at the way life had made her mother willing to settle for so little, Lana's indecision once again turned into determination as the bus headed into the center of the city and Lana realized that she knew one thing for certain. She realized that she would never forgive herself if she got scared and went back to Wilcom because, if she did, she would end up like her mother.

Lana got off the bus and tried not to think about what she was seeing: the pimps and whores and drug addicts who made the Eighth Avenue bus station a nightmare come true. Dragging her suitcase with her, Lana went to the row of phone booths and found a torn, tattered directory. Dahlen,

Russell. There it was. The name was real and the address was the most expensive there was, right on Park Avenue. Number 999 Park.

Lana dialed the number and when Russell Dahlen came to the telephone, he knew immediately who she was.

"I knew you'd call one day," he said, sounding happy to hear from her. "I hoped and prayed that you would."

Russell Dahlen's voice was warm and pleasant and he said that of course he wanted to see her. As soon as possible. He asked if she would meet him at his office. He gave her the address and said that he would be there in half an hour.

Lana hung up in ecstasy. Russell Dahlen had known exactly who she was. He said that he had hoped and prayed that one day she would call. He said that he wanted to see her right away. As soon as possible, he had said!

Her mother's concerns had been for naught. Her own last-minute fears had been ridiculous. She was welcome in Russell Dahlen's life. From the happy way he'd sounded, she was *more* than welcome! Everything was going to be fine! Everything was going to be perfect!

V

DIFFERENT
WORLDS

Wall Street had no building more elegant than that which housed Lancome & Dahlen. Luther Dahlen and Hamilton Lancome, Sr., had bought it at a bargain price during the thirties and in the intervening years had turned down increasingly large offers for the property. Designed in Greek Revival style by Haynes Whittier Apthorpe and built of white granite in 1873, its columned façade and stately proportions made it an architectural masterpiece, a state of place as well as a state of mind, a structure that spoke of prestige, money and tradition.

The name of the company that owned it, Lancome & Dahlen, was chiseled into the white marble over the broad double doorway in elegant Roman letters. A uniformed security guard, obviously instructed to expect her, opened the heavy front door for Lana as she stood there, unable to find a bell and not quite sure whether or not a knock would be heard.

"You're here for Mr. Dahlen?" he asked. His red potato face was Irish, Lana knew. An Irish face that was, like Will's, no stranger to the bottle. An Irish face that had been in the basement sipping whisky when Slash Steiner and Pete Oney had quietly let themselves into the building through the employee's entrance.

"I'm Miss Bantry," Lana said nervously. The awe Lana felt at the sight of the palatial building rendered her almost tongue-tied. Through the partially opened door she could see shimmering marble floors and polished antique furniture. She felt she had wandered into a palace, not an office building, and the stirrings of intimidation she had felt at the Paul Revere earlier that day were multiplied by a thousand. She felt awkward, out of place and inferior. She was filled with an unwelcome surge of resentment at the comparison she couldn't help but make between the physical evidence of her father's riches and the relentless, remorseless life-draining financial struggles with which she had grown up. The endless self-denial, the constant penny-pinching, the always ending up with second best and doing without had all been unnecessary.

"Mr. Dahlen's already here," the watchman replied, cutting off Lana's thoughts. "He's waiting for you upstairs."

With a gesture, he directed her toward the stairs and Russell Dahlen's second-floor office. Picking up her suitcase, Lana, sick to her very soul at the unnecessary unhappiness and deprivations of her childhood, began to mount the stairs.

As Lana made her way up the ornately carved, exquisitely curved staircase, the evidence of her father's weath mounted. She caught enticing and tantalizing glimpses of the polished Chippendale, the massed bouquets of fresh flowers, the English landscapes, the working fireplaces and the rich Oriental carpets that decorated the private rooms and offices. Lana had never heard the word Chippendale, did not know the names of the English nineteenth-century landscape painters and was unfamiliar with the terms Shiraz and Kirman. Yet the sense of wealth and luxury, safety and security was overwhelming and, as Lana reached the top of the staircase, she could not help but be profoundly bitter at the way fate had so cruelly cheated her.

As Lana came to a stop at the landing, a man came out of the office at the very end of the wide, richly carpeted corridor. He was tall and well built with even, clean-cut features. His wavy chestnut hair was just like her own. He wore an elegant dark suit and conservative silk tie and Lana found it hard to believe that she was in any way related to this man who looked so rich and so invulnerable that he might almost have belonged to another species of being.

"Lana?" Russell Dahlen asked, realizing that she was his daughter and that he didn't even know her last name.

"You're Russell, aren't you?" Lana replied, putting down her suitcase. She had decided on "Russell" on the bus. She had decided that she wouldn't call him anything as formal as Mr. Dahlen. On the other hand, she certainly couldn't call him father, either. At least not yet.

"Yes. I'm Russell Dahlen. I'm your father," he said, sounding terribly formal and very distant. His voice on the phone had been warm and pleasant. He had sounded so happy to hear from her. Now everything was completely different. His tone was tentative, his faint smile cool and remote.

Inside, deep down, Russell Dahlen knew instinctively that the girl facing him was his daughter. The person he saw, however, a person with flaming red hair who carried a shabby leatherette suitcase and wore a uniquely unbecoming, garishly colored cheap dress, was someone he didn't know or recognize. She came from a world he didn't know, a different world of which he had no experience. She seemed an alien being to whom he could have no possible connection.

Having spoken, Russell stood there motionless, still shocked at the sight of the stranger who faced him. For a moment, he had an overwhelming sense of being trapped by the past and by a child he didn't know. He didn't move toward Lana. He didn't extend his hand to shake hers. He didn't open his arms to her and, as father and daughter hesitated for a moment suspended in time, Lana was suddenly bitterly aware that she wasn't at all what he had expected or hoped for. In some way, she knew but didn't at all understand, Lana sensed that she was a terrible disappointment.

The moment of silence dragged on uncomfortably and it was Lana who finally spoke.

"Some father," she said bitterly, remembering how he had wanted the abortion. Putting down the suitcase, she walked toward him and, glaring at him, dared him to love her.

* * *

"I've often thought about you," Russell said, inviting Lana into his private office. Sitting opposite her, he took a good look at her. Except for Luther's broad, intelligent forehead, she didn't even look like a Dahlen. She was small and curvy and her eyes were a brilliant sapphire blue like her mother's. Her hair was a raw hue of red and her dress, obviously brand new, was too tight and too bright. Russell was ashamed to admit even to himself that he was embarrassed by the sight of her but he was. He was glad that he had invited Lana to the office, where no one he knew would see them together. "I've thought about coming to Wilcom to see you."

"Then why didn't you?" Lana challenged immediately, even though she knew the reason perfectly well. She hung on to her anger fiercely. Her anger protected her against other feelings, feelings of being inferior and inadequate, feelings of being a terrible disappointment to this rich and powerful man. "It's on every map."

Russell raised his eyebrows in a surprised salute. She was bright, he realized. And quick.

"Touché," he said with a wry smile.

Lana had never heard the word before and, feeling defensive and intimidated, she stared at Russell belligerently. His intention had been to compliment her and to acknowledge her point. Lana, however, had interpreted his unfamiliar word and self-mocking gesture as derision and dismissal. It would be the first of many misunderstandings between them.

"I didn't come to see you because I was afraid of your father," Russell said, wanting to explain his behavior and realizing immediately that of course he didn't mean father. "I mean . . . Mildred's husband," he amended, realizing that he didn't even know whether or not Mildred had married.

"Afraid?" asked Lana contemptuously. "Of that drunkard?"

"He threatened to kill me," Russell said, remembering the checked lumber jacket, the smell of whisky, the pink receiving blanket that told him that his other child was a girl, too. That he had failed not once, but twice. The sound of a shotgun echoed in Russell's memory even after all these years. "I wanted to come. I wanted to know you. I wanted to take care of you. But there was no point in getting shot. Surely you must understand."

"No, I *don't* understand!" said Lana, growing agitated. She moved back and forth aggressively as she spoke. "Not at all! After all, you *are* my father. You could have called. You could have written. You could have acted as if you knew I was alive!"

"Your mother warned me not to," Russell said, confirming what Mildred had said earlier. "She was afraid of what he might do. Not only to me if I ever came to see you or tried to get in touch with you. She was also afraid of what he might do to you."

"He already did plenty! He made my life miserable," Lana said, verging wildly between anger and tears. "He yelled at me and he cursed me for as long as I can remember. He told me I owed him four thousand dollars and then he stole from me!"

Russell raised his hands in a gesture of compassion.

"I'm sorry. So sorry. It must have been terrible for you," he said, appalled at what Lana had just told him. "Now that you've come to me, perhaps I can try to make it up to you. Perhaps we can . . ."

As Russell spoke, Lana jumped up suddenly, cutting him off in midsentence.

"Do you smell smoke?" she asked, moving swiftly toward the door.

As Lana spoke, she pulled open the office door and looked out into the hall. She saw that in the large area behind the elegant offices, there was an open bullpen filled with desks and filing cabinets. Fires blazed in the wastepaper baskets and were already spreading toward the curtains.

"Fire!" Lana screamed as Russell, now smelling the smoke himself, jumped up, too. "The office is on fire!"

"There's a bathroom through that door," Russell told Lana, pointing toward the door behind his desk. "I'll call the fire department. Meanwhile, wet some towels. We'll put them over our faces to protect ourselves. We'll use the front stairs . . ."

As Lana turned to follow her father's instructions, her hand accidentally brushed the sleeve of his jacket. Acting from an instinct so deep and so profound, an instinct he could neither control nor resist, Russell suddenly reached out and took her into his arms.

"I'm sorry," he said, overcome by regret and sympathy. There were tears in his eyes and his voice caught. "I've thought of you so often. Can't we make up for the past?"

"I don't know," Lana said, choking on her own sudden tears. "How could I? After the way you treated us?"

"I felt I had no choice," said Russell, once again defending himself, once again explaining his absence. "It wasn't only my safety I thought of. It was your safety, too."

As Russell spoke, a young man, realizing there was someone in the private office at the end of the hall, came running around the corner and down the carpeted hall. He had die-straight dark hair, pale skin and piercing gray eyes. Russell Dahlen had never seen him before, and Lana would never forget him.

It was obviously he who had started the fires that were beginning to spread out of control and threaten them all. He looked dangerous and determined and for a moment both Lana and Russell feared for their lives.

Lana pulled away from her father's embrace and ran toward the bathroom as the young man stood in the office doorway and Russell Dahlen found himself face to face with a dangerous-looking stranger who knew his deepest, darkest secret.

"Who are you? What do you want?" Russell demanded. His fingers went to his tie in order to straighten it.

"I could ask you the same thing," the young man replied arrogantly. He had seen the embrace and he was aware from the guilty way Russell Dahlen straightened his tie that he had interrupted a pretty hot scene. He looked at Russell brazenly, realizing that he had caught the rich bastard at a highly embarrassing moment and wondering how he could use his knowledge.

"Lana!" said Russell, addressing her over his shoulder as she stood there, stock still. "Hurry!"

Lana turned and ran toward the bathroom as Slash Steiner realized that he had the goods on the man who had fired his father.

A few moments later Russell and Lana stood safely on the sidewalk, thanking God that they had gotten out of the burning building unharmed, although Lana's suitcase and everything in it had been destroyed. Russell flagged a passing taxi and, opening the door, helped Lana in.

"We'll have lunch tomorrow. At one o'clock," Russell told Lana closing the door behind her. "In the dining room of your hotel."

"Take the young lady to the Roosevelt," Russell told the driver crisply, handing him a bill and cutting off his complaint about going off duty. Then he handed Lana another bill through the open window, the first hundred dollar bill she had ever seen in her life.

"That's for the room and your expenses," he told Lana. "Tomorrow we'll begin to get to know each other. After lunch, we'll spend the afternoon shopping. We'll replace your suitcase and everything that was in it. I owe you a great deal, Lana, and one way or another, I'll try to make it up to you."

With that, Russell Dahlen headed back to the building his father had bought thirty years ago, the building that was in flames. The building that was his heritage, his responsibility, his legacy, his burden.

Lana did not sleep that night. Too much had happened. From the meeting with her father to the fire that had almost killed them both. From the promise to make up for the past to the hundred dollar bill so casually thrust through a taxi window. From the loss of all her material possessions to the discovery of a different world. From the shock of confronting the criminal who had wanted to burn the building down to the luxury of the hotel room, the first one Lana had ever been in in her entire life.

Lana tossed and turned. Got into bed and got out. Sat in the comfortable upholstered chair and opened all the drawers in the pretty little desk. Took a bath in the unfamiliar luxury of a bathroom that was all hers. Tried to remember all the things that had happened and tried to understand.

There were a thousand questions Lana wanted to ask her father. Had he really wanted to kill her? Had he loved her mother? Why had he come to Wilcom on the day she had been born? Was he married? Did he have any children? Did she have a sister she had never met? A brother she didn't know?

Lana couldn't wait until the next day to ask the questions that burned at her. Russell Dahlen was her father; yet he was a stranger. She wanted to know everything about him, to get to know him, perhaps even to love him and one day to have him love her. Through him, Lana hoped to reclaim the identity that fate had so cruelly ripped away from her. The identity that meant that her father was no ordinary drunkard but someone kind and loving, rich and powerful, the identity that meant that she, too, was someone who deserved a chance to be happy.

VI
ONE O'CLOCK

ana went downstairs at dawn, anxious for one o'clock. She spent the whole morning exploring the city. The rich shop windows of Fifth Avenue, the elegant buildings along Park, the bustle of Madison, the well-dressed businessmen, the sleek-looking career girls all seemed to belong in a movie, not real life. The motion, the vitality, the energy of the city was a magnet for Lana and she dreamed one day of being part of it. More than any other single thing, though, Lana was enthralled by actually seeing the famous beauty salons that, until then, had just been names in magazines like *Vogue* and *Harper's Bazaar.*

She stopped at Michel of Paris, Enrico Caruso and Enzo de Perugia. She made mental notes of the decor, the stylists' uniforms, the attitude at the reception desk and, above all, the kind of hairstyles clients were leaving with. She paused at Kenneth's—he was famous for doing Jackie Kennedy's hair—and dropped in at Helena Rubenstein's Fifth Avenue salon, where Michel Kazan was the star stylist. As Lana stood in front of Elizabeth Arden's salon looking into the window, a woman emerged from a limousine and the uniformed doorman opened the famous red door for her. Lana, too intimidated to enter the imposing mansion, caught a glimpse of the elegant marbled and chandeliered interior. Just walking into a place like that, Lana thought, would make a woman feel special. One day, she promised herself, she would own a salon as beautiful, a place so magical that by simply entering it, women would feel important.

Glancing at her watch, Lana returned to the Roosevelt Hotel anxious to begin the rest of her new life.

Lana glanced around as she entered the hotel dining room, disappointed to see that Russell Dahlen wasn't already there, waiting for her. She checked her watch against the big clock over the reception desk and saw that it was right on time. Both said that it was exactly due. When the headwaiter approached, Lana said that she would wait.

"I'm meeting someone," she said, proud to be in the city, proud to have an appointment, proud to have, at last, a father she could be proud of. A father who cared about her.

At five past one, Lana told herself that Russell was caught in traffic. At ten past one, she suddenly wondered if perhaps there was another dining room in the hotel. Could she be in the wrong dining room? However, when she asked, she was told that there was only the coffee shop.

Russell Dahlen was not there, either.

At quarter past one, the early stabs of disappointment began to curdle Lana's mood and she stopped making excuses for Russell's tardiness. She began to wonder if Russell Dahlen had had second thoughts about getting to know her.

It had been clear from the expression on his face and the tone of his voice that she was, in some way, a terrible disappointment to him. Was it her hair? Her clothes? The suitcase she carried? It couldn't have been anything else because, at that moment, Lana hadn't said a single word. Russell Dahlen didn't know one thing about her and about what she was like. All he knew about her was what he could see.

Lana felt guilty about mentally accusing her father of such snobbish superficiality and she began to wonder if he had forgotten that he had said that he would meet her for lunch at one o'clock. Could an appointment that meant so much to her be so insignificant to him? Could she have been that unimportant to her father?

Could she have been *such* a disappointment? Lana couldn't even think about that without beginning to cry.

* * *

Standing by the headwaiter's station, feeling increasingly embarrassed and awkward, Lana sternly told herself that she was being too critical, that she was judging prematurely and too harshly. She fought back the tears and the disappointment. She told herself that Russell couldn't possibly have forgotten.

Hadn't he said that he would try to make up for the past? Hadn't he specifically said that they'd have lunch and then spend the afternoon shopping? Hadn't he made a point of promising that he'd replace her suitcase and everything that was in it? He hadn't been the least bit vague, Lana reminded herself. He had been very definite.

Still, no matter what Lana told herself, the weight of Russell Dahlen's failure to arrive grew steadily heavier. At twenty past, embarrassed at the way people in the dining room seemed to be staring at her, Lana squared her shoulders and, as if she had urgent business, retraced her steps to the coffee shop and walked through the entire lobby. Russell Dahlen was nowhere to be found.

At twenty-five past, unwilling to give up hope, Lana asked at the front desk if there were any messages for her.

The reply was negative.

At one-thirty, Lana telephoned the office of Lancome & Dahlen but the switchboard informed her that, due to fire, the offices were temporarily closed. When she telephoned 999 Park Avenue, a maid told her that Mr. Dahlen was at the office. When asked if she wanted to leave a message, Lana couldn't think of what to say and, in a failure of words and courage, had mumbled no and hung up. Then she went back to the dining room and asked the headwaiter one more time if anyone had come by and asked for her while she had been gone.

"No," the headwaiter replied, feeling sorry for her. She had apparently been stood up and it obviously hurt. "No one."

* * *

Still refusing to think the worst of her father, Lana went out to the reception desk and asked once again if there were any messages for her.

"No," the clerk replied, looking through the boxes and reminding her that she'd bothered him just ten minutes ago. "Nothing."

"You're sure?" asked Lana timidly, afraid that if she offended him too much, he'd tell her that she had no message even if she *did* have one.

"I'm sure," he snarled. He had the physique of a marshmallow and the demeanor of a bureaucrat. "You've got eyes. You saw the box yourself. It's empty."

"Could you please check again?" she asked with as much authority as she could muster.

"I said there are no messages, miss," he replied, heavy and huffy. "Don't you understand English?"

He turned away and walked off, leaving her alone.

All sorts of angry and bitter vengeances passed through Lana's mind as she checked out of the hotel, paying for the room with the hundred-dollar bill her father had given her the night before. She thought of going to 999 Park Avenue and waiting until Russell Dahlen returned and then confronting him at his home, embarrassing him in front of his family. She thought of waiting for him at his office and embarrassing him in front of his colleagues. She thought of hiring a lawyer and suing him for money and recognition. However, Lana's fantasies of vengeance vied with the realities of her situation. Obviously, the plain fact was that, no matter what Russell Dahlen had said in an emotional moment of reunion, her father wanted nothing to do with her.

Lana was afraid that if she went to 999 Park Avenue and confronted Russell that he would say that he did not know who she was and call the police and have her bodily removed. If she went to the office, she was sure she would be refused admittance and thrown out. She realized that she didn't even know a lawyer and that, if she did, she had absolutely no money with which to pay one.

She remembered with bitter clarity the moment in which Russell Dahlen had first seen her and she had realized from his voice and his expression that she was not what he expected, not what he wanted. She would not force herself where she clearly wasn't welcome. She had suffered enough humiliation in her life at the hands of Will. She would not invite further humiliation at the hands of Russell Dahlen.

Instead, Lana decided that she had been foolish to try to resurrect a history she had never been a part of. She decided that she would do the wise, the adult thing. She would do what her mother had done: she would let the past stay locked away and buried.

Russell Dahlen, Lana decided, was a coward, afraid to face the daughter he had ignored for sixteen years, and a snob who judged people by their looks and clothes. Sixteen years ago he had been unable to stand by her mother when she had needed him and today he was unable to face his daughter. Russell Dahlen wasn't even, Lana told herself in disgust, worth hating. Despite his money and his fine clothes, Russell Dahlen was not one bit better than Will Bantry.

Lana left the Roosevelt and told herself that one day she would be back. One day she would be part of the city whose energy and glamor had already addicted her. One day she would be someone her father would long to know. One day, when he came to her, she would shut the door in his face. One day, when he needed her, she would treat him the way he had treated her. One day, she would make him feel the way she felt.

Humiliated. Insignificant. Unimportant. Unloved.

Lana boarded the Greyhound, heading back for Worcester and her original plan. She was, she thought bitterly, a woman with nothing. She was leaving New York with even less than she had when she had arrived the evening before. Her suitcase had been burned in the flames along with all her clothes. Except for what she wore and the purse she carried, she owned nothing. She was a woman who had been deprived of everything: of money, of possessions, of a father, of love.

There were, Lana told herself, refusing to indulge in self-pity, far worse destinies. However, as the bus headed north, Lana wept and wept, unable to stanch the tears that came and came as if from a limitless reservoir of pain. No matter how hard Lana tried, she could not think of what those destinies might be.

VII

SILVER

AND PLATINUM

It was another freaky New York story and Lana's bitter tragedy was someone else's pathetic comedy.

That morning, because the subway stopped in the middle of nowhere between Union Square and Grand Central for half an hour, Ruby Goldstein was almost twenty minutes late for her job operating one of the two switchboards at the Roosevelt Hotel. Her boss, Peaches Barton, who was no peach, looked up sourly as Ruby took her place at the switchboard already lit up like a Christmas tree because of the big aluminum siding salesmen's convention that had taken over the hotel for the week.

Ruby waited for Peaches to scream at her, but Peaches, busy at her own board, never had the chance to say a word. By noon, swamped with calls all morning long, Ruby had not even had her morning break. She was looking forward to lunch, not to mention a visit to the ladies' room, as she got up and stretched.

"If you go to lunch," Peaches said, addressing Ruby for the first time. "Don't bother to come back."

Ruby hesitated for a moment. She needed the job. And even if she lost the job, she would need the reference.

"I'm going to the john," Ruby said.

"Then you're fired," said Peaches who hadn't been able to stand Ruby from Day One. Because she smoked. Because she snapped her gum and cracked her knuckles. Because she took off a million cockamamie Jewish holidays that Peaches bet even rabbis didn't take off. Because when she didn't show up because of a religious holiday, she didn't show up because she had the cramps, the flu or the pip. Good riddance to bad rubbish was Peaches's opinion. And not a moment too soon at that.

"Well, screw you," said Ruby, picking up her purse and deciding that for the kind of crummy job she could get she could fake a reference anyway. "*And* the hotel you work in!"

With that, Ruby picked up the entire stack of messages she had taken that morning, put them into her ashtray, lit a match to them and, when the blaze was going to her satisfaction, marched out, heading straight for the ladies' room. At least she'd get a free pee out of them before she left, she thought as she flounced through the lobby and made up her mind to use a slug in the pay toilet.

Peaches took the cardboard carton with the now-cold morning coffee she had been too busy to drink and drowned out the small fire. The messages were reduced to a pile of soggy ashes. She hoped to hell that none of the messages was about the Russians invading Chicago or the atomic bomb blowing up Seattle because, if they were, everyone was in big trouble. Fortunately for the inhabitants of Chicago and Seattle, none of them was.

One of them, however, was a message from Russell Dahlen for Lana. Since Russell hadn't even had time to learn his daughter's last name, he had asked that the message be delivered to her in the dining room promptly at one o'clock. The message said that, due to the fire at Lancome & Dahlen which would keep him busy all day, their appointment would have to be postponed. In his message, Russell Dahlen told Lana to stay on at the Roosevelt, that he would pay for it, and that he would telephone her again just as soon as he had the chance. He also asked her to leave a home phone number or address where he might be able to reach her in the future.

Russell Dahlen spent the entire day with the fire marshals, insurance adjusters and his partners, dealing with the fire that had burned out the interior of the Lancome & Dahlen building the night before. However, as Russell answered questions and decided company policy, his mind kept returning to Lana.

Russell had gotten over his initial shock at first seeing his daughter. He was ashamed at the way he had judged her so quickly by the narrow standards that had been formed by the only world he had ever lived in. With a bit of time to revise his judgment, Russell realized from her cheap dress and shabby suitcase that money was obviously a problem. He knew from her harsh New England accent that she hadn't been able to go to the best schools. He could imagine what she must have thought when she entered the Lancome & Dahlen building and inevitably compared it with what she was apparently familiar with. Russell remembered Wilcom as a sick and dying town, as a place where people struggled without much hope. In view of that, Russell could now understand her anger and her resentment toward him and he wanted to try to make it up to her in every way he could. With help. With money. With acceptance. Perhaps, one day, with love.

Russell called the Roosevelt at four o'clock, the first free moment he had all day. Not even knowing his daughter's last name, but needing somewhere to start, Russell began with the supposition that Lana might have adopted her mother's name. He asked the clerk to check the register for Lana Neill.

"Sorry," the voice replied. "No Lana Neill."

Russell thought for a moment.

"Can you check first names? Lana is an unusual name."

The clerk turned Russell over to the reservations manager.

"There *was* a Lana registered," she said after a moment. "Lana Dahlen. She's checked out though."

"Did she leave an address?" asked Russell, touched at the way Lana had used his name.

"Only the one she registered under," said the manager. "It's local—999 Park Avenue."

"Did she leave a forwarding address?" asked Russell, saddened at the further evidence of Lana's longing.

"No, none."

"A telephone number?"

"I'm sorry, sir. No telephone number."

Russell thanked the manager and hung up. The stranger who was his daughter had left no name, address, or telephone number at which he could reach her. According to the Roosevelt's records, she had paid for the room in cash. There was not even a check with a bank address that might lead him to her.

Lana had, Russell realized, simply appeared from nowhere, borrowed his name and his address, and then disappeared to nowhere. Even though he had asked her to leave a number and an address, she hadn't. Russell realized then how much she must have resented him. How much she must have hated him. He hadn't been much of a father and Russell, more than anyone, knew it all too well. Perhaps, he told himself, he shouldn't have been so afraid. Perhaps he should have confronted Will. But the fact was that he hadn't. Because he was afraid for himself, for Mildred, for Lana. And because he was ashamed of himself for what he had done and for what he had failed to do.

Nevertheless, despite the years of his apparent indifference, Lana had looked for him and found him. Now, driven by guilt and longing, Russell decided that he would look for her. Even after all these years, Russell still remembered Mildred's mother's phone number from sixteen years before when he and Mildred had been madly in love. Russell Dahlen began his search for his daughter by calling that long-ago number.

"No Mrs. Neill here," said the voice that answered, the voice of a teenaged girl. The theme from *A Summer Place*, haunting and evocative, played in the background.

"I'm looking for her granddaughter. For Lana," said Russell. "She has red hair."

"No Lana here neither," the girl added and hung up. For the next three hours, the phone was busy.

At midnight, Russell gave up. Tomorrow, he would begin again.

* * *

As soon as she could, Lana went to the public library in Worcester. She looked through the microfilms of the *New York Times* starting with 1944, the year in which she had been born. From its pages, she learned that Lancome & Dahlen had been founded in 1926 by Russell Dahlen's father, Luther, a man who was, Lana realized, her grandfather. She also learned that Russell Dahlen had a daughter who had been born in the same year and the same month that she had. A girl whose name was Dolores. A girl who had been born with a silver spoon.

Like Slash, Lana would be haunted by a photograph in a silver frame. Like Slash, Lana would not forget the photograph on the cabinet in Russell Dahlen's office. The photograph that was autographed *To Daddy with love.* The photograph of a girl with blue-black hair, a girl who had everything while Lana had had nothing. A girl who had a name and a place in the world, fame and fortune and, most of all, a father.

Lana hated that father for what he had done to her. She hated that girl, a girl who had everything she should have had, even more.

Several weeks after she got back to Massachusetts, Lana bleached her hair the palest shade of platinum available as a way of distancing and differentiating herself from the dark-haired half-sister she so bitterly resented and so desperately envied. The platinum hair would become Lana's trademark. A badge of identity, a declaration of independence, a sign of determination because, on the night she had met her father and discovered that she had a sister, Lana had glimpsed a different world, a world she was determined, one way or another, to conquer. A world, she was determined, that would notice her and pay attention to her. A world that would praise and love her. A world that would give her everything she had never had. Her father's riches. Her sister's privileges.

VIII
LOVE AND
WORK

*A*lthough the calendar said 1960, the mood was very much that of the fifties. Although a new decade had begun, the attitudes of the previous decade continued to reign, and Lana was no more exempt from their influence than anyone else.

Nineteen sixty was the year the Pill, the pacemaker and Valium made news, but their real impact on everyday life remained very far in the future. Hair was teased and bouffant and bras and shoes both had stiletto points. The miniskirt and the pants suit, uniforms of the sixties, were yet to be designed, manufactured, sold and accepted by millions and millions of women. Men wore their hair and their sideburns short and their boxy suits were cut of gray flannel.

The icons of the sixties were still waiting in the wings of history. Jane Fonda's image was that of Barbarella: a blonde bombshell with falsies and false eyelashes. The antiwar crusader nicknamed Hanoi Jane and the exercise guru with the bionic body were more than a decade away. The Beatles were playing to rowdy audiences in dank and dingy Liverpool cellars, and Jackie Susann had yet to write that emblematic best seller of the sixties, *Valley of the Dolls*. Timothy Leary and H. Rap Brown, Martin Luther King and Billie Jean King, Twiggy and Betty Friedan may have been already doing their thing, but they were doing it in obscurity.

On television, cosy domesticity, white-bread style, both set and reflected the mood of the times. Lucy was America's favorite housewife, and Ozzie and Harriet were still bringing up David and Ricky. Bubble gum music dominated the *Cash-box* charts with gems like "Itsy Bitsy Teenie Weenie Yellow Polka Dot Bikini" and "Teen Angel." The Stones and Jim Morrison, growling and snarling revolution and sex, had not yet been heard from. Although scientists had just developed the laser, it was romance that was on everyone's mind. Liz was still wed to Eddie and Royal Wedding Fever gripped the country as Princess Margaret married a commoner, Anthony Armstrong-Jones.

In 1960, modern men still wanted an old-fashioned woman around the house. In 1960, the only women who worked were women who had to. The only jobs they could get were the ones men didn't want and the few women who hired other women didn't treat them any better than men did.

Within four hours of arriving in Worcester, Lana found two jobs. The first was in a shabby-looking beauty salon on Main Street called the Beauty Box. The second was in the Frostee Cone across from the bus stop. Located between a tavern and a five-and-ten-cent store, the Beauty Box had three stations, a manicure table and a Help Wanted sign in the window. It was owned by a tough-faced bleached blonde named Rose Scorvino, whose cigarette seemed permanently glued to the corner of her mouth.

"Two bucks an hour. Cash. Off the books," Rose told Lana, after she called Cut 'n Curl in Wilcom to ask if they'd ever heard of Lana Bantry. "You supply your own uniforms and you split your tips with me. You understand?"

Lana nodded unhappily.

She understood perfectly. She understood that it was an outrageously unfair offer and that she had no choice. Lana had used what was left of the hundred dollars Russell Dahlen had given her to pay for a room in Esther Flynn's boarding-house on Elm Street around the corner from the Beauty Box. Other than that, thanks to Will and thanks to a burglar and arsonist who had stumbled into the offices of Lancome & Dahlen at the worst possible moment, Lana had nothing. No money and no possessions. The only clothes she owned were the ones on her back.

Lana could not afford to wait and she could not afford to be choosy. She accepted Rose Scorvino's offer and started work at the Beauty Box that same afternoon. Memories of raised expectations and dashed hopes, of a father found and an identity lost, of silver spoons and silver frames were still fresh, still brutally bitter in her mind.

Rose Scorvino had a hard little body and a hard little mind. Like Mildred and like thousands of other women who labored in pink-collar jobs, Rose had worked hard for as long as she could remember and never gotten anywhere. She had no money in the bank and no future and no prospects. She had divorced two husbands and outlived the third. Her son had been killed in a motorcycle accident when he'd been a teenager. Her daughter, whose parking lot attendant husband had left the house one day never to return, was struggling to support two young children by working as a cocktail waitress in Boston.

Life had indeed been tough for Rose and it had made her cynical and suspicious. Like Will, she had a sharp, critical tongue; like Will, she was eternally convinced that she was being cheated—out of money, out of respect, out of a day's work for a day's pay.

"I know how many customers come in here a day," Rose warned Lana at six-thirty on her second day of work when Lana dutifully divided the tips with her. "The least anyone dares tip is a quarter. If I catch you holding out so much as dime, you're fired! You understand?"

Lana nodded. "I understand."

What Lana understood was that without money, life was brutal. That without money, there were no choices and no options. She remembered a building so rich it was like a palace and she contrasted it to the shabby place she worked every day. She remembered an elegant father and a photograph of a beautiful stepsister in a polished silver frame and felt the poison of hatred and resentment.

Lana did all the things for Rose that she had done back home at the Cut 'n Curl. She swept the floors, scrubbed the shampoo basins, polished the mirrors, kept the shampoo and conditioner bottles refilled, answered the phone, kept the appointment books, helped the clients on and off with their coats, got them coffee from the percolator in the back room and doughnuts from the nearby bakery, watered the snake plants in the window and passed out movie magazines to clients under the driers. She also shampooed, occasionally set hair, sometimes brushed out a set and even, now and then, gave a permanent although, until she had her license, touching a client was technically illegal.

At night, after the salon had closed, Lana worked the 7 P.M. to 2 A.M. shift, dishing out Frostee Cones in vanilla, strawberry, coffee and chocolate plus the flavor of the day. Not wanting to spend a cent that she didn't have to, Lana subsisted on coffee, doughnuts and all the Frostee Cones she could eat.

As soon as Lana had saved enough money, she registered at the Acme School of Beauty Training. In order to attend the thirty hours of night school a week, Lana had to quit the evening shift at Frostee Cone and, instead, worked there only on Sundays and Mondays, juggling her two jobs and night school. It was physically exhausting and a financial squeeze, but Lana gritted her teeth and stuck with it, knowing that one day a license would be well worth her struggles.

Working harder than she had ever worked in her life, Lana completed the thousand hours of training in hairstyling, permanent waving and straightening, cutting, tinting, shampooing and manicuring in the minimum time of eight months. She received no mark in any class lower than 97. Once again, she graduated at the top of her class. Once again, no father came to her graduation ceremonies, proud to applaud her achievements.

"I want a raise. I got the best marks in the class," Lana told Rose as soon as she had graduated. "I want to keep my tips and I also want to be put on the books now that I have my license."

More than anything else about her job at the Beauty Box, Lana had hated working off the books. She had had enough of being a second-class citizen. It reminded her too painfully of being Will Bantry's shunted-aside stepchild and Russell Dahlen's ignored wrong-side-of-the-tracks child.

"I'll give you a five-dollar raise and you can keep your tips, but no way I'm going to put you on the books," Rose said, hands on hips, eyes squinched against the smoke that rose from her cigarette. Rose was resigned to the raise and the tips. Like hell was she going to cough up Social Security, withholding and the rest of the bullshit. She wasn't running General Motors, just a small-town beauty parlor. "It'll cost me a fortune."

"I don't like working off the books. It's not legal," said Lana in her first show of independence. Now that she had a license, she wasn't so completely dependent on Rose and her job at the Beauty Box.

Rose glared at her. She had never much liked Lana, even though she was honest, reliable and a hell of a good worker. There was something about Lana that said that she thought she was better than anyone else. Lana had a way of acting that made Rose feel that she was looking down at her.

"Legal!" exclaimed Rose, spraying ashes down the front of her uniform in her outrage. "Who the hell do you think you are? J. Edgar Hoover?"

"I just want to be treated properly," said Lana firmly, standing her ground and playing her ace. "Since you won't give me what I deserve, I'll work for someone who will. You're not giving me any choice. I'm going to take the job Ed Hilsinger offered me last week."

Ed Hilsinger's salon, Vogue Beauty, was the fanciest and most expensive in Worcester and Ed himself had a reputation as a fair employer and a nice man to work for. Everyone at Acme had hoped to work at Vogue Beauty. Ed Hilsinger was, like many small-town salon owners, a family man who found that owning and operating a salon was an excellent way of supporting his family. From the first day Lana, her luxuriant, shoulder-length platinum blonde hair gleaming and arranged in a sensuous Veronica Lake dip, came to work at the Vogue

Beauty Salon, Ed knew that Lana Bantry was the one-in-a-million kind of hairdresser every salon owner dreams of.

She was good with her hands and good with people. She was honest, smart, reliable and creative. She could do everything from delicate double-process color to the kind of shampoo with scalp massage that clients loved. As one of the few beginners who had both a beautician's license and several years of salon experience, Lana drew a better-than-average regular salary. Her tips, because the clients liked her so much, were generous and Lana saved every single penny.

"Nice to see you, Lana," Lorraine O'Day, the teller at Worcester Savings would say every Monday morning at nine sharp. Lorraine had become one of Lana's clients and had a standing appointment every Friday at five-thirty, just as Lana had a standing appointment—made with herself—to add to her steadily growing savings account. "The truth is, I can set my watch by you."

In just the same way she had once pored over textbooks and homework, Lana now studied the beauty trade magazines Ed subscribed to. She kept abreast of the newest styles and products, the latest trends in salon design and decoration and the most modern notions about employee training and salon management. By the time Lana had turned seventeen and was going on eighteen, she had a thousand ideas about how a salon should be run and what it should look like. With Ed's encouragement, she quickly began to put those ideas into practice. When Ed mentioned that the salon was going to be painted on Monday, the day it was usually closed, Lana had an idea.

"Why don't we paint it pink?" she asked, recalling the interior she had admired in New York at Michel of Paris. "It would be much more feminine than the beige we have now."

The new rosy-pink paint was very pretty and extremely flattering. Clients said that they loved it and their enthusiasm gave Lana another idea.

"Have you seen these mirrors?" Lana asked Ed, showing

him an ad in *Modern Salon* magazine. "The ad says that they're polished in a special way that softens wrinkles and lines. They're not really that much more expensive than the regular kind."

Business had improved since the salon had been repainted and Ed was in the mood to go along with almost anything Lana suggested. The customers loved the way they looked in the new mirrors. They liked the pretty new pink shampoo gowns Lana had stitched up on Mrs. Hilsinger's sewing machine, the free samples of shampoos and conditioners that the beauty supply salesmen gave Lana and which Lana passed along to the customers. They liked the soft music Lana kept on the radio and the Friday and Saturday afternoon fashion shows she arranged with Worcester's dress shops.

By the time Lana had worked for Ed Hilsinger for eighteen months, business had almost doubled. Ed had hired two more stylists, raised his prices and given Lana two raises. He was beginning to worry that she would take one of the other jobs that were now being regularly offered to her.

"I have a chance to buy another salon," Ed told Lana in the fall of 1962. "It's sort of rundown now but I can buy it at a good price. I'd like you to manage it for me," he said, offering her still another raise.

"I'd like the job," said Lana firmly, "but not the raise."

Ed looked at her, not sure he had heard correctly.

"Did you say you don't want the raise?" he asked, his thick eyebrows shooting upwards toward the sky. Ed was shocked. In the more than twenty years Ed Hilsinger had been in business, no one had ever turned down a raise.

Lana nodded.

"I'll work for my current salary and fifty percent of everything I bring in the way I do now, but I'd like ten percent of the overall profits," Lana said, telling him the idea she had gotten from an article about a profit participation plan in *Today's Salon*. "It'll be a good deal for you now because there won't be any profits for a while and you'll save the amount of my raise. It'll be good for me because I intend to make your second salon just as successful as this one and I'm willing to take less now to make more later."

"You're a good businesswoman," Ed said, impressed by Lana's willingness to put off an immediate raise for future profits. In the end, if she were successful, she would make much more money. "You're very smart about money."

"I come from a poor background. I better be," Lana said. "Now, tell me, what salon are you planning to buy?"

"The Beauty Box. It's not doing well and Rose Scorvino wants to sell," Ed told her with a grin. "I think you worked there once."

Lana knew that Rose would resent her—and she didn't care. She knew that Rose would try to give her a hard time—and she didn't care. Business was business and, for Lana, business came first. The first thing Lana did was tell Rose that from now on, everything would be on the books—including Rose's own salary since Rose wanted to stay on as an employee.

"No way!" said Rose, almost choking on her Lucky. "I'm not giving Uncle Sam a dime of my hard-earned money."

"I'm sorry, Rose, but that's the way Ed and I do business," said Lana. "If you don't like it, you'll have to leave . . ."

Rose hesitated for a moment and glared at Lana suspiciously.

"I suppose I have to split tips with you, too?"

"No," said Lana. "Your tips are yours to keep."

Rose squinted at her cynically from behind her screen of cigarette smoke.

"You're sure?"

"I'm sure," said Lana.

Then she informed Rose that there was to be no more cigarette dangling from her lower lip while she worked on clients and that she was to smoke only in the supply room during her breaks. She also told Rose that her old dye-stained uniforms would have to go. They were to be replaced by fresh, spotless ones. In addition, Lana informed her, her dark roots would have to be regularly touched up.

"Your own hair should be an example of what the clients can expect," Lana said.

Rose, by now too shocked to argue, simply nodded.

"Now why don't you start by cleaning up the counters behind the shampoo basins and Windexing the mirrors?" Lana said briskly. "Your first client is due in at ten."

The next thing Lana did was, literally, clean the place up. She swept it out and waxed the floors, threw out the dog-eared movie magazines, scoured the ladies' room, threw away the dusty snake plants and, that Monday, painted it the same pink as Michel of Paris.

"It's still a dump," Lana told Ed a month later. The old clients were continuing to patronize the Beauty Box but, despite Lana's clean-up efforts, the salon was not drawing any new business. "If you can let me have a three-hundred-dollar advance, I can make some changes that will attract new clients."

Little by little, getting her ideas from the trade magazines she read religiously and using her memories of the big New York salons she had seen on the day she had still had dreams of having a real father and a real family, Lana fixed up the Beauty Box. She installed pink Formica counters, new flooring that looked like pale marble, strings of flattering chrome makeup lights, the same polished mirrors she had bought for Ed and comfortable, cushy chairs in cream-colored vinyl.

Almost half of Lana's former customers eventually followed her to the Beauty Box and gradually, as word of mouth got around about the salon's face lift, new clients began to come. After eight months, Lana told Ed that it was time to raise the prices. A year later, when the tavern next door went out of business, Lana suggested that they rent the vacant space. It would double the size of the salon.

"We have enough business to warrant another stylist," Lana told Ed, going over the books with him. "I also want to add a manicurist on Fridays and Saturdays. According to my figures, we'll be able make an additional two and a half dollars per square foot."

* * *

No matter how much money she made, Lana always wanted to make more. She had not given up her dream. She still wanted a salon of her own. She still wanted to save her mother from her dead-end life. She still wanted to live her own life in the different world she had glimpsed in New York. She still wanted to hurt her father as he had hurt her and she still wanted, one way or another, to outdo the half-sister who had all the things Lana felt she should have had.

Lana got the idea for her first real success from the private-label brands of detergent and cleanser that she bought in the supermarket in order to save money. She shared her idea with Tom Morello, the Premiere Beauty Supplies salesman who served the Worcester region. What Lana wanted was a private label shampoo and conditioner. What she wanted to do was to sell them in the Beauty Box.

What Tom wanted was Lana. She was a dazzler and a knockout. She looked like someone who belonged in the movies. She had a body that just wouldn't quit and platinum blonde hair that looked like a movie star's. She was, without doubt, absolutely the most glamorous girl Tom had ever seen. But her looks were only the beginning. Besides being utterly, traffic-stopping gorgeous, Lana was clearly a go-getter and her ambition and industriousness ignited Tom's own half-formed dreams.

Tom Morello knew what he was and he was tired of it. He was sick of being a small-town second-rater, tired of getting B's instead of A's, fed up with being a minor leaguer when he might have been a major leaguer. All his life Tom had heard that he had potential. So far, though, he had never figured out a way to fulfill that potential. He knew he could do better than he had been doing. Much better. The more he got to know Lana, the more time he spent with her, the more he watched her in action, the more he thought that, with Lana as an inspiration and a helpmate, he might be able to achieve the success he thought he deserved but that, so far, had eluded him.

* * *

"I can guarantee that I'll buy fifty dollars' worth a month *if* I can get what I want," Lana told Tom, sketching out her plans for the private-label products. As always, when talking business, Lana was intense and single-minded.

"I want dispenser-top plastic bottles," she continued, oblivious to her effect on Tom, his hormones and his dreams. "The shampoo should be packaged in an eight-ounce size and the conditioner in a four-ounce size."

Lana had learned from her clients that most of them shampooed in the shower and that screw-off tops accidentally dropped into the tub were a pet peeve. She had also noticed that women tended to overuse conditioners, which left their hair heavy and greasy. Lana realized that if she packaged twice the amount of shampoo to conditioner and instructed her clients to make sure they started and finished both bottles at the same time, they wouldn't overuse conditioner—and she would make more money.

"You really know what you want, don't you?" said Tom, impressed at the way Lana had everything already figured out.

"It's my business," said Lana earnestly, concentrating on her idea, seeing in it a way to add to her income. "I'd be in a lot of trouble if I didn't know what I wanted. And, by the way, I want both the shampoo and the conditioner scented with rose. Women love the way it makes their hair smell."

Lana also knew exactly what kind of label she wanted. Shocking was the pinkest pink there was and that was the color Lana chose for her label. Shocking pink and a border of red roses.

"Women love pink," she told the staff designer at the printing shop, knowing from hundreds of conversations with clients just what women liked and didn't like. "And roses are a sign of love."

Women, Lana had learned, were suckers for love. She, personally, had more faith in money and her most important relationship was still with Worcester Savings.

Lana began to use the private-label brands exclusively, and right away the clients commented on how good the shampoo and conditioner smelled and how shiny and well behaved their hair seemed. They said they wished they could use the same rose-scented products at home. All Lana had to say was that the items were for sale at the cash register. For as long as a client sat in her chair, Lana had, she realized, a captive audience. She did not intend to let the opportunity for a single sale pass her by.

Lana made a point of selling the private-label shampoo and conditioner for twenty-five cents less than the regular brands. To introduce her new shampoo and conditioner, Lana gave every client a fresh red rose with her first purchase and a free bottle after every fifth purchase. The private-label shampoos and conditioners quickly outsold the other brands and soon were the only ones Lana stocked in the salon.

"Why don't you let me sell them at Vogue Beauty, too?" asked Ed, impressed by Lana's hustle and seeing in the private-label products another profit center for Vogue Beauty. Lana agreed, and her income from the private-label products quickly doubled.

The Beauty Box and Vogue Beauty were soon two of Premiere's best customers. Tom, knowing a good thing when he saw it, gave Lana's idea about private-label products to his other accounts along with the pink-and-red label Lana and the designer had worked on. Lana, flattered that Tom thought so much of her idea, gave him her permission.

The specially packaged, rose-scented private-label products sold almost as well for other salons as they did for the Beauty Box and Vogue Beauty. Tom, whose commissions were increasing every month, was making more money than ever.

"I can hardly handle all the business," Tom told Lana happily. Tom had always felt that he was destined to be successful. With Lana on his side, the kind of success Tom felt he could achieve was suddenly within his grasp. He was thrilled that he had finally done something that was turning out well. "The paperwork is going to kill me."

"Why don't you let me represent the line for you in Worcester?" Lana suggested immediately, pointing out that,

that way, she'd be taking on a lot of the paperwork. "I already sell to Vogue Beauty. We can split the commissions fifty-fifty."

"As long as the boss goes along, you've got a deal," said Tom happily. Lana could handle Worcester. He'd have more time to devote to the rest of his territory. It sounded like a good deal all around. Tom showed Lana how to do the paperwork, gave her a stack of Premiere order forms and told her that the boss had gone along with the idea. The boss's name, Tom told Lana, was Stan Fogel.

"Stan's a real go-getter, too," said Tom admiringly. "And tough as nails. You two would really speak the same language."

Then he asked Lana if she'd like to have dinner with him when the Beauty Box closed.

"We could go to a movie after, if you want," Tom added, thinking of the local drive-in where the action in the cars was always better than the action on the screen. Somehow, he promised himself, he would get through the iron curtain that Lana Bantry seemed to have built up around herself.

IX
LOVE AND
ROMANCE

*L*ana *married Tom Morello on a Monday in June 1964*
at Worcester's town hall. The bride glowed with happiness,
but it was the groom who was bursting with pride. Tom
Morello had, for once in his life, reached out and up and
gotten what he wanted. Success, the big, head-turning success
Tom had always known would be his, seemed to be in reach
at last.

The adored son of working-class parents, Tom had always
done well at everything he had tried. His successes, though,
in school, in sports and in business, had always had limits.
Tom was always able to get halfway up the ladder. The
problem was that he inevitably seemed to fall short of climbing all the way to the very top. Tom had been a star first
baseman of his high school team. He was good with the
wood, good with the leather, but his dreams of getting a pro
contract with a major league team never quite materialized.

"The kid has talent, all right," the Red Sox scout told
Tom's father, "but he's got an attitude problem, too."

Tom, the scout continued, didn't seem as hungry as some
of the other young prospects. He was not as willing as they
were to hustle, to put out, to hew to the discipline professional sports demanded. The Pirates' scout agreed and so did
the Braves' scout. Tom blamed the coaches for being too
tough and for bad-mouthing him. He told himself that if he
just waited the scouts would see for themselves just how
talented he really was.

In the classroom, Tom coasted along easily with straight

B's. With a bit of extra effort, the guidance counselor told him, he could get A's and be admitted into a top college like Brown or even Yale. Tom, however, wasn't so sure that college interested him and he stuck with the B's, knowing that he had no reason to be ashamed of anything. When Tom graduated from high school, he attended the State University at Fitchburg for two semesters and then, deciding to return to his first love, sports, dropped out.

Tom played first base for the Danbury semipro team for the next two years, but the major league scouts who had once been interested now told Tom that he was too old. They were busy signing promising young prospects right out of high school. When an uncle told Tom that he was wasting his time chasing a ball, Tom reluctantly agreed.

Tom's off-season job as a salesman in a sporting goods store also seemed a dead end. When the same uncle told Tom that he could get him a sales job with a company owned by a friend of his, a friend who had made a fortune selling permanent waves to beauty parlors, Tom thanked him, grateful to have another chance.

He had blown college and he had blown his athletic ability. Not that Tom saw it that way. He just said that he hadn't gotten the breaks. The new job would be different, Tom knew. He'd paid his dues. This time, his luck would change.

Sure that this time he would succeed, Tom took the job at Premiere. He had looks and charm to spare and he knew that selling was basically just a matter of getting people to like you. And at *that*, Tom knew, he was a genius. When he first met Lana, he had just turned twenty-six and was beginning to think about getting married and starting a family. The people who knew Tom best thought it was a good idea.

"You ought to get married and stop whoring around" was the way his cousin Freddy put it.

"Get married, at least," joked Tom whose pattern of limited success had one dazzling exception: women. With women, Tom never failed, and he didn't fail with Lana.

"Married?" said Lana ecstatically, when Tom proposed.

She felt like a starving woman who had just been offered a feast. "Do you really mean it?"

Tom Morello was Lana's first boyfriend. The boys in Wilcom had found her too snobbish and too standoffish. The ones she had liked had ignored her; the ones who might have been interested, she dismissed. Tom was the first man who paid extravagant, almost obsessive attention to Lana and she was dazzled by him.

Tom was dark-haired and dark-eyed and extremely handsome. He had long, long black eyelashes and a gypsy's wild, exotic appeal. His good looks, his beautiful clothes, his smooth way with words and his sensitive, oh-so-sensuous hands made him seem almost too good to be true. He told Lana that her eyes were the blue of a summer sky, that her hands were so beautiful an artist would long to paint them. He sang romantic songs into her ear when they danced and he never arrived for a date without a gift: a bouquet of flowers, a love poem he had written especially for her, a bottle of toilet water or a pretty piece of jewelry. For the first time, Lana felt the stirring of romance. For the first time, she didn't sneer when people talked about love.

Beneath the charm and the glamour, Tom also seemed to have substance. He had a good job and, as he told Lana over and over, he dreamed of a much better one not too far in the future. He was sure that one day, with just a few breaks, he could really be somebody. In the meantime, he was doing well at Premiere and already making a good living. He told Lana that his boss really seemed to like him.

"Stan hinted that I might have a chance to make assistant sales manager," Tom told Lana, sharing his ambitions with her. If he got the promotion, Tom said, he'd have a title, a fancy office, a company car.

"Who knows," he said tenderly, putting his arms around her, "maybe you'll even be married to a vice president one day."

Tom was filled with romance and dreams that, this time, seemed as if they might really come true.

* * *

Together, Lana thought and Tom agreed, she and Tom could and would have everything: health, wealth and a happy family. Money would not be a problem the way it had been when she was growing up because both she and Tom worked and were good earners. They both wanted children, and several of them. In addition, Tom's parents had been married for thirty-two years and, to Lana, the stability and obvious affection in their marriage was another good omen.

"My sisters are already talking about our parents' thirty-fifth anniversary party," Tom said with an indulgent smile as he told Lana about the huge party that had marked their thirtieth.

"I'm looking forward to *our* thirtieth," said Lana, thinking that her future seemed brighter than she could possibly have imagined. For a while, Lana even forgot about the life she had been cheated out of and the girl who had everything she should have had, too. Shared dreams and shared happiness were an antidote to the poison of envy.

Tom and Lana got married in a civil ceremony at the town hall. After, Mildred took them and Tom's family to lunch at the Paul Revere. Will attended neither the ceremony nor the lunch after. Lana was glad.

"He'd only have gotten drunk and ruined everything," Lana told Mildred. "We'll live happily ever after. And so will you. I promise," she said and kissed her mother.

Tom and Lana's honeymoon was the typical hairdresser's weekend of Sunday and Monday. They spent it in Lana's single bed in her small room in Esther Flynn's Worcester boardinghouse. The sex was, as usual, spectacular and there seemed no need for conversation since Lana and Tom so obviously agreed about everything.

They were so much in love.

They didn't need to talk.

Their lips and their bodies said it all.

Tom wasn't an athlete only at first base.

* * *

At four-thirty on the following Friday afternoon, Tom surprised Lana by arriving unexpectedly at the Beauty Box. He presented her with a passionate kiss and a large gold foil-wrapped box of chocolates to celebrate their one-week anniversary. Then he asked her where she wanted to have dinner that evening and named two of the most expensive restaurants in Worcester.

"After dinner we'll go to the movies," Tom said, planning their evening. *"The Spy Who Came in from the Cold* is playing. I want to get a load of Richard Burton. I want to figure out what Liz Taylor sees in him."

"That's sweet of you, but I can't leave here," Lana said, thinking that Tom was very romantic but completely unrealistic. She was solidly booked until seven o'clock and Tom knew it. Beside, Lana couldn't help but wonder why Tom wasn't still out calling on accounts. It wasn't even five and all the salons stayed open until eight on Friday nights. Shouldn't Tom have been working, too? Shouldn't he have been calling on customers, taking orders, servicing the accounts?

"I'm booked all afternoon," Lana said, telling Tom that she couldn't just drop everything and leave the Beauty Box. "I can't just dump my clients."

"But you *can* dump your husband?" Tom replied, obviously hurt. He was shocked that his wife didn't automatically put him first.

When Lana wouldn't change her mind and leave the Beauty Box early to go out with him, Tom, unaccustomed to being turned down by a woman, left by himself. All he wanted was to have a good time and to share it with his new wife whom he adored. However, if Lana wasn't interested in having some fun, Tom was sure that he could find someone who was. He did not come home until four that morning.

Six weeks later, when, for the second month in a row, Lana got her period right on schedule, Tom was disappointed.

"I was hoping we'd made a baby," he said unhappily,

coming out of the bathroom where he'd seen the newly opened box of Tampax on the bathroom shelf. "We sure did plenty of work on it."

"But we just got married," Lana said, thinking that babies were a few years away. Lana wanted to put some more money in the bank before she got pregnant. She didn't want their baby to grow up in a household filled with financial struggles the way she had. She took it for granted that Tom felt the same way, too. "I can't get pregnant now. You know that Ed and I have been talking about my buying the Beauty Box from him. We've just about reached an agreement. If everything keeps going along smoothly, we'll probably sign the papers soon. If we do, I'll be busier than ever. I won't have time for a baby for a few years."

"Hey! I didn't get married just for some legal screwing," Tom said, turned off by Lana's answer. He did not even bother to reply to Lana's big news about her approaching agreement with Ed Hilsinger. Tom was already sick and tired of Lana's constant talk about the ins and outs of her negotiations with Ed and all the changes and improvements she'd make if she ended up buying the Beauty Box. All Lana could talk about, it seemed, was the goddamn Beauty Box and how much money she could make.

Tom wanted a wife, not a business tycoon. He wanted someone to support him in his career, not be obsessed with her own. He wanted someone like his mother, only younger, of course, and sexier. He didn't mind if Lana had a job, but she should put him first. It was the way Tom had grown up. It was the way everyone Tom knew had grown up.

"I got married to have a family," he said bleakly, not comprehending Lana's obsession with success and money. Wasn't he enough for her?

"So did I. I didn't say I didn't want babies. I only said that right now just wasn't the time," said Lana, wanting to soothe him. After all, they didn't disagree about anything. Just the timing.

Torn between her desire for financial security, her love for her husband, her wish to have children and her drive to be successful, Lana stopped using her diaphragm. She decided to let fate make the decision for her.

By the time Tom and Lana had been married for five months, they were a marriage counselor's nightmare. Their union was a spectacular mismatch. They disagreed about everything: money, sex, children, family, and leisure. Neither was wrong, neither was right. Tom and Lana saw life differently, their values were different and so were their ambitions and expectations.

Stan Fogel did not expand Tom's territory as Tom had hoped, and when the job of assistant sales manager came up, Tom found out that he had never even been considered. The job went to the man who covered New Hampshire and Vermont. Tom was furious and felt that Stan Fogel had been stringing him along.

"Stan's a bullshitter," Tom complained bitterly. "I'll never believe a word he says again."

Lana, however, wasn't sympathetic. She was on Stan Fogel's side.

Lana thought that Tom just plain didn't work hard enough, and she and Tom began to argue incessantly about what she now saw as Tom's laziness and what Tom saw as Lana's obsession with work and the way she delayed gratification and sacrificed present pleasure for the future.

In addition, Tom's charm had worn very thin very fast. He no longer sang in Lana's ear when they danced. In fact, they no longer danced. The love poems, Lana had learned, had been copied from Hallmark cards, and the costume jewelry and toilet water seemed corny and pathetically inadequate in the face of the serious problems they and their marriage now faced.

X

LOVE AND
MARRIAGE

"*You live and die for that goddamn salon!*" Tom swore when Lana told him she wouldn't be able to leave work early on a Saturday afternoon so that they could go to Tom's high school reunion back home in Danbury. Tom wanted to show off the turquoise Thunderbird he'd just made the down payment on.

Lana had no interest in nonsense like high school reunions. She had more important things to think about. She and Ed had finally agreed on all the terms for her to buy out the Beauty Box. They had an appointment to go to Ed's lawyer's office on Friday afternoon for her to sign the papers. Between the loan she'd gotten from the bank, her savings and the projected profits, Lana calculated that she would own the Beauty Box free and clear in three years.

"You might have made assistant sales manager if you had some of that attitude toward *your* job," Lana counterattacked.

Tom had thought that because Lana was stacked, she might be dumb. He had thought because she was feminine, she might be passive. He was shocked at how wrong he had been. He thought he had married a sex goddess. Instead he found himself in bed with a woman who, he swore, read herself to sleep with her bankbook.

The only thing Lana spent money on was a clipping service she had found listed in the Yellow Pages. The service sent a thick envelope to Lana every other month. Those envelopes, filled with newspaper stories and photographs of a New York socialite named Deedee Dahlen, always put Lana into a terrible mood that lasted for days. When Tôm, not understanding Lana's strange obsession, told her to stop wasting her money and making herself miserable, Lana told him to shut up and mind his own business.

Tom and Lana argued constantly about money. Tom accused Lana of being cheap. Lana accused Tom of being a spendthrift.

"You'd live in this two-by-four forever to save money, wouldn't you?" Tom snarled, feeling increasingly boxed in. He and Lana were still living in Lana's old room at Esther Flynn's boardinghouse while they were looking for an apartment of their own. Every apartment Tom liked, Lana thought cost too much. Every one she liked, Tom called a dump. They finally compromised on one neither liked.

Tom wanted to buy a new car; Lana thought the one he had was plenty good enough. Tom said that his extra earnings on the private-label products would cover the down payment. Lana said that he ought to put the money into a savings account for a rainy day. When Tom drove home in a brand-new turquoise T-bird, they had had a fight that ended with their not speaking for ten days.

Tom wanted to take a vacation and go to Puerto Rico; Lana thought a vacation was an outrageous waste of money. Tom liked to get dressed up and go out to dinner; Lana liked to stay home and cook because it cost less. The less she spent on herself, the faster she could pay off Ed and own the salon.

"You and that fucking salon!" Tom exploded, sick of living on macaroni and cheese and tuna casseroles so that Lana could pay off the Beauty Box sooner.

"You and that stupid car!" screamed Lana, thinking of all the sensible ways they could invest the money as Tom mailed off another hefty car payment check.

Their differences over money were nothing compared to their differences over sex. Tom told Lana she was frigid. Lana thought Tom was a sex maniac.

"You're always 'too tired,' " Tom said in disgust one night after they'd been married almost five months.

Lana had gotten home from the Beauty Box at nine, cooked, served and cleaned up dinner, vacuumed the apartment, done two loads of laundry, closed out the day's books and, at one-thirty, glazed with fatigue, had gotten into bed. She set the alarm for six so she could do the week's payroll and withholding before she went to the salon at eight to wax the floors before opening for business. Tom had reached over and, with no preliminaries, began to knead her breast. Lana pushed his hand away.

"What's the matter?" Tom jeered. " 'Too tired' again?"

"The only time I ever said I was too tired was after I'd worked two straight weeks of fourteen-hour days over Christmas and New Year's," Lana replied, wondering what on earth had happened to his sensitive lips and skillful hands. Did a marriage license turn a man into a barbarian? Or was it just Tom? *Me Tarzan, you Jane, let's fuck* seemed to have become Tom's postwedding style.

"You can't even come half the time," he snarled, rejected.

"How can I come?" Lana sneered, turning her back on him. "You're already finished by the time I'm just getting interested."

The sensitive and passionate lover who had courted her had turned into a horny husband who expected sex on demand whether or not she happened to be in the mood. A horny husband, Lana realized, who already had other girl-friends.

She found lipstick on his shorts, love notes in his jacket pockets and credit card receipts for dinners she hadn't shared with him. She found a pair of blue nylon bikini panties in the glove compartment of his T-bird. She served the panties on his dinner plate.

"I assume they're yours," she told him sweetly, putting the dish down in front of him. "They're not my size."

Lana was beginning to think that if they had a six-month anniversary, it would be a miracle. Never mind thirty years.

* * *

By the time they'd been married eight months, Lana had stopped trusting in fate. She began to use her diaphragm again and when Tom felt it inside her, he yanked it out of her and threw it across the room.

"We're here to make babies!" he told her, wanting to assert himself. Tom thought if he got her pregnant, maybe she'd settle down and become a real wife. "The fun fucks are over!"

The next day, Lana went to a doctor and secretly got a prescription for birth control pills. When Tom found them hidden behind her moisturizer in the medicine cabinet, they had a bitter, screaming argument that ended with Tom flushing the pills down the toilet.

"You're not killing my children!" Tom shouted, coming out of the bathroom, beside himself with fury and frustration. He wanted a wife. An obedient, adoring wife. Not a wife who constantly undermined him and put him down. "I'll kill you first!"

Tom pushed Lana toward the bed, slamming her against the sharp corner of the bureau. She stumbled and Tom came after her. He twisted her arm up behind her back, making her scream with pain. Terrified that he would break her arm and that she would be unable to work, Lana managed to get her foot behind Tom's ankle and wrest him momentarily off balance. In shock, Tom released her arm but immediately raised his fist and punched her in the face.

Momentarily thrown off balance by the assault, Lana almost fell. Tom took advantage of her shock and threw her to the bed. Ripping her skirt, he shoved his knees between her legs and pushed her panties aside. He held her hands over her head with one hand and unzipped his fly with the other.

"You bitch! You frigid bitch!" he screamed.

His penis was purple with engorged blood and Tom forced his way into her. Tom had married for love and sex and a family. He had wanted to settle down and be the man of his family. However, instead of being first, Tom found himself a distant last to ambitions he didn't understand and obsessions he didn't share. His career was going nowhere and Lana kept rubbing his face in his failures, telling him he was lazy and trying to slide by on charm. Tom's frustration and disappointment turned him wild as, driven by fury and resentment, he pounded and pounded away at Lana. He used his hot, rigid penis as a weapon at the same time that he slapped her face and pummelled her body, trying to subdue her and bend her to his will.

"Stop!" screamed Lana, struggling under him and trying to force him off her. "Stop!"

Her vagina felt raw and torn, her eyes swollen, her lips bloodied, her breasts sore from Tom's furious assault. Half crazed by a thousand memories of Will hitting her mother, Lana twisted around violently under Tom and grabbed desperately for the lamp on the night table. Picking it up, she smashed it over Tom's head in a shower of broken glass and flying sparks. Tom didn't make a sound but his assault on her body instantly ceased and he crumpled toward the floor, blood dripping from his scalp.

For a moment Tom lay motionless, blood staining the rug beneath him. Lana, terrified that she had killed him, knelt down and touched his head gently. Tom opened his eyes and glared at her.

"Bitch!" he snarled.

"Get out of here!" Lana said, pulling back and standing up again. She prodded him with the toe of her shoe. "Get up," she repeated. "And get out of here."

Tom got up slowly and, holding his bleeding head, stumbled toward the front door, Lana beside him, propelling him along. At the last minute, she ran into the bedroom, pulled his clothes from the closet and threw them out on the lawn after him.

"You're going to pay for this!" Tom screamed, picking up his clothes, furious at the way she had treated them, throwing them around as if they were nothing more than rags. "Money is all you care about and I'm going to make you pay!"

As Lana slammed the front door, she noticed that Tom's girlfriend, whom she recognized as a client of Rose Scorvino's, was sitting outside waiting for him in the turquoise T-Bird. She had obviously heard the whole thing.

* * *

"Mr. Morello's lawyer said you tried to kill him," said Mario Rizzuto a week later. Mario Rizzuto was Catholic and a divorce lawyer and apparently saw no conflict between the two. He did not seem particularly impressed by Lana's accusations that Tom had beaten and raped her, telling her that if judges gave divorces on the grounds of husbands beating up wives and then having sex with them, there wouldn't be any marriages left in the state of Massachusetts. Rizzuto pulled some official-looking papers and several 8 × 10 black-and-white photographs out of folder.

"Your husband's lawyer gave me these," Rizzuto said. He shoved the papers across the desk. The photographs were of Tom, blood running down his face and spotting his shirt. The papers accompanying the photographs were a detailed medical report. "The doctor mentions cuts and contusions," said Rizzuto.

"*He* threatened to kill me! Did he tell his lawyer that? And did he tell his lawyer that he almost broke my arm?" replied Lana. Her arm was still sore and, under the beige concealer, her eye was still bruised and purple.

"Do you have any medical records?" asked Rizzuto, perking up, seemingly slightly more interested in accusations of assault and battery than mere adultery, wife beating and rape.

"Medical records! What medical records? I cleaned myself up and went to work," Lana said, outraged.

"Were there any witnesses?" Rizzuto asked. He gave Lana the distinct impression that he was more sympathetic to Tom's problems than hers.

"Sure," said Lana. "My husband's girlfriend. She was outside in the car. She heard the whole thing."

Rizzuto raised his eyebrows and shrugged, unimpressed.

"I doubt she'd testify against him," he said.

"I bet she would," said Lana, her blue eyes cold and flinty. "Particularly if I threaten to tell her husband . . ."

Even Rizzuto had no answer to that one.

The haggling over the settlement lasted longer than the courtship, and there was more talk about money than there

ever had been about love. In the end, Tom got the T-bird—
and the payment book—and Lana got the washer and dryer.
The real struggle was over the Beauty Box and the commissions from the private-label shampoos and conditioners.

Lana had built the salon's business up from zero and was
buying it with money she had earned herself. She felt that the
Beauty Box was hers. Tom, knowing how much money the
Beauty Box took in, was determined to get it for himself. He
was less interested in the commissions and he knew that Lana
wanted to continue to represent Premiere in Worcester. He
was willing to let Lana have the commissions as long as he
ended up with the Beauty Box. Lana insisted that the Beauty
Box was hers—and so were the commissions on the private-
label shampoos and conditioners.

Rizzuto warned Lana that she was being greedy.

"You'll never get both," said Rizzuto, and he seemed to be
right, since Tom refused anything less than full and outright
ownership of the Beauty Box in return for the divorce.

"Yes, I will," said Lana stubbornly even as she reluctantly
signed the papers turning over the Beauty Box to Tom while
retaining the Premiere accounts and commissions for herself.

Rizzuto shrugged and didn't bother to reply.

He was damn glad he was just her lawyer, not her boyfriend. With the platinum-blond hair and hairpin curves, she
looked hot as a pistol, but underneath she was tough as nails.
Who needed it?

The first thing Lana did after her divorce was to send a
handwritten note on shocking pink stationery to every one of
her clients at the Beauty Box. She informed them that she had
sold the salon and that she would be back at Ed Hilsinger's.
She concluded by saying that she hoped that she would see
them there.

In his first month of ownership, Tom found that business
at the Beauty Box was down 10 percent.

The second thing Lana did was to take a trip to Providence, where she met with Stan Fogel. The divorce
agreement had given Lana the right to sell the private-label

products in Worcester. Lana was determined to get them for the whole New England territory.

"My ex-husband has been selling the private-label shampoos and conditioners," Lana told Stan Fogel. "He's used my shocking pink and rose label, my sales pitch and my gimmick of giving away a free rose with every sample. It's one thing to copy an idea, it's another to do a lousy job of it."

"You could do better?" Stan asked. He had a gruff, gravelly voice and piercing brown eyes. He liked Lana's feistiness and thought she seemed like a hell of a go-getter. Like every man who met her, Stan Fogel was almost blown away by Lana's sheer physical allure. With her pale, shining hair, lush breasts and ripe hips, she was nothing less than a knockout. The fact that she also obviously had brains and plenty of them made her seem almost too good to be true. Stan, unlike Tom, loved nothing more than a challenge.

"Try me," Lana said, all single-minded determination. As usual, Lana was oblivious to her effect on the opposite sex. "I'll work the first month for nothing. If you don't like the results, we'll shake hands and say goodbye. No hard feelings. If you do, we'll make a deal."

Lana worked at Ed Hilsinger's from Tuesday through Saturday. On Mondays, the traditional closed days for most salons, she sold private-label shampoo. Since she didn't have the time to call on each salon manager individually, Lana decided to have them come to her, and she organized what she called her dog and pony shows.

Lana established seminars for hairdressers and invited top stylists and colorists from Boston and Providence to give demonstrations on live models from the audience. For a modest registration fee, hairdressers from Massachusetts, Vermont, Rhode Island and Connecticut got a chance to learn new styles and new techniques, to mix and to mingle.

On every chair Lana placed a shocking pink long-stemmed rose along with a complimentary sample package of private-label shampoo and conditioner. That next week, every hairdresser who attended got a follow-up phone call and an opportunity to place an order. Within six months, Lana had increased the private-label division of Premiere by almost 20 percent.

"Well, now what?" she said to Stan Fogel. "Is it goodbye or have we got a deal?"

"We've got a deal," Stan said and he knew damn well that whatever he offered Lana would turn down. Not that the prospect of being turned down bothered him in the slightest. Stan was tired and bored and the prospect of a little tough horse trading turned him on.

It had been a long time since doing business had been any fun. It had been a long time, come to think of it, that anything had been any fun.

The third thing Lana did was buy a salon she had seen advertised for sale in one of the trade magazines.

"How would you like to spend the summer in Hyannis?" Lana asked her mother, barely able to contain her excitement at the prospect of liberating her mother from Will, from his threats and criticism and drunken binges.

"In Hyannis? Isn't that very expensive?" her mother asked. All Mildred knew about Hyannis was that millionaires like the Kennedys spent summers there.

"Very," said Lana, explaining that she had just bought a salon there.

"Then how will you make the down payment?" her mother wanted to know.

"Out of my savings account," said Lana.

"But didn't Tom didn't get half of it in the settlement?"

"What Tom didn't know about," replied Lana. "Tom couldn't get."

Lana was twenty-four and divorced and the first of her dreams had finally come true. She had taken the first step toward the rescue of her mother from her marriage and now, with the purchase of a salon in an elegant resort, she was ready to launch her next assault on the different world, the world of privilege and power and money and happiness, that still haunted her. The world which, except for a brutal quirk of fate, should have been hers all along.

X I
WOMAN   ON
HER   OWN

The salon in Hyannis for the summer season led to a salon in Palm Beach for the winter season, and Lana's reputation for success gradually began to grow. The gossip, half admiring, half envious, wasn't always flattering.

The story making the rounds was that Lana Bantry had gotten her start by cheating her first husband on their divorce settlement and then, still not satisfied with her revenge, putting him out of business. Talk also had it that Lana's relationship with her ex-husband's boss wasn't just business. They said that first she seduced Stan Fogel and then she blackmailed him. Although that wasn't the way Lana saw it at all.

The story began in Europe. In the summer of 1966.

Ed Hilsinger had gone home to visit his family in Copenhagen that summer of pot, protest and psychedelia and come home with a Danish invention Lana had never even heard of before: electrically heated curlers. The curlers were wired for 220-volt European current, and in order to demonstrate them to Lana, Ed had to buy a converter and transformer.

Lana was fascinated by the possibilities of the new gadget and began to experiment with her own hair. She quickly realized that the hot curlers would be an enormous boon to salons. Hairdressers would be able to create instant hair styles. Clients would be liberated from time under the drier. Last but definitely not least, salons would be able to book more appointments in the course of a day with time saved per client and thus increase their profits.

"Can I buy them from you?" she asked Ed, telling him to name his price.

"Take them," he said, handing the curlers to her along with the converter and transformer. "Consider them a present."

Ed considered the hot curlers strictly a novelty. Lana saw in them vast possibilities. *If* she could find a manufacturer able to adapt the product to American standards. *If* she could find a distributor willing to take a gamble on an untried appliance. They were—and Lana knew it—two great big ifs.

Stan Fogel was that uniquely American phenomenon—the small-town millionaire. He was the quintessential example of the big frog in a small pond, of the local boy who made good, of the high school hotshot who became a leading businessman and pillar of his community. Stan stood out in Providence. He was comfortable in the local restaurants, where his preferences in food and drink were well known. He was sure of himself in meetings with local lawyers, politicians and businessmen. He liked cruising around town in his big light blue Cadillac. Everyone in Providence knew who Stan Fogel was and waved a friendly greeting.

Stan liked to tell people that he worked hard and played hard. He enjoyed the two annual trips—to Israel and Bermuda—taken with his wife. He enjoyed even more the half-dozen jaunts to Las Vegas, where he sampled everything—the crap tables, the floor shows and the services of the hotel hookers. He was, all in all, an enviably happy man as long as he didn't have to move outside the confines he had so surely and completely conquered.

However, amid the daily satisfactions of Stan's life, the gratifying sense of having made it, the comforting feeling of having plenty of money in the bank, the knowledge that his sons would one day follow him in the business he had built from nothing, there was a dead spot. Stan missed the fun he had had back in the good old days and, over a few drinks, he would wax nostalgic.

Stan had started out as a traveling salesman for the Revlon jobber in New England during the Depression. Cosmetics was a Depression-proof business and Stan made a good living selling nail polish and lipstick to drugstores and beauty parlors. Stan remembered his youth fondly and he missed the road. He missed the camaraderie, the drinks, the deals, the pussy. Stan was facing—not with much relish—the big five-oh, and he frequently asked himself the question that Peggy Lee had made famous: Is this all there is?

Stan secretly dreaded that the answer was yes, pal, that's all there is. There ain't no more.

Stan didn't want to believe it. He didn't want to believe that he was over the hill. However, his spreading paunch, the diminished frequency and duration of his erections, his graying hair, his apparently evaporated zest for life all told a different story.

Stan Fogel didn't know it, but he was just waiting for Lana.

Lana didn't know it, either. If she had, she would have done everything differently.

Stan Fogel had made his first fortune in the early 1950s, when American women by the millions wanted the Poodle Cut, the latest look from Europe. The cold wave, which had been around since World War II, had been languishing on salon shelves for years as color had superseded permanents as the profit center for salons. The Poodle Cut changed all that, and Stan Fogel, who was always ready for anything, was ready for the Poodle Cut.

Stan made a quick deal with a Boston beauty supply wholesaler to take a warehouse full of permanent waves off their hands. Glad to get rid of the inventory, the wholesaler was happy to sell cheap. The cold waves that Stan sold to a salon for one dollar cost the client ten to twelve dollars. Over the next decade, Stan sold millions of cold waves, salons sold millions of perms and everyone got rich. Particularly Stan. He quit his job with the Revlon jobber and founded his own company, Premiere.

Stan, who had a sexy good guy/bad guy, cop-and-crook aura about him, was something of a hero in the beauty trades.

He was known as the man who had seen the change coming and who had been ready to cash in on it. By the time Lana Bantry came into his office and started to tell him about the revolutionary new product Ed Hilsinger had brought back from Copenhagen, Stan couldn't have cared less.

"I've been rich for so long, I'm not interested in money any more," Stan told Lana before she could get down to the details. Stan leaned back in his big leather executive-model chair and, with his posture, dared her to contradict him. Lana leapt at the chance.

"Bullshit," she replied, her blue eyes glittering with intensity. "I've got an idea that's going to make me rich and you, too, if you're interested."

"I'm already rich. I'm not interested," said Stan, instantly beginning to get interested despite himself. "But, what the hell? I've got some time to waste. What's your great idea?"

"Electric curlers," said Lana excitedly, as if she were telling him the password to paradise.

"Electric curlers? You've got to be joking," Stan snorted. "I've been in the beauty business for longer than you've been alive and I've never heard of them."

"Just because you never heard of them doesn't mean they aren't going to change your life," Lana said, unconsciously telling Stan exactly what he had been wanting to hear for several years now. "They were invented in Copenhagen," Lana continued and then went on to describe her discovery in detail.

"So maybe these curlers have possibilities, but the fact is I'm still not interested," Stan said when Lana had finished. "Hell, making money isn't fun any more. All it means is tax headaches."

Stan hated the IRS with a passion and always said that every dime he managed to hide from Uncle Sam was worth a dollar to him. He also liked to joke that he kept a permanent ticket to Rio in his vest pocket in case the IRS ever caught up with him. He did not want to repeat the experience of a friend of his who had whiled away several highly unpleasant years in jail as a result of tax fraud.

"I'm too old to fight the IRS and I'm too old to go to jail," Stan said, ready to drop the whole subject.

"But you're not too old for a big-time success," insisted Lana. "And I mean big!"

"You're ambitious, aren't you?" asked Stan, finally coming off his macho stance and for the first time addressing Lana as if he had really noticed her and who she was.

"Why not?" she replied. "Aren't you?"

There was silence for a moment as Lana looked Stan straight in the eye. This time, it was she who dared him. She dared him not to be her equal. It was a dare Stan could not resist.

"So tell me more," Stan sighed, feeling badgered and put upon. Stan thought that Lana Bantry had real pain-in-the-ass potential, but he also admitted to himself that he was sort of beginning to enjoy parrying with her.

Lana told Stan everything she had been able to find out about the electric curlers, from the name of the Danish manufacturer to the fact that American rights had not been tied up. She even demonstrated them on her own hair right in front of Stan's eyes.

"If you go ahead right now, Premiere will have the exclusive," Lana said intensely, as she demonstrated the hot curlers and the different styles that could be created almost instantly. As with Tom in the very beginning, Lana was so wrapped up in her idea that she did not notice the mesmerizing effect she was having on Stan. She went on to describe the potential she saw in the electric curlers. "This product will bring hair care into the twentieth century. It will revolutionize the beauty care market. *And*, because of it, Premiere will go from being a small-time success into being a big-time success."

Stan sighed heavily. Just listening to her exhausted him. She came on like gangbusters. The thing was, it turned him on. So did she.

"Well, you beat me down," Stan finally said grudgingly. "What the hell? Let me sleep on it. Come back tomorrow and we'll talk some more."

Lana got up and, as she was leaving his office, Stan had a sudden last-minute question.

"Don't you ever smile?" he asked. He noticed that she had been as grim as a gravedigger the entire time she had been pitching the electric curlers.

Lana turned and looked at Stan for a moment.

"Give me a good reason," she replied, challenging him once again, "and I'll smile."

With that, she opened the door and walked out.

Stan leaned back in his chair and watched her retreating figure. Never mind the silky, platinum blonde hair that he wanted to walk through barefoot, thought Stan, Lana Bantry was, as they used to say in high school, built like a brick shithouse. Stan could hardly keep his hands off her and the stirring in his groin sent him a message that he wasn't over the hill. Not yet. Far from it.

As Lana left his office, it was Stan who smiled. She wanted a reason to smile? He'd be delighted to give her one. Just delighted. All she had to do was give him a chance.

Emma Sparling, a blond socialite, had been one of Lana's first clients in Hyannis. Emma and her family lived in Boston, summered in Hyannis and wintered in Palm Beach. It had been through Emma, in fact, that Lana had bought the Palm Beach salon.

Emma's husband, Franklin, a businessman with an Ivy League background, had made his fortune by building up a small family-owned company that manufactured small appliances—toasters, blenders, irons, electric can openers—and then going public with it. After her initial conversations with Stan, Lana took the Danish curlers to Franklin Sparling's factory just on the outskirts of Providence.

Franklin Sparling was the opposite of Stan both physically and psychologically. Stan was built like a bulldog and had a bulldog's tenacity and surface ferocity. Stan had a gruff voice and a harsh New England accent. His brown eyes were sharp and watchful and his beautiful olive skin was strong and large-pored. Stan's dark beard, always impeccably shaved, was heavy and aggressively masculine. His clothes were inevitably expensive and carefully tailored. For a man who prided himself on being hard, Stan was unusually fond of soft fabrics like silk and cashmere. He considered himself, with reason, as being something of a fashion plate.

Franklin Sparling, on the other hand, resembled a greyhound and had a greyhound's lean and aristocratic bearing. He was tall and slim with a bony Anglo-Saxon face, intelligent light blue eyes and thin, sensitive skin. His style was well-worn Brooks with a touch of English country. His view was worldly rather than provincial, and he was the first man Lana would come to know well who had graduated from college. His manners were impeccable not only in the sense of knowing which fork to use but because, more important, Franklin Sparling treated everyone from janitor to ambassador with the same polite and genuine interest.

Once again, Lana repeated everything she had been able to learn about the curlers. Then, still using the converter and bulky transformer, Lana demonstrated them on her own hair. She then asked Franklin Sparling if he would be able to recreate and adapt the product for American use.

"Probably. But why?" he asked, in the elegant Harvard-Yale-Princeton accent that had instantly explained Russell Dahlen's accent to Lana. It was an accent that only money could buy. Before Lana could answer his question, Franklin did, adding his own no-nonsense Yankee opinion: "Who's going to use them? Women aren't going to want to cook their hair."

"Wanna bet?" replied Lana.

Women would *fry* their hair if frying would make it look better.

The development, copyrighting and trademarking of the electrically heated curlers ate up more and more of Lana's time, until eventually she had no choice except to put her mother in charge of the day-to-day workings of the two salons she now owned. Mildred divided her time between Hyannis and Palm Beach while Will stayed home in Wilcom. Even though she worked hard, Mildred seemed to become younger as her lifelong financial problems eased. The lines around her mouth gradually seemed to relax and the tension in her body began to disappear. After several attempts, she succeeded in stopping smoking, and her roses-and-cream complexion seemed clearer and finer than it had in years. At almost forty-five, Mildred seemed to have found a new lease on life. To Lana's surprise, however, she did not divorce Will.

"He begged me not to leave him," Mildred said, trying to explain the loyalty that even she didn't quite comprehend. Was it loyalty? Was it guilt? Was it a need to be needed? Mildred didn't know. All she knew was that Will had a hold on her she didn't understand and didn't seem able or even willing to free herself from. "He's even talking about joining AA."

In order to meet the demands on her time and energy, Lana moved from Worcester to Providence.

"I feel like a tennis ball," Lana told her mother, "bouncing between Premiere's offices and Frank Sparling's factory."

At the same time that Lana was working with Franklin Sparling on the development of a manufacturing prototype for the curlers, she entered into a formal agreement with Stan. Stan would create a brand-new division of Premiere to market the curlers. Lana would be an employee of that division. She agreed to a small salary in return for an eventual royalty override on every unit sold. Lana foresaw the same kind of eventual reward she had received in her arrangement with Ed Hilsinger when she agreed to manage the Beauty Box for a smaller salary up front but a percentage of the profits later on. She was more than willing to work for Stan for less now in exchange for more later.

"It will be well worth it in the end," said Lana when Franklin asked her if she was sure she was making a good deal.

"I hope you're right," Franklin said, upset that Lana had refused his advice to consult a lawyer before she signed her agreement with Stan. Lana had feared that bringing in a lawyer would alienate Stan and end her dream before it had even started. Beside, lawyers were expensive and Lana hated to spend any money that she didn't absolutely have to.

"Stan Fogel's a tough cookie," Franklin warned.

Lana shrugged her shoulders confidently, dismissing Franklin's warning.

"That's all right. So am I."

After all, Lana reminded herself, she had overcome Will, who had stolen from her, Russell, who had ignored her, and Tom, who had tried to outbargain her. Her success so far was proof of her brains and toughness. What could Stan Fogel possibly do to outwit or to defeat her?

XII
RUBIES AND
ROSES

*A*t first, *Premiere marketed the electric curlers only to* salons. However, as soon as clients saw how fast and easy to use the curlers were, they wanted to buy them to take home. One year after Premiere began to sell the curlers to salons, it began for the first time in its history to sell to retail distributors and wholesalers. The electric curlers, now available in drug and appliance stores, were a consumer sensation. From 1966 until the end of the decade, Premiere had the United States exclusive on the sale and distribution of the electric curler.

Lana, of course, won her bet with Franklin Sparling. It turned out that women, millions of them, had no objection whatever to cooking their hair. Eventually, the big personal appliance companies copied the electric curlers, and by 1970 Premiere lost its exclusive. Nevertheless, as Lana had predicted to Stan, the curlers turned Premiere from a small-time success into a big-time success. Thanks to the electric curlers Ed Hilsinger had brought home from a vacation and to Lana's insistence, persistence and vision, Premiere had begun its transformation from a regional beauty supply company serving a limited number of accounts into a personal appliance company with a newly expanded product base and national penetration.

"I've been offered three and a half million for the company," Stan told Lana. "What do you think?"

"I think you should tell them to stick it in their ear," she said, talking Stan's language.

Stan laughed. "You know what I like about you? You think like a man."

Stan was becoming more and more aware, however, that Lana did not look like a man. Lana had decided when she was fifteen years old that dieting was idiotic and that the fleshy, voluptuous body God had given her was beautiful no matter what so-called style dictated. She did not believe in suffering—either at the dinner table or in the fitting room—and she enjoyed both her food and the brightly colored, highly designed clothes that demanded attention.

She was a petite and curvy woman on whom too much seemed to be just enough. Too much jewelry, too much perfume, too many ruffles and flourishes. She loved wildly printed scarves, bold, horizontally striped T-shirts, big hoop earrings and armsful of oversized silver and ivory cuff bracelets. She broke the "rule" that said that curvy women should wear dark, slenderizing colors—and got away with it. She wore fire engine red, cyclamen pink, sapphire blue and vibrant fuchsia and looked wonderful in all of them. She wore the highest-heeled shoes she could find, and she was addicted to dramatic, wide belts that supposedly "cut" a woman but didn't. Not her. Not at all.

Lana may have been small in stature, but she dressed big and she thought big. She was the kind of woman men noticed and Stan was no exception. He noticed, also, that despite her glamorous style and voluptuous body, Lana never gave the slightest indication that she even knew that sex existed.

"You'd be a very attractive woman if you'd loosen up a little," Stan said, trying the protective, paternal approach.

"I'm not interested in being attractive," Lana replied curtly.

Ever since her divorce, Lana had made a point of turning away men who might have been interested in her. Just as she had hardened her mind to Russell Dahlen and the bitter disillusion the meeting with him had represented, Lana had hardened her mind to any further ideas of men and romance when her marriage had broken up. Love and sex had been sour disappointments and Lana had purposely deadened the part of her that yearned for them. She had decided, instead, to devote herself to business.

"There's no law that says that brains and beauty can't mix," Stan said instantly, dropping the paternal crap and trying flattery instead. "Particularly in your case."

Lana did not reply and pretended not to have heard but Stan's words pierced, just a little, the hard shell with which she had protected her bruised and unusually tender feelings.

Lana reacted by being even more formal than usual with Stan when, for her twenty-sixth birthday, he gave her twenty-six of her favorite red roses. Tucked into the bouquet was a ruby-and-diamond pin in the shape of a rose. The pin, from Providence's best jeweler, was Lana's first piece of valuable jewelry and she was ecstatic with it.

"It's absolutely beautiful! Thank you!" she bubbled, thrilled with the gift and immediately fastening it to the lapel of her jacket. She didn't care if diamonds in daylight were supposedly vulgar. Lana loved glitter and flash at any time of day or night. She did not, though, as Stan had hoped, throw her arms around him in appreciation. Instead, Lana stepped back a pace, wanting to make sure that Stan didn't confuse her appreciation with any other emotion. "But I'm not going to go to bed with you."

"Who asked?" Stan replied.

Stan was being flippant, but he knew and she knew that just as Lana had revived his interest in business, she had also revived his interest in life. Since he had met Lana, Stan had taken up jogging, lost twenty pounds, colored his hair and begun wearing Johnny Carson–style turtlenecks on all but the most formal occasions.

Stan now radiated vigor and a primitive but unmistakable sexual magnetism. Because of Lana, because of the new excitement, new energy and new success she had brought into his life, Stan had transformed himself from a gray, overweight man who looked every minute of his fifty years into a lean, supercharged dynamo who just smiled when people mistook him for thirty-eight or maybe forty.

As for Lana, she ultimately made almost a hundred thousand dollars from another present—the "present" Ed had given her when he handed her the electric curlers. The hundred thousand dollars represented Lana's share of the royalty override deal she had made with Stan, and that hundred thousand dollars was the first big chunk of money Lana had made in her life.

"Don't you feel awfully rich?" her mother asked when Lana proudly showed her the check. Mildred was extraordinarily impressed with her daughter's accomplishment. As always, though, she found herself inhibited from showing Lana the full extent of her pride.

Lana shook her head.

"Not really," she admitted, surprised herself with her answer. "Not as rich as I felt on graduation day when I had five hundred dollars in my purse and was buying you lunch."

Mildred nodded, realizing that Will had stolen more from Lana on that day than just money. He had stolen an essential part of her innocence. Russell Dahlen, she knew, had completed the theft.

Although she did not have to, Lana gave Ed a check for 10 percent of the amount, ten thousand dollars.

"You don't have to do that," Ed said, touched and surprised at the gesture.

"But I do have to," Lana replied. "I would never have earned the money without you."

Ed planned to use the money to help with college tuitions for his children and, although Lana would inevitably have her detractors, she would also have passionately loyal defenders. Ed Hilsinger would always be one of them.

Lana invested all her earnings in treasury bills, among the most conservative of investments.

"You're too young to be so conservative," Stan told her,

impatient with her caution. Stan loved playing the market and loved to regale Lana with the details of his machinations. He chortled over his profits and moaned over his losses. Barely a day passed when Stan, along with Lana, did not pay a call on Stan's stockbroker.

"I spend almost as much time with your broker as I do with you," Lana complained teasingly.

"Pay attention," Stan replied in an irritated tone, unwilling to be teased about anything as important as money. "Maybe you'll learn something that will be worth money to you one day."

Stan's words would turn out to be prophetic. At the time, though, Lana could not imagine any circumstances in which she would play the market. Nevertheless, she took Stan's advice and paid rapt attention to all of Stan's stock market maneuvers. Without even being aware of it, Lana was not only learning the beauty business, she was beginning to learn about the ups and downs and ins and outs of stock and the stock market.

Meanwhile, Lana's two salons prospered. Her investments grew slowly but surely. As the sixties turned into the seventies and horizons for women broadened, Lana gradually began to believe that, unlike her mother and Rose and a million other women who had worked hard in pink-collar jobs and menial clerical positions all their lives and ended up with nothing, she might be different. Her dreams of one day conquering her father's world became less and less outrageous and more and more realistic.

Meanwhile, Lana continued to learn everything she could from Stan, and she learned that the beauty business, dedicated to women, was run by men and that not all of their business practices were beautiful. Far from it.

Three years after their divorce, Lana got a telephone call from Tom Morello. Three years which had not been good to Tom. Having won the Beauty Box in the divorce, Tom immediately quit his job at Premiere. The Beauty Box, Tom knew, generated plenty of money and would support him in real style. Tom had been starved for fun and affection during his brief marriage, and he planned to make up for it on the money that poured in from the Beauty Box.

However, from the moment ownership of the salon was transferred to Tom, its earnings began to dry up. Month after month, receipts fell and the income Tom had planned to enjoy gradually eroded. As Tom had more or less anticipated, Lana's personal clients stopped coming almost immediately. He did not anticipate other problems or other losses. Nevertheless, problems and losses plagued the Beauty Box from the moment Lana turned it over to him.

Without Lana's personal presence at the salon, Tom had trouble keeping good help. Every one of his best stylists eventually quit to take jobs elsewhere. Each one who left took even more clients away from the Beauty Box. Although Tom did not understand why, new clients did not appear to replace the ones who had left even though, in an attempt to stimulate business, he began to advertise and, when advertising didn't work, he offered cut prices.

Tom blamed Lana for bad-mouthing him all over Providence and he accused her of stealing clients. Blame and accusation did not improve business, however, and Tom came to feel that he had been stuck with the raw end of a bad deal. By the time a year had passed, Tom was having trouble meeting his monthly notes. Remembering how badly Lana had wanted to hold on to the Beauty Box, Tom called and told her that he would be willing to sell it back to her.

"At the right price," he warned, knowing who he would be dealing with.

Lana drove to Worcester, looked over the books and visited the salon. Tom had left its management to Rose, and the Beauty Box was once again run-down and tired looking. The six operators Lana had once employed had dwindled to three, and the manicurist now came in only on Saturday afternoons. The salon itself needed a complete freshening up—fresh paint, up-to-date equipment and new fixtures. Tom named a price of eighty thousand dollars. It was, he thought, a fair-and-square price.

"Fifty," Lana offered.

* * *

Lana and Tom met face to face for the first time since their divorce in a restaurant in Worcester to discuss business. Tom ordered a Seven and Seven, a mixture of 7-Up and Seven Crown and then, with a flourish, he presented Lana with a long-stemmed red rose.

"For old time's sake," he said with a poignant smile. Lana took the rose and thanked him, thinking that his gesture was sweet and sad and utterly inappropriate. After all, this was a business meeting, not a romance.

The way Tom looked shocked Lana.

Tom's clothes, which Lana had once thought so sharp and stylish, now seemed cheap and flashy. Since she'd seen him last, Tom had lost weight and developed a slight paunch simultaneously. His skin, once so healthy and tanned, was pale and slack. Lana tried to remember the handsome young man with the wild, gypsy appeal. What, she wondered, had happened to him? Tom seemed tired and confused and Lana wondered whether he was still so successful with women. Somehow, she doubted it. As she sat opposite her former husband, Lana found it impossible to remember the passions, positive and negative, that had once flowed between them.

"Fifty? You've got to be kidding!" Tom said, outraged at Lana's offer. He couldn't believe it! She had screwed him on the divorce and now she was trying to screw him out of the salon.

"I'm not kidding," said Lana. "The place looks crummy. It needs paint and renovation. All the good stylists have left. The clients have gone along with them. Receipts are down. Fifty is all it's worth."

Tom ordered a second drink and leaned down to take his first sip of it without picking it up from the table. His eyes, Lana noticed, were red-rimmed and bleary and his hands trembled.

"Seventy-five?" Tom said hopefully, looking up at her and batting his lashes.

Lana shook her head.

"Fifty," she repeated.

"No way!" exploded Tom. "I thought I was doing you a favor! I'll find another customer."

"Fine," said Lana pleasantly. "I wish you luck."

What killed him was that the bitch sounded as if she really meant it.

Lana and Tom eventually agreed that Lana would buy back the Beauty Box for forty thousand dollars the week after a fire that started in the middle of the night burned out the interior. The fire had started at four in the morning. By the time the fire department arrived, the Beauty Box was beyond rescue.

Tom always swore that the fire had been the doing of one of Stan's goombahs, but a fire department inspection concluded that one of the driers had shorted out and that the fire was electric in origin. Nevertheless, the rumor got started that Lana Bantry, backed by Stan Fogel, was not to be crossed.

"Why don't you wear the pin I gave you anymore?" Stan asked on the day that Lana signed the papers and wrote the check buying back the Beauty Box.

"It's too expensive," she said unconvincingly. Then, referring for the first time to the swirling rumors about their relationship, she added: "Beside, I don't want to look like a kept woman."

"It's not being a kept woman you should worry about," Stan said mysteriously in his gravelly voice.

"Then what *should* I worry about?"

"You really think that fire was an accident?" he asked, sounding as if he thought she was being dense.

"That's what the fire department said," Lana replied. Having seen for herself how run-down Tom had allowed the Beauty Box to become, Lana had accepted the fire department's ruling at face value. Never, until that moment, had she given the fire or its origins a second thought.

"Fire departments can be bought," Stan informed Lana. He then refused to utter a single additional word on the subject.

Lana looked at him and wondered. Had the fire really been accidental? Had the old, frayed wiring simply shorted out? Or had Stan paid off the fire department? Lana didn't know and, the more she thought about it, the more either alternative seemed possible. Still, no matter how often she questioned him, Stan refused to tell Lana what had really happened, and Lana realized that Stan's mysteriousness and the possibility of his ruthlessness made her both slightly afraid of him and very excited by him.

"You're not the only tough one around here," Stan said shrewdly, instinctively understanding Lana's reaction. "Now don't bug me with any more questions because I'm not going to answer them."

That night Lana went to bed with Stan for the first time. It was the first time Lana had slept with a man since her divorce and she shocked both herself and Stan with her wild abandon. She scratched his back with her long nails and seemed to suck the very essence out of him with her hot, wet mouth and darting, agile tongue. She was capable of orgasm after shuddering orgasm that left her spent and breathless and almost at the point of tears.

"Are you always this hot?" Stan asked sometime in the middle of the night, in ecstatic amazement.

"Just with you," Lana said honestly, no longer able to remember the good times with Tom.

Stan was electrified and rejuvenated by his sexual power over Lana. He was surprised and delighted to see that Lana also dyed her pubic hair platinum. It was suddenly and unexpectedly Stan's turn to be slightly afraid of her and very excited by her.

"I suppose you think I ought to divorce my wife for you," Stan said the next morning as, drained, they lay quietly watching the sun come up. The last thing Stan wanted was a girlfriend making ultimatums and demanding marriage. He wanted to get things straight right from the beginning: he was interested in an affair. Period.

"No," Lana said immediately, thinking of Tom and remembering how marriage had turned a passionate love affair into a nightmare. "That's the last thing I want. My freedom means everything to me."

Lana's words and the certainty with which she uttered them shocked Stan.

"Suppose I said that I wanted to divorce Florence for you?" Stan asked, several weeks later. Their lovemaking had become more and more torrid, leaving Stan drained, satisfied and hungry for more all at the same time. He bragged to his friends that he was walking around with a perpetual hard-on, a man his age!, and he realized that he could not get enough of her. He also realized that he was in love with her.

"I'd tell you not to," Lana said flatly, seeing the love and the need in Stan's eyes and running from them. Tom had been a needy man and Lana did not want another.

"My marriage has been empty for years. We'd be something together, Lana. Really something. I love you. I want to marry you," Stan said, letting his emotions show, throwing himself at her, putting himself at her mercy.

"I love you, Stan, but I don't want to marry you," Lana said. Then, seeing the crushed expression in his brown eyes, Lana added, and it was the truth: "I don't want to marry anyone. I've been hurt too much."

Emotion, Stan began to realize, did not soften Lana. Instead, it seemed to harden her, to make her pull away even further. Once again, Lana unconsciously gave Stan what he most wanted: a goal and a challenge. The more distance Lana tried to put between them, the more determined Stan became to have her. The more independence Lana tried to assert, the more deeply Stan fell in love with her.

"A divorce would be a good thing for me. And it would be good for Florence, too," Stan said, changing his tactic and pressing his case. If Lana wouldn't go for emotion, Stan would try logic. It was a logic Lana immediately attacked with the unsparing bluntness that had always devastated Tom. She told Stan that he was handing out the line men have used since time immemorial to justify their own last-gasp, middle-aged grab at fantasies of youth and freedom.

"A divorce would not be good for your wife any more than it would be good for any middle-aged woman without a career who has devoted thirty years to a marriage and a family," Lana said, shocking Stan by taking Florence's side.

Lana was right, but that reality was not something Stan could face deep in the clutches of his current sexual rebirth and his increasing realization that lust wasn't all that he felt. He had started out insisting on an affair. Now, realizing that Lana could mean everything, including, literally, life to him, Stan fell more and more deeply in love with her.

"We'd get married," Stan continued, spelling out the dream that had become an obsession and, unwilling and unable to let any challenge go unconquered, trying to persuade Lana to change her mind and agree to marry him. "Believe me, after that, nothing could stop us!"

"Nothing can stop us now," Lana replied, cutting him off, keeping her guard up. Maybe Stan *did* love her but love, Lana had learned, went out the door the minute a man felt he owned a woman. She had been married once and the way she felt now, once was enough. Love and marriage, she had learned the hard way, had nothing to do with each other. Love seemed to survive better *without* the ring, *without* the commitment. After all, as Lana knew better than anyone, Stan had no compunctions about cheating on Florence. If she agreed to marry him, Lana was sure that one day she would find herself in Florence's position. She had already been humiliated by a man who turned to other women. The memory of that particular pain was still too sharp, still too fresh, and Lana continued to turn aside Stan's proposals.

"I love you," Stan kept saying as if the words themselves could have an hypnotic effect. He couldn't believe that Lana didn't feel his sincerity, couldn't see the genuineness of his emotion, couldn't sense the depth and strength of his passion. "Don't you love me? At least a little?"

"Of course I love you," replied Lana. "I love you a lot."

"Then marry me," said Stan. He wanted her. He wanted to give her everything. Love and money and a place in his world. Didn't she want him, too? Didn't she understand what he was offering? Didn't she realize that he wanted to give her everything she had most wanted for her entire life?

"No," said Lana, turning him aside. "Marriage isn't on my list, so forget it."

She was to regret her words a thousand times.

XIII

THE OTHER

WOMAN

*B*y early 1970 the major appliance companies had put their manufacturing and marketing muscle behind the electric curlers and Premiere had lost its exclusive. However, anticipating the competition, Lana and Stan had been visiting beauty trade shows all over the United States and Europe looking for a follow-up product. At a beauty trade show in Geneva, Lana found just what she had been searching for: a hand-held, pistol-grip hair dryer manufactured by a small company in Belgium.

Lana tied up the American rights and Premiere, once again, was first with a product that would revolutionize hairdressing. The pistol-grip hand-held hair dryer, first mass marketed in 1971, coincided with the London-originated trend to more casual hairstyling. Old-fashioned rollers and floor-standing helmet hair dryers became obsolete almost overnight. Premiere's sales zoomed upward in an almost straight trajectory as not only women but eventually men, too, came to regard the hand-held hair dryer as an everyday grooming necessity.

The dazzling success of the hand-held hair dryer turned Premiere from a solid regional company into an industry pacesetter and, ironically, transformed Stan and Lana's relationship from a satisfying combination of love affair and business relationship into a battlefield.

By early 1972, just as Stan had finally resigned himself to the fact that Lana would never agree to marry him, Lana was beginning to regret not having accepted Stan's repeated offers to divorce his wife and marry her. Now that Stan no longer threw himself at her, Lana began to believe that he really did love her and that a second marriage might be far different from her first marriage. After all, both she and Stan were older and more mature. They had both learned from the past and wanted to reshape the future in a different, more satisfying way. Now that Stan no longer begged her to marry him, Lana began to think she had made a mistake in turning Stan down. As always, she covered her longings for love with concerns about money.

Lana, until now single-mindedly preoccupied with Premiere's success, became increasingly aware that although she had been instrumental in turning Premiere from a regional company into a national corporation, she did not own one single share of Premiere's stock and did not even have an official title. Stan, stung by Lana's rejection, did not seem the least bit anxious to provide her with either.

"I found the hair dryer. I tied up the rights. You sneered. You said that women would never give up their weekly salon appointment," Lana reminded Stan, asking him to name her a vice president of Premiere and give her shares of its stock.

"So I was wrong," Stan shrugged, refusing to share money or status. Lana hadn't given him what he wanted. Now he wasn't going to give her what *she* wanted.

The tables had turned. Lana offered to live with Stan but he said that he wasn't interested. She even said she'd consider marriage but Stan replied that it was too late. He'd gotten comfortable at the center of his wife-mistress triangle. He'd been deeply hurt by Lana's repeated rejections and, just as Lana had once kept part of herself shut away from Stan, Stan now held himself slightly aloof from Lana.

"I love you," Lana would say, imbuing her words with almost painful intensity.

"Now you tell me!" Stan would jest, holding her at a distance now that she opened herself to him.

* * *

Lana and Stan's conflicts weren't only personal. There were professional disagreements, too. Lana wanted to expand Premiere by buying a chain of beauty schools, but Stan refused. Lana wanted to branch out—to Boston, to Chicago, eventually to New York—but Stan was opposed.

Stan was comfortable in the familiar world he had so completely conquered. His recent successes with Premiere had only further consolidated his position at the very top of the local heap. Stan, moreover, had no interest in testing unfamiliar waters. He had no interest in taking any chances that he didn't have to. The different worlds that fascinated Lana frightened Stan, although he would have been the last to admit it. On the other hand, he didn't want to lose Lana and one way to keep her was to keep her dependent on him.

Neither Lana nor Stan understood why, but the more she wanted to move ahead, the more Stan held back.

The royalty override agreement that had once seemed so lucrative to Lana now seemed like peanuts. The good deal now seemed like a bad deal. The partnership that had once seemed ideal now seemed terribly unfair. Lana had done the work, but once again she'd been cheated out of the rewards.

Lana told herself that she should have had a big salary, a fancy title, a cushy office and a safe deposit box full of company stock—after all, she had more than earned them. Hadn't the electric curlers been her idea? And hadn't she been the one who had discovered the hand-held hair dryer? Hadn't she practically had to break Stan's arm to make him go along with the curlers? And hadn't she finally had to threaten to take the hair dryer to the competition before Stan would agree to take a chance on it?

Lana, who had considered herself a hardheaded businesswoman ever since her divorce from Tom, now accused herself of being a fool. She bitterly regretted not having taken Franklin Sparling's advice about having a lawyer represent her in her deal with Stan. She remembered Tom's cynicism about Stan and his promises and she was ashamed of herself as she remembered how utterly unsympathetic she had been. For the first time, Lana began to realize that she, too, had been at fault in the unraveling of their marriage.

Unintentionally, Lana had put herself in a position where she was totally dependent on Stan's goodwill if she were to have any hope of getting what she had worked so hard to earn. If Lana was angry at Stan, and she was, she was nothing less than furious at herself. Stan had offered love and Lana had refused it. Stan had offered marriage and she had been afraid to take it. Afraid to love and be loved. Afraid to let her guard down, afraid to trust. She wanted everything—the love and the money, the shell and the distance, the freedom and the independence—and she had ended up with nothing.

Stan was not getting any younger, and if anything ever happened to him, Lana realized that she would be legally entitled to exactly nothing. Even if Stan lived a long and healthy life, Lana was still nothing more than a highly paid employee who slept with the boss. She continued to ask and even beg Stan to name her vice president of the company and Stan, having the upper hand, continued to refuse. Desperate to get what she felt she had earned and deserved, Lana finally offered to buy some stock in Premiere.

"I'm not asking you to *give* it to me, for Christ's sake!" Lana told Stan, her frustration mounting as he shuffled his feet and said he'd have to think about it. "I'm asking to buy it."

"I know. I heard you. I said I'll think about it," Stan said crankily, his ulcer nipping relentlessly away at him as he sensed his wife-mistress paradise inexorably slipping away from him.

The paradise of being loved by two women was being replaced by the reality of loving two women. Both of them had legitimate demands to make of him and Stan could neither resolve the conflict nor rescue himself from it. Florence, aware of the local gossip, was beginning to demand to know what he was doing and who he was seeing when he wasn't at home. Lana was threatening to expose their affair to Florence if he didn't give her what even he agreed she had more than earned. Stan now dreaded a divorce—a divorce would wipe him out financially and emotionally. He also feared losing Lana. He still loved her, he knew, more than he had ever loved anyone. However, his tender and so recently wounded pride would no longer let him admit it.

Just as Lana floundered in impotent anger, Stan found himself washed one way and then the other by longing and pain, a victim of equally powerful, totally conflicting emotions.

No matter what Lana said or did, Stan hemmed and hawed and crapped around. He was unable to come to a decision, unable to satisfy both wife and mistress, unable to share the money and the success he had once said didn't even interest him. As 1972 turned into 1973, Stan was still procrastinating. In desperation, Lana thought about suing Stan for what was morally and ethically hers. She consulted three lawyers, each one of whom told her the same thing: that when it came to Premiere, she had no legal leg to stand on.

"I can't believe I was so stupid. Me!" she told her mother in utter disgust.

For the first time in her life, Lana was aware of feeling scared.

In 1974, Premiere, in a co-venture with Franklin Sparling, built a factory just outside Providence. In 1975, it built an 80,000-square-foot shipping and warehousing facility next door. The shakedown and start-up period for the factory involved dozens of emergencies and unanticipated crises. The construction of the warehouse was fraught with union problems, cost overruns and a construction accident in which one laborer was killed and two injured when the brakes on a fully loaded cement mixer failed.

At the same time, Stan and Lana, needing to raise capital for Premiere's present and future expansion, were working on plans to take the company public. They spent hours with lawyers, accountants and prospective underwriters sifting through complex plans, proposals and strategies. Lana, learning by osmosis, was becoming more and more knowledgeable about all the ways in which the value of a company's stock could be driven up or down.

The sixteen-hour days and the unrelenting series of problems and crises combined with the difficulties of their personal relationship exacted their toll on both Lana and Stan. At thirty, Lana felt the stress; at fifty-five, Stan showed it. Lana had trouble concentrating and difficulty sleeping. Stan complained of pains in his chest and of occasional difficulty breathing, and Lana noticed that sometimes he seemed terribly white around the mouth.

"Maybe you ought to see a doctor," Lana suggested, worried about the way Stan looked. She was furious at him; she was also in love with him.

"I'm tired, that's all!" Stan snapped, refusing.

Consulting doctors, in Stan's opinion, was a sign of weakness and soft-mindedness, acceptable only for women, children and the elderly. Stan was stubbornly determined to keep up with his young mistress, and Lana, for her part, did not insist. She did not want to think of her vibrant and energetic lover as a middle-aged man who might be struggling to maintain her pace.

Snared by the exigencies of illusion and denial, Stan and Lana, united in unspoken collusion, permitted the dangerous impasse to continue.

In 1976, the impasse came to a shocking end. On the Saturday of the Labor Day weekend, Lana got a midnight telephone call from Kenny Conlon.

"Stan's in the hospital. He's had a heart attack," said Kenny. "A serious one."

Lana hung up the phone with the dread feeling that not only was she about to lose her lover but that all of her worst fears were about to come true. She lay awake that entire night wondering what she could possibly do to protect herself and get what she had worked so hard for years to earn. She tried to think of what weapons might conceivably be at her disposal.

* * *

"Mrs. Fogel?"

It was the afternoon of the day Stan had his heart attack. Florence Fogel had just returned home from the cardiac intensive care unit. Surprised to hear her name, Florence turned as she was putting the key into the front door of the red brick mansion she shared with her husband. Although she had never met Lana Bantry, she knew instantly who the flamboyantly dressed platinum blonde with the big breasts was. Local gossip had been, as usual, dead solid accurate.

"My husband is seriously ill," Florence Fogel said with dignity. "I don't think that you and I have anything in the whole world to talk about."

With that, Florence Fogel turned her back on her husband's mistress and pushed the front door open to let herself inside.

"I'm sorry to disagree with you, Mrs. Fogel, but I think we do," said Lana politely but insistently, stepping a bit closer to her lover's wife. "If you're as smart as I think you are, you'll invite me in."

The look on her rival's face and the utter determination in her tone of voice made Florence Fogel decide that it would be wise to change her mind. Reluctantly, she invited Lana Bantry into her home, the home she had shared for so many years with Stan.

The home, Lana realized as she walked through the front door, that might have been hers if only she had accepted Stan's offer of a divorce and remarriage. Getting everything she had worked so hard to earn would have—and could have—been so easy if only she had agreed to marry Stan when he had offered. She would have been a wife and not a beggar. Law and custom would have been on her side. Instead, it was going to be risky and dangerous. Lana followed Florence Fogel through the expensively decorated foyer with her heart in her mouth.

XIV

MIXED

BLESSINGS

lorence Fogel was buxom and heavily boned but not fat. She was expensively dressed in a well-cut navy-blue gabardine dress with a matching jacket, shoes and handbag. Her hair was cut short and becomingly colored and styled. Her makeup, although overly conservative, enhanced her exceedingly well-preserved prettiness.

Florence Fogel had been married for thirty-two years and understood her husband very well. Although she hardly approved of everything Stan did, she loved him and was intensely loyal to him. She was devastated by his affair and by the fact that her rival was all the things she wasn't and couldn't possibly be: young, a business associate, and, worst of all, new. Florence dreaded that Lana would take Stan away from her and, in self-defense, she did not bother to hide the fact that she considered Lana Bantry a tramp and a gold digger.

"Now just what is it you think we have to discuss?" Florence asked when she and Lana had sat down on facing chairs in the Fogels' attractively decorated and pristinely neat living room.

"What we have to discuss is how we're going to divide Stan's estate," Lana said. As she lay awake the night before, she had rehearsed not only the words but the straightforward tone in which she said them. She was determined to keep the conversation as pleasant and businesslike as possible. It was her best and certainly only hope of getting what she wanted and what she deserved. She was bitterly aware that had she

305

agreed to marry Stan, she would never have been in this position in the first place. She was bitterly aware that if she had accepted Stan's proposal, Florence Fogel would have been a defeated rival rather than a woman whose cooperation she desperately needed.

"Stan's not even dead and you're talking about dividing his estate?" Florence replied in open disbelief. Her gold bracelets, bought on a trip to Israel, jangled in annoyance. "You've got even more nerve than I thought! I beg to disagree with you, Miss Bantry, but I don't think we have one thing to talk about."

Florence Fogel rose, indicating that the conversation was over. She went to the door, stood next to it, and waited for her unwelcome guest to leave.

Lana did not move. She sat in Florence Fogel's living room as unbudgingly as if she had been planted there.

"As you may or may not know, the company that Premiere is today is largely due to my ideas and my work," Lana said, as if Florence Fogel had not spoken and were not standing at the door to the foyer with her hand on the doorknob, ready to usher her out. "Stan was virtually retired when we met and, as far as I know, you have never set foot in Premiere's offices. I want to make it very clear that I think you should get the house, the stock, the bonds and all the other assets Stan accumulated during your marriage. However, I do think that Premiere should be mine."

"Yours? You're outrageous! Stan is my husband and I intend to inherit every single penny," said Florence. "After all," she added sweetly, giving into her outrage over the invasion of her home and her marriage, "I'm Stan's wife. You're just his whore. Stan's will leaves everything to me and the children. There isn't a way on earth that you will get one cent!" Florence said, speaking quickly and making her position absolutely clear. She unlatched the front door. "Now I really think you had better leave."

"I'm sure you know that a great deal of Stan's business was conducted on a cash basis," said Lana patiently, not moving an inch from her chair. She spoke as softly and as politely as if she were discussing the weather.

"I know everything about my husband's business!" Florence Fogel snapped. Stan's affair was enough of a humiliation. To have his girlfriend in her living room trying to pry money out of his estate was really too much. Florence wished to God Stan had handled his embarrassing affair a bit better. It was one thing to be humiliated. It was another to have to put up with his girlfriend's blatant attempts to wring blood money out of him as he lay somewhere between life and death in an intensive care unit.

"Then I suppose you also know that that cash is now invested in bearer bonds and deposited in Bahamian bank accounts," Lana said matter-of-factly. "The last Stan told me, they total more than two and a half million dollars."

"So?" Florence began to tap her foot impatiently. She could not believe how insanely indiscreet Stan had been. Getting sex outside their marriage was bad enough. Making a fool of himself over a younger woman was a public embarrassment. Blabbing about their finances to an outsider was absolutely unforgivable. Didn't Stan know any better? Had he completely lost his mind?

"And you do know, don't you, that Stan never reported the cash part of his business to the IRS?" Lana asked. Her tone was still pleasant. However, the expression in her eyes wasn't. It was an expression that Stan would have respected.

"My husband was in a dog-eat-dog business," said Florence, defending Stan and beginning to flush slightly. She was beginning to realize that Lana wasn't just a floozy.

Florence Fogel relatched the door and took her hand from the doorknob. She began to fidget with her gold bracelets, turning them around and around on her wrist. She wished Lana Bantry would get to the point and get the hell out.

"Tell me, Mrs. Fogel, do you and your husband file joint tax returns?" asked Lana.

"Of course! I'm his wife!"

"And you signed those returns?"

"Of course!"

"Then you realize, don't you, that you're legally responsible for whatever Stan did?"

Florence Fogel looked at Lana and finally realized exactly what she had been driving at. The hand that had been fidgeting with her bracelets suddenly stopped moving, and Florence Fogel turned pale under her makeup.

"You don't mean you'd go to the IRS?" Florence asked in shock, returning to the living room and sitting down again.

Florence, too, had heard Stan brag about his ticket to Rio. For thirty years, she had listened to his crazed speeches about how much he hated the IRS and all the ingenious ways he had figured out to escape their greedy clutches. Over the years, she had begged Stan not to do anything that might get him into trouble. She had told him that the money he might save wasn't worth the risk. He had refused to listen and now look!

"Not if I get what I want," said Lana pleasantly.

Florence Fogel was silent for a very, very long moment. She was an extremely intelligent woman, and she understood perfectly the dangers of the situation in which she now found herself.

"You were right, Lana. We do have a few things to talk about," said Florence calmly, speaking just as pleasantly as Lana had. Florence Fogel's reasonable tone hid a pounding heart and trembling, suddenly weak knees. "But first, would you like me to get you a cup of tea?"

Lana thanked her but refused the offer.

"Actually, I could use a real drink," Florence said, making up her mind to make the best of a bad bargain. Adopting the role of gracious hostess, she turned to Lana. "Would you like me to get you one, too?"

"Yes, as a matter of fact, I would," said Lana, accepting.

Florence Fogel went to the bar in the den to get the drinks, leaving Lana alone for a moment in the living room. If Stan had been there, he would have seen Lana smile. However, it probably would not have made him feel too terrific to know that he was the reason.

One week after Stan Fogel was released from the hospital, he suffered a second, fatal heart attack. His funeral was a large one as befitted a man of his local stature. It was attended by employees, business associates, prominent local figures, fellow members of the charities which Stan helped support and, of course, his grieving family.

Many people noticed how cordially, not to say even graciously, Florence Fogel accepted the condolences of Lana Bantry. Was it possible, people asked themselves, that Stan, always known to be extremely shrewd, had somehow, in a city as small as Providence, managed to keep his wife from finding out about his mistress? Obviously he had, they decided, unable to reach any other conclusion.

In death, Stan's reputation soared even higher than it had in life. Lana, thanks to the friendly agreement she and Florence Fogel had arrived at in Stan's own living room, finally had what she worked so hard to earn: the million and a half shares in Premiere that had once been Stan's.

Victory was sweet but it would turn out to be tainted, and Lana would find that her blessings were mixed indeed. Before the end of the year Lana would realize that, in fact, what she had won when she had won the Premiere stock was frustration, hassle and aggravation. She had simply exchanged one problem for another. To be specific, she had exchanged Stan for Stan's board of directors.

Although Lana did all the day-to-day work of actually running Premiere, it was the board that had the final say-so. The board had been assembled by Stan and consisted of Stan's two sons, Stan's lawyer, Stan's accountant and Stan's banker. Acting on Stan's wishes, they not only refused to give Lana the title, salary and stock options she deserved but, not having the knowledge of her abilities that Stan had had, they tied her hands in a dozen ways and Lana soon complained that she felt like an atomic engine trapped in a Model T.

"I own a million and a half shares. The board owns another million and a half. There are three million shares outstanding," Lana told Franklin Sparling, talking over her frustrations with him over lunch. "If I can buy up another half million shares, I can call a meeting and tell them to go fry ice."

Franklin Sparling nodded. He had faced a similar problem when his father died, leaving the company to him and a board that had no confidence in a twenty-two-year-old Yale graduate with a major in classical languages. "The stock is selling at seven. What you need is three and a half million dollars."

Lana looked at Franklin for a moment as she felt her heart sink to her knees. Then she told him what he had already guessed.

"That's exactly three million dollars more than I've got."

When Lana returned to her office an hour later, wondering if she would have the drive and the strength to overcome one more hurdle, Kenny Conlon was waiting for her. The news was bad, he said, as he waved the 13-D at her and told her that a corporate raider was making a run at Premiere. The raider's name, Kenny informed Lana, was Slash Steiner.

X V
S I L V E R
L I N I N G S

*W*hile *the Premiere board bickered over how to handle the* threat posed by Slash Steiner, Lana, spending sleepless night after sleepless night, lay awake remembering. She thought of Slash Steiner—and of his wife. Lana tried never to think about her sister because when she compared her life with her sister's, Lana felt almost eaten alive with envy. Through the years, Lana had received dozens of envelopes from the clipping service and she thought she knew everything there was to know about her sister.

Lana knew that Deedee Dahlen was a woman who had it all—a rich father, an adoring husband, two beautiful children. For years she had lived in a gorgeous town house and then moved to a fabulous Park Avenue triplex apartment. Both residences had been lovingly photographed by every magazine from *Vogue* to *Architectural Digest.* She wore the most expensive designer clothes and furs. She was a member of New York's most exclusive clubs and vacationed in the world's most glamorous resorts. She was a hostess of renown and entertained socialites, celebrities, political figures and important businessmen. Her parties, her clothes, her luncheons, even her choices in perfume and caterers and florists were all slavishly reported by the press.

Over the years, the clippings had included dozens of photographs of Deedee—at horse shows, at charity balls, at cocktail parties, at benefits for various charities, at innumerable fashionable openings and first nights. Deedee Dahlen had gotten married in 1964, the same year, coincidentally, that Lana herself had gotten married. However, Lana's "wedding" had taken less than ten minutes in Worcester's drab city hall. Deedee's had been a lavish extravaganza followed by a glamorous honeymoon that seemed simply a fitting interlude in the glittering life that had come before and after.

Deedee's husband, Lana had learned, had the curious name of Slash Steiner and, although it seemed absolutely impossible, the photographs made it clear that Slash Steiner was the same young man who had almost cost Lana her life on the night she had met her father. Slash Steiner received almost as much attention from the press as Deedee did. He was called the man with the Midas touch, and his money added to Deedee's made them a golden couple, showered with every material blessing imaginable.

The bitter and inescapable conclusion Lana drew as she lay awake thinking of her sister and the husband who was out to destroy Premiere was that Deedee Dahlen had been handed everything on a silver platter. She, Lana, on the other hand, had had to work and struggle and overcome a thousand bitter setbacks to get where she was, and even though she had come a long way, Lana was still far from rich.

It wasn't only money that represented the gulf between Lana and her sister. It was the comparison of the rest of their lives, too, that rankled. Lana was divorced and childless. Lana was still grieving over the untimely death of her lover, a grief made more bitter by the realization that when love had come along, she had been too wounded and too angry to recognize it.

Deedee Dahlen, on the other hand, had everything. She had love *and* money. A husband and a father, two beautiful children and a million dollars in the bank—just for being born. One day, Deedee Dahlen would inherit another immense fortune, a fortune Lana should have shared. Instead, not only would she inherit nothing but now Deedee Dahlen's husband was trying to take away what Lana had struggled so hard to earn.

Literally sick with resentment as the board finally decided

to give in to Slash Steiner, Lana mused bitterly about silver. Silver spoons, silver frames and silver platters. It was the thought of silver that suddenly gave Lana the idea she had been searching for, the plan that would, at last, make her the equal of her sister, the counterattack that would lead, at last, to her own triumph.

Lana smiled to herself as she suddenly thought of another kind of silver: silver linings.

"Goddamn son of a bitch! Double-crossing shithead!" It had been back in 1972 and Stan was not in a good mood. Counting his losses never did Stan's disposition any good. It got him right where it hurt most—in the ulcers.

What Lana remembered as her mind wandered during the board meeting was the way Stan had howled and cursed when his broker had suckered (Stan's word) him into buying stock in a small local company that made silver and silver-plate for the many costume jewelry manufacturers located in Rhode Island. The state traced its position as a center of the jewelry and silverware industry to the arrival in the seventeenth century of French Huguenots who were skilled in metalcrafting. Paul Revere, one of their more famous sons, was, of course, a silversmith as well as a Colonial patriot.

Subsequently, losing faith in the company, the broker had sold a few hundred thousand shares for various clients. Stan, however, had been in Bermuda at the time and had never received the broker's message warning him to get out of the stock. The massive sale of stock in the thinly held company had caused the stock's price to go south. Far south. Down past the Equator. The missed message had cost Stan a major bundle.

"Shit!" Stan had fumed, popping Tagamet and swilling Maalox. "A hundred grand gone! Down the tubes! Just like that!"

Stan, however, like the elephant, never forgot.

"The company's still a good company and a bargain is a bargain," he told Lana when, to her amazement, he began to buy back the stock a few weeks later.

Stan had methodically repurchased the stock at the depressed price. He then sat back and rode the price back up, making a small fortune in the process, turning what looked like a defeat into a big, big profit. The way Stan's curses had turned into cackles of joy gave Lana just the idea she had been searching for.

Lana stopped going into her office and camped out in her broker's office. She watched the Premiere stock as it moved across the tape. Trade by trade, its price, pushed upward by Slash's buying, went from seven to nine to ten. At ten and a half, Lana made her move.

"I want to sell my Premiere stock." Lana told her broker.

"How many shares?" he asked, automatically punching up the price on his Quotron.

"All of them," said Lana.

"Profit taking?" he asked, a ratty grin on his face as he calculated the commissions. "You always were shrewd, Miss Bantry."

Shrewder than even he imagined, thought Lana, knowing that the sale of her million and a half shares would cause the price of Premiere stock to deflate rapidly. When it had sunk to rock bottom, she would move again.

Lana left her broker's office, went home and immediately called her mother in Palm Beach.

"I want you to buy one and a half million shares of Premiere," Lana told Mildred. "Offer four dollars a share and divide the orders through brokers in Hyannis, Palm Beach and Worcester."

Lana wanted to break up the purchases. She did not want to leave too obvious a trail.

"Do it right now," she instructed Mildred. "Before the news gets out!"

Lana had waited a lifetime and it all happened in less than eighteen hours. The price of Premiere stock fell from ten and a half to ten to nine to eight to six. It finally stopped its free-fall at four, just as Lana had calculated.

With the fifteen million dollars she had made selling her stock at ten and a half, Lana bought back all the shares from her mother at four. Then she purchased an additional million shares that had been dumped on the market as the price had begun its nosedive.

In one afternoon, Lana made five million dollars in cash profit and bought complete control of Premiere at a rock-bottom price. She had also, she was sure, cost Deedee Dahlen her fortune and possibly even her marriage. Lana knew that her coup would have exploded through the Dahlen family like dynamite detonating. She told herself with satisfied anger that finally, finally, they would have to pay attention to her.

She wasn't the least bit surprised when, two days later, Russell Dahlen telephoned. She was certain that Russell Dahlen would know about Slash's losses in Premiere. The name Bantry was sufficiently uncommon so that Russell would have no trouble realizing who she was the minute Slash Steiner used her name. Although Lana did not know it, Russell had been searching for her for years. In a shocking twist of fate, it was she who had come to him.

"This is your father," he began awkwardly. "Russell Dahlen."

"I know who you are," said Lana, cutting him off. Russell Dahlen's accent was so distinctive, Lana would have known it anywhere. The sound of his voice had burned a hole in her memory. "What do you want?"

What Russell wanted was to talk to Lana and to find a way to restore Deedee's money and Slash's reputation while, at the same time, finally introducing Lana into the family. He told Lana how he had searched for her for years and how every trail had turned into a dead end. He told her how overjoyed he was to have her back in his life and how sorry he was that it had been a bitter business battle that had finally led him to her.

"I'd like to see you. I'd like to talk to you," Russell said. He wanted to tell Lana that he would do anything in his power to make things up to her. He would offer her money, recognition, acceptance, love. What he also wanted, Russell

Dahlen would explain, was to find a way to turn disaster into triumph and to have both halves of his family come together in healing mutual acceptance. "I'd like to have lunch with you. I believe I still owe you one from several years ago."

"Yes, indeed you do," said Lana, thinking that it hadn't been several years. It had been seventeen. Seventeen long, lonely, angry years of struggle and oblivion.

Russell was delighted when Lana agreed to meet him for lunch at the Paul Revere.

"There's something I want to show you. I have a surprise for you," said Russell. He sounded relieved and happy as he hung up. Lana smiled grimly. She, too, had a surprise for him.

That afternoon, Russell visited his lawyer.

"I want to change my will," he told Van Tyson. "I have a daughter no one knows about. I want to bring her into the family. I want to give her what she deserves. I want her to inherit half of the Dahlen stock in Lancome and Dahlen."

The change in Russell Dahlen's will made Lana equal to Deedee. Its wording officially acknowledged Lana's existence and accepted her into the Dahlen family. The will directed that half of the Dahlen shares in Lancome & Dahlen be turned over to Lana. Deedee, Russell knew, would be more than happy to share her vast inheritance with a sister who was a brilliant businesswoman, a woman who had out-smarted even Slash. With Lana as a partner, Deedee's own fortune would multiply infinitely.

When the new will was typed, signed and witnessed, Russell asked for and received a copy of it which he put into his jacket pocket. That will was the something he wanted to show Lana. It was the surprise he had promised her. It was his way of turning disaster into victory and bringing his family together at last.

In the years since Lana had treated her mother to a gradua-tion-day lunch, the Paul Revere had become a prominent local attraction. What had once been simply a restaurant had, over the years, expanded into a tourist complex comprising an entire reproduction Colonial village. The Paul Revere Village had a working foundry and brick-oven bakery, an old-fashioned mill that stone ground the flours used in the bakery, a yarn and candle shop. The original restaurant had grown into three large dining rooms surrounding a cobbled courtyard that was used for open-air dining during the warm summer months.

Russell drove up from New York and arrived for lunch right on time. Lana, as she had promised, had made a reservation and the headwaiter showed Russell to her table. He sipped a drink while he waited for Lana, anxious to see her, anxious to tell her his brilliant idea, the idea that was elegant in its simplicity and triumphant in its implications.

He would arrange for Lana to merge Premiere with Marx & Marx. The new, combined company would make Lana even richer, Deedee's fortune would be restored, Slash's reputation would be repaired and the Dahlen family would be united at last. It was the kind of masterstroke Russell had been looking for his entire life, the kind of masterstroke that would make Luther at last applaud with unreserved admiration and give him reason to point at his son with joyous, wholehearted pride. All Russell needed was Lana's cooperation, cooperation he was certain to receive when he showed her his new will.

Ordering a second drink, Russell glanced at his watch. Lana was now almost fifteen minutes late. At first, Russell ascribed her tardiness to traffic. When half an hour had passed, he asked the headwaiter if there was a message for him. There wasn't. Then Russell became concerned. Had she been hurt? Had she been in an accident? He cautioned himself not to overreact. He wondered if she'd mixed up the date, although that seemed impossible since it was Lana who had made the reservation. Russell Dahlen finally got up and telephoned his daughter's office. He was surprised when Lana herself answered the telephone.

"Is everything all right?" he asked, surprised to hear her voice.

"Everything's fine," she said.

"We have a lunch date," Russell said, confused to find her still in her office. He began to feel awkward. "I'm here at the Paul Revere. Have you forgotten?"

"No," she said. "I haven't forgotten."

Russell was perplexed.

"I've been waiting for you," he said, touching the copy of the new will in his jacket pocket. He was anxious to give it to her, anxious for her smile, anxious for the happiness they had both been cheated out of. The happiness they had both waited a lifetime for and deserved.

"I know."

"Then why aren't you here? Is something the matter?"

"Nothing's the matter," replied Lana coldly. "I just want you to know how it feels to wait for someone who never comes, how it feels to be a nobody."

Before Russell could say another word, she hung up.

The next morning Russell Dahlen resigned from Lancome & Dahlen. No one understood why and Russell refused to speak about his mysterious trip out of town and his sudden, unexpected resignation from the company his father had founded. He also told Van Tyson that he wanted to come in and change his will again. However, he never quite got around to it, postponing appointment after appointment. Russell was sure that somehow he and Lana would find a way to overcome their hurt feelings and reconcile. Reconciliation and happiness had been so close. Russell did not want to give up. Not completely.

A thousand times, Russell picked up the telephone to call Lana. A thousand times, he hung up before he dialed. He remembered the coldness and the anger in her voice, the coldness and the anger that chilled him, the coldness and the anger that were just like Luther's.

The next time, he promised himself as he hung up, he would complete the call. The next time, he promised himself, things would be different. The next time, he promised himself, he wouldn't feel so intimidated and so guilty.

* * *

People who knew the Dahlens thought that the family had suffered setbacks from which it would never recover. Russell Dahlen, they said, was a defeated man. They talked about his stooped posture and the way, almost overnight, his hair had turned white. They talked about the way he now spent all his time in his greenhouse, rarely leaving and rarely speaking. They talked about the way, sometimes, Russell Dahlen would begin to weep for no apparent reason at all.

Deedee, they said, was a broken woman, devastated by the loss, within less than six months, of her son, her husband and her fortune. They talked about the sudden, shocking way passion had turned to bitterness and how Deedee had brutally cut Slash out of her life. They talked about the way she shut herself up in her apartment, about the way she refused to see people and no longer accepted invitations, about Claire's obvious sadness and the way Deedee seemed unable to cope with the avalanche of problems Slash had left behind. They spoke about a nervous breakdown, a suicide attempt, a sanitarium.

PART FIVE

New York Rich / 1976–1988

"*When I was younger, there were millionaires. Now there are billionaires.*"

—BILL BLASS

"*Deedee's and Lana's lives intersected at those crucial moments in life when money doesn't matter and love isn't enough—the moments that leave everyone naked and defenseless. The moments, tragically, that made the two of them at last equal.*"

—ANNETTE GWILYM

I

ROLLS-ROYCES AND RICKSHAWS

On the same day that Deedee had screamed that she should have married Trip, Slash had gone to Providence. He wanted to meet the woman who had outsmarted him. He wanted to find out what she was like. He wanted to know if *this* Lana was *that* Lana. He wanted to know if Lana Bantry's Premiere coup was simply hard-nosed business or whether it was something more.

One look told Slash that Lana Bantry was the girl he had seen in Russell Dahlen's arms. Then she had been shabby and scared, an out-of-place redhead looking lost and scared in the lavish office and the luxurious surroundings. She was blond now but not brassy, and although she obviously thought big she was surprisingly petite.

"We've met before," Slash said as he entered Lana's pink, white and silver office. "In June 1960. Aren't you Russell Dahlen's . . . ?" Slash let the sentence trail off, not knowing himself what word he had intended to use.

"Enemy," Lana said, completing the sentence and answering the question. "You just happened to get in the way."

Her eyes and her voice warned Slash not to ask any more questions. Instead, he told her why he had come to Providence.

"The Premiere deal was just the beginning. The real problem was Trip Lancome. He double-crossed me," Slash told Lana, explaining that the losses in Premiere in themselves hadn't been what had cost him his wife, his money and his career. It was Trip who had turned a loss into a disaster, a miscalculation into a catastrophe. Slash had seen Trip not only pull the rug out from under him, but Trip had walked away with the huge profits in Marx & Marx, the deal Slash had set up in the first place. Slash was obsessed with his rival and unable to get over the fact that he had actually been naive enough to trust Trip. "I made him rich and he double-crossed me."

"I know the feeling," Lana said, thinking of Stan and understanding Slash's sense of betrayal. "Now what are you going to do?"

"Get it all back," Slash said. "And settle my score with Trip Lancome."

"What made you come to Providence?" asked Lana, thinking that the difference between Russell Dahlen and Slash Steiner was all the difference in the world. Russell had telephoned. Slash had made the trip. Russell had asked. Slash had acted. Russell had made a lunch date. Slash confronted her in her office.

"To give you a chance to get rich," Slash said. Even in defeat, Slash knew his value.

"I'm already rich," Lana reminded him. Their exchange was an eerie echo of Lana's earliest challenge to Stan and Slash's initial offer to Deedee.

"No, you're not," said Slash. "Not New York rich."

Slash's gray eyes were burnished steel and the tone of his voice dared Lana not to take her next step into the different world that still excluded her. It was a dare it did not occur to her to refuse.

Just as Lana had tempted Stan, Slash tempted Lana. New York rich wasn't millions. It was tens of millions, hundreds of millions. New York rich wasn't quiet rich or shy rich. New York rich was outspoken rich and can-you-top this? rich. New York rich was Slash's kind of rich. It was Lana's kind of rich.

He was going to start over, Slash told Lana. This time, Slash told Lana, he would do it on his terms. This time, he would do it by himself. This time, no one would be able to say that he had married his way to the top. He was still in his mid-thirties, he pointed out, young enough to have dreams, old enough to have experience. He would get Deedee back. He would get the money back. He would get his reputation back.

Slash then went to Boston and took the first plane out. It went to Seattle where, wanting to protect Deedee from the mess he had left behind, Slash hired a lawyer. Then he took the next flight to Singapore. He would begin his quest for redemption in the place where he had once begun a marriage.

Rolls-Royces and rickshaws, the Confucian work ethic combined with Western capitalism, confidence bordering on arrogance, Western skills and Asian patience, Chinese imperial luxury, American efficiency, French fashions, Japanese management techniques, fortune tellers, noodle makers, herbal medicine shops, spicy satays, the Singapore sling, a golden-domed mosque, Hindu shrines, Chinese festivals for the living, the dead, the ghostly and Lady Luck—Singapore is an amalgam of Chinese, Malay, Indian, Arab and British colonial influences shot straight into the twentieth century.

Nineteenth-century wooden houses painted blue or orange or pink with massive wooden shutters stand in the shadow of gleaming brass-and-glass vertical shopping malls. Skyscrapers housing the international financial district look down on a harbor serving the vessels of over three hundred shipping lines. Multilane highways lead to the Tiger Balm gardens, and for every Givenchy and Dior boutique, there is a fortune teller, or a tiny hole in the wall selling Hindu festival cards or live birds or handmade wooden clogs lacquered red for good luck. Tiny food stalls serving memorably delicious Szechuan, Nonya, Cantonese, Hokkien and Punjabi specialties hunch up together a chopstick's length away from the Overseas Banking Corporation's building, designed by I. M. Pei. Singapore seemed a Switzerland with Chinese food, a boom town with a difference—a past and a future.

In the summer of 1977, Singapore was in the middle of an extraordinary building boom that was transforming its shape and skyline. The statistic was that a new building was begun every seventeen minutes. The noise of jackhammers, pile drivers and fully loaded dump trucks drowned out even the blare of Chinese funeral trucks. So feverish was the building fever that traditional neighborhoods that had existed for scores of years were bulldozed in half an afternoon. Korean, Vietnamese and Malaysian laborers lived right on the construction sites and worked three shifts in constant rotation, twenty-four hours a day, seven days a week, fifty-two weeks a year.

The crisis of confidence that had undermined Slash's judgment in the months following Russ's death had passed, and Slash felt like his old self again. A sleepless night led to his decision to relocate.

"I had gone to Singapore to try to remember what I had been like when Deedee had fallen in love with me when I woke up and heard jackhammers going at three in the morning," Slash told Adrian Adams, who was on a swing through Asia with his current lollipop. She was listed on his expense sheet as a secretary, and she seemed to think that duty free meant free. Slash had invited Adrian to his penthouse office on Singapore's prestigious Orchard Road, an office whose design, in time-honored Asian style, had been supervised by a *feng shui* monk who repositioned the entrance doors at angles to fend off sinister spirits which, according to tradition, travel only in straight lines.

"It didn't take a genius to realize that real estate was the place to be. Using a suite in the Shangri-la that I couldn't afford as an office, I began buying options on buildings that weren't even a hole in the ground yet with money I didn't have," Slash continued, squinting a hawklike smile from behind his dark sunglasses.

"The way it worked was that the Chinese developers sold options to investors to raise money to pay for the construction costs," Slash continued, giving Adrian a crash course in getting rich quick, Asian style. "The investors, in turn, waited until the building went up and then made their profits by reselling the options—to art galleries, restaurants, camera shops, department stores, boutiques.

"It was just like the bull market of the sixties: people were turning money over every six to eight months. It was get-rich-quick time, and everyone was cashing in: English employees of London companies, Japanese executives of Tokyo corporations, Chinese wheeler-dealers and Malay government officials. They were all making more money in Tanglin Road and Orchard Street real estate options than they were in their own businesses.

"Eventually, so was I. And Lana, too, because after I made the deals, I had to find the money, and the richest person I knew at the time who I was still on speaking terms with was Lana," Slash concluded as Adrian, a notorious gossip, lapped up every last detail. He could hardly wait to get back to New York to spread the word.

"Singapore? Real estate options? Tanglin Road mixed-use towers?" replied Lana dubiously when Slash proposed that she invest some of her profits on the Premiere deal to help finance him in Singapore's booming real estate market. "What do you know about that?"

It was just the kind of question Slash had been asked a thousand times and even though he was the one who needed the money, he felt on safe, familiar ground.

"I can count," he said bluntly, treating her to his best fuck-you smile. "That's all I need to know. Now, are you in or out?"

Lana remembered all the times she had been told she was too cheap and too conservative. She also remembered what Kenny had found out about Slash Steiner: that he had come from nowhere to make a fortune in the sixties, a fortune he had multiplied in the seventies. Despite his miscalculation with Premiere, Slash Steiner was, after all, the man with the Midas touch and he had offered her a chance to get rich. New York rich.

Slash Steiner was certainly smart, Lana realized. And she had changed. Taking over Premiere in the dazzlingly shrewd way that she had had made a quantum difference in Lana's opinion of herself and her place in the world. She was no longer Stan's apprentice, no longer bound by the talents and the limits that had made Stan a small-town millionaire—and kept him one. Lana was no Stan, content to find a niche and stay comfortably in it. She never had been. Lana's ambitions were big and her horizons bigger.

"In," she told Slash, taking her own sweet time to give him her answer and matching his fuck-you smile with one of her own.

Slash's first partner was Tan Siah Lee, and the first thing Tan told Slash was that the deal was sold out. Tan had a fat, smiling Buddha tattooed on his chest from nipple to nipple, collarbone to belly button and wore his shirts open to the navel to display the artwork. Tan was called a liar and thief by the people who liked him. The ones who didn't like him just shook their heads and tried to stay away.

Everyone agreed, though, that whatever Tan's shortcomings and liabilities, he was a very, very good businessman who always had very, very good luck. They also said that Tan had the largest space reserved in the cemetery because Tan never went anywhere without his white Mercedes and his six-foot-tall black Senegalese driver—including the hereafter. Tan, it was said, did not intend to meet his maker anonymously.

"Come on, Tan. Don't shit me," chided Slash. They were lunching on dim sum at the Shangri-la's elegant ground floor restaurant. In Singapore, as in many Far Eastern cities, the best restaurants are often found in the expensive hotels. "I know that the ground floor southwest corner is still available. I had dinner with your lawyer's secretary last night. He types up all the option contracts and he knows what's sold and what isn't . . ."

"You must be Chinese," said Tan nodding his head, impressed at Slash's resourcefulness.

"I wish you'd tell that to all the people who think I'm Jewish," Slash said, thinking of the uptight WASPs who ran Lancome & Dahlen and remembering when he had been referred to as the house yid.

Tan, from the Teochew minority himself, recognized an ally when he saw one. After a good laugh that shook Tan's belly—which was just as big as the Buddha's—Tan admitted that the southwest corner might possibly be made available and, over crab fingers, steamed dumplings and Johnny Walker Black Label, he and Slash began to talk price.

When the time came to cash out, Slash shared his profits on the southwest corner of Fortune Plaza with the lawyer, the lawyer's secretary and Tan himself. When Slash handed Tan the check, he said: "Next time, come to me first."

When he handed Lana her check, he said: "I've got another deal going. Are you in?"

"Why not?" she replied, looking at the check and seeing that Slash had doubled her money in six months. "I can count, too."

Slash's second partner was Kok Kah Kee. Kok Kah Kee was a small, spare man whose ego more than made up for his lack of size. He liked to be known as the J. Paul Getty of Asia. His pearl-gray suits matched his pearl-gray Rolls and his business interests ranged from rubber and copra plantations in Malaysia to marine salvage companies and fast-food franchises that spanned the crescent from Tokyo to Karachi. Despite what he had heard about Slash's shrewdness, Kok tried to sell him the less desirable back part of the combined vertical shopping mall and condominium apartment tower he was building and not the more desirable front side.

"Back or front. It's all on the ground level. It's all the same. Prime real estate," Kok Kah Kee told Slash during a thirty-five-course banquet in an ornate red-and-gold private dining room at the Imperial.

"If you believe front and back are the same, maybe I could interest you in buying a bridge," replied Slash, wondering if Kok Kah Kee really believed what he was saying or if he simply thought that Westerners were incredibly dumb. "It connects lower Manhattan with Brooklyn . . ."

Kok Kah Kee, busy with his guests, either did not hear, pretended not to hear or chose not to hear and Slash, finding his place card, sat down. He noticed that every other chair was left empty as Kok Kah's other businessmen guests found their place cards and took their places. When the public doors were shut and the guests were alone with their host, Slash found out why: At the sound of a gong a file of exquisitely beautiful young Asian girls elaborately gowned, bejeweled, made up and perfumed came in and took the empty seats. Each girl then proceeded to feed the man to her right choice delicacies morsel by morsel with solid gold chopsticks.

"You want her, she's yours," Kok Kah told Slash as he made the rounds, working the room. He indicated the lovely girl who had been assigned to Slash, to feeding him, to seeing that his glass was full, to engaging him in conversation, to laughing at his jokes and smiling appreciatively at his every word. Kok Kah Kee was known as a gracious and generous host, a quality much admired by the Chinese, and Slash accepted his host's offer.

The next day, Kok Kah Kee showed his other side.

"Take the back side of the building," he said, trying to cajole Slash.

"No way!" said Slash.

"I don't see why not," persisted Kok Kah Kee.

When Slash stubbornly held out for the front, Kok Kah finally intimated that he would not be above blackmail. The girl, according to Kok Kah Kee, was only thirteen.

"Americans, I think," mused Kok Kah Kee, "would not approve."

"Are you kidding? Next time take my picture! You'd be doing me a favor," replied Slash.

Kok Kah Kee blinked, not quite understanding. Slash spelled out his meaning.

"Listen, Mr. Kok, my reputation's already so lousy no one would be the least bit shocked," Slash said. Then he leaned forward and spoke very, very clearly so that the elegantly dressed Chinese could not possibly misunderstand. "In fact, back home they'd be impressed."

Between outmaneuvering Tan and standing up to Kok Kah Kee, Slash acquired what Asians respect most: face. Slash's word was often better than other men's signed promises, and his performance backed up his façade. In Singapore as on Wall Street, Slash's style often shocked, but his honor and integrity, in Singapore as on Wall Street, were never doubted.

From then on, the best deals went to Slash first and at Kok Kah Kee's dinner parties Slash was inevitably seated at the tables with the red cloths and the prettiest girls. Among the Chinese the tables with red cloths are reserved for the most honored guests. So are the prettiest girls.

"They know they can trust me," Slash explained to Lana, telling her that in the Orient, once a man is trusted, a handshake is better than a 150-page contract vetted by a dozen lawyers. "And they know I'll share the profits."

Slash loved doing business with the Chinese and the Chinese loved doing business with Slash. When Tan gave a two-day party to celebrate the completion of a factory for the manufacture of denim jeans that would carry an American label and be shipped back to the States for sale, Slash got an idea.

"You could do Premiere's manufacturing cheaper here than you can in Providence," he told Lana after he'd done a bit of research. "Even including shipping costs back to the States, your manufacturing costs would be half. You'd get a price advantage over all your competitors."

"And what would you get?" Lana asked.

"Half," said Slash.

Thus it was that Premiere, until then a New England-based company, took the first step from being a regional business to being an international corporation. Lana's dream of making Premiere into the pacesetter in its field took its first step toward becoming a reality, and Lana and Slash, who had started off as adversaries, officially became partners.

They were two of a kind. He was unconventional and so was she. He was frightened of nothing and neither was she. He had just survived a stunning turning point in life and so had she. He was looking for further horizons and so was she.

He was a man who had just lost a wife and she was a woman who had just lost a lover.

Lana, Slash had long since realized, was no million-dollar baby. She was a million-dollar woman with a checkbook all her own. She was no old-fashioned woman looking for a sugar daddy or a meal ticket. She was an independent woman comfortable in a man's world—and with a man's attitude toward romance. That combination, volatile and unpredictable, explosive with unspoken secrets and vast amounts of money, quickly made, was what made it all so exciting.

That—and the fact that Slash and Lana were in a strange culture where all the restraints of home were temporarily suspended. They were playing a dangerous game, and both of them wondered which of them would make the next move first.

I I

SHAMBLES

In May of 1977, barely one month after Slash's depar-
ture, the board of Lancome & Dahlen unanimously voted
Trip Lancome the company's new president. The heir had
been anointed. Tradition had been upheld and Slash Steiner,
a comet that had briefly blazed through the skies, was forgotten and condemned to the limbo of nonpersons.

"He worked here for a while," Trip would admit if anyone
asked about Slash. "But he wasn't that important. After all,
he never even made partner."

In that same month, Deedee received a letter from a lawyer
in Seattle informing her that her husband had left the country. The letter said that Slash would be in touch with her. It
did not say where Slash had gone or when she would hear
from him again. Because of the pending lawsuits, the letter
concluded, it would be better if she did not know of his
whereabouts.

Deedee had always had love and money in abundance. She
had never imagined that she'd ever be without them. She had
never dreamed that she would be penniless and alone. She
had never thought that Slash would leave. She had never
dreamed that a woman she had never heard of named Lana
Bantry would turn her life upside down. However, in the
spring of 1977, right after the Premiere debacle, Deedee was
face to face with disaster—financial disaster and emotional
disaster.

The money was gone and so was Slash. Deedee's life had become a void, and into the void came the terror. Deedee, who had never written a check in her entire life, never held a job and never stood in a check-out line in a supermarket, woke up every morning with a leaden feeling of dread and emptiness. She did not answer the telephone and she did not go out. She became a recluse, and some said that she was having a nervous breakdown. Others went further and said that she had entered a sanitarium.

"I don't answer the phone because it's usually someone wanting money and I don't know what to tell them," she told her mother. "I don't go out because I'm too embarrassed and ashamed to face people. I'm not a widow and I'm not a wife. I'm not separated or divorced. I'm no one and I'm nowhere."

"Yes, you are! You're still Deedee Dahlen," insisted Joyce, reminding Deedee of her past and her future. Joyce feared for Deedee and wanted to give her a reason not to give in to despair. "You have a name that means something and one day you'll inherit the Dahlen stock. Nothing and no one can ever take that away from you."

Nevertheless, despondent and depressed, Deedee began to hoard sleeping pills and tranquilizers. She thought about death and sometimes talked about suicide.

Deedee, with no choice, accepted financial help from her parents and grandparents, help that was never enough in the face of the tremendous debts, expensive lawsuits and gargantuan overhead Slash had left behind. Despite her fury at Slash, she even accepted the occasional checks that Slash mailed through his Seattle lawyer, checks that still didn't make a dent in the mess he had left behind.

Deedee put the triplex and the Southampton house on the market. She fired her help, returned her credit cards and canceled her charge accounts. She shopped for bargains, clipped coupons and sold her furs and designer clothes to resale shops for a fourth their original cost while she waited for someone to rescue her.

"You're turning yourself into a martyr," said Nina in the summer of 1977, the summer when Manhattan was revealed to be a vulnerable island. The summer of a massive power failure that closed stores, offices and tunnels, a power failure that was followed by massive looting and arson in a wild, angry spree. A brutal summer of the Son of Sam murders that made women afraid to go out alone. A summer when everything seemed to come to a dead end, including Deedee's hopes and fantasies.

Nina told Deedee that her *nouveau* poverty was excessive. "No wonder you can't find a man."

The comment was devastating. Particularly, Deedee realized, because it was true. She did feel like a martyr. She felt as if she had been singled out by fate for terrible punishments she had done nothing to deserve. She blamed Slash for everything that had gone wrong, and even though she realized that her attitude was making her unattractive, she seemed helpless to change it.

What was also devastating was her discovery of the shocking differences between being single, rich and beautiful and being the abandoned wife of the high-flying man with the Midas touch who had disappeared in the middle of a sensational financial scandal. The men she had once relied on to court her and cater to her were now married, gay, preoccupied with business or interested only in an affair.

Trip had remarried shortly after he'd been named president of Lancome & Dahlen, and although Deedee sometimes had fantasies of taking him away from his new wife, he was clearly not interested. He told her point-blank that he was furious at the cowardly way she had withdrawn her portfolio at the first weakening in the market, and he informed her that she had only gotten what she deserved.

"I told you so," Trip said, not even bothering to suppress his gloating pleasure at the fact that he had turned out to be right. "I warned you about Slash Steiner a long time ago."

Deedee was devastated each time a new romance begun with high hopes crashed on the shoals of reality.

"You're too old," one man told her bluntly. "I'm interested in someone in her twenties."

"Claire is too much of a burden," another man said, referring to Claire's alternate clinginess and rebelliousness and her problems at school—both in and out of the classroom. "One look and I can see she's trouble."

One potential romance after another died stillborn as men told Deedee that they had met someone else, someone younger, freer, richer, more famous, more successful, more talented, more interesting, more with-it. The good news was that by the late 1970s, women had been liberated. The not-so-good news was that men's expectations of women had soared to stratospheric heights.

Women were expected to be successful—and sexy. To be able to run a business—and a house. To be domestic—and devastating. To be moms—and mistresses. To take a meeting—and take out the garbage. Women who knew only how to be perfect wives were as out of style as the Model T. Everyone was on the fast track now, and no one cared about million-dollar babies anymore, particularly million-dollar babies who had lost all their money.

Barbara Hutton had died, frail and alone, after seven husbands, the whereabouts of her fabulous jewelry collection a mystery. Brenda Frazier of the red lips and white strapless dresses was also dead, her youthful marriage to Shipwreck Kelly just a sidebar in yesterday's society news. Doris Duke had withdrawn completely into private life. Gloria Vanderbilt had emerged from a privileged and painful childhood to become a well-known artist and successful businesswoman. The era that had made them the gossip column celebrities they had once been was gone along with the Stork Club and the Colony, coming-out parties and convertibles, hats from Lily Daché and solid gold swizzle sticks. By the time Deedee turned thirty-four and Slash had been gone almost a year, she felt like a relic.

She had no money and few friends. Her social life had dwindled to nothing. Claire was clearly in trouble and so, if something didn't happen soon, was she. Nothing in her entire life had ever prepared Deedee to take care of herself. She didn't feel sexually desirable; it seemed clear that she wasn't socially desirable. She no longer had money, looks or youth. Her life was a mess. She was a mess. Deedee knew it all too well.

She drifted through her days in a cloud of numbness punctured by fits of weeping and bouts of regret. She was paralyzed by indecision and conflict. She wanted Slash to take care of her, but she never wanted to see him again. She kept the love letters he sent and wrote replies which she never mailed. She wanted a divorce so that she could be free but free for what, she asked herself bitterly, postponing appointment after appointment with her lawyers. She wanted to get her broker's license but couldn't even concentrate enough to read a newspaper. She wanted to earn money but didn't even know how to get a job.

She would go to her bathroom cabinet and, like a miser, count the pills she had saved. She would wonder if she had enough. She would wonder if she would have the courage to take them. She would wonder how much worse things could get.

By the winter of 1978, Deedee had not been able to find a buyer for either the apartment or the house. Both were too big, too expensive and too difficult to maintain to be easily sold. In the summer of 1978, the co-op board in Manhattan threatened to take legal action unless Deedee paid the arrears in maintenance in full. In the autumn of 1978, Deedee almost lost the Southampton house because of long overdue property taxes. Living from hand to mouth, a beggar in her own family, Deedee lurched along until the autumn of 1979. Right before Thanksgiving, the roof of Deedee's flimsy house of mirrors caved in when Prudence Mars, the headmistress of the Epson School, told Deedee that Claire was simply too difficult and too disruptive to remain in the classroom.

Deedee was shocked to hear that Claire had stolen one girl's book bag and thrown her homework away, appalled to learn that Claire had deliberately spilled milk on another girl's brand-new winter coat. She listened in silence as Prudence Mars told her that Claire talked back to teachers, walked out of classes and would be getting the first failing grades in her entire life.

"Claire's behavior is disturbing the other girls and, unless Claire gets both extra tutoring and psychological counseling, we're going to have to ask you to take Claire out of Epson," Prudence Mars told Deedee at the midterm parents' conference.

Deedee nodded silently and wondered where she would get the money. She was already desperate for money. Money to pay the maintenance. Money to pay property taxes. Money to pay the debts Slash had left behind. Money to pay for all the things that Luther's budget didn't allow for and that Russell's clandestine checks and Slash's erratic ones didn't even begin to cover. And, now, on top of everything else, Prudence Mars had told Deedee what she had known all along: that Claire needed help. Expensive help.

Deedee could just imagine what Luther would say if she asked him to pay for a therapist for Claire. Russell's reaction, if he could pull himself out of his own depression long enough, would undoubtedly be the same. If only she could call Slash, she would. But Slash was gone and Deedee was desperate.

In January of 1979 not knowing if she was right or wrong, brave or foolish, self-sufficient or self-destructive, Deedee swallowed the tatters of her pride and went downtown to the white granite building at the corner of Wall and Broad. By the time she walked up the elegant, richly carpeted staircase to the big office in the corner, she had convinced herself that she had nowhere else to go.

"It isn't just for myself," Deedee said, twisting the chain handle of her handbag into hard little knots just like the hard little knots in her stomach. She was sitting opposite the big, polished antique desk in an elegant visitor's chair. She felt like what she was: a supplicant. "It's for Claire. She's getting failing grades and she's going to be expelled from school. She needs extra help and I can't afford it."

"You knew that Slash was an outlaw when you married him," said Trip unsympathetically, reminding her of her dereliction. The sound of his voice from across the expanse of the desk seemed to come from a thousand miles away. The gold wedding ring on his left hand seemed to mock her.

That past January, on a business trip to Paris, Junior Lancome had died peacefully in his room at the Ritz. Trip was now chairman, as well as president, of Lancome & Dahlen. He was running the company he had inherited with no interference from anyone now that Luther, in his mid-eighties, was only a figurehead and Russell had retired. The vacuum that Slash had once predicted had come to pass, only it was Trip, not Slash, who was there to fill it.

"Please, Trip," Deedee said, hearing herself beg. "I'm desperate."

Trip smiled and shrugged. He looked expensive and invulnerable in a Savile Row custom-tailored suit, an immaculately pressed shirt and a subtle silk tie. Not one blond hair was out of place, and he looked as if he had never been tired or ill and never felt a moment's fear or apprehension in his entire life.

"I won't insult you by offering you charity. Instead, I'll make you an offer," he said finally, acting as if he were doing her a favor. "I'll give you an advance, a very generous advance, on the Lancome and Dahlen stock you will inherit when your father dies. I'll give you the money right now, today, if you want. You can leave here in an hour with a check—a large check. That way, you and Claire will never again have financial problems."

"And you'll end up owning all of Lancome and Dahlen?" Deedee asked. Even through her pain and humiliation, Deedee remembered what Slash had always said about Trip wanting to take over the entire company one day.

Trip nodded.

"It's a good deal for you, Deedee. After all, you don't know the first thing about the company," Trip said, reminding Deedee of her incompetence.

"But the stock is my inheritance. It's all I've got," Deedee said, thinking that Russell wasn't even dead and Trip was already trying to take over the Dahlen share of the company Luther had helped found.

"It's your choice, Deedee. You can leave here with enough to live on for the rest of your life or you can leave here empty-handed," Trip said coldly. He had the upper hand now and he was unsparing and unforgiving in its use.

Deedee stared at him for a moment, and she finally shook her head silently. The Dahlen stock meant more than just money to her. It represented an identity, a family, a history. The Dahlen stock wasn't just hers. One day, it would be Claire's.

"No, Trip. I won't sell it to you. If you won't help, Slash will," she said, getting up to leave. If she had to go to Seattle to get Slash's address, she would. If she had to hire a detective to find Slash, she would. If she had to turn the earth upside down to find him, she would.

"I wouldn't be too sure of that," said Trip.

Deedee looked at him.

"What do you mean?" she said, refusing to take one more insult, one more condescending remark. "Of course he will!"

"Not as long as he's in love with another woman," said Trip. He took Deedee firmly by the arm and, guiding her carefully, almost as if she were crippled, he walked her toward the door.

"What other woman?" Deedee demanded, stopping in her tracks to face Trip.

"Lana Bantry," said Trip, repeating the name he'd heard from Adrian Adams. As Deedee's face crumbled, Trip smiled and twisted the knife. "They're partners. In and out of bed."

As Deedee made her way back down the marble staircase, almost blinded by tears, she thought of the pills in her medicine chest. They were waiting for her. Slash had been gone for two years. He had found someone else. He wasn't coming back. All she had was herself and herself, as had been made clear to her since childhood, wasn't nearly enough. It was time, Deedee thought. She had a way out. She had the solution. She had the courage. Trip had given it to her.

As she hailed a taxi and gave the driver her address, Deedee felt the lifting of an unbearable burden. She would go home. She would take the pills. She would no longer be a burden to her family, an inadequate mother to her daughter.

Deedee leaned back in the taxi and sighed in relief. She felt that she had made the right decision. Her parents would take care of Claire and she would, at last, find peace.

III

FOREIGN

AFFAIRS

*D*uring the worst of her struggles with Stan, Lana had sworn never to get involved with another married man. Love with a married man had broken her mother's heart. Love with a married man had broken her own heart. Married men were trouble. Married men were poison. Married men were heartbreak.

Even though Slash Steiner was half a globe away from the wife who was openly speaking of her plans to divorce him, he was, thought Lana, no different from any other married man. In fact, he was even more dangerous. More dangerous because, unlike Stan, he was no middle-aged married man in search of love and a second chance. More dangerous because his wife was no stranger but a sister.

A thousand times, Lana wanted to tell Slash that she and Deedee were sisters but she was afraid. Afraid he wouldn't believe her. Afraid that he would. Afraid he would tell her that it didn't matter. Afraid he would tell her that it did.

Every time Lana made love to Slash, she felt an electrifying combination of triumph and shame. Triumph over the sister she hated and envied since she had been sixteen. Shame at the shocking secret she was keeping from her lover. Every time Lana made love to him, she told herself that it was the last time.

Those secret thoughts and feelings of Lana's, never shared with Slash, gave each of their sexual encounters an intense and almost desperate edge.

"Are you always that passionate?" Slash asked Lana in amazement during their first weekend together. They had clawed and sucked each other. They had clutched and grabbed at each other and, at the moment of climax, they had cried out and then collapsed, exhausted and at the point of tears. Deedee was the most responsive woman Slash had ever made love to. Lana, however, was the wildest and most uninhibited. "Are you always like that?"

"No," said Lana, still shaken herself from the intensity of their lovemaking. She had never been to bed with a man as sexually charged as Slash and she had never had so much at stake as in this secret competition with the woman she so desperately envied. "Just with you."

Even after the very earliest weeks of their affair, their lovemaking continued to have a mysterious, almost violent quality that Slash could never understand but which never failed to electrify him. The man who prized control above all had finally met a woman who could make him lose control, and the seducer found himself being seduced.

"You're already a success," Slash told Lana, "but I can help make you more successful."

"You're already rich," he told her, "but I can help make you richer."

The first thing Slash did was to help Lana negotiate a deal with a Singapore manufacturing company to make electrical products—hair dryers, hot combs, drying lamps—for Premiere at half the United States cost. The second thing he did when it became clear that their relationship was about to become more than just business was to tell her that he could never marry her.

"I want to be honest with you. I don't want to mislead you. I want you to know the truth," Slash said the first time they had dinner alone. "I'm madly in love with my wife."

"From what you say, all she seems interested in is divorce," Lana said, reminding Slash that he had told her that Deedee had already hired lawyers.

"She'll change her mind," said Slash confidently. He

thought of his separation from Deedee as temporary. He thought of Deedee's anger as temporary.

"Don't be so sure," Lana replied, wondering whether Slash, who was usually so realistic, might be indulging in a bit of wish fulfillment. "Besides, has it ever occurred to you that *you* might change yours?"

"And you think you're the woman who can make me?" asked Slash with a sudden challenging smile.

"Why not?" said Lana, accepting the challenge as she took him into her arms.

Once again, triumph conquered shame and Lana, justifying her behavior, told herself that if Deedee didn't want Slash, she did.

Slash said one thing and did another. He kept telling Lana that he didn't want to get involved with her or with anyone, but he spent all his free time with her. He kept telling her that their romance was strictly business, but once he helped set up the manufacturing company for her, he made sure that she had to spend more and more time in Singapore. With him.

"The labor contracts have to be signed," he told Lana over the telephone. He was in Singapore. She was in Providence. "You'd better come a few days early so that we can go over them first."

After the labor contracts were signed and Lana had returned to Providence, there were problems of quality control, questions of design and color, decisions about which vendors to buy switches, plastics and wirings from, choices about packaging, shipping and printing, as well as the necessity for constant meetings with local management, tax experts and legal authorities. All of them, it seemed, needed Lana's personal attention.

By the spring of 1978, Slash and Lana were treated as a couple all over Singapore. Slash introduced Lana to his business associates and acquaintances—to hard-working and hard-living Chinese real estate tycoons, to elegant English executives deceptively shrewd behind their perfect manners, sophisticated Japanese entrepreneurs driven to excellence, beautifully educated Indian lawyers with sensitive eyes, handsome Malay politicians both honest and otherwise.

"The English are smarter than they look," Slash told Lana, sharing one of his shrewder insights. "And the Japanese are dumber."

Slash and Lana were invited everywhere together—to ul- traexpensive restaurants overlooking the Strait, to the pala- tial homes of rich Chinese swarming with silent servants and the latest in Western luxuries, to dinner dances at private clubs and weekend parties in exclusive hideaways on the long white beaches on the China Sea between Kuantan and Mers- ing on the east coast of Malaysia.

"The east coast of Malaysia is the Riviera of the Orient," Slash said, singing its praises. "It's Southampton with curry, the Caribbean with soy sauce, the Greek Islands with coco- nuts."

And a married man's vacation from his wife, Lana added bitterly to herself as Slash continued to talk about how much he loved Deedee, about how much he missed her and how he would never be really happy until he got her back. Lana was sick and tired of hearing Slash sing Deedee's praises. She expressed bitterness and resentment and told Slash that she was fed up hearing him talk about how much he adored his wife. One day, Lana said, she was going to hand him an ultimatum.

"One day," she threatened, "I'm going to force you to choose between us."

What neither Slash nor Lana understood was that Slash's longing for Deedee was an essential part of their relationship because Lana's bitterness, however sincere and deeply felt, was a screen. A screen behind which lay Lana's own doubts, hesitations and ambivalences. She felt both guilty and victori- ous at being in bed with her sister's husband. She was ashamed of herself and proud of herself at the same time.

Lana's private life, in contrast to her business life, had been filled with pain and failure. She had been divorced once and had been, for years, a married man's back-street girlfriend. In a decade of diminished expectations, Lana was a skittish seventies lover, one foot out the door at all times. She longed for commitment but she was wary of it. She wanted love but she had been burned by it. She yearned for happiness but doubted whether it existed. She knew from experience that she hadn't been able to distinguish love from lust and that she had confused romance with reality.

Just as Slash said one thing and did another, Lana often felt one thing and said another. When she wasn't threatening Slash with ultimatums, she was telling him that she actually preferred an affair that was more business than romance.

"Business lasts," Lana said, telling Slash about her marriage to Tom and her affair with Stan. Both had started as irresistible romances, she said. Both had ended as resistible hassles. "Romance doesn't."

She told him that for a woman as busy as she was, a part-time lover was better than a full-time husband.

"A husband is a luxury I can't afford," Lana explained, saying that the demands of domesticity were more than she had the time or energy to cope with. "A lover is a necessity I can."

When Slash told Lana that they had no future, she replied that the future didn't interest her. When he warned her that what they were enjoying was strictly an affair, she replied that an affair was all she had time for. When he told her about how much he loved Deedee, she told him that she'd been there before: the girlfriend of a man who wasn't available. She told him that she knew all about it: the pluses and the minuses, the advantages and the disadvantages, the perils and the pleasures.

"I can handle it," Lana told Slash, assuring him—and herself—and relieved, deep down, that Slash wasn't asking her to make any permanent commitment.

"I don't want either of us to get hurt," Slash said, because however much he loved Deedee, he was beginning to care for Lana more than he wanted to admit and she sensed it. Her ambivalence expressed itself in alternating bouts of pride and shame. Her pride told her to continue. Her shame told her to get out. The war between pride and shame and her deepening attraction to the man who was now the most important person in her life prevented Lana from acting.

Instead, she drifted in even closer at the same time that she told herself that she could walk away any time she chose. She was still telling herself that the next time she went to bed with Slash would be the last time.

As the emotional connection deepened between Slash and Lana, so did their business relationship. Frequently, the demonstrations of Slash's feelings for Lana took a material and practical form. He oversaw her Singapore factory when she wasn't there and he invested for her in its booming real estate market.

Because of Slash, Lana's thinking became even bolder, her horizons wider. The small-town millionaire she had once been gradually disappeared under Slash's influence. Lana's vision became more and more global and her references increasingly international.

"If you really want to build Premiere," Slash told her, "the best way to do it is to buy up other companies and merge them into Premiere."

With Slash's advice and encouragement, Lana bought a California company that made high-quality organic shampoos, setting gels and mousses and a Georgia-based company that made decorative hair accessories ranging from elegant barrettes to colorful clips and clamps. She merged both companies into Premiere.

"Premiere has doubled in size in less than fifteen months," said Lana. "Thanks to you."

"There's still plenty of potential for growth," replied Slash and mentioned the name of a company that manufactured the aerosol cans hair sprays and mousses came in. "It would be a perfect fit for Premiere," he said and, after looking into the situation, Lana agreed.

The more business Slash and Lana did together, the more reasons there were for them to spend time together. There would be a problem at the factory, a cash flow crisis, a crucial financial or manufacturing or marketing decision to be made.

Lana would go to Singapore and to Slash because Slash was always the one with the answers, the one who could always see the way out of a problem, the one with the solutions, the contacts, the vision.

Business concluded, there would once again be champagne and flowers from Slash and the whole increasingly disturbing, increasingly electrifying affair would begin again.

By the summer of 1979, Slash and Lana's new-style romance had survived some old-style arguments. When Slash needed a woman at a big social event, he took Lana. When it was an important business function and other men brought their wives, Slash went alone and left Lana at home. It happened more than once.

"I'm not just your girlfriend!" Lana fumed when she learned that Slash had attended an important dinner for the president of the Straits Bank without her. Everyone who mattered at all in Singapore's business community had been there—except for Lana. "I'm also your business partner."

"The only women there were wives," replied Slash. "You wouldn't have fit in."

"I fit in well enough in bed!" Lana said, infuriated. "I can goddamn well enough fit in at the dinner table! Besides, if we got married, it wouldn't be a problem!"

"Is that a proposal?" Slash asked, suddenly serious.

"I don't know," said Lana, shocked at the words that had come out of her mouth. "What if it were? What would you say?"

Slash thought for a moment.

"I don't know," he said. "But what if I said yes?"

Lana didn't answer and Slash backed off.

The next morning when she woke Lana realized that she had forgotten to use her diaphragm the night before. She saw no connection between their conversation about marriage and her own mental lapse.

Not, Lana reminded herself, that the diaphragm was really necessary in the first place. Pregnancy was apparently not even a possibility. She had never become pregnant during her marriage, not even during the early times when she had taken chance after chance. And later, in a pathetic attempt to tie Stan to her when he refused to allow her the Premiere stock she felt she had earned, she had tried—and failed—to become pregnant by him. That had been eight years ago. Lana had been only twenty-seven years old then. She was thirty-five now, and the biological clock was ticking loudly. Lana did not think that her oversight was important, and the next months when she got her period right on schedule, she wasn't the least bit surprised.

Meanwhile, she remembered what Slash had said about saying yes to a marriage proposal and pride seemed to win a definitive victory over shame as Lana told herself to be patient. With increasing confidence she began to tell herself that, if she wanted to, one day she would have everything Deedee Dahlen did—including her husband.

IV

APPOINTMENT
IN SAMARA

*A*s the cab made its way uptown from Wall Street
through Little Italy and the Village, Deedee sat back and
relaxed. For the first time in months, she actually felt happy.
She felt happy that she had made her decision, happy that she
had saved the pills, happy, even, that Trip had given her the
courage to do what she had lacked the courage to do. As the
taxi threaded its way up Irving Place and around Gramercy
Park, though, the perimeters of Deedee's happiness began to
fray.

Now that she was relaxed and off guard, Deedee began to
remember the venomous stab of fury she had barely let herself feel when Trip had condescendingly refused to give her
charity and had, instead, offered to buy her Lancome &
Dahlen stock. The stock that wasn't even hers yet. The stock
that would belong to her only after her father's death.

Russell was just sixty-three and, despite his early retirement from Lancome & Dahlen, he was in perfect health and
seemed destined to live as long as Luther. Trip's offer was
ghoulish and revolting. Deedee realized that if she had accepted, Trip would have hovered like a vulture, waiting for
Russell to die, counting the days, counting the dollars. The
thought was repellent and, as Deedee began to consider all
of its consequences and implications, she fought off a wave
of nausea and disgust.

Deedee's anger and distaste were only amplified by the
memory of the way Trip had mishandled her money and his
obvious pleasure in wounding her with the news of Slash's

affair. Not that Deedee was really surprised. Not that she couldn't have guessed as much. Adrian Adams had dropped enough hints and there had already been plenty of gossip. What wounded Deedee even more was Trip's deliberately malicious way of telling her, the way his pleasure in inflicting pain had been so obvious. That realization unleashed a feeling of fury toward Trip and, with it, the beginnings of a revision of the attitudes that had kept Deedee prisoner since the day Slash had told her that her money was gone.

Deedee had focused her rage at Slash and she had been wrong, all wrong. It wasn't Slash who had hurt her. It was Trip. Trip, Deedee suddenly remembered, who had pulled the rug out from under Slash. Trip, who had turned a sure thing into a disaster. Trip, who had broken a promise. Trip, who had stood by and watched Deedee's fortune and marriage disintegrate and Slash's reputation crash while he had profited and gained control of Lancome & Dahlen.

As the taxi travelled north through Murray Hill and stopped and started its way through the midtown office blocks of the Forties and Fifties, Deedee's feeling of relief and happiness disintegrated completely. It was replaced by anger, an emotion Deedee had been brought up to fear and repress, an emotion she had been so frightened of she had only rarely permitted herself to feel it. Anger was a stranger to Deedee, and she did not know how to experience it.

At first she felt her anger tentatively, afraid of it, unfamiliar with its shape and outline. Then, little by little, she allowed her anger in and found that she welcomed it. The anger was cleansing, and it cut away at the numbness she had felt since Russ's death. The anger, healthy and full-blooded, replaced what Deedee now realized was the pseudohappiness she had felt at the thought of suicide. Her anger, her enemy for an entire lifetime, felt good.

Deedee's anger, so long pent-up and now finally unleashed, triggered a whole chain of thoughts as she experienced an unfreezing of blocked emotion that traced its way back to the weekend of Russ's death and perhaps even further back than that. Back to the time Deedee had first met Slash and fought for the right to marry him. Back even further to all the times she had been told it was too bad she was only a girl. Back to all the times she had been told that if only little Luther had lived, the Dahlens would have had an heir worthy of them, an heir to carry on the Dahlen name and increase the Dahlen fortune.

But what about me? Deedee had cried. Don't I count? She had asked. We love you, she had been told, but it's too bad. Too bad you're only a girl. Too bad you're not a boy. Too bad you can't replace little Luther. Too bad, Deedee had concluded, that little Luther had died and she had lived.

The entire punishing cycle had been repeated with Russ's death, a cycle in which Deedee had been blamed and, unable to bear the blame, had, in desperation, projected it onto Slash. Slash, who had seemed strong. Slash, who had seemed invulnerable. Slash, who had made up for little Luther. Slash, who had been entrusted with the family fortune and the family reputation. Slash, who had seemed able to do everything Deedee couldn't do.

As the taxi broke free of the strangling traffic at midtown and leapt forward through the Sixties, Deedee broke free of the strangling of emotion that had led her to think that she didn't really matter and that suicide might be a solution. She realized that she *did* matter and she *had* replaced little Luther. She had replaced him with Slash.

She was the one who had defied her family to marry Slash. *She* was the one who had sensed Slash's talents. *She* was the one who had had faith in Slash's abilities. *She* was the one who had known, before anyone else had known, that Slash was the heir the Dahlens had been looking for.

The Dahlens needed her but they didn't know it. The Dahlens had depended on her but they hadn't known it. Deedee hadn't known it, either, but now she did, and as she made the decision that would change her future and the future of the entire Dahlen family, Deedee leaned forward and, in an urgent voice, told the driver that she had changed her mind and gave him another address.

* * *

Deedee entered her parents' apartment and made a brief telephone call on the telephone just off the foyer. Then she asked for her mother. Deedee intended to speak to Joyce about Trip's offer, about the future of Lancome & Dahlen, about the state of her marriage.

Instead, because Joyce had a dental appointment, Deedee confided in her father. First she told him about Trip's offer to buy her Lancome & Dahlen stock. Then she told him about Lana Bantry.

"She's having an affair with Slash," Deedee said, sounding angry and agitated in a way Russell had rarely heard. Russell noticed the physical changes in her as she spoke. Ever since Russ's death, Deedee had been pale and lifeless, drifting through her days like a sleepwalker. Now there was color in her cheeks and fire in her eyes. "That bitch is having an affair with my husband!"

Russell turned pale, a reaction Deedee interpreted as shock at her blunt language.

"I don't believe it!" he said in a choked voice.

"I do and I'm going to go to Providence," Deedee told her father. They were standing in the greenhouse where Russell had been starting a tray of seedlings.

"Providence?" asked Russell. A chill went through him, cutting icily across the warm, humid air of the greenhouse.

"Yes," said Deedee. "That's where Premiere is." A call to local information had yielded Premiere's address and telephone number. A secretary had volunteered the information that Miss Bantry was out of the country but was expected back that same afternoon.

"I'm going to sit down with Miss Lana Bantry and I'm going to tell her to stay the hell away from my husband," said Deedee, leaning against a lath bench.

"How can you do that?" Russell blurted. "Won't it be too humiliating?"

"Absolutely! Humiliating to Miss Bantry. Particularly when I show her the love letters Slash has been writing to me during their so-called romance!" said Deedee, intent on her own determination. She had been numb too long, passive too long. "I just telephoned Lana Bantry's office. She's getting back from Singapore tonight and when she gets home, I'm going to be waiting for her!"

"Don't!" said Russell, dreading the thought of Deedee and Lana meeting for the first time without him. Sooner or later—and probably sooner—Lana would tell Deedee that they were sisters. *He* wanted to be the one to tell Deedee. *He* wanted to be the one to bring his two children together. After all, Lana and Deedee were not only sisters, but the only Dahlen heirs to Lancome & Dahlen. It was essential that they meet as friends not enemies, as allies not rivals, as sisters not strangers. After all, not only did the future of the Dahlen family depend on it, so did the future of Lancome & Dahlen itself.

"Why not?" Deedee asked, sounding uncharacteristically defiant. How could her father not want her to confront her husband's lover? How could her father not want her to do everything humanly possible to save her marriage?

"I'll go," said Russell, putting down the packet of seeds. "Let me talk to her."

"But Slash is *my* husband. It's *my* marriage and my problem," Deedee said, thinking not only of herself but also of the necessity of getting Claire's life back on track. She wanted to give Claire the father and the stable family life she so clearly missed. "Claire needs Slash, too. I was wrong when I sent him away. I'm the one who should fight for him."

"It will be an ugly scene," Russell said flatly, pulling off the heavy linen smock he wore over his shirt when he worked in the greenhouse. "The least I can do is spare you that. You've been through enough. Let *me* talk to her. Let *me* take care of you."

"Are you sure?" asked Deedee, touched at the way her father was so ready to stand up for her.

"Of course I'm sure," said Russell. "Your marriage is as important to me as it is to you."

Deedee smiled, grateful for the love and protection her father was once again offering. Deedee embraced him and thought how much she loved him. As always, he put her and her feelings first. As always, he wanted to take care of her. As always, he wanted to protect her.

Russell called the garage and had his car readied. It had been years since he had made the drive to New England and he was glad there was still time. Time to change things. Time to make up for his mistakes. Time to rewrite the past as he had rewritten his will. He was glad he hadn't changed it. He had known all along that if he waited long enough, life would present him with the perfect opportunity to see Lana and reconcile his entire family. If he had to use the will as a bribe to get Lana to stay away from Slash, he would even do that.

He should, Russell told himself regretfully, have gone straight to her office from the Paul Revere. But he hadn't. He had been too hurt, too guilty, he had allowed himself to be too easily turned away.

This time, things would be different. This time, *he* would be different. This time, he would insist. This time he would face Lana and set things straight. Too much anger and too much misunderstanding had taken place between them. This time he would not take no for an answer.

When Russell got to Providence, Lana's secretary told him that Lana had changed her plans and gone directly to Worcester from the airport. The secretary wasn't exactly sure whether Lana would be at Lana's mother's house or at the Beauty Box. It was Thursday evening. The Beauty Box would be open late.

"But try the house first. It's at Thirty-five Willow Drive," said Roseann when Russell asked. "Lana and her mother sometimes meet there first for coffee and then go to the salon together."

As Russell Dahlen got into his car and headed for Willow Drive, Will Bantry sat in the living room of the pleasant, Colonial-style house Lana had bought for him and Mildred. He hated the house. He knew that Lana had meant well but, to him, the expensive house, with its big lawn and tall shade trees, was just another proof of his own failures. He had told Mildred that he didn't want to live there but Mildred had insisted, saying that Lana would have been terribly hurt if they turned down the gift she took so much pleasure in giving. Will felt trapped. By the house, by his life. He had joined AA for a while but he had dropped out. He had failed even at that.

Will poured himself another drink and, as usual, thought about the unfairness and injustices of his life and the way he had never had the breaks. His anger focused on Franklin Sparling and the job he had just lost.

Sure, he'd missed a few days of work. Sure, he was late some of the time. And, yeah, sure, he'd shown up a few times in the afternoon with whisky on his breath after he'd had a few. But, what the hell. It wasn't the end of the world, was it? He was a damn good mechanic. So what right did Franklin Sparling have to fire him?

Will freshened his drink and cursed under his breath as he missed the glass at first and slopped the amber liquid on the table.

He hated Franklin Sparling. He hated those rich bastards who thought they had the right to run other people's lives just because they had some money in the bank. If he had any balls, he'd tell Franklin tight-ass Sparling just what he thought of him. In fact, if he had any real balls, he'd shoot his ass off. Not to kill him or anything like that. Just enough to show him that money wasn't everything.

Will leaned back in his easy chair and smiled, savoring the image. The more he thought about it, the more he liked the idea of Franklin Sparling flat on his stomach in the hospital, buckshot up his ass.

Unsteadily he got up and, holding onto the wall for balance, went up to his room and got his shotgun out of its rack. It was a nice piece of equipment and he kept it in A-one condition. Cleaned and oiled, loaded for action. Will caressed its gleaming wooden stock and went back downstairs. He wondered what Franklin tight-ass Sparling would say when he showed up in his fancy office with a gun under his arm.

Just then Will thought he heard someone knock, but he

wasn't sure. No one ever came around in the middle of the afternoon. Then he heard the knocking again.

Sure as shit. Someone was there. Wouldn't it be a hoot if it was Franklin coming back to apologize and beg him to take his job back?

Well, thought Will, heading toward the front door and taking the shotgun with him just in case, he'd tell old tight-ass just what he could do with his precious job.

"All right! All right! Keep your pants on!" Will yelled, bumping into the fancy breakfront and rattling some of Mildred's beloved dishes but finally making it to the front hall. The knocking continued, and Will opened the door.

"Your daughter's secretary said she might be here," Russell began, realizing even as he spoke that Lana was *his* daughter and that now that he had finally accepted the idea, he'd have to get used to the words, too.

"She's not my goddamn daughter!" Will snarled and then he realized who it was.

It had been over thirty years but Will Bantry remembered the la-di-da accent that cut through the swirls in his alcohol-fuddled brain as if it had been yesterday. It was the rich prick who had deprived him of a perfect wife. The rich prick who had left him to raise the kid who wasn't his, the kid whose ideas were just as fancy as her old man's.

Franklin Sparling and Russell Dahlen. They were two of a kind with their fancy clothes and snotty attitude. They thought they were doing you a favor giving you a two-bit job or dumping their goddamn kid on you and letting you pick up the bills. He'd warned Russell Dahlen that if he ever saw his face again, he'd shoot him just the way he'd been thinking of shooting Franklin Sparling. They both deserved it.

Will Bantry stepped back half a pace, raised the gun to his shoulder and fired.

V

NEXT OF KIN

Her scream pierced the quiet of her Park Avenue apartment and subsided into nothingness as Deedee swayed, almost fell, and then, with a visible effort of extraordinary will, pulled herself together again. The two policemen had knocked on her door and told her, as gently as they could, that her father was dead. He had been murdered by a man she had never heard of called Will Bantry.

The two officers stood in the large, rectangular foyer, police caps in their hands, ready for anything. Some people fainted. Others threw things. Some withdrew, others attacked. Informing the next of kin was not the physically most dangerous part of their jobs. It was, however, emotionally the most hazardous. No cop ever got used to it. None ever got good at it.

"It's not possible. There must be a mistake," Deedee said, looking from one to the other. She willed herself to believe that denying their words would render them untrue.

The two policemen looked at each other, knowing what they had to say—that it was not only possible but that it was true and that there had been no mistake—but not quite finding the words. The taller one licked his lips. The other swallowed and cleared his throat.

"Then it's true," Deedee said, before either could speak. She spoke in an almost inaudible tone, the tone of death and acceptance. Her father had gone to Worcester—gone to meet death—because of her.

* * *

That evening Deedee went into her father's greenhouse and cut a white rose, his favorite flower. She kept the fragrant blossom by her bedside until its petals lost their scent and turned the color of tea.

"Will and Russell don't even know each other!" exclaimed Lana in initial disbelief when she arrived at the Beauty Box from the airport. Her mother, already alerted by the local police, told her that her stepfather had shot and killed her real father. Will was in custody. Russell was dead. "Will Bantry and Russell Dahlen have never even met!"

"Yes, they have," said Mildred, quietly, remembering the hospital room and the fight. She recalled, as if it had been yesterday, shielding her newly born baby from the brawling men and her subsequent terrifying fall from the high, hospital bed to the floor. "Once."

Lana had been shocked and stunned to learn that it had been Will Bantry, keeping an old promise, who had shot Russell Dahlen, but it was Mildred, even more, who stood at the center of the tragedy. She was shattered by the way her long-ago romance had exploded in violence.

Russell was dead and Will, scared and humiliated at being in jail, did not understand why and how his drab, failed life had ended in catastrophe. More than thirty-five years after a Cinderella romance that had been followed by a marriage of necessity, Mildred's husband had killed her lover. Mildred's roses-and-cream complexion faded to gray as the color drained from her face and her blue eyes turned the color of ashes as, once again in the back room of the Beauty Box, she told Lana long-buried secrets, the final, violent secrets of the day of her birth.

"Will and Russell met on the day you were born. Russell came to see you. He and Will got into a fight in the hospital. Will threatened to kill Russell if he ever saw him again. He even shot at him. Will went to jail," Mildred told Lana, revealing for the first time the violent events that had taken place so many years before.

"Russell came to see me?" asked Lana, absorbing the

shocking story her mother had just told her. "Why did he come? I thought he wanted you to have an abortion. I thought he gave you money to have me killed."

"He did. Then when Deedee was born and she was a girl, your father hoped you'd turn out to be a boy," Mildred said, telling Lana what Russell Dahlen had told her mother over the telephone so many years ago. "In the Dahlen family, boys were everything. Girls were nothing. Russell desperately wanted a male heir."

"So I was nothing more than a second disappointment," Lana said softly, realizing that her sex, over which she had no control, was at least part of the reason Russell Dahlen had abandoned her to the shadows of his life.

"According to Russell's father, the continuation of the Dahlen name and the Dahlen fortune depended on Russell having a boy," said Mildred bleakly, confirming Lana's words and thoughts.

Lana swallowed, unable to speak, and embraced her mother, taking as she had so often taken, the role of her parent's parent. As Lana comforted her mother, it also occurred to her, for the first time ever, that perhaps Deedee Dahlen hadn't had everything. Apparently, Deedee, too, had been a disappointment to her father and to her family. Both she and her sister had been born girls in a family that valued boys.

Nevertheless, Lana's realization didn't change the way she felt toward Deedee. Nothing could. Nothing would.

Not even her unexpected inheritance, the inheritance that made her, at last, her sister's equal. The inheritance—and the acceptance it signified—that had come more than thirty years too late.

Van Tyson called Lana on the telephone several hours after her father's death. Lana was still at the Beauty Box. Mildred had gone to meet with the lawyer she had retained to represent Will.

"Russell Dahlen changed his will on March 28, 1977," the lawyer told Lana. "The will acknowledges you as his daughter and leaves you one half of the Dahlen shares in Lancome and Dahlen."

The date was a date engraved on Lana's mind, the date she had finally paid her father back for the years of rejection and indifference, the date she had finally made him feel the way she had felt, the date they were to have had lunch at the Paul Revere.

"I didn't know," said Lana as the breath went out of her. Why hadn't Russell told her? Why hadn't he given her the chance to reconcile when he was alive?

"You didn't?" the lawyer asked in surprise. "Russell told me he was going to give you a copy of the will. He told me he was going to have lunch with you. He planned to give it to you then. Didn't he do it?"

"We never met that day," said Lana softly. "We never had that lunch."

Almost inaudibly, Lana thanked the lawyer for calling and hung up the telephone. Her unasked questions had just been answered. Russell hadn't told her about the will because she hadn't permitted him to. They had not reconciled during his lifetime because she had clung so fiercely and so ferociously to her anger.

Lana did not cry. She did not weep. Instead, she left her office in the back of the Beauty Box and, going to the shampoo station, gave the young assistant the rest of the evening off.

Lana shampooed client after client in a blind attempt to wash away her feelings of shame and guilt. As she washed and rinsed, Lana thought obsessively of her last conversation with her father. She remembered the exact degreee of frigidity and finality in her voice, the confusion and hurt in Russell's. At the time, she had felt so utterly vindicated in her anger, so righteously justified in her deliberate cruelty. And she had been, she now realized, so wrong. So desperately and tragically wrong.

Even after the last client and stylist had gone and the salon was empty, Lana stayed at the Beauty Box. Rolling up her sleeves, first climbing the stepladder and later getting down on her hands and knees, she began to scrub and polish the salon, leaving no detail neglected and no corner untouched.

She cleaned the windows and the mirrors, the floors and the walls, the styling stations and client chairs, the shampoo and color areas, the manicure tables and chairs, the reception and waiting foyer, the storage and rest rooms. The pads of her fingers became wrinkled and her hands raw with water and strong detergent as she cleaned and polished, attacking dust and soil as if they were the material incarnations of her own unbearably painful emotions. Still, no matter how hard she worked or how aggressively she cleaned, the feelings of shame and guilt—so much, much worse even than the shame and guilt she felt every time she made love to Slash—did not disappear.

Once again, Lana realized, someone had offered love and, once again, she had been too hurt and too angry to recognize it and to accept it. The surprise her father had promised, she now understood, was not only an inheritance of money but the love and acceptance she had had hungered for her entire life.

Lana remembered that the Chinese had a saying: the one who seeks revenge should dig two graves. Lana realized with a sick sensation that in her implacable lust to get even, she had dug them both. A literal grave for her father. A living one for herself.

She went home exhausted and cleaned her house the way she had cleaned the salon. Nothing changed. She could not forget what she had done. She could not forgive herself.

Will Bantry, in jail, didn't remember getting the gun. He didn't even remember answering the door. In fact, he didn't even remember coming home early from work that day. The last thing he remembered was having a few at the Shamrock Tavern, just across the street from the Sparling Manufacturing Company.

"Only a few," he kept insisting to the lawyer Mildred had hired for him. "I didn't even think I was high."

*　*　*

"Half-sister?" Deedee exclaimed, turning white in utter shock when Van Tyson read her the will. "But I'm an only child. I have no sister!"

"Apparently you do," the lawyer said, correcting Deedee gently and showing her the document with her father's signature. "And she's inherited half of the Dahlen stock."

"Half! Never! I'll contest the will!" Deedee said. Her green eyes glittered emerald against the sudden pallor of her skin. "I'll fight it in every court in the country!"

"On what grounds?" asked Van Tyson quietly. He understood Deedee's shock. He also understood the realities. "Your father was of sound mind. He was under no duress. He acted of his own free will."

Deedee stared at him silently. For an instant, Deedee directed her shock and bitterness toward Van Tyson, the messenger, the bearer of terrible tidings. Tidings that told Deedee that she would inherit only half of the Dahlen fortune. Tidings that also answered the question Deedee had asked for as long as she could remember, a question that had never been answered. Tidings that told her why her father had not been present at her birth. Tidings that revealed, at long last, the identity of the person who had been more important to him than she had been.

Deedee sat in the paneled, almost Dickensian office of her father's lifelong lawyer, and realized what the consequences of her father's shocking last will and testament really entailed. She would have to share not only her wealth but her very identity with the woman who had stolen her fortune and her husband. The woman Deedee despised more than any other, a woman she perceived as an interloper, a rival, the bitterest of enemies was, she learned, her sister.

Deedee vowed she would never have anything to do with Lana Bantry. Her father had never included Lana in the family, had never during his entire lifetime recognized her as his child. Using her father's behavior as a justification for her own, Deedee saw no reason to acknowledge Lana Bantry's existence. Deedee continued to blame Lana for the death of her father, the loss of her fortune and the shattering of her marriage.

Joyce, however, far more realistic, reminded Deedee that it was Russell who had gone to Worcester and Will Bantry who had pulled the trigger. Lana had had nothing to do with Russell's death. In addition, Joyce reminded Deedee that it was Trip who had been behind the loss of her fortune and Slash's defeat, and not Lana. Speaking firmly and almost sharply, Joyce advised Deedee to think with her head and not with her emotions.

"Your father left Lana Bantry half of the Dahlen stock. There's nothing you can do to change that," Joyce pointed out. "If you work with her, you can exert some control over the future of Lancome and Dahlen. If you don't, Trip is going to be able to do everything his way. You might just as well have sold your stock to him when he offered to buy it."

"She's an interloper," Deedee said stubbornly, refusing to accept her mother's clearheaded analysis of exactly who had been responsible for what. She clung fiercely to the blame that relieved her of responsibility. "She's not a Dahlen."

"But she *is* a Dahlen," said Joyce relentlessly, refusing to hide from the facts. "She's asked to come to Russell's funeral. I told her that she would be welcome."

"You did? How could you?" asked Deedee, appalled at the thought of having the stranger she despised at her father's funeral.

"How could I not?" replied Joyce with inexpressible sadness. "She's Russell's daughter, too."

Joyce now knew where Russell had been on the day of Deedee's birth. She now knew that Russell had had not one child but two. She now knew that her plan never to conceive again so that Deedee would inherit everything had been an empty and pathetic vengeance. From a poor family herself, Joyce understood how shunned Lana must have felt, how much of an outsider she must have considered herself in comparison to the rich and self-absorbed Dahlens.

Always a practical woman and now a wiser, more compassionate one, Joyce realized that, if for no other reason than the future of Lancome & Dahlen, the entire Dahlen family would one day have to accept the existence of Lana Bantry. As far as Joyce was concerned, the sooner that day arrived, the better. She continued to urge Deedee to be realistic. Deedee continued to refuse to listen.

VI

SISTERS AND
STRANGERS

Sisters and strangers, heiress and orphan, Park Avenue debutante and drunkard's battered child, Deedee and Lana met for the first time on the day of their father's funeral. Lana Bantry was much smaller than Deedee had envisioned. Deedee had imagined Lana as a giant, aggressively striding through life grabbing whatever she wanted. Instead, Deedee was surprised to find that even in high heels, Lana Bantry was tiny. She had a high, girlish voice and blue, wounded eyes. Nevertheless, Lana's hair was too flashy, her makeup too bright, her black dress too highly fashionable. Even in mourning, Lana could never fit in, could never belong.

Lana was surprised at how tall Deedee was. From the way Slash had spoken about her, Lana had imagined her to be a porcelain doll, fragile and dainty, wispy and insubstantial. Instead, she was poised and dignified and exuded a kind of authority that Lana knew she would never possess. Deedee Dahlen possessed the kind of authority that only money, a lifetime of money, could buy. Lana resented her background, her lifetime of privilege and the look that told Lana that she was, and would always be, an outsider.

Their mutual resentment and suspicion hardened as they were introduced to each other by the man they both loved at the graveside of the father they both mourned.

"You should never have met. Not like this," said Slash without irony. He had come from Singapore for the funeral, wanting to be there for Deedee, for Claire and for the family with whose fate his own had been so inextricably linked. Claire had greeted him with tears and kisses and Deedee, pale and barely controlled, had embraced him. The rest of the Dahlens had turned toward Slash for consolation and comfort.

Standing at the graveside of the man who had first understood his abilities and given him the chance he needed, Slash was somber and visibly shaken. The planes of his face seemed more sharply etched than ever before as he stood between the two women he loved. Two women linked by murder and money. Two women who shared a father and a lover. Two women who shared a vast inheritance, a vast pain and a vast animosity. Two women who were heiresses and victims of the same fortune, the same shocking crime, the same shocking revelations.

"Why did he do it?" Deedee asked Lana. Russell's grave was next to Russ's and little Luther's. Her father's funeral reminded Deedee painfully of her son's funeral and the premature death of a brother she had never been able to replace. Deedee's complexion had an unusual pallor and her makeup, although subtle, only seemed to exaggerate her ghostliness. "Why did Will Bantry shoot my father?"

"*Our* father," said Lana, correcting Deedee immediately and almost angrily. She had hidden her platinum hair under a black hat. A few pale strands had escaped and framed her face like a platinum halo. In a severe black dress, she looked like a lost angel. "Russell Dahlen was *my* father, too."

"Our father," Deedee replied almost inaudibly, accepting the correction grudgingly. "But why? Why did Will Bantry do it?"

"He was drunk," said Lana, who had visited Will Bantry in jail the day before. "He says he doesn't remember."

"Do you believe him?" Deedee asked, appalled. Will Bantry had taken one life and shattered half a dozen others and said he didn't even remember doing it. Deedee could hardly believe it.

"Yes, I do," said Lana. She sensed Deedee's disbelief and realized that Deedee had always been safe, always been protected. She had never lived with a drunkard, did not know and therefore could not comprehend the violence, the rage, the lethal destructiveness, the blackouts and amnesia of an out-of-control alcoholic.

"What was Russell Dahlen doing on Willow Drive anyway?" Lana asked, still thinking of the brutal way she had repaid Russell for that long-ago lunch at the Roosevelt. How could she forgive herself? How could she have hated that much? How could she have been so angry? How could she have hung on to her hurt feelings for so long? How could she make up years of anger to a dead man? Now that it seemed too late, Lana asked herself questions that had no answers and looked to Deedee for clues to the crime. "What made him come to Worcester?"

There was a flicker of pain in Deedee's eyes and she turned away and avoided Lana's eyes as she answered the question.

"He went there because of me," Deedee said, thinking that once again she had allowed herself to be taken care of, that once again she had retreated instead of advancing. When would she learn? When would she change? When would she grow up? When would she fight her own battles? "He was going to ask you to stay away from Slash."

Lana's eyes stung with tears of guilt and shame and she turned away.

As the minister began the somber service, the two women stood apart from each other, filled with emotions too raw to be expressed and too painful to be faced. Not yet. Not for a while. Not while money and murder tied them together and suspicion and blame held them apart.

As Russell Dahlen's body was lowered into its grave, Deedee, unable to watch, turned away. She broke down and her shoulders heaved spasmodically as she sobbed in Slash's arms. Sobbed for the father who had always tried to be a good son and a good father and for the way his efforts had brought him frustration rather than joy, pain rather than pleasure, death rather than life. Sobbed for the brother she had never known and whose death she had spent a lifetime vainly trying to compensate for. For the son she had lost and could never replace. For the marriage that was in ashes. For the family that was, once again, shattered by an untimely death.

Sensing and sharing Deedee's agony, Lana touched Deedee gently on the shoulder, wordlessly offering comfort. Deedee pulled away and shook her head.

"Please go away," she said coldly through her tears. "You've already caused enough destruction."

Unwilling to risk one more rejection, Lana backed silently away. Luther Dahlen had refused to acknowledge her. Edwina, following his lead, had barely spoken to her. Only Joyce, weeping quietly, had allowed her to express her condolences. Lana, condemned to grieve in isolation, left the gravesite alone, overwhelmed by the old feeling of being ignored, of being a nobody.

As Lana turned to glance back at the family that, except for Joyce, had united to exclude her, she saw Trip Lancome walk over to Deedee. Lana looked on with an almost unbearable sense of rejection and envy as Trip put his arm around Deedee and murmured quietly to her. Deedee tilted her head toward Trip, listening carefully. Lana wondered what Trip was saying to Deedee, what memories of Russell they shared, what ties of affection bound them, what words of consolation he was uttering. Trip's soft words and gentle touch were so obviously intended to comfort Deedee and to take care of her that Lana turned away, unable to watch.

Everyone had someone, Lana thought as she walked to her car alone, bitterly recalling the gentle way Trip spoke to Deedee and the tender way Slash held her. Everyone. Except her.

When Lana was finally alone and no one could see, she too broke down and wept. For the father she had never known and never understood, the father who had been the focus of her most extravagant fantasies and her bitterest disappointments. For the sister she had envied and hated and who had sent her away. For the family she had never been part of and now never would be part of. For the man she feared she would inevitably lose to another woman. For the baby she carried inside her.

* * *

Doctor Ashani Mitali in Singapore had told Lana that just because she had gotten her period didn't mean that she wasn't pregnant. One week later, Dr. Kathleen McNally in Providence said the same thing.

"People think that the moment a woman gets pregnant, the menses automatically stop. It just isn't true," Dr. McNally said. "Some women continue to have what seem to be normal menstrual periods for the first few months of a pregnancy. It's not normal but it's not all that unusual, either."

"So now what?" asked Lana, stunned by what had happened to her. Shaken by Russell's murder and Will's guilt. Shocked by the discovery that she had inherited half the Dahlen shares in Lancome & Dahlen. And staggered now by the confirmation that she was, indeed, pregnant.

"You can go ahead and have your baby," said Kathleen McNally. "You're healthy and all the tests are normal."

"But I'm thirty-six," said Lana, wanting a reason to end the pregnancy.

"So are a lot of new mothers these days," said the doctor briskly, telling Lana to make another appointment in a month. It would be a sensible precaution, Kathleen McNally said, to undergo amniocentesis.

Except to discuss business, Slash had not called Lana since he had returned to New York and, except for business, she had not attempted to reach him. Their whole anxious, electric, ambivalent affair had ended by mutual, almost wordless consent with a single shot from a drunkard's gun.

"I have to go back," Slash had said. "To Deedee. To Claire. To my family."

"I know," said Lana, feeling a simultaneous and almost overpowering surge of combined loss and liberation. The loss Lana felt was the knowledge, this time final, that she had lost Slash. The liberation was from the angry sense of retaliation toward Deedee that had been, from the very beginning, a silent, invisible but potent part of her affair with Slash.

"I'm seeing Deedee," Slash told Lana several weeks after Russell's funeral. Now that Slash knew that Lana and

Deedee were sisters—something Lana had known but never confided during their entire affair—Slash realized even more than ever how tough and tough-minded Lana could be. He admired her for that toughness and he respected her for it. That toughness had been the key to her success and to her survival.

"I knew you would," replied Lana, not entirely surprised to find that she was relieved to have the end of the guilty and shameful affair taken out of her hands. She had been acutely aware of the longing in Slash's eyes as he had looked at Deedee at the funeral and the tender way he had held her in his arms.

Lana had known then that whatever was between Slash and Deedee was not over, that their ending had yet to be written. She had known then that Slash had not been lying when, all along, he had said that he was still in love with Deedee. She had known then that her hopes of having everything her sister had—including her husband—were the hopes of a vengeful fool.

Then she told Slash about the baby.

"I'm going to go ahead and have it," Lana said, more calmly than she felt. She had wrestled with her conscience, longing for a way out of bearing Slash's child yet unwilling, as her mother had been unwilling, to kill the life within her. The tests Dr. McNally ordered had shown that everything was normal. They had also revealed the sex of the child.

"It's going to be a boy. He'll be born in July," she told Slash. "I'm going to name him Joel. I picked it out of a book. No one in the Dahlen family or my mother's family has that name. I want him to have a new name and a fresh start."

Slash swallowed.

"I love you," he finally said.

"I know," Lana replied. "But not enough."

Slash did not answer. They both knew that she was right.

Then Lana firmly turned the conversation to business. Business was safe. Business was comfortable. And what remained between them was business—quite a bit of business.

The Singapore factory. The real estate investments in the Far East and on the West Coast. The money that Slash needed to go back into business in New York. He wanted to start an investment firm. He wanted to outdo Lancome & Dahlen at its own game.

"Isn't it about time you backed me in a business I actually know something about?" Slash asked Lana as they discussed the possibility of her putting up the financing for Slash's return to Wall Street. It would be a loan, he told her, and an opportunity.

"But I already own a fourth of Lancome and Dahlen," Lana said. "Wouldn't I be competing with myself if I helped put you back into business?"

"Lancome and Dahlen isn't what it used to be. It's coasting on its reputation," said Slash. "Now, tell me, are you in or out?"

VII

UPTOWN

Other people would have hidden. *Other* people would have drawn the shades and shut the doors. Other people would have hung their heads and been grateful for whatever crumbs they could feed off. Slash wasn't other people. Once again, he intended to be the right man in the right place at the right time.

The first thing Slash did when he returned to New York was to pay back Deedee's debts and the debts he himself had left behind. He also paid back—with interest—every cent he had lost for his clients in the Premiere debacle. It was his way of announcing that he was back and of forcing Trip to drop the Lancome & Dahlen lawsuit.

"He can't sue me for debts that have been paid," Slash told Deedee.

The second thing he did was to go into business again. With financial backing from Lana, Slash leased offices on Park Avenue and Fifty-seventh Street, pointedly far away from Wall and Broad and all the traditional attitudes that address symbolized. To make the point even more apparent, Slash named his new company Uptown and he opened for business as the new decade began. Once again, Slash's timing would be nothing short of miraculous.

Slash infuriated Trip by hiring Arthur Bozeman and his small, highly trained and motivated staff of research analysts away from Lancome & Dahlen. In the process, Slash did something he thought Trip should have done long before: he made Arthur a full partner. Slash continued to build his own staff at Uptown and his hiring practices, he always pointed out proudly, were exactly the opposite of Lancome & Dahlen's.

"I never ask them who their father was or where they went to school," Slash told Lana. He still remembered a thousand slights, a thousand snubs as if they had happened only the day before. "The only degree I give a damn about is the one I graduated with: PSA. Poor, Smart and Ambitious."

Slash repeated his comment to a writer from *Forbes*. As usual, Slash was highly quotable. As usual, Slash got the headline. It read:

PSA: BETTER THAN AN MBA?

Slash's first clients at Uptown were associates he'd known from Singapore, men like Tan Siah Lee and Kok Kah Kee. The takeover mania was just heating up and the new heroes of the business press were T. Boone Pickens, Carl Icahn and Saul Steinberg. American business seemed to be on the auction block with big companies swallowing small, small annexing big and the raiders and arbs standing by ready to swoop in for the big gains.

Slash guided Uptown's clients through the ups and downs of Wall Street's merger mania of the first half of the 1980s. Gulf/Chevron. Conoco/DuPont. Warner/AmEx. Bendix/Martin Marietta. City Service/Phillips. Marathon Oil/U.S. Steel. General Foods/Philip Morris. Just as the seventies had been the decade of real estate, the eighties, said Slash, would be the decade of common stock.

Slash was, once again, right. The stampede, triggered by a drop in interest rates, began in August 1982 on, ironically enough, Friday the thirteenth. A twelve-point rise brought the Dow to 788. It rose in almost a straight vertical line to 800, 900, 1,000. Trading records were regularly broken, volume was up and Slash swore that the end was nowhere in sight.

"The party is just beginning," Slash told a reporter from the *Wall Street Journal.* "By 1987, the Dow will break 2,500."

As always, Slash's timing was impeccable and his profits were sensational, but Uptown was not the one-man band it sometimes seemed to be. On its staff were investment bankers, security lawyers, stock analysts, public relations specialists and traders. There was even, it was said, an employee whose sole job consisted of keeping track, via Federal Aviation Agency data, of movements of corporate jets in an attempt to monitor who was seeing who and who might have been talking merger, takeover or buyout.

However, it was Slash who got all the attention and all the notoriety and while he was making money for his clients, he was also making it for Uptown. His investment moves were bold, risky and, most of the time, highly lucrative. He also had, and he was always the first to admit it, his share of bowwows.

"My clients are widows and orphans," he told a reporter from *Forbes.* "Widows and orphans in the fifty percent bracket."

As always, Slash made good copy and the quote was used as a headline.

"Aren't you fed up with Slash?" Michael de Rosnay asked Trip. "He gets all the headlines and all the attention."

"No," said a tight-lipped Trip. "He's welcome to them. I was never interested in personal publicity."

Trip was very calm and very confident and Michael wondered what Trip *was* interested in. When he asked, Trip said that he was interested in Lancome & Dahlen.

"After all, Lancome and Dahlen is in my blood," Trip said, explaining his apparent lack of jealousy. "I'm its chairman and president. I don't need headlines to tell me who I am."

Michael nodded and thought, not for the first time, that the right genes and the right pedigree were sometimes worth more than money in the bank.

* * *

Michael was right about the genes and the pedigree. Trip Lancome looked very much the same as he had when he was in his twenties. His blond hair was still thick and strong, his physique still trim and athletic. He moved like a much younger man and his tennis opponents and hunting companions knew that his eye was just as keen and his reflexes just as good as they had ever been. However, under Trip's blond perfection, where no one including Michael de Rosnay could see, there was a scar as disfiguring as the birthmark he always hid.

The scar was a psychological darkness. It was a darkness people sensed when they saw Trip's second wife in gym class, unexplained bruises visible above the scooped neckline of the long-sleeved leotards she always wore, even on the hottest days of summer. It was the darkness that had caused his first wife to divorce him after only three years of marriage. It was the darkness Deedee had seen when Trip had beaten a horse and when, in rage, he had stopped just short of hitting her and had, instead, picked up an iron poker and vented his anger on a newspaper and a glass vitrine.

It was the darkness that had shocked Deedee, once again, when she had called Trip to tell him that Russell had been shot and, in the unguarded moment that had followed, Trip had said: "They shot the wrong man."

Michael de Rosnay wondered, however, if the right genes and the right pedigree could do anything about the gradual but increasingly apparent erosion in Lancome & Dahlen's profits and the desertion of some of its clients to Uptown. Money, Michael knew, had no loyalty. Money had no morals. Money had no memory. Money went where the profits were. Money was going Uptown.

VIII
MEMORIES AND
HOPES

Slash seemed to be almost magic with Claire. He saw her every day after his return from Singapore. Slash was living at the Belgravia Hotel on Madison Avenue and Seventy-second Street, and he came over to Deedee's apartment every morning to have breakfast with Claire and to walk her to school. He had dinner with her almost every evening and spent every weekend with her. The life and the humor had crept back into Claire's gray eyes and her ivory skin seemed warm and luminous once again.

"If you don't hate me too much, why don't you join us?" Slash asked Deedee after he'd been back several weeks. They had been polite with each other. Polite and wary. Deedee knew about Lana and Slash knew that Deedee knew. The subject of Lana Bantry was a minefield both were afraid to tread.

"Please, mommy! Won't you come?" asked Claire, her eyes lighting up. Even Julia Krauss, Claire's therapist, agreed—Claire had seemed transformed since her father's return. Even if for no other reason than that, Deedee felt grateful to Slash. "Pul—eaze!"

They began to have dinner—the three of them—at restaurants carefully chosen by Slash and approved by Claire. At Shun Lee West. The Russian Tea Room. John's Pizza. Raga. Anita's Chili Parlor. The Hard Rock Cafe. They were restaurants perfect for a courtship—if you were courting a hip Manhattan child. They were restaurants that had nothing to do with romance of a conventional kind and Slash made sure that he and Deedee were never alone, that she never felt crowded, that she never felt pressured. He wanted her back. The last thing he wanted was to scare her away.

Slash did not make the mistake of ignoring the past. He told Deedee that his affair with Lana was over and, for the first time, he and Deedee spoke about Russ. Slash told Deedee how bitter he had been at the way the Dahlens, and finally Deedee herself, had seemed to hold him responsible.

"I'm not going to pretend none of it ever happened," Slash told Deedee, his gray eyes dark with remembered pain. Enough time had passed for Slash to be able to talk about his feelings. Enough time had passed for bitterness and resentment to lose some of their power. "And I'm not going to pretend that I wasn't devastated by the way you sided with your family against me."

"Is that what I said? Was I that cruel?" Deedee asked, shocked. She had been in a state of numb shock in the months after Russ's death. She could not remember—exactly—how she had acted, what she had done and what she had said.

"Yes," said Slash. "You behaved as if you were the only one who suffered."

Slash also talked about the Premiere debacle and about how Lana Bantry had outsmarted him. He talked about the money he had lost and explained his behavior in psychological terms. He equated the loss of money with the loss of Russ and his guilt over not being able to save his son. There was also, he admitted, a wish to pay Deedee back for the way she seemed to blame him.

"Crazy as it sounds, I think part of me may have *wanted* to lose the money," Slash said, trying to explain his miscalculation with Premiere. "I wanted to punish myself. I wanted to punish you. I wanted you to hurt the way I hurt."

"But why didn't you tell me how you felt?" asked Deedee, sadly, remembering that every time she had wanted to talk—

about Russ, about her family, about the way she felt—Slash had refused.

"Because I couldn't," he admitted. "I just couldn't find the words. I hoped that, with you, I wouldn't need them. I hoped that you, of all people, would understand me."

For a moment Deedee said nothing.

"I'm sorry," she finally said quietly. "I should have been more compassionate."

"So should I," he said softly.

She realized that they both had been ensnared in their own pain, unable to reach out for the other. She wondered if the future could be different. She wondered if there really would *be* a future.

Little by little Deedee became more comfortable in Slash's presence. Slash was still, after all, legally her husband. He was the father of her child. He was still the most attractive man she had ever met in her life. A gentleman gangster with the right-side-of-the-tracks connections and the wrong-side-of-the-tracks accent, a brooding Hamlet in a black turtleneck, a tycoon in a three-piece suit, a lover with a poet's sensitivity in jeans and an open shirt. He was the hero with a thousand faces, the chameleon with a thousand colors, the man with the Midas touch.

Gradually, Deedee began to tell Slash what had happened while he was gone. She quoted Luther's speeches about independence and self-sufficiency. She told him about Russell's retirement and retreat from life. She told him about Claire's problems in school and out.

"Her marks fell and she said she didn't care. She dropped out of the swimming team and she said she didn't care. She abandoned her chemistry experiments for science club and she said she didn't care. She no longer got invited to any birthday parties and she said she didn't care," Deedee recalled, on the verge of tears, upset even by the memories of her daughter's devastated reactions to the loss of a brother, a father and a way of life. "I tried everything. And nothing worked. Then Prudence Mars called me in for a conference..."

"Claire's better now," said Slash gently. "Thanks to you."

"And thanks to you," replied Deedee. This time, when he reached out for her, she didn't pull away.

She remembered the way he smelled and the way his body fit so perfectly against hers. She remembered the way he liked to caress her until she lost control and the way he liked her to come first. She remembered where he liked to be touched and the words he liked her to whisper. Sharing a bed with Slash once again seemed comfortable in its familiarity and exciting in its newness. It was a combination of the old and the new, the strange and the familiar, a mélange of memory and hope, of experience and experiment.

"I love you," Slash murmured into Deedee's glossy hair, pinning her hands with his. "I always have. I always will."

"I know," Deedee said, remembering Slash's letters, letters filled with love and longing. Then she remembered her own replies and knew that all along, not so deep down, she still loved Slash.

"We belong together," Slash said.

"Did you think that when you were in Lana's arms?" Deedee asked. It was a question she didn't want to ask. Yet she couldn't help herself. She had to know.

"Even then," he said.

Deedee reminded herself that Slash never lied, but she didn't know whether or not to believe him. She was still too wounded. Still too bruised. And with reason. Slash had also told her that Lana was pregnant and that she planned to have the baby. Their baby. A son.

"The affair is over," Slash said.

"But not the relationship," said Deedee, unable to forget that Lana was going to give Slash the one thing she couldn't: a child.

Deedee also told Slash about Trip.

"He offered to buy the Lancome & Dahlen shares from me twice," Deedee said, describing the humiliating scene in Trip's office. "My father was still alive and Trip was already trying to grab everything for himself."

"Even back then?" Slash hadn't known. "What did you do?"

"I refused. I thought it was disgusting. I knew he'd just wait around for Russell to die." Deedee smiled ironically and realized that if she'd agreed to Trip's proposal, she would have had no connection with Lancome & Dahlen. Lana, the interloper, would have been the only Dahlen to own stock. "Unfortunately, Trip got his wish. Sooner than even he probably dared hope."

"And what was the second time?" Slash asked.

"On the day of my father's funeral," replied Deedee bitterly.

As Deedee spoke, Slash wondered whether Trip had made the same offer to Lana. And, if so, how she had responded.

"I told him his offer wasn't good enough," said Lana, confirming that Trip had telephoned her on the day after Russell Dahlen's funeral, offering to buy out her share of Lancome & Dahlen.

"Whatever Trip offered," replied Slash. "I'll double it."

"Forget it," said Lana. "I'm not selling. Not to Trip. Not to you. Not to anyone."

The Dahlen stock was the one tangible link Lana had to her father and her family. It was the one thing she would never let go of. Besides, its value wasn't only sentimental and symbolic. The Dahlen stock had material value as well as potent clout in the world of business and high finance. To buttress her decision not to sell even further, Lana quoted Slash's own remark about the eighties being the decade of common stock back to him.

"Why should I sell something that's going to go up in value?" she asked.

"That's the point. It won't go up in value," said Slash. "Not as long as Trip is running the company."

"In that case, Lancome and Dahlen ought to get rid of Trip," said Lana.

"You'll need Deedee to do it," Slash pointed out.

Lana smiled bitterly.

"Deedee barely speaks to me," she said. She had sensed

from the beginning that Deedee felt about her the way Russell had felt: that Lana was from a different world, a world Deedee neither comprehended nor wanted to comprehend, a world of poverty and struggle that Deedee looked down on and was extremely frightened of. "I think Deedee would rather lose her fortune than admit that she and I are sisters."

"Deedee is not that much of a fool," said Slash.

Lana did not hear him. She insisted on her own point of view.

"Deedee thinks I'm low class. I think *she's* a revolting snob."

"You *always* retaliate, don't you?" asked Slash.

"It's how I survived," said Lana, refusing to be defensive.

"This time, it's how you're going to sit idly by and let your inheritance be worth less and less," Slash warned, refusing to let her shut him out.

Slash told Lana that her resentment of Deedee was childish and self-destructive.

"So Deedee grew up rich," Slash said, knowing the basis of Lana's jealousy. "Don't for one minute confuse rich with happy because one hasn't got anything to do with the other. If you and Deedee can forget your personal animosities and work together, you can save Lancome and Dahlen. If you don't, you can kiss the company your father gave up his life for goodbye."

"I hate to admit it but, you're probably right," said Lana grudgingly. Nevertheless, she still loathed the way Deedee had treated her as a nonperson, just the way Will had treated her, just the way Russell had treated her. The thought of having to be in the same room with Deedee, of having to find a way to work with her, of, finally, helping to make her even richer, filled Lana with her old fury and resentment. Yet, as Slash pointed out, not to do it was to destroy her own inheritance.

"Of course I'm right," Slash said with a straight face. This time, the killer expression was in his words, not on his face.

* * *

Slash told Deedee that her refusal to accept Lana was not only bad manners but financial suicide. Lancome & Dahlen was losing clients and losing profits. Although Trip blamed Slash for stealing business from Lancome & Dahlen, no client had ever left Lancome & Dahlen except by his own free choice.

"My mother has been telling me the same thing," Deedee admitted. She had tried to speak to Trip about Lancome & Dahlen's falling profits and shrinking capital, but he had contemptuously told Deedee to stick to what she knew best: dinner parties and small talk.

Nevertheless, the thought of sitting down with Lana, of talking business with her, of sharing her inheritance with her brought a feeling of deep bitterness and a profound sense of having been cheated out of her birthright. However, not acting in a way that was best for Lancome & Dahlen would be almost willfully to stand by and allow the company that was her birthright to be destroyed.

"Joyce is no fool," Slash said. After all, it had been Joyce who had maneuvered Luther into setting up Deedee's trust fund. It had been Joyce who had kept together a shaky marriage for Deedee's sake and for the sake of Deedee's inheritance. It had been Joyce who had helped engineer Deedee's engagement to Trip and Joyce had been among the first to accept Slash and to recognize his talents. Behind her candy-box prettiness and slightly vague manner, Joyce was as hard-headed as Luther, a more than even match for her formidable father-in-law and for the complicated family she had married into. "Your mother is a shrewd woman."

"So am I. After all, I married you, didn't I?" Deedee said, finally deciding after weeks of argument and indecision to put the welfare of Lancome & Dahlen before her personal feelings. She told Slash that she'd agree to talk with Lana.

Lana and Deedee met for the second time in the living room of the Park Avenue triplex Slash had once shared with Deedee. Lana was as intimidated by Deedee's elegantly furnished triplex as she had been by the white granite Lancome & Dahlen building. Now, as then, she concealed her intimidation behind an aggressive manner.

What was different, though, was that in 1960 Lana had been a prisoner of her fantasies. Now she was a captive of nothing and the exact equal of the woman she faced. As Lana entered her sister's apartment, she realized with a shock that Russell had left her the only inheritance she had ever really wanted: the chance to be accepted as an equal. Her success in getting that acceptance, however, was entirely up to her.

Deedee, too, was intimidated. She was intimidated by Lana's enormous success and independence and she also feared Lana's hold over Slash: Lana and Slash were not only business partners, now they were the parents of a son. Deedee feared there was no way she could compete with Lana and yet she also realized that she had never once in her life fought her own battles, not even when her marriage was at stake. She had willingly allowed her father to fight for her and, in the end, to die for her.

Now, however, there was no one to turn to and Deedee hid her fears and anxieties behind a strained and exaggerated politeness. As they spoke, Deedee gradually realized, to her surprise, that the sister she had never known existed was giving her the chance she had been waiting for her entire life: the chance to grow up.

Lana wore a short black leather skirt with a jacket whose shoulder pads would have made Dick Butkus feel at home. Her shoes had sky-high heels and her jewelry could be weighed by the pound, not the carat. Deedee wore Chanel and pearls. A tea tray went untouched as the two women sat in Deedee's formal living room. An air of mutual distrust and discomfort pervaded the atmosphere as Lana got down to business.

"Trip is doing a lousy job of running Lancome and Dahlen," Lana said, reeling off the facts and figures and recapping the conversation in which Slash had persuaded her to put aside her hurt feelings and meet with Deedee. "More and more of the big clients are deserting. Profits are down and so is the value of our stock. Trip asked to buy my stock but I turned him down. I understand he made you the same offer and that you also refused."

Deedee nodded. Lana continued.

"I figure, why the hell should I sell my inheritance and I thought you figured the same," said Lana, her soft, feminine voice at extreme contrast with her no-nonsense content. "Uptown is making money hand over fist. There's no reason Lancome and Dahlen shouldn't be keeping pace. Trip, though, acts as if he's back in the middle ages when Wall Street was an old boys' club. He's running Lancome and Dahlen for himself and his cronies. 'Screw the other stockholders' seems to be his attitude. That means us, Deedee. You and me."

Deedee nodded again. She would never have expressed herself in the same way, yet when she heard Lana speak she had the uncanny feeling that she was almost listening to herself think.

"I don't like you any more than you like me, but Slash is right. If we were smart, we'd vote our stock as a block. Together, we would have a good shot at persuading the board to get rid of Trip. Slash has already said that he'd agree to run Lancome and Dahlen," Lana proposed. "What do you think?"

"I think Slash is right," said Deedee, remembering what not only Slash but also her mother had said about the necessity of her and Lana working together. As always, when it came to business, Slash seemed to be right. As always, when it came to the practicalities of life, her mother seemed to be right.

"Shake?" asked Lana, holding out her hand. Her chunky silver and ivory cuffs clanked heavily.

Reluctantly, but knowing it was the right thing to do, the smart thing to do, the grown-up thing to do, Deedee extended her own hand.

Deedee wasn't comfortable with Lana. Her style was too outrageous, her words too blunt, her manner too direct. It didn't make any sense to her, but all the things that Deedee loved in Slash offended her in Lana: the outrageousness, the outspokenness, the willingness to break the rules and challenges to the status quo. She also knew that she was jealous of Lana and that she certainly didn't trust her. After all, Lana had once tried to take her husband and she had gone ahead and had Slash's baby out of wedlock.

However, whatever else Deedee thought about the stranger who was her sister, as she worked with her to save Lancome & Dahlen, she realized that she was beginning to respect her. When it came to the mechanics of running a business, the cutting of costs, the maximizing of profits, the creation of new sources of income, Lana was, Deedee quickly realized, a wonder woman. She was, thought Deedee, a chip off the old block. Lana was Luther's linear descendent.

Lana, on the other hand, found Deedee cold and distant. She thought that Deedee was uptight and passive. She had depended all her life on men; she had never had to fight, never had to struggle. Never could they be friends, thought Lana, never could they find anything in common except the stock that they had inherited equally. Lana couldn't begin to understand what Slash saw in Deedee, but she also realized that whatever Deedee's lure was, she, Lana, could never hope to compete.

Nevertheless, despite all of Lana's resentment, as she and Deedee, out of necessity, began to plan the turnaround of Lancome & Dahlen, she had to admit, however grudgingly, that Deedee Dahlen had class, character and contacts and plenty of them. Deedee knew everyone, everywhere: new money and old, Palm Beach and Westhampton Beach, the Racquet Club and the Vertical Club, the working rich and the idle rich, Seventh Avenue and Park Avenue.

In the fifties and sixties, it was said that the Dahlens had the brains and the Lancomes had the contacts. In the eighties, Lana and Deedee began to realize that it was Lana who had the savvy, Deedee who had the contacts. Lana conceived the plans to revitalize Lancome & Dahlen. Deedee knew the people who had the power to put those plans into action.

When Lana's plans were finalized, Deedee smiled and said that she was going to take Trip's advice.

"I'm going to stick to what I know best. Dinner parties," she said. Then she smiled and added: "Only that talk isn't going to be so small."

Deedee knew every single board member at Lancome & Dahlen. She knew their names and birthdays, their favorite drinks and their golf handicaps, their wives and their children, their alma maters and the names of their yachts, dogs and clubs. At a large, formal dinner party, given with the style and panache for which Deedee had always been renowned, Deedee introduced Lana to the members of the Lancome & Dahlen board.

"My sister and I think it's time for a change of leadership at Lancome and Dahlen," Deedee said, addressing the board when dinner was over. She used the word *sister* deliberately, knowing that presenting a united front to the board was crucial. Still, the word *sister* stuck in her craw. "We have a plan to present to you."

"I own one fourth of Lancome and Dahlen and one half of Uptown," Lana said when it was her turn to speak. "I've secured Slash's agreement to merge the two companies. Such a merger would bring Uptown's profits to Lancome and Dahlen and enhance Uptown's status with Lancome and Dahlen's longtime Wall Street reputation. Of course, we need your agreement to go ahead with such a merger."

There was a murmur in the room as the partners remembered the performance of the Partners' Portfolio and contrasted it with the recent shrinking profits at Lancome & Dahlen. They also looked at the Uptown profit and loss statement Lana passed around. They recalled Slash's brilliant performance during the sixties and the seventies and the way he had gone to Singapore to recoup his losses after the Premiere debacle. They also thought about the way Trip Lancome seemed to feel that the company was his fiefdom and the way he made it clear that their opinions and their preferences meant little or nothing. Luther and Ham Senior had never made such a mistake, and both Junior and Russell had always made a point of getting along with the board and punctiliously soliciting the board's opinion on every major matter.

At the Lancome & Dahlen board meeting the next day, overriding Trip's lone dissenting vote, the board passed a resolution to initiate merger negotiations with Slash.

The profits Slash had amassed in Uptown provided the money. The stock owned in Lancome & Dahlen by Lana and Deedee provided the leverage. In the summer of 1985, the two companies merged officially. Trip was kicked upstairs and given the honorary title of consulting partner. Slash was named president and CEO. Trip's shares of the stock in the new company made him one of the richest men on Wall Street. Slash's shares of stock gave him control.

"I'm surprised you agreed to stay on at Lancome and Dahlen," Michael de Rosnay told Trip when the papers were signed and the announcement of the merger made public.

"Why should you be surprised?" replied Trip, concealing his bitterness at being the victim of a power play he felt Slash had masterminded. Trip, as always, kept his emotions to himself and played his cards close to his vest. "I'm still a stockholder and a partner in Lancome and Dahlen. I have nothing against letting Slash make me rich."

Michael shrugged and nodded. *That* he could understand. *That* anyone could understand.

Slash, however, was not really satisfied. He told Lana that, ironically, he found himself in almost the same situation she had faced at Premiere. He ran the company but he was not even a major stockholder. It really wasn't fair, he said. There was still something he wanted that he didn't have, he said.

He wanted the other half of Lancome & Dahlen. The Lancome half.

IX
LOVE AND
MONEY

The beach, one of the Caribbean's most beautiful, was a pristine miracle of crystal water, shimmering white sands and rustling palm trees. Except for a picturesque, thatched-roof beach bar that served rum punches, grilled crayfish and French-fried plantain chips, it was completely deserted. The island, near Anguilla, was so remote that only those with private planes or yachts had access to it. It was on that beach that Slash met, accidentally on purpose, a girl who had been born with a platinum spoon.

Nina Lancome had married and divorced a third time, an extremely scandalous and ultimately very expensive divorce that had cost her much of her fortune. She was surprised when Slash said that he was interested in buying her Lancome & Dahlen stock.

"But the company's finally doing well. Why would I want to sell stock now?" Nina asked as she and Slash walked along the dazzling white beach. Since its merger with Uptown, Lancome & Dahlen had become a high-profile firm, a darling of the heavy hitters, a headline-producing sweetheart of the business press. The financial world used words like rejuvenation and renaissance to describe the spectacular comeback of the old-line firm. The dazzling bull market run-up of the eighties had benefited Lancome & Dahlen's clients tremendously. As Slash had predicted, former clients, drawn by the perfume of profit, were returning to Lancome & Dahlen and new ones, wanting to be where the action was, were opening accounts in record numbers. Megabucks and monopoly money deals had become the order of the day and Lancome & Dahlen was in the center of the action. "Why would I want to sell?"

"Because I'll pay you more than your stock is worth," Slash said. If Nina wanted one dollar, he'd give her three. If she wanted one million, he'd give her three million. If she wanted ten million, he'd give her thirty million. Slash had always known when to pay—and when to overpay. Now was one of those times.

"What about Trip?" Nina asked, wanting to know what would happen to her brother if she sold her share of the Lancome stock.

"I'll make Trip the identical offer I make you. He'll be richer than ever," promised Slash, dismissing Trip as one of the least of his concerns. Slash had not noticed the dark side of Trip. He had not noticed the way Trip brooded and the way Trip looked at him. He had not noticed the white line of rage that was now permanently etched around Trip's mouth. Now that he had defeated Trip, Slash was not in the habit of noticing Trip.

He left the island with Nina's promise of her support when he went to Trip.

Slash kept his promise to Nina and even let Trip stay in the prestigious corner office that had once belonged to his father, a man who had been doomed to go through life with the name Junior. Nevertheless, although Trip was becoming richer than ever and although he retained all the trappings of power and prestige, he found that once Slash moved into the office that had been Luther's, his influence was methodically stripped away.

Trip's title was "consultant," but the only things he was consulted on were colors for the new carpets, the wordings of public relations announcements concerning hirings and promotions and the menus for the annual Christmas party. He read about Lancome & Dahlen's most recent coups in the newspapers along with everyone else, the arbs no longer called pumping for information, and the young hotshots in the office no longer came only from Yale and were no longer all male and all white. The appearance of power was all that Trip retained and nothing of its substance.

He blamed it all on Slash. He remembered how Slash had once, long ago, seduced Deedee away from him with love and how, more recently, he had seduced Nina with money. Even when Deedee pointed out to him that it was she and Lana who were behind some of the massive changes at Lancome & Dahlen, Trip had refused to believe her.

"What do you girls know about running a business?" Trip had asked, dismissively, with the same patronizing tone he had always used when the talk turned to what he considered "men's business."

Trip's bitterness, concealed by his unlined, blue-eyed good looks, festered silently but lethally. Trip dwelled on Slash's comeback, on the way Slash had outmaneuvered him with Lana and Deedee, on the way Slash had grabbed the headlines and the profits and the attention. He was bitter at the way Deedee had taken Slash back and furious at the way Slash had forced the first female partner down his throat. Trip realized that Slash had made him rich as a way of destroying him and he burned with rage and resentment and a plan for revenge.

When Trip was skeet shooting in East Hampton, he imagined Slash in the sights of his gun. When he rode at his farm in South Salem, New York, he imagined Slash being trampled under the hooves of his horse. When he sailed in the cold waters off Dark Harbor, he imagined pushing Slash overboard.

He wondered how his life would have turned out if he had had the courage to defy his father and gotten rid of Slash Steiner in the first place.

As for Slash, although Uptown, now the venture side of the company, would always make the most money, it was the restoration of Lancome & Dahlen as one of Wall Street's most prestigious and highly regarded firms that gave him the most satisfaction. The man who had grown up an orphan had found a family to rescue. That rescue was one of the enormous satisfactions of his life.

In 1986, applying the lessons he had learned in Singapore, Slash entered into an agreement with one of the city's princes of real estate. Together they purchased the site next to the classic Haynes Whittier Apthorpe Greek Revival building of white granite erected in 1873. As a result of a complex deal involving zoning variances, the purchase of adjacent air rights, massive tax abatements and advantageous interpretations of the city's building codes, the Lancome & Dahlen building would be preserved but, over it, a brand-new glass-and-steel tower would be erected. On that site, on the corner of Broad and Wall, would stand the tallest building on Wall Street. No building in the entire world would be so expensive and no building in the entire world would have the influences on worldwide financial trends the tenants of that building would have.

"Is the fact that your building will literally tower over Lancome and Dahlen one of the reasons you entered into the deal?" asked a reporter who covered the groundbreaking.

"Let's put it this way," Slash said, smiling that fighter pilot's grin. "It's not a negative."

"And do you consider yourself a member of the establishment now?" asked another. She was blond and pretty and very intelligent—a fixture on one of television's top-rated prime time news shows. She was also the great-granddaughter of the founder of the network, one of the world's richest men. No one, though, had ever said that she had gotten where she was any way except by her own hard work, perseverance and talent. As she herself had said in response to an interviewer's question, her name had gotten her in the door. After that, it had been up to her.

"What?" asked Slash, laughing, perfectly aware of who she was. "And ruin my reputation?"

She made a note of the answer. She would suggest to the producer that the show do a feature on Slash and she wondered, as she folded her notebook, what all that energy and all that intensity would be like in bed.

The architect's plans called for the Lancome & Dahlen building to act as a base for the new tower, the monument to Slash's success and his phoenixlike reemergence from the ashes of scandal. Trip considered the design vulgar and showy. However, it was the removal of the name Lancome & Dahlen and its replacement with the name Steiner on the façade of the Haynes Whittier Apthorpe Greek Revival building that was the one step too far, the one slap in the face of tradition too much, the one final symbol of Slash's success Trip could no longer swallow.

"Slash?"

Slash turned, surprised to hear Trip's voice as he stepped into his waiting limousine after the groundbreaking ceremony that signaled the start of construction of the new tower. Trip had not spoken to him except in public in the years since the final merger of Lancome & Dahlen and Uptown Securities.

"Yes?"

Slash assumed that Trip would finally offer his congratulations and say something about letting bygones be bygones.

However, if Trip said anything else, Slash never heard it over the roar of the subway train passing underneath. He felt the searing heat of the bullet enter his flesh and then he felt nothing more.

It seemed, said Slash's driver later, to have happened in slow motion. Slash fell facedown, his body at first covering the stain of blood that seeped slowly on to the sidewalk. It took Slash's driver a moment to realize what had happened. By then, there was no trace of the gunman. He had been absorbed into the swirling rush hour crowd that hurried past.

The dazzling career of Slash Steiner, the legendary man with the Midas touch, seemed to have come to an end on the streets of the financial district over which he had once reigned.

For three days, Slash lay unconscious in the intensive care unit of the Carnegie Hospital, where Deedee had been born. The doctors were not optimistic about Slash's chances, and the tabloids were filled with headlines about the mysterious shooting, in broad daylight, of the Wall Street superstar.

Meanwhile, despite police interviews with Slash's wife and business associates, his employees and the scores who had known him, either socially or through business, there were no solid leads and no real suspects in the shooting. Although Slash had been unconventional and outrageous, although he had upset the status quo, he had never cheated anyone, never double-crossed anyone, never gone back on his word.

Slash's offenses had been sins of style, never sins of content. Almost everyone who had done business with him had ended up richer. Slash Steiner was that rarity: a successful man with no real enemies.

It had been easy. He had attended the groundbreaking ceremony by Slash's personal invitation and in his well-tailored three-piece suit, he had, as he always did, fit in perfectly. He carried the gun, one of his hand-tooled Purdeys, in a briefcase, and he left the podium at the same time that Slash had. He had called to Slash just as the subway passed underneath and he was about to get into his car. When Slash had looked up, he had fired. The gun was concealed under the raincoat he carried over his arm.

Then he had simply replaced the pistol in the briefcase and melted into the 5:30 P.M. flood of Wall Streeters rushing to get home, to get to the gym and work out, to fall into a nearby bar and talk about the day's trades.

When the police interviewed him in his prestigious corner office at Lancome & Dahlen, they noticed how remarkably young he looked for his age. His body was trim and the blond hair that fell over his forehead was as thick and as strong as it had been when he had been in his twenties. He told them how much he had admired Slash.

"He brought Lancome and Dahlen into the eighties and we'll miss him," he said. He was calm and poised, the kind of man people would instinctively trust with their money. "Nevertheless, Lancome and Dahlen is a company with a long tradition and, as Slash was always the first to say, it is the future that counts."

Trip Lancome's presence at the groundbreaking ceremony was attested to by a dozen witnesses, all of whom were from the highest echelons of the city's financial world, all men of impeccable honesty and reputation. The shooting had taken him only seconds, seconds that had been easily lost among the distractions of brass bands, speeches and celebrations. Since it was Slash who had increased Trip's wealth so tremendously, there was really no motive that anyone, if he had been of a mind to, could have pointed at. The police respectfully thanked Trip for giving them his valuable time and, with apologies for disturbing him, left.

There was only one man who knew what Trip had done, and that man was unconscious. The prognosis, according to the hospital spokesman, continued to be bleak.

Deedee kept a tearful vigil at Slash's bedside. Two days passed and then three. There was no change in Slash's condition. There was no sign of improvement and the doctors' voices grew quieter, their expressions more guarded. The articles that appeared in the newspapers now began to read like obituaries and the board members of Dahlen & Steiner began somberly to speak of plans for a smooth succession. Slash Steiner, it seemed, had come to the end of an incredible run of luck. Nevertheless, late in the afternoon of the fourth day after the shooting, Slash suddenly opened his eyes.

"What the hell are you crying for?" he asked Deedee, his killer grin weak and wan but still in perfect shape. "Don't you know they're going to have to use a silver bullet to get me?"

* * *

Trip Lancome had always disdained publicity. He was of the school that believed that a gentleman's name appeared in the newspapers only three times in life: at birth, marriage and death. However, the photograph of him in handcuffs, being led to prison to serve seven years for attempted murder, made not only every newspaper in the country but the cover of *Time* magazine. Never in history had a multimillionaire scion to a great American fortune who sat in the chairman's office of a powerful Wall Street firm gone to prison for a crime other than a financial one. The expression on Trip's face in the photograph finally revealed to the world the psychological darkness within. It was a chilling mixture of outrage and contempt.

Eight months into his prison term and two months before he would be eligible for parole, Trip Lancome was brutally murdered in the prison laundry. The weapon was a shiv. The motive was an argument over a pair of socks. The killer was a teenaged Hispanic, a previous offender who had a long record of violent assaults. Trip Lancome was forty-two years old.

Many would recall the untimely deaths of Trip's grandparents in a light plane crash on the British Virgin Island of Tortola and talk about fate.

"Trip Lancome had the money but not the luck" people would say, forgetting that there had always been a certain darkness about Trip.

X
RECONCILIATIONS

*A*s soon as *Slash was out of the hospital, he and Deedee* officially reconciled. Although Slash's style, his sense of humor and his Midas touch stayed with him, he emerged from the shooting with a limp. Refusing to give in to the first physical disability he had ever suffered, Slash adopted a black ebony cane with a silver handle which he used as a prop and a trademark. The cane, the dramatic shooting and the limp all added to Slash's glamor and mystery. He and Deedee resumed their glittering lives at the top of Manhattan's social pinnacle, where the times had finally caught up with them.

In the more than twenty years since Slash and Deedee's first meeting, the Dow had risen from 610 to almost 3,000. New money had replaced old and the working rich had replaced the idle rich. Earned money had supplanted inherited money and the term nouveau riche was no longer an insult, merely a statement of fact.

Slash, as always, had been in the vanguard and Deedee was widely admired as the perfect high-profile Manhattan wife, not only aiding and abetting Slash's increasingly dazzling career but helping to run the company her grandfather had founded. Deedee was now that ultimate Manhattan heroine, a glamorous member of the working rich. Her clothes, her charities, her business activities, her parties, her marriage were written about with slavish adoration. However, only Deedee knew the realities behind the glitter. Only Deedee knew the depth behind the surface. Only Deedee knew the pain behind the pleasure.

There were even some who never realized that the marriage had been interrupted by scandal and separation. Those who did welcomed the reconciliation as a triumph of love and money.

Despite the shooting and Trip's violent death, Nina and Deedee continued their relationship. Through three decades of unimaginable changes, through marriages and separations, divorces and disasters, the two women maintained the links that had made them friends since childhood. Friendship, they realized, often lasted longer than either love or money. Friendship was not to be put easily aside.

"Aren't you jealous of Lana and Slash?" Nina asked, amazed at the triangle which was the focus of gossip at lunches and dinners all over Manhattan. Unlike Russell, Slash, the pain of being an unwanted child ever fresh inside him, made no secret of his out-of-wedlock child. He and Lana and little Joel were often seen together. "Aren't you afraid they won't be able to resist each other a second time?"

"Of course, I'm afraid," said Deedee. "Who wouldn't be?"

But Nina didn't really believe her. Deedee didn't *seem* afraid. Not the least bit.

Love and money. Ultimately, they seemed to be all anyone really understood. At least, thought Lana, love and money were what she and Slash understood. Love and money had, after all, brought them together and it was what kept them together, since Lana had not only inherited 25 percent of Lancome & Dahlen but still owned 50 percent of Uptown. Her share of the new, combined company was enough in itself to make her an enormously rich woman.

However, Lana's sole ownership of Premiere, now one of the country's largest manufacturers of beauty supplies and the owner and franchiser of salons in shopping malls throughout the country, made Lana the only woman to earn her own way into both the *Forbes* 500 and the *Fortune* 500.

In 1987, Lana added to her wealth when she bought Marx & Marx and merged it with Premiere.

"Your father wanted to buy Marx and Marx for you a long time ago," said Leon Marx at the closing. Now in his late seventies, Leon's notorious temper had mellowed slightly, diminishing from the nuclear to the merely volcanic. However, still five feet five, he had not grown an inch, nor had his outsize, compensatory ego shrunk so much as a millimeter. He had driven a hell of a good bargain with Lana who, herself, was known as a tough dealmaker. In each other, Leon and Lana had met worthy adversaries and respectful negotiators. Both already tremendously rich, their merger agreement added to their respective wealth.

"He did?" asked Lana in amazement. "When?"

"In March 1977. He wanted to merge Premiere with Marx and Marx. He said it would be good for everyone. For you, for Deedee, for Slash. He wanted to make selling worth my while. He even offered to overpay. That's how badly he wanted the deal. Then, of course, he died before anything could be finalized," said Leon sadly. "It's too bad, isn't it? We both would have been a hell of a lot richer a hell of a lot sooner."

Lana nodded, avoiding Leon's probing gaze. She choked back the sickening realization that once again Russell had been thinking of her and that once again, in her anger and resentment, she had refused to allow him to help. She had been, she realized, a bitter and resentful daughter who had refused to let Russell be a father. She wondered when she would learn. She wondered when she could put the bitterness behind her. She wondered when she could forgive herself. She wondered *if* she could forgive herself.

Pitied as the daughter of the town drunk in Wilcom, socially snubbed as a lowly beautician in Worcester, shunned as a married man's mistress in Providence and gossiped about behind her back in Singapore, where she was neither wife nor concubine, Lana was fully accepted in New York, where a whiff of scandal never hurt, particularly when accompanied by blinding success, reams of publicity and *beaucoup dinero*.

Successful men, including Pete Oney and Paul Gwilym, a recent widower, courted her and interesting women invited Lana into their circles where she was a welcome addition to corporate boards, political groups and charitable endeavors. Lana had her own money, her own empire, her own world. She had worked hard for them all and she was now ready to enjoy them all. Without guilt. With gusto. She deserved it, she told herself. It was a right she had long since earned.

She had been, she told herself, for far too long a woman who had been denied rewards. She had won prizes in school but her father hadn't been there to applaud her. She had made a success of the Beauty Box but Tom had resented her accomplishment and tried to deprive her of it. She had made Premiere a huge success but Stan had always withheld praise and participation. Then she had loved Slash, knowing all along that he loved Deedee. She seemed to have an infallible instinct for getting hurt, being cheated and ending up second best.

For a long time, Lana had blamed the world for not recognizing her for what she was and for what she had accomplished. Now she was beginning to realize that she would have to accept at least part of the blame.

Over and over, Lana had turned down the possibility of love and its rewards when it had been offered. As a child, she had turned aside a teacher who had sensed her isolation and interested herself in Lana's happiness. During her brief, early marriage, she had confused charm with commitment, romance with reality. As an adult, she had rejected Stan when she should have accepted him. She had deliberately hurt her father when she should have opened her arms to him. The next time, Lana promised herself, if love were offered, she would know how and when to accept it.

Claire Steiner and Joel Bantry would grow up far differently from their mothers. Deedee was determined that Claire would not be brought up in the total ignorance of basic finance that she had been. Lana and Slash agreed that Joel would never be the ignored guilt child Lana had been.

Claire and Joel knew from their earliest years that they would, one day, inherit equally the company their parents owned. A company founded by a great-grandfather in the twenties. A company to which a reluctant heir had given his life. A company brought into the eighties by a man from nowhere who, unlike Trip, liked to break the rules as long as no one got hurt. A company inherited and influenced by two women who knew what it was to be rich and poor, loved and ignored, hurt and happy, women who knew that love and money weren't everything.

Luther Dahlen's ninety-fourth birthday party took place in the autumn of 1988. The party, as it had for as long as anyone could remember, would be held at "21." Deedee insisted that Lana be invited.

"It's about time you acknowledged her," Deedee told Luther. Luther, angry at Russell for his sad secret, had continued to refuse to acknowledge Lana's existence. However, ever since Deedee and Lana had joined forces to exert their will over the company whose stock they had inherited, Deedee was no longer so intimidated by the old man who had run his family for generations with an iron hand and tight purse strings. "For her sake, for Joel's sake and for your own sake. It's time you forgave Russell for not being the man you wanted him to be. It's time you accepted him for being the man that he was."

The old man surprised Deedee by agreeing.

"I was a horse's ass," he said, echoing words from long, long ago. A mist of tears blurred his still-young voice. "In fact, I owe Lana an apology. She's Russell's child and I've treated her like an outsider."

"Apology?" repeated Deedee amazed. "Did I hear you correctly? I've never heard that particular word cross your lips."

Luther smiled and nodded.

"I'm stubborn but I'm not stupid," he said with the outspoken bluntness so much like Lana's. "Besides, you're never too old to change. My only regret is that Russell isn't here. I owe him an apology, too. He was a good son and a much better businessman than I ever gave him credit for."

Then the old man with the young man's voice smiled wistfully. There were regrets he would have to live with and mistakes he still had time to change. Luther Dahlen had wheeled and dealed, used his money to interfere in other people's lives, had gone through life doing whatever he had to to get his way. He had been selfish and altruistic, stingy and generous, self-centered and compassionate. Sometimes he had done the right things from the wrong motives and at other times the wrong things from the right motives. He had never been bored and he had never given up.

He was, in fact, already thinking about his ninety-fifth birthday. He thought that maybe, for a change, the party ought to be held somewhere other than "21"; "21," despite the renovations, was still for old folks. Luther was thinking about Nell's on Fourteenth Street. He had never been there but, he told Edwina, confiding his heretical idea, all the young people seemed to like it very much.

Toward the end of Luther's birthday party, Deedee went over to Lana. She had been thinking about how she felt and what she wanted to say to the stranger who was her sister.

"We've been partners, but that's all," Deedee told Lana as Luther's birthday party drew to a close. Luther's words and Slash's respect for Lana had made an enormous impression on Deedee, as had her own experiences in working closely with Lana. Joyce's compassion toward Lana had influenced Deedee, too. All of them—along with the enormous increase in her wealth which Russell had foreseen—had caused Deedee gradually to reconsider her own distant and detached attitude toward Lana. "The coolness has been my fault. I'd like to change things. I'd like to feel that we were sisters."

"I've been at fault, too," said Lana, her throat closing with an intensity of emotion that took her off guard. She knew she had held Deedee at arm's length the way she had held everyone who had ever mattered to her at arm's length. "I resented you for being born."

"I felt the same way," Deedee said sadly. "I was afraid of you. I was afraid that you'd take my husband the way I thought you took my father. I was afraid that you'd take my money and that I'd end up in the world you left behind. I didn't think I could rescue myself the way you rescued yourself. You seemed to be everything I wasn't."

Deedee smiled sadly in recognition of her own deepest fears and most primitive anxieties. Then she wordlessly extended her hand in a gesture of reconciliation. Lana took it in hers and then, impulsively and acting from the same deep instinct that had once impelled their father on a night in June so long ago, Deedee moved a step forward and opened her arms.

Lana swallowed and moved toward her sister. Lana had just been offered love once again and this time she knew enough to accept it. In the moment that she opened her arms to her sister, Lana forgave herself at last for rejecting the father who, despite his flaws, had clearly loved her. Russell Dahlen had been far from perfect, Lana realized, and so was she. The time had come at last to let go of the anger, to set the resentment free.

The hurt in Lana's blue eyes finally lifted as bound by more than just love and money, bound by shared blood and common heritage, the two women moved into each other's arms and embraced.

Slash, standing nearby and leaning on his silver-handled ebony cane, watched them and smiled. Not a killer smile and not a wise guy smile. Not a smile that held people away or a smile that challenged them but a lover's smile. He loved them both and he loved them in different ways. Lana reminded him of who he was. Deedee reminded him of who he could be.

He loved Lana because he understood her. He had come from nowhere and so had she. He had been born poor and so had she. He had not even had a name and neither, really, had she. He had had to fight every inch of the way and so had she. He had been abandoned and so had she. He was used to struggling and so was she. He didn't care about breaking the rules and neither did she. He was used to winning and so was she. He had a secret and so did she. His was the death of a son. Hers was the identity of a father. He loved her because he knew how she thought and how she felt and he loved her because her existence and the existence of the son she had borne for him made him feel that he wasn't quite so alone.

But he loved Deedee in the unique way a man can love a woman who has the power to make all his dreams and fantasies come true. He had loved her from the moment he had first seen her photograph in a silver frame, and he loved her now. She was his ideal, the heiress he had seduced, the fair princess he had won, the woman whose existence in his life proved to him that he was valuable, that he, although an orphan and a man from nowhere, was worth loving. Every time she walked into a room, Slash felt the magic and he knew that she, and only she, was the one.

ABOUT THE AUTHOR

Ruth Harris is also the author of HUSBANDS & LOVERS (Fawcett, '86), A SELF-MADE WOMAN (Fawcett, '84), THE LAST ROMANTICS, THE RICH AND THE BEAUTIFUL and DECADES. She lives with her husband, Michael, in New York City.

There's a time for husbands . . .
There's a time for lovers . . .
Every woman needs to know when.

Once a shy and insecure girl, Carlys Webber has blossomed into a rich, savvy, successful woman. Now she can afford two of everything—

KIRK ARNOLD—Carlys's husband, a fast-track, corporate trouble-shooter. He gives his all at the office and is becoming more aloof at home.

GEORGE KOURAS—Carlys's lover, a passionate architect, who is everything Kirk isn't; he's sensitive, expressive and he needs Carlys.

A modern gifted woman, tangled in her own web of want and wealth—having too much, loving too many, wanting more than she could ever learn to manage.

HUSBANDS AND LOVERS

Every woman needs both.
Every man should be both.

HUSBANDS AND LOVERS

by Ruth Harris

SBN 20972-5, $4.50

Available in a bookstore near you, or call toll free

1-800-733-3000

Use your American Express, MasterCard, or Visa.

To expedite your order, please mention Interest Code "MRM 5". Postage charges are $1 for the first book, 50¢ for each additional book.

To order by mail, send check or money order (no cash or CODs please) to: Ballantine Mail Sales, 8-4, 201 E. 50th St., New York, NY 10022.

Prices and numbers subject to change without notice. All orders subject to availability of books. Valid in U.S. only.